"Are you okay?"

"Never better." Shane grinned. "The bull barely nicked me."

She studied him critically. "You're limping."

He laughed, he couldn't help it, and lowered his voice. "I appreciate the concern, Cassidy. It means a lot to me."

"Of course I'm concerned. That was a close call."

"Is that the only reason?" He leaned in. A mere fraction at first, then more.

She drew back. "I don't know what you're implying."

"That you're worried about me because you might like me a little."

"Well, I don't."

His grin widened. "Could have fooled me."

"You always did have a big ego."

"Matched only by my..." He let the sentence drop.

"Shane!"

"Confidence," he finished with a chuckle.

ARIZONA

COUNTRY LEGACY

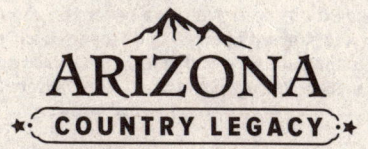

THE BULL RIDER'S HONOR

New York Times Bestselling Author

Cathy McDavid

Heidi Hormel

Previously published as *The Bull Rider's Son* and *The Bull Rider's Redemption*

HARLEQUIN

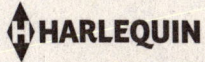

If you purchased this book without a cover you should be aware that this book is stolen property. It was reported as "unsold and destroyed" to the publisher, and neither the author nor the publisher has received any payment for this "stripped book."

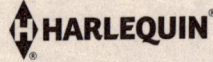

ISBN-13: 978-1-335-18993-6

Recycling programs for this product may not exist in your area.

Arizona Country Legacy: The Bull Rider's Honor
Copyright © 2020 by Harlequin Books S.A.

The Bull Rider's Son
First published in 2015. This edition published in 2020.
Copyright © 2015 by Cathy McDavid

The Bull Rider's Redemption
First published in 2016. This edition published in 2020.
Copyright © 2016 by Heidi Hormel

All rights reserved. No part of this book may be used or reproduced in any manner whatsoever without written permission except in the case of brief quotations embodied in critical articles and reviews.

This is a work of fiction. Names, characters, places and incidents are either the product of the author's imagination or are used fictitiously. Any resemblance to actual persons, living or dead, businesses, companies, events or locales is entirely coincidental.

This edition published by arrangement with Harlequin Books S.A.

For questions and comments about the quality of this book, please contact us at CustomerService@Harlequin.com.

Harlequin Enterprises ULC
22 Adelaide St. West, 40th Floor
Toronto, Ontario M5H 4E3, Canada
www.Harlequin.com

Printed in U.S.A.

CONTENTS

The Bull Rider's Son
by Cathy McDavid — 7

The Bull Rider's Redemption
by Heidi Hormel — 247

Since 2006, *New York Times* bestselling author **Cathy McDavid** has been happily penning contemporary Westerns for Harlequin. Every day, she gets to write about handsome cowboys riding the range or busting a bronc. It's a tough job, but she's willing to make the sacrifice. Cathy shares her Arizona home with her own real-life sweetheart and a trio of odd pets. Her grown twins have left to embark on lives of their own, and she couldn't be prouder of their accomplishments.

Books by Cathy McDavid

Harlequin Western Romance

Mustang Valley

Cowboy for Keeps
Her Holiday Rancher
Come Home, Cowboy
Having the Rancher's Baby
Rescuing the Cowboy
A Baby for the Deputy
The Cowboy's Twin Surprise
The Bull Rider's Valentine

Harlequin Heartwarming

The Sweetheart Ranch

A Cowboy's Christmas Proposal
The Cowboy's Perfect Match

Visit the Author Profile page at Harlequin.com for more titles.

THE BULL RIDER'S SON

Cathy McDavid

To Mike and Friday nights.

Chapter 1

Few people receive a second chance in life. Shane Westcott was one of them—three times over—and he had no intention of squandering his good fortune. He was lucky to be alive, lucky to be gaining shared custody of his four-year-old daughter and lucky to have landed the job as bull manager at the Easy Money Rodeo Arena.

"Keep him moving," he called to Kenny, the young wrangler in charge of herding Wasabi from the large, open main pen into one of the smaller adjoining holding pens. It was imperative they isolate the bull from the others. "Don't let him dawdle."

The solid black Brahma-longhorn cross had other ideas and stepped slowly, almost daintily, through the gate. His actions were so far removed from his normal fiery temper, Shane hardly recognized the bull.

"He don't want to move," Kenny complained when Wasabi stopped completely.

"Tickle him on the hocks."

Kenny gawked at Shane as if he'd suggested hopping onto the bull's back and taking him for a leisurely spin. "You can't pay me enough to get in there with that monster."

The monster in question bellowed pitifully, sounding more like a calf missing his mama than an eighteen-hundred-pound bucking machine capable of launching world champions twelve feet into the air with a mere toss of his head.

"Use the rake over there," Shane instructed.

Kenny turned and, spotting the rake leaning against the back of a chute, gave a comical double take. "Well, lookie there."

Shane resisted rolling his eyes. With help like this, it was no wonder the rodeo arena needed someone competent in charge.

Grabbing hold of the rake, Kenny bent and poked the handle through an opening in the fence then tapped Wasabi on his back hocks. The bull promptly grunted with annoyance and banged his huge head into the gate hard enough to rattle the hinges.

"Again," Shane said, and the teenager complied, grimacing as he did.

Bred for bucking, twisting and spinning, Wasabi had the ability to earn money hand over fist for his new owner, but only if his injury was correctly identified, diagnosed and treated. This was Shane's chance to prove his new boss had made the right decision in hiring him.

Not a lot of pressure for his first day on the job.

"He's favoring his left front foot." Mercer Beckett,

co-owner of the arena, stood beside Shane at the fence. Resting his boot on the bottom rung, he chewed a large wad of gum—a habit left over from quitting smoking years ago.

"You're wrong," Shane said. "He's favoring his shoulder."

Mercer squinted skeptically. "You don't say?"

"Watch how he hesitates after taking a step, not before."

Shane climbed the fence for a better view. He knew Wasabi personally. In fact, he'd taken his last competitive ride on the bull. If not for split-second timing and fate stepping in, Shane might have been carried away from that harrowing fall on a stretcher instead of walking away under his own steam. He'd decided then and there to retire a champion and find a new profession. Six months had passed since, and it turned out to be the best decision he could have made.

"Seems Doc Worthington agrees with you," Mercer said. He'd mentioned the arena's regular veterinarian before, on their way over to the bull pen.

Shane frowned. "If he's already figured out what's wrong with Wasabi, why'd you ask me?"

"Isn't it obvious?"

To see if Shane was worth his salt as a bull manager. Understandable. He'd been at it a mere five months. "What's his treatment course?"

"Anti-inflammatory injections. Rest." Mercer shrugged. "Time."

"Which you don't have."

"Our next rodeo is three weeks away. Wasabi's our main draw. Going to be a lot of disappointed cowboys if I have to pull him from the lineup."

Not a promising beginning for a rodeo arena with a relatively new bucking bull program.

"Three weeks is cutting it a little close," Shane said. "Injuries don't heal overnight."

"Joe Blackwood mentioned you worked wonders at the Payson Rodeo Arena, and their bull had a ruptured disc."

The longtime rodeo promoter and friend of the Becketts had recommended Shane for this job. Shane didn't want to let either man down.

"Have you heard of Guillermo Herrara?" Shane stepped off the fence and onto the ground.

"Vaguely. He's a rodeo vet out of Dallas."

"Not just a rodeo vet. He's a specialist in bovine sports medicine."

"There's such a thing?"

"There is. And he's had a lot of success in treating chronic joint injuries with massage therapy."

Mercer laughed. "You have got to be kidding."

Shane shrugged. "How important is it to you Wasabi is sound and ready to go in three weeks?"

"You're planning on massaging that bull's shoulder?"

"With a little help from your veterinarian."

Mercer's laugh simmered to a low chuckle. "This I have to see."

They spent another thirty minutes with Wasabi. Unlike Kenny, Shane had no qualms about crawling into the pen. True, the bull was in pain, but Shane didn't consider the threat to be too great. Mercer's only response had been to raise his brows and chew his gum faster.

"Okay," the arena owner hollered when they were done. "You can put him back now."

Kenny didn't appear any happier about returning

Wasabi to the main pen than he had been about fetching him.

"Let's head to the office and start on your paperwork." Mercer led the way. "Sunny is a stickler about having all the proper payroll forms filled out."

It was well known among people in the rodeo world that Mercer and Sunny Beckett, divorced for twenty-five years, were in business together. An unusual arrangement, for sure, but a successful one. Sunny oversaw the business side of the arena and Mercer the livestock.

Their three grown children worked alongside them. Ryder, a former ad agency executive, handled the arena's marketing and promotion. Their youngest daughter, Liberty, taught riding and supervised trail rides. Cassidy, their oldest daughter and the Beckett family member Shane knew better than the others, was in charge of the bucking jackpots, team penning competitions and roping clinics.

He half hoped to see her in the office. The stab of disappointment he felt when he didn't took him by surprise. He'd always liked Cassidy. In fact, they'd dated briefly in their late teens for about a month.

In those days, both of them were focused on their rodeo careers and the relationship quickly fizzled. Some years later, she and Shane's brother Hoyt began dating. Their relationship had lasted longer and was more serious, though it, too, had ended. Shane remembered being a little jealous and thinking his brother a fool to let her go.

But that had been a long time ago. After Cassidy and Hoyt's breakup, she'd quit barrel racing altogether. Shane crossed paths with her periodically, mostly when he came to the Easy Money for a rodeo. Their chats never lasted long, he assumed because of whatever resentment she still harbored toward his brother.

"Sunny, it's a pleasure to see you again." He flashed the arena's other co-owner his best smile, which she returned along with offering him a firm handshake.

"Welcome, Shane. Come into my office. I have your employment package ready."

Mercer waited in the reception area while Shane accompanied Sunny. He thought about asking after Cassidy, then decided against it.

Once Shane was seated in the visitor's chair, Sunny handed him a slim stack of papers. "There's a lot of reading, I'm afraid. Employee policies and procedures. Withholding tax forms to complete. A noncompete agreement. Take everything home tonight and bring it back in the morning. All I need for now is the I-9 form completed and to see two forms of ID."

Shane fished his driver's license and Social Security card from his wallet.

When they were done, he asked her a few general questions about the arena. Sunny was friendlier than Shane had anticipated. He'd been warned by both Joe Blackwood and Mercer that the matriarch of the Beckett family wasn't in favor of the new bull operation. Shane had more to prove than his ability to manage. He needed to ensure the operation was run safely and profitably.

"About my daughter," he began.

"Mercer mentioned you'd be having her for visits."

"Yeah, alternating weekends."

He didn't add, *temporarily*. Eventually, Shane was hoping to have Bria for considerably longer visits. He'd need larger, more permanent living quarters than the fifth-wheel trailer that came with this job. Bria's mother had insisted, and he didn't blame her. Rodeo was no lifestyle for a four-year-old girl.

The fall from Wasabi had prompted Shane to leave the only career he'd ever known. Discovering he was a father—something Bria's mother had revealed *after* Shane quit—required him to settle down and find a new occupation. The Easy Money Rodeo Arena, the heart and soul of Reckless, Arizona, and the small town's most popular Wild West attraction, could be the place where Shane carved out his future.

"Is it against policy for me to take my daughter riding on arena horses?" he asked.

"Of course not." Sunny's expression warmed. "We have plenty of kid-friendly mounts. But you'll be required to sign a waiver. And provide proof of health insurance."

"No problem." He'd remind Judy to bring the card with her when she dropped off Bria next weekend.

Judy was usually very accommodating, and he couldn't be more grateful. It might be guilt motivating her since she had kept Bria a secret from him all those years. Or it could be she was about to get married to a guy with children of his own. Shane didn't care. All that mattered was they were working together for Bria's best interests.

"Speaking of your daughter…" Sunny rose from her chair. "I'll let Mercer show you the trailer now."

Shane shook her hand. "Thank you again for the opportunity."

"All set?" Mercer waited by the door leading to the barn, a look of expectation on his weathered and whiskered face.

Expectation, Shane noted, directed at Sunny. Not

him. It was obvious Mercer cared deeply for his ex-wife. She, on the other hand, was not as easy to read.

Mercer led Shane behind the main barn to where an older-model trailer was parked in the shade. A green garden hose ran from a spigot to the hookup beside the trailer's door. A heavy-duty orange cord connected the trailer to an electrical outlet. The door stood slightly ajar and the folding metal steps were lowered.

Shane didn't need to go inside to know he'd hung his hat in far worse places than this. In fact, it was a step up from many.

Mercer handed him a key on a ring. "Make yourself at home."

"Mind if I park my truck here?" Once Shane had a look around the trailer, he'd unload his belongings and unpack.

Before Mercer could answer, his cell phone jangled. Listening in silence to the caller for several seconds, he barked, "Be right there," and disconnected. "Sorry, I have an emergency. One of the calves got tangled in some wire."

"Anything I can help with?"

"Naw." He dismissed Shane with a wave of his hand. "Get yourself settled."

Shane watched a moment as Mercer jogged in the direction of the livestock pens located on the other side of the arena. When his new boss was out of sight, Shane climbed the trailer's two steps, opened the door wide and entered his new home. His first sight was of the small but comfortable living room–dining room combo. His second sight was of the tiny kitchen.

His third sight, and the one cementing his boots to the carpeted floor, was of Cassidy Beckett, pushing aside the accordion divider separating the sleeping area from the rest of the trailer.

She swallowed a small, startled gasp, and her hand fluttered to her throat where it rested. "Sorry. I wasn't expecting you yet. Mom asked me to put fresh towels in the bathroom and change the sheets on the bed."

"You don't have to go to any trouble." The words caught in his throat before he choked them out.

Shane had always thought of Cassidy as pretty. Sometime during the intervening years she'd grown into a striking beauty with large dark eyes and shoulder-length hair the same chocolate brown shade as a wild mink.

He stopped thinking about why his brother let her go and began wondering why he shouldn't ask Cassidy out himself. No reason not to. She was exactly the kind of woman he fancied. More importantly, she had no lingering attachments to his brother—who'd married someone else shortly after he and Cassidy split. She also had a son close in age to Bria and would probably be understanding of his single-dad responsibilities.

"It's good to see you again," he said and strode forward to greet her with a hug.

Suddenly, Shane's new job had an altogether different perk. One which quite appealed to him.

The initial alarm Cassidy experienced upon seeing Shane tripled when he swept her up in an enthusiastic embrace. It was bad enough her father had hired him. Worse that her mother insisted she stock the trailer with fresh linens. Disastrous that he'd caught her here. With him blocking the narrow passageway to the door, escape was impossible. She had no choice but to surrender to his powerful hold on her.

"Good to see you, too," she managed to reply.

He didn't immediately release her. Cassidy worried he'd sense the tension coursing through her and attempted to extract herself. He let her go long enough to take in the length of her from head to toe before hauling her against him a second time.

"You look great."

"Thanks," she mumbled, refusing to return the compliment by admitting how incredible he looked. And smelled.

Good heavens, the man had been out with the bulls for at least an hour by her estimation. He should reek to high heaven. Instead, with her face firmly planted in the crook of his shoulder, she inhaled the spicy and appealing scent of whatever aftershave he'd used this morning.

With their broad shoulders, lean, muscular builds and ruggedly chiseled profiles, both Westcott brothers were head-turning handsome. Back when the three of them were competing on the rodeo circuit, Cassidy had considered Hoyt to be the more attractive of the pair. No longer. Shane not only held his own in the looks department, he'd surpassed his older brother.

Finally, thank goodness, his grip slackened and he freed her. "How have you been, girl?"

"Umm...okay."

Girl? To her horror and chagrin, her heart gave a small flutter at the endearment he'd used during their short-lived romance. She dismissed it. Being attracted to Shane was impossible. For too many reasons to list.

"Sorry I interrupted you." She attempted to pass

him. "Let me get out of your way. I'm sure you want to unpack."

"Stay a while." He didn't budge. "We can catch up."

"I promised Liberty I'd help with her riding class this afternoon." Surely her sister would forgive this one small fib, considering the circumstances.

It was then Cassidy remembered her sister didn't know the circumstances. No one did for certain except their mother, and Cassidy had sworn her to secrecy.

"That's not for another hour." Shane smiled sheepishly and—dang it all—appealingly. "Your dad mentioned the schedule earlier."

Her father. Of course, Cassidy thought with a groan. He alone was responsible for hiring Shane and throwing her life into utter turmoil.

"We have a new student signing up."

"Come on." Shane gestured to the dining table. "It's been years since we had a real talk."

It was true. Cassidy had avoided him and Hoyt like the plague, determined not to let either of them near her son, Benjie. It hadn't been easy. Shane had competed regularly until recently and often visited the Easy Money.

"Five minutes." Shane removed his cowboy hat and tossed it onto the table.

She hesitated. The one thing more dangerous than being alone with Shane was being alone with his brother. To refuse, however, might raise Shane's suspicions. She couldn't chance it.

"Okay." She slid slowly onto the bench seat, the faded upholstery on the cushions pulling at her jeans, and repeated "Five minutes" for good measure.

He plunked down across from her, a pleased grin on his face.

Cassidy swallowed. The small dining table didn't provide nearly enough distance. Shane's appeal was infinitely more potent up close. His sandy brown hair, worn longer now than when he was competing, didn't quite cover the jagged scar starting beneath his ear and disappearing inside his shirt collar—a souvenir courtesy of his last ride on Wasabi. And those green eyes, intense one second and twinkling with mirth the next, were hard to resist.

Currently, they searched her face. Cassidy tried not to show any signs of the distress weakening her knees and quickening her breath.

"What's Hoyt up to these days?" She strove to sound mildly interested, which wasn't the case.

"Same as always. Heading to a rodeo in Austin this weekend."

"Still married?"

At the spark of curiosity in Shane's eyes, she wished she'd posed the question differently. Now he'd think she cared about Hoyt's marital state. Well, she did. But not for *that* reason.

"He and Cheryl are doing fine. Bought a house in Jackson Hole last year."

Jackson Hole. In Wyoming. Good, Cassidy thought. Plenty far from Reckless, Arizona.

"Any kids yet?" She cursed herself for needing to know.

"Nope." Shane shrugged. "Still trying. Hoyt wants a big family. Or so he says."

A jolt shot through her. She attempted to hide it with a show of nonchalance. "Tell me about your daughter."

Shane instantly brightened. "Bria's four. Not sure yet if she wants to be a princess or a soccer player when she grows up."

"What? No cowgirl?"

"I'm hoping to change her mind."

Cassidy's son, Benjie, wanted to be a champion bull rider. Like his grandfather before him and, unbeknownst to all but Cassidy and her mother, like his father and Uncle Shane.

She quickly shoved her hands beneath the table before Shane spotted them shaking. How was she ever going to keep him from finding out about Benjie and telling Hoyt? She vowed to find a way.

There were those who'd disagree, claiming she should have told Hoyt from the beginning about Benjie. That he had a right to know. Others, admittedly not many, who would side with her. It wasn't just Hoyt's nomadic lifestyle and partying ways, which had been one of the reasons for their breakup. Cassidy couldn't take the chance of him fighting for, and probably winning, joint custody of Benjie.

She'd seen firsthand how parents living in separate towns divided a family. When her brother, Ryder, had turned fourteen, he'd left to live with their father. Up until last fall, Ryder had rarely seen or spoken to Cassidy, Liberty and their mother. Their father's return had reunited the Becketts, but they were far from being a family. Not in the truest sense. Too much hurt and betrayal, and too many lies littered their past.

No way, no how, was she putting her son through the same broken childhood she'd endured. She would not suffer the same heartbreak that had devastated her mother when they'd lost Ryder. And it would happen. Of that, Cassidy was certain.

"Mom mentioned Bria will be visiting soon." Cassidy forced a smile.

Shane, on the other hand, beamed. "Every other weekend to start."

To start? Was he planning on obtaining full custody of his daughter? Cassidy's anxiety increased. If Hoyt followed his brother's example...

She pushed the unpleasant thought away. "She's close by, then?"

"Mesa."

"Ah." A forty-five-minute drive.

"That's why I accepted this job." A glint lit his eyes as his gaze focused on her. "Now I have even more incentive."

Oh, dear. Cassidy steeled herself, determined to resist him. "Bria's mom is okay with you taking her more often?"

"Judy's been great. She wants Bria and me to have a relationship."

"But she lied to you about having a child."

The uncanny similarities between Benjie and Bria weren't lost on Cassidy.

"I understand her reasons," Shane said. "I wasn't what you'd call good father material. Now that I've quit my wild ways and found a job which keeps me in one place, Judy's willing to work with me."

His brother, too, had quit his wild ways to become a rodeo announcer, but Cassidy didn't feel inclined to work with him. Not yet, and maybe not ever.

"It can't be easy for you, seeing Wasabi every day."

"He's just another bull under my care."

Her gaze was automatically drawn to his scar. She'd seen the pictures posted on their mutual friends' Facebook pages. The gash, requiring forty-four stitches, traveled from beneath his right ear, down his neck to his chest. Miraculously, Wasabi's hoof had just missed an artery. Otherwise, Shane might have bled out.

"I'm glad you're all right." Her voice unwittingly softened.

Shane responded with a heart-melting smile. No surprise he'd inspired a legion of female fans during his years on the circuit. Was that the reason for Bria's mother's secrecy? It wouldn't surprise Cassidy.

"Not my day to die," Shane said matter-of-factly.

"All the same, it was a terrible fall. How can you bear to look at Wasabi?" Cassidy still shuddered when she passed the well house, even though the accident involving her and her father happened twenty-five years ago. Like Shane, she'd walked away when things might have gone horribly different.

He shrugged. "He was just doing his job. Like any bull. I didn't take it personally."

More charm. He could certainly lay it on thick. And Cassidy was far more susceptible than she liked.

She abruptly stood. "I need to go."

Reaching for his cowboy hat, he also stood and waited for her to leave first. "Drop by anytime." The invitation was innocent. Not so his tone, which hinted at something else altogether.

When she spoke, *her* tone was all business. "If you need something, let me know."

"How about having dinner with me?"

She blinked. He didn't just ask her on a date, did he? "I beg your pardon?"

"Your dad mentioned a couple good restaurants in town. I could use someone to show me around. Help me get the lay of the land. Seeing as we'll be working together—"

She shook her head. "Benjie, my son, has homework tonight."

"You could bring him along."

"Thanks, but no. He has enough trouble with school as it is. I'd never get him to finish his homework if we went to dinner first."

"Maybe another night this week."

Did the man never give up? "We'll see," she said, planning to stall him indefinitely.

Outside the trailer she allowed herself two full seconds to gather her wits before heading to the arena in search of her sister. Should Shane come searching for her, he'd find Cassidy doing exactly what she said, helping with the riding lesson.

Fortunately, Liberty was there, talking to a student's mother. She finished just as Cassidy approached and met her halfway.

"What's wrong?" Liberty asked.

Cassidy shook her head. "Nothing."

"You look like you've seen a ghost."

Not a ghost. The brother of one, perhaps. "I was talking to our new bull manager."

"Shane? Do tell."

Cassidy planted her hands on her hips. "What does that mean?"

"He's a nice-looking guy."

"We work at a rodeo arena. There are a lot of nice-looking guys here."

"But none of them have ever left you flustered. Didn't you two date once?"

Cassidy ignored the question. "I'm not flustered. I'm annoyed. I have a lot to do and can't afford the time it takes to babysit a new employee."

"Right." Liberty laughed gaily before turning on her heel and leaving Cassidy to stew alone.

She hated it when her baby sister was right.

Chapter 2

Seven-point-three seconds into his ride, the young cowboy came flying off the bull's back. He dropped to his knees as the buzzer sounded, then pitched forward onto his face. Recovering, he pushed to his feet, grabbed his fallen hat and dusted off his jeans, a fierce scowl on his face.

Cassidy couldn't be sure if he was mad at himself for failing to reach the full eight seconds required to qualify or if he was in pain. Perhaps a little of both. He hobbled slightly on his walk of shame from the arena. Behind him, a trio of wranglers chased the bull to the far end and through a gate. A fourth wrangler swung the gate shut on the great beast's heels.

Score: bull one, cowboy zero.

"Better luck next time," a buddy hailed from the fence where he'd been watching.

A second pal slapped the cowboy on the back while a third offered him a bottled water and hearty condolences.

Moving as a group, the two dozen participants from the Tuesday night jackpot slowly made their way to the open area where either their families, friends or pickup trucks waited.

Cassidy switched off her handheld radio and tucked her clipboard beneath her arm. She, too, was almost done for the evening.

Bull-riding jackpots, along with bucking horse, calf roping and steer-wrestling competitions, were popular events at the Easy Money. Especially in the weeks preceding a rodeo. If a participant performed well, he could earn enough winnings to cover his entry fees and perhaps a little extra. If not, well, at least he got in some good practice.

Tonight, Shane had worked closely with Cassidy's father, learning the ins and outs. He also studied each bull, noting the personalities and traits of those new to him and re-familiarizing himself with those he'd previously ridden.

Cassidy knew this for a fact because she'd taken her eyes off him only long enough to perform her tasks of calling out the participants' names and communicating with her sister in the announcer's booth. Even now she had to look away for fear of Shane catching her staring at him with doe eyes. Again. He had already, twice.

Damn, damn, damn. Why did her father have to hire Shane Westcott of all people? She should have said something when she'd had the chance. But, then, she would have had to tell her father why, and that was out of the question.

Okay, Shane was competent at his new job. Cassidy noticed he took time to converse with each cowboy, offering tips and pointers and, more importantly, listening to the cowboy talk about his ride.

Shane entered every piece of information into a small spiral notebook he constantly removed and replaced in his shirt's front pocket. No fancy-schmancy handheld electronic device for him.

Somehow, Cassidy thought that fitting. Shane didn't strike her as a high-tech kind of guy. No wonder he and her father got along like twins separated at birth.

They also dressed alike, though Shane's shirt fit his broad shoulders better and his jeans hugged his narrow hips with drool-worthy closeness.

Stop looking at him!

Slamming her mouth shut, Cassidy wheeled around, intending to return the handheld radio to the registration booth and do a final total on tonight's runs. Instead, she came face-to-face with her mother.

"Keep staring at him like that and you're going to draw attention to yourself."

"I'm not staring," Cassidy insisted.

"Sure. And I'm a natural blonde."

"You *are* a natural blonde."

"Was. These days, my color is courtesy of Pizzazz Hair Salon." Her mother linked an arm through Cassidy's and led her away from the chutes. "Come on. Let's get out of here before he's any the wiser."

"It's not what you think."

"You did date once."

"I'm just curious."

"About him or Hoyt?"

"Not so loud," Cassidy admonished and glanced nervously about. No one appeared to have heard, but she couldn't be too careful. "Hoyt, of course," she continued in a half whisper. "I asked Shane about him the other day."

"And?"

"He's still married. Still childless. The good thing is, he and his wife bought a house in Jackson Hole."

The two of them walked to the registration booth. There Cassidy removed the wristband key ring she wore and unlocked the door. Breathing a sigh of relief, she entered the one-room modified office. Finally, they were out of earshot.

"Just because he has no children," her mother said, "doesn't automatically mean he'd seek custody of Benjie."

"You can't be serious." Cassidy entered numbers on a ten-key calculator, tallying the evening's scores for her father. And probably, Shane as well. She'd have to explain their system to him.

Drat. Yet another reason for them to work together. She paused and leaned against the counter. "To quote Shane, 'Hoyt wants a big family.'"

"Me not telling your dad about Liberty is no reason for you to keep Hoyt in the dark regarding Benjie."

Cassidy gawked at her mother. "I thought you were on my side."

"I am on your side and will support any decision you make."

"Except now that Dad's back, and he and Liberty are all cozy and comfy, you're having second thoughts."

"I've always had regrets. It wasn't an easy decision to make, lying all these years."

The story was well known throughout Reckless and

by plenty of others in the rodeo world. Sunny Beckett sent her husband and business partner packing when his acute alcoholism nearly ruined them, personally and financially. What she didn't tell him, or anyone else, was that she had been pregnant with their third child. Rather, she lied about the father's identity, claiming he was some cowboy passing through.

Then, last summer, Liberty had accidentally discovered Mercer Beckett was her biological father and tracked him down. He used a reconciliation with her to worm his way back into the lives of his ex-wife and daughters.

One good thing *had* happened in the wake of Mercer's return. Cassidy's brother, Ryder, also came home. They still didn't agree on their father—Ryder trusted their father's sobriety and she didn't—but otherwise the two of them had grown close during the last few months.

How could they not? Ryder was engaged to Cassidy's best friend, Tatum Mayweather, after all. Cassidy hadn't seen that one coming, but she was pleased for both her brother and best friend. They proved differences were superficial when it came to love.

Theirs was actually the second of two upcoming Beckett weddings. Liberty was also engaged. To Deacon McCrea, a former employee of the arena and now their legal counsel. Cassidy, conversely, remained single and planned to stay that way.

She'd been asked to be maid of honor at both affairs, the dates of which had recently been set for this summer and fall respectively. She would be pretty busy during the coming months, assisting with the thousand and one details, hosting bridal showers and making short day trips to pick out dresses.

Thank goodness she didn't need to worry about her parents. Since his return, her father had made it clear he was still in love with her mother and intended to remarry her. So far, her mother was resisting. One of her parents, at least, was behaving sensibly.

"Well, I have no regrets." Cassidy powered off the ten-key calculator and tore loose the paper tape.

"Hoyt has a right to know he's a father," her mother said.

"And Dad didn't?"

"You deserve child support."

"I don't see the big deal. You didn't get any from Dad for Liberty and managed just fine."

Her mother compressed her lips in a show of impatience. "That's not entirely true and you know it. He didn't take any money for his share of the arena all those years—which is basically the same as paying child support."

"He stole Ryder from us."

"Ryder went to live with him when he was old enough to legally choose."

Cassidy's chest grew tight making it hard to breathe. "I won't lose Benjie."

And there it was. The crux of the matter. Cassidy's greatest fear. What would happen if she told Hoyt about Benjie? Even if he didn't come after her for some sort of custody, Benjie could one day decide he'd rather live with his father and leave her just like Ryder.

"Shane's not stupid." Her mother's manner was less judgmental and more sympathetic. "He's bound to put two and two together."

"Not if I can help it."

"You can't keep Benjie hidden from him forever. They'll meet eventually. What if Shane tells Hoyt?"

"I'll lie if I have to." Leave Reckless if necessary.

"You've been lucky so far. One day Benjie's going to ask about his father, and you won't be able to put him off like you have in the past."

"I'll figure something out."

"Cassidy—"

"Believe me, Mom, I've weighed the pros and cons. I'm not ready to tell Benjie or Hoyt."

Her mother sighed. "You didn't always feel that way."

No, she hadn't. When she was eight months pregnant Cassidy had gone so far as to locate Hoyt and drive to where he was living, only to learn he was engaged to Cheryl, a young widow who'd lost her first husband unexpectedly. Putting herself in Cheryl's shoes, Cassidy had turned around and driven back to Reckless. She wouldn't be a home wrecker. Been there, done that, and she refused to compound the guilt she already bore.

"I came to my senses."

As if reading Cassidy's thoughts, her mother said, "You weren't the reason I divorced your father."

"I know."

"Do you? Really?"

"He was a drunk. If you hadn't divorced him, he'd have driven the arena into bankruptcy. I may have been ten, but I remember. Everything."

The smell of alcohol clinging to him like a layer of heavy sweat. Finding him passed out in the back of his pickup truck behind the barn. Or on the living room couch if he managed to stagger inside. Once in the middle of the kitchen floor. Twice in the chaise lounge on the back patio when her mother had banished him from the house.

Worst of all were the outbursts, which, to this day, still rang in her ears. The yelling. The fights. The breaking down into gut-wrenching sobs, his and her mother's. The constant apologies.

"He regrets the accident."

Cassidy wheeled on her mother. "He could have killed me. And himself."

"I'm not defending him."

"Sounds like you are." She wiped at the tears springing to her eyes, angry at herself for letting her emotions get the best of her.

"What's important is that you weren't hurt. Either of you. Just scared. No less than I was, trust me."

Memories surfaced. They were never far away. Especially since her father's return.

One night, shortly before her parents' marriage imploded, her father fetched her from a friend's house when her mother couldn't get away. The people lived less than a mile away. Nonetheless, he shouldn't have been driving. Cassidy refused to go with him at first. When he raised his voice, she acquiesced rather than have him cause a scene in front of her friend.

Misjudging the distance, he ran the truck into the well house. Granted, they weren't going fast, twenty-five miles an hour at most, and the well house suffered the most damage. There was a small dent on the truck's front fender. Cassidy's seat belt saved her from injury.

When the truck rolled to a stop, she jumped out the door and sprinted the entire way to the house, yelling at her mother to make her father leave. Two weeks later, her mother did.

At first Cassidy had been glad. Good riddance. Then, seeing how miserable her mother and brother were, she was consumed by guilt. The feeling intensified when, two years later, Ryder left. When she was older, she'd wondered if her reaction to the accident had driven her mother into the arms of another man within days after her father left. Learning that was all a lie had affected Cassidy more than she let on.

"I put up with the drinking and the bad business decisions," her mother continued. "But I couldn't let him endanger my children. Once the trust is gone, there's no getting it back."

"You trust him now. At least, you act like you do. You let him purchase the bulls when you swore we'd never own them again." And that purchase had led her father to hiring Shane.

"There's no letting or not letting," her mother said. "We're partners. An arrangement requiring give and take on both sides."

"What did he give?" From where Cassidy stood, her mother had done all the compromising.

"He agreed to put money aside for Benjie's college education."

Cassidy was taken aback, especially when her mother named the amount.

"His own personal money," her mother added. "Not the arena's."

She quickly recovered. "He can't buy my affections. Or my forgiveness. And he can't buy off his responsibility for what happened."

"Did it ever occur to you that he's simply doing something nice for his grandson? He does love the boy. And Benjie adores him."

He did, which rankled Cassidy to no end. "I'll tell him no."

"You can't stop him. It's his money. He can do with it what he wants. And when the time comes, Benjie can accept it, with or without your consent."

Cassidy liked that less.

During these past six months her life had been slowly spiraling out of control. First her father returned. Then both her siblings met their future spouses. Lastly her father had hired Shane.

Cassidy vowed anew to keep her son from his uncle's path as much as possible. The benefit would be twofold. In addition to keeping the identity of Benjie's father a secret, she'd quell this wild and inexplicable attraction to Shane. Anything else was unacceptable.

"Atta boy," Shane crooned. "Steady now."

Wasabi swayed from side to side, but managed to remain standing—which was a good thing. If the bull collapsed onto all fours, his massive weight could compress his lungs and cut off his breathing. It was imperative that every move be precisely executed, every step accomplished at the exact right moment or Wasabi might die.

"We're done," Doc Worthington said, visibly relaxing as the tranquilizer took effect.

Getting the bull sedated had been a tricky process, to say the least. With few choices, and to be as humane as possible, the Becketts' vet had used a tranquilizer gun, aiming the feather-tipped dart at Wasabi's muscular hind-quarters. The bull hadn't felt a thing.

Turned out, the initial dose hadn't been strong enough, and the vet had to administer a second one, which had worried Shane. Stress and excitement could cause the tranquilizer to run through the bull's system at an incredible rate. Shane had once seen a bull require five doses.

Now, he carefully monitored the entire procedure from his place beside the wizened country vet. So far, so good, and his respect for the older man grew.

Two of the arena's most capable wranglers had been recruited to act as spotters, along with Mercer. If Shane appeared to be in any trouble during the bull's massage therapy, they'd jump right in. Shane was glad for their presence. Despite his show of confidence, this type of therapy was relatively new to him. A phone call yesterday with the bovine sports medicine specialist had yielded some helpful advice.

The older veterinarian considered Shane a bit crazy to take this on, especially since he had limited experience.

Yes, there were risks. In more ways than one. Shane might get injured, or, worse, he could make a fool of himself in the eyes of his new employer and possibly lose his job.

"You ready?" Mercer called from the sidelines.

"Let's do it." Taking a fortifying breath, Shane crawled through the fence rails.

"There's still time to tie him up."

"I don't want to upset him more than he already is."

Shane didn't have long. Twenty minutes at most before Wasabi came out of the sedation. No telling how the bull would react. Dazed and disoriented, he'd likely attack the nearest object with horns or hooves. In this case, Shane.

Straightening, he surveyed his surroundings before

slowly approaching Wasabi. A small crowd had gathered to watch from a safe distance, Cassidy among them. Their gazes briefly connected before Shane looked away. He couldn't afford any distractions, and Cassidy was a big one.

Since their encounter in the trailer four days ago, it seemed as though she'd made it her mission to avoid him. Often, like at last night's bull riding jackpot, he'd sensed her presence, only to turn and find her staring at him or, more often, quickly averting her head.

She was obviously drawn to him, if nothing else, out of curiosity. And the feeling was mutual.

Why, then, did she run for the hills every time he approached? Her behavior just piqued his interest further, and Shane wasn't a man to be put off indefinitely.

"Watch it," Mercer hollered when Wasabi opened his bleary eyes and swung his head clumsily to the side. Mercer, along with the two wranglers, had formed a circle around Wasabi and Shane. "Maybe you should dose him again," he said to the vet.

"I don't dare. Not unless you have a crane handy we can use to lift him."

That elicited a round of nervous chuckles from the wranglers. They, too, were on high alert.

A moment later, the bull calmed, and his eyes drifted closed. He rumbled as if snoring. Shane waited another minute, positioning himself near Wasabi's shoulder, avoiding both the bull's hind end and head, either of which could be deadly.

When the bull didn't react, he tentatively stroked Wasabi's back. Other than a slight twitch, the animal remained motionless. Growing bolder, Shane removed first one, then the second dart. Wasabi continued sleeping, and Shane skimmed his palm down the bull's thick neck to his shoulder. Probing gently, he searched for any lumps, swelling or other signs of a contusion. Wasabi's injury could have been the result of a kick from another bull, requiring a potentially different course of treatment.

"Find anything?" Doc Worthington asked.

"Nothing yet." Shane increased the pressure, kneading methodically.

Wasabi snorted lustily. A moment later, he quieted.

"He probably just sustained a sprain."

In Shane's opinion, the vet was being optimistic. Wasabi could have a torn tendon or ligament. Trauma of that nature would end his career.

"Guess we'll know soon enough," Mercer said.

They would, if Wasabi didn't improve quickly. Like, within days.

Knowing he had little time left, Shane continued with the massage. It might be his imagination, or wishful thinking, but he swore the bull relaxed beneath his touch.

"Get the tape," he said.

Mercer delivered the roll from the vet. During Shane's phone call yesterday, the bovine sports medicine specialist had recommended elastic therapeutic tape, the same type human athletes used for their injuries. Wasabi would look a little funny, but if it helped, who cared?

Just as Shane finished affixing the last strip, the bull started to rouse.

Doc Worthington raised his tranquilizer gun. "I can dose him again."

"Don't bother, I'm done."

More correctly, Wasabi was done. Grunting angrily, he jabbed the empty air in front of him with his horns. Shane jumped out of the way, though the dazed bull missed him by a mile.

The reprieve didn't last. Wasabi awakened quickly and, finding himself confronted by hated humans, charged the closest one, which happened to be Shane. And, like that, the race was on.

Shane bolted for the fence. From the corner of his eye, he saw Mercer and the wranglers attempting to distract Wasabi. The bull ignored all but his tormenter and bore down on Shane, his loping gait growing steadier and faster by the second.

"Look at him move." Doc Worthington slapped his thigh. "He feels better already."

At the moment, it was little consolation to Shane that his efforts had yielded the desired results.

With the fence in sight, he executed a high-flying leap. Grabbing the top railing, he hurled himself up and over and onto the other side, landing with a loud thud. Only then did he notice the sharp pain shooting up his left calf.

Wasabi had clipped him in the leg. Nothing was torn, either his jeans or his flesh, but Shane would be sore for the next few days.

Mercer ambled over to check on Shane. "I say we call it a tie."

Doc Worthington chuckled. "Or a payback."

Shane called himself plain lucky. "Anyone see what happened to the roll of therapeutic tape?" His last recollection was of it sailing out of his hand.

"In the dirt." Mercer hitched his chin at the holding pen. "We'll get it later when the coast is clear."

The two wranglers had convinced Wasabi that his interests were best served back in the main pen with the other bulls and not causing trouble for them.

"My hat's off to you, young man." Doc Worthington eyed Shane's leg. "You all right?"

"Fine." He glanced at the crowd, which had shrunk to a small gathering. Good, Shane thought. His leg did hurt, and the fewer people who knew it, the better.

All at once, Cassidy rounded the chutes, passing her father and the vet on their way to the pen, and made straight for him. It was a nice change from her recent habit of avoidance. The expression of concern on her pretty face made him almost forget about the pain shooting up his leg.

"Are you okay?" she asked in a rush.

"Never better."

"I'm serious, Shane."

"He barely nicked me."

She studied him critically, her eyes traveling from his head to his boots. "You're limping."

He grinned, he couldn't help it, and lowered his voice. "I appreciate the concern, Cassidy. It means a lot to me."

"Of course I'm concerned. You had a close call."

"Any other reason?" He leaned in. A mere fraction at first, then more.

She abruptly drew back. "I don't know what you're implying."

"I'm thinking you're worried about me because you might like me a little."

"Well, I don't."

His grin widened. "Could have fooled me."

"I mean, I do like you. As a fellow employee." Her

cheeks flushed, and she tripped over her words. "And as an old friend."

He'd flustered her, and though it shouldn't, the thought pleased him. "Right."

"You always had a big ego."

"Matched only by my...." He let the sentence drop.

"Shane!"

"Confidence," he finished with a chuckle.

"I guess you are okay. Don't know why I worried."

She spun and would have left him in the dust if he hadn't grabbed her arm and pulled her swiftly to him.

"Thanks." Lowering his head, he pressed his lips to her cheek, letting them linger.

The contact wasn't much. Not as far as kisses went. No more than a light caress. Yet, it sent a shock wave coursing through him with the kick of a lightning bolt.

She must have felt a similar shock, for she let out a soft "Oh" and, for one incredible moment, melted against him. The next instant, she tensed. "I—I have to g-go."

"Why, Cassidy?" He searched her face. To his surprise and concern, he noted fear in her eyes. "What are you afraid of?"

"Nothing."

He wanted to contradict her, but this wasn't the time or place. Not with her acting like a skittish colt and not with her father standing close by, watching the two of them like, well, like a father watches a man who's just kissed his daughter on the cheek.

What would Mercer think if he knew of Shane's attraction to Cassidy? He might approve. Then again, he might oppose it.

Maybe Shane should take a moment and step back

from the situation. This job was too important for him to mess up right out of the gate.

The thrill of his encounter with Cassidy faded. Unfortunately, his attraction to her didn't. Try as he might, Shane couldn't stop staring as she walked away.

Then again, he wasn't trying very hard.

Chapter 3

"I sure appreciate the use of ole Skittles." Shane tugged on the brim of Benjie's too-big cowboy hat. "I know it's rough sometimes, letting someone else ride your horse." He lifted his daughter and planted her on Skittles's broad back, then faced Benjie again. "Bria will treat him right, I promise."

"It's okay." The boy kicked at the ground with the toe of his boot, leaving behind a large gouge in the dirt. "I can ride Rusty."

Cassidy bit her lower lip to keep herself from speaking. She knew how much her son disliked riding the potbellied, swaybacked mule. Not because Rusty was mean or difficult or stubborn, as were many of his breed. But because he wasn't a horse. That, in Benjie's opinion, made him the object of ridicule from his peers. Like a kid forced to wear no-name sneakers while everyone else in school owned expensive, celebrity-endorsed athletic shoes.

Cassidy had been getting plenty of flak from Benjie this past school semester. He complained nonstop about his discount store footwear. The thing was, she didn't have money to spare for nonessentials.

Her mother's words came back to haunt her. If she told Hoyt about Benjie, she'd be able to collect child support from him. Possibly for the years since Benjie's birth.

No, no, no. She wasn't about to share, much less risk losing, custody of her son. And Hoyt would no doubt insist on some form of custody.

"You need a leg up, too?" Shane asked Benjie.

"I got it." Nimble as a monkey, Benjie grabbed the side of the saddle and scrambled up onto Rusty's back.

"Good job."

Though Benjie would argue differently, Skittles was barely better than the mule. One of the arena's oldest mounts, the horse's slow, steady gait and docile personality made him perfect for a novice like Bria. Truthfully, Benjie was ready for a more advanced horse. But he loved Skittles and was loath to part with his pal.

"I want to go, Daddy," Bria exclaimed gleefully and jiggled her turquoise cowboy boots.

A tad on the chubby side, she sported a generous mop of curly brown hair and an impish grin that reminded Cassidy a lot of Shane.

"Okay, okay. Give me a second." Shane patted Benjie's leg. "You want to ride in the arena or come with us to the round pen?"

"With you." Benjie gazed longingly at Skittles, not

at Bria, who was combing her fingers through the old horse's stringy mane.

"If it's okay with your mother." Shane glanced at Cassidy, his green eyes twinkling.

She knew at once he'd been aware of her scrutiny the entire time and said nothing. Guess she wasn't nearly as clever as she thought.

Rather than avoiding him, as was her plan when he'd first arrived, she'd gone about the arena with a business-as-usual approach these past few days. She refused to let him think their kiss had been anything other than mild and meaningless.

Truth be told, it had rocked her to her core. She couldn't remember a time when a simple peck on the cheek had turned her limbs to liquid.

Maybe her mother was right when she said Cassidy had gone too long without dating. What other reason could there be for her racing heart every time he neared?

Cassidy's view of Shane, Bria and Benjie was obstructed when a woman astride a leggy thoroughbred rode up beside her.

"Cassidy, dearie, can you help me adjust my stirrups? They're a little long."

"Sure," she answered automatically and did as requested.

"Mom," Benjie hollered as if she'd been swallowed whole and not momentarily out of sight. "Can I go with Mr. Shane?"

The name was a compromise. Cassidy insisted her son address adults formally, one of the few holdovers from her father's strict teachings. Shane, however, wanted Benjie to call him by his first name.

She stepped around the horse and into view. What

if Shane asked Benjie about his father? Better she was there to intercede. Then again, what if her going sent Shane the wrong message about them? Cassidy couldn't decide on the lesser evil.

"You're welcome to join us," Shane said affably. "If you're worried about him."

"I'm not worried." Not about Benjie.

"Then come on. The more the merrier."

"Um, I need to, ah…"

The woman on the thoroughbred leaned over her horse's neck. "For Pete's sake, go with him," she said in a loud whisper. "Don't ever turn down an invitation from a handsome man."

Seventy, if she was a day, the woman was a regular at the Easy Money and one of their few English hunter-jumper riders. Rumor had it she'd been married—and divorced—four times.

"Mom," Benjie pleaded.

Feeling pressured from all sides, Cassidy relented. "Okay, fine."

"Good decision," the woman said. "You won't regret it." Pulling on the reins, she turned her horse away and nudged him into a trot.

Wrong, Cassidy thought as she caught up with Shane and saw his satisfied grin. She regretted it already.

He walked beside his daughter, holding on to the side of Skittles's bridle. He didn't look over at Cassidy, which somehow irritated her all the more. What? Invite her and then ignore her? The next instant she reminded herself she couldn't care less. She had no interest in him.

Luckily, or unluckily, depending on one's opinion, no one was using the round pen. Benjie, familiar with the drill, entered the pen first and rode Rusty in a clockwise circle.

Cassidy tugged her short denim jacket snugger around her waist, the gesture the result of nerves and not the cool January breeze blowing in from the west.

"Daddy, I want to ride by myself," Bria said, her eyes on Benjie. "I can do it."

"In a minute. First, we need to get Skittles used to the pen."

The old horse couldn't be more used to the bull pen if he'd been born in it. Shane, Cassidy realized, was being protective, but not so protective he smothered Bria. He also engaged Benjie in friendly conversation. Her son responded as he always did to attention from cowboys at the arena. He lit up.

Did Benjie miss having a father in his life? Was she wrong to deny him?

"Race you." He passed Bria at a slow, bumpy trot.

"No, Benjie," Cassidy warned. She'd climbed the fence to a built-in bench seat, installed so parents and instructors could sit comfortably while monitoring the goings-on in the pen. "Bria isn't ready to race yet."

"But I want to," the little girl protested and kicked Skittles in the sides. The saddle's wide, thick cinch prevented her boots from making any real contact.

Like father, like daughter, Cassidy decided. The little girl was fearless. Shane had always been like that. The quality had earned him a world championship bull-riding title on three separate occasions. It had also darn near cost him his life.

Shane brought Skittles to a stop. "If you promise not to race," he told Bria, "you can fly solo."

The little girl stopped giggling in order to stare at

him, an expression of bewilderment on her cherub face. "I'm not flying, Daddy. I'm riding."

"Yes, you are. And doing well, I might add."

He adjusted the reins, placing them firmly between her plump fingers. "Don't let go and don't move your hands all over the place. You'll pull on Skittles's mouth, and he won't like it."

Shane continued instructing his daughter for several minutes until she was fidgeting with excitement.

"Daddy," she whined. "I'm ready."

"All right." He stepped back and let her go.

Cassidy could see the struggle on his face. As a parent, she understood what he was going through. It wasn't easy, giving up control. Even, evidently, for Shane, who'd been a father only these last four months.

Bria completed her first circuit on her own with no mishaps. A second and third progressed just as smoothly, considering Benjie followed closely, daring her to go faster. Cassidy hadn't been aware that she'd let her thoughts drift until the bench shifted beneath her. With a loud creak, Shane plopped down.

Right beside her. She hadn't realized how small the seat was. Her pulse quickly soared. Really?

Cassidy pretended Shane's proximity made no difference to her. "She's a chip off the old block."

Indeed, Bria took to horse riding as one might expect from the offspring of a rodeo champion.

"Not bad for a first time out."

"Her mother doesn't ride?" It seemed a reasonable question to Cassidy and not her being nosy, though she was.

"Never been on a horse."

"Huh. I take it you didn't meet her on the circuit."

He leaned back, pushing his cowboy hat off his face and giving her a less obstructed view of his profile. His strong, rugged features were pronounced in the bright afternoon sun, as was his scar. Both stole her breath.

"Actually, I did. Right here. She and a friend came to the Wild West Days Rodeo."

"Wow." Cassidy hadn't noticed his interest in anyone. Then again, she'd steered clear of Shane during the rodeos he'd attended. Less chance of people talking about her son and him hearing. "Were you angry with Judy for not telling you about Bria?"

Of all the disagreements Cassidy's parents had had since her father's return, not one had been about her mother lying to him about being Liberty's father. Why was that? Surely, he was angry. She could easily imagine how furious Hoyt would be with her if he discovered her deception.

"Yeah," Shane admitted, "at first, I was angry." His tone gentled. "I got over it once I met Bria."

Cassidy doubted Hoyt would be as forgiving. Her glance returned to Bria. "She's adorable."

"She's something else, all right. I was scared to death she'd hate me. Be mad at me for abandoning her all these years."

"How could she? You didn't know about her."

"I wasn't sure she'd understand. But turns out I didn't need to worry. We hit it off from the start. Like she'd always been a part of my life."

"Was she upset with her mother?" That possibility concerned Cassidy almost as much.

"No. Judy and I concocted a story to tell her. She accepted it. I suppose because she's four."

Like Cassidy's sister. Liberty had accepted the story

their mother had made up. Also like Benjie, when Cassidy put off his occasional queries.

"And Judy's willing to share custody with you?"

Shane gave Cassidy a curious look. "She is."

When he didn't ask why Cassidy wanted to know, she pushed on. "What changed her mind?"

He raised his eyebrows, his curiosity noticeably increased. Still, he didn't ask. "The accident and me walking away from rodeoing. When I decided to settle down, she thought maybe I'd grown up enough to be a father."

"Have you?"

He laughed good-naturedly. "Depends on who you ask."

"I think you have," Cassidy said, quite seriously. "You're not the same man I once knew."

"Thank you. I'll take that as a compliment."

"I meant it as one."

A spark of attraction flashed in his eyes, causing her breath to hitch. They were close. So close she could discern each and every laugh line bracketing his eyes. Feel the raw energy emanating from him. Sense the weighty pull of their mutual attraction. It wasn't easy to resist.

"What about Benjie's father?" he asked. "Is he in the picture?"

"He isn't."

And, like that, the attraction fizzled. Shane had ventured into forbidden territory.

"Sorry," she said, "I have to go. *We* have to go. Benjie," she called to her son. "Grandma's fixing dinner."

"Aw, Mom. Not yet."

Cassidy stood—and realized too late she was caught between Shane's knees and the fence railing. She couldn't pass unless he allowed it. Would he? Her gaze was drawn to his handsome face.

"Stay," he said in a voice like warm honey. "Please."

"We can't."

"You haven't given me a chance to apologize."

Before she could ask what for, two high-pitched squeals split the air. The first from Skittles, the second from Bria. In a flash, Shane vaulted from the bench. Cassidy grabbed the wooden seat before losing her balance. She twisted sideways just in time to see him reach Skittles and his daughter's side.

"I'm sorry." Benjie hung his head.

"It's all right, buddy." Shane held Bria tight in his arms. "No harm done."

Indeed, his daughter had quickly calmed down once she realized Skittles had merely taken a brisk hop-step when Benjie tugged on his tail.

"It's not okay." Cassidy came up beside him, her mouth tight. "He was teasing her horse. That's against arena rules and *my* rules."

"She's fine," Shane insisted. "And, besides, he apologized."

"Just because she's not hurt is no excuse for what he did."

Something was off in Cassidy's tone. Shane couldn't quite put his finger on it. As if she was talking about something other than her son and the teasing incident.

"All right. Then how 'bout we punish him? One hour of mucking bull manure after school tomorrow."

Cassidy nodded in agreement. "Seems fitting."

"Do I have to?" Benjie pouted.

"Yes, you do, young man."

Bria giggled. "Ha, ha. You have to clean up cow poo."

Shane set her back atop Skittles. When he patted the horse's rump, the pair moseyed off.

Benjie followed on Rusty, his attitude adjusted.

"He's just being a boy," Shane told Cassidy.

"A misbehaving boy."

Rather than returning to the bench, he and Cassidy exited through the gate and continued watching from outside the round pen. He was glad to see she'd forgotten about leaving. For the moment, at least. Experience had taught him she'd flee at the tiniest provocation.

Shane struggled to repress a smile. The women he typically met on the circuit were transparent, making their wants and wishes crystal clear. Cassidy, on the other hand, was a mystery. He liked that about her. Then again, he'd always appreciated a challenge.

Since she hadn't brought up his apology, he did. "I'm sorry about the kiss the other day. I got carried away."

"I've forgotten all about it."

"Why don't I believe you?"

"No big deal, Shane."

Wasn't it? He'd felt something when his lips brushed her cheek. A rather enjoyable, no, exciting, sensation unlike any before. He'd been certain she'd felt it, too.

"In any case, I was out of line."

"Okay. Apology accepted. Now can we talk about something else? How's the massage therapy with Wasabi coming along? Dad says he's improving daily." She kept her voice light, though the underlying tension in it was unmistakable.

Which made Shane reluctant to abide by her request. He wasn't ready to drop the subject.

"Remember that time in Albuquerque when I got thrown? You came running to my rescue then, too."

She gaped at him, proving she also remembered.

"Why did we stop dating, Cassidy?"

"I don't know. We were young and ambitious and both wanted championship titles."

She focused her attention on the children. The two reliable lesson mounts were placidly circling with their young passengers.

"We had a few good times," he said. "You and me."

"We did."

"I was jealous when you started dating Hoyt."

"Really?" Surprise flared in her eyes. "You never said anything."

"Maybe I should have."

Her eyes widened. "I didn't think you cared."

Shane nodded. Hoyt had been the better choice, or so he'd told himself.

"Do you miss competing?" he asked.

"Not at all. My life now is the arena and my son."

Had Hoyt's engagement so soon after he broke up with Cassidy hardened her heart? Shane didn't think so. Cassidy had been the one to end things. And she'd obviously dated other men. Pretty quickly after Hoyt, given she had a five-year-old son.

"If you don't mind my asking, what happened with you and Hoyt? One minute you were in love, the next you walked out on him."

"I do mind you asking."

"It's been a long time." What was the harm? Unless she still cared about Hoyt. The thought didn't sit well with Shane for reasons he'd rather not examine.

"Exactly. It's been a long time and doesn't matter

anymore." Grabbing the top fence railing, she placed her foot on the bottom one and hauled herself up. "Come on, Benjie. We really need to go."

Shane waited until she lowered herself to the ground before stating the obvious. "Every time I say something you don't like or that makes you uncomfortable, you run off."

He half expected her to deny it, but she didn't.

"Then stop saying things I don't like and that make me uncomfortable."

He chuckled and shook his head. "You're something else, Cassidy Beckett."

"I'll take *that* as a compliment."

"It was intended as one." More so than she probably realized.

She entered the pen and fetched her reluctant son. It seemed Benjie wasn't done playing with Bria. Shane was glad the two were getting along. He wanted his daughter to fit in at the Easy Money and to make friends.

"I supposed we should call it a day, too." He took hold of Skittles's bridle and led the horse through the gate. "I promised your mother I'd have you home by seven thirty."

Bria's features fell. "Can I stay over again?"

How he wished he could accommodate her. Nothing would make him happier. But he didn't dare push the boundaries of his agreement with Bria's mother, who'd been adamant that their daughter attend preschool on weekday mornings. Once he'd proved himself, then, yes, he'd insist on more time. Shane was smart enough to take things slowly.

"Sorry, kiddo. But maybe your mom will let you

come back this weekend." Judy had mentioned attending a real estate class on Saturday. She might appreciate Shane babysitting.

While he and Cassidy unsaddled and brushed down the mounts, the kids played a game of tag in the barn aisle. Benjie could have easily won, but he let Bria catch him more than once.

"He's good with her," Shane told Cassidy. "Considering he's a year older and a boy."

"Benjie's used to socializing with kids of all ages. They're a staple at the arena." Untying Rusty's lead rope, she walked ahead. "Come on, Benjie. Help me put Rusty in his stall."

Bria stared after them, her expression bereft. Shane cheered her by lifting her up and setting her on Skittles's bare back.

"Hold on to his mane," he instructed and returned the old horse to his stall, three down from Rusty's. Shane used the opportunity to continue conversing with Cassidy.

"Maybe next Saturday we can take them on a trail ride together?" He'd heard a lot about the rolling mountains beyond the Easy Money's back pastures, but had not yet found the time to ride them.

"I'm working. The Jamboree's in two weeks."

She was referring to the arena's next big rodeo. Shane would be busy, too. Yet, he couldn't take no for an answer.

"How much would it hurt if we quit an hour early?" He removed Skittles's halter and lifted Bria from the horse's back. She scampered over to Benjie.

"I'm not going on a date with you," Cassidy said.

"It's not a date. We're talking a trail ride with Benjie and Bria. Invite your friend Tatum and her kids if you want."

"Bad idea." She shut the door on Rusty's stall. "Besides, I have other plans. A...family function."

"We were friends once. We can be again."

"It's complicated."

"Only if you make it complicated."

"No."

"Why? Because of Hoyt?"

"Of course not."

"You still care for him."

"I don't. He means nothing to me."

Shane recalled their brief kiss the other day and the sparks that had ignited between them. "What about me, Cassidy? Do I mean anything to you?"

Her sharp intake of breath and flustered denial should have been enough of an answer for him.

It wasn't, and Shane was more than prepared to see exactly how deep—or not—her feelings for him ran.

Chapter 4

Most women who owned SUVs did so because they had a pack of children to tote around. That was true for Cassidy and her friend Tatum. Cassidy didn't understand why her sister drove one. Liberty had always struck her as the consummate cowgirl, more comfortable behind the wheel of a pickup truck than anything else.

Yet, here they were, Cassidy, Liberty and their mother, heading into Mesa for a girls' afternoon, riding in style—*not*—in her sister's SUV. The vehicle was a mess. But instead of toys scattered across the floor of the back seat, there were a pair of old boots, a hoof pick, a bridle with a broken buckle, a spray bottle of mane detangler, bride magazines and an assortment of loose CDs.

The empty snack food wrappers, however, were the

same as the ones in Cassidy's car. Literally, the same. Apparently, Liberty subscribed to a similar on-the-go diet as Benjie.

Cassidy rolled her eyes from her seat in the back. In the front, her mother and sister chatted nonstop about Liberty's wedding plans. They paid little attention to Cassidy, as long as she interjected the occasional comment about flowers or menu selections or veil versus no veil.

The wedding wasn't until the end of August—a date had finally been set—but, according to her mother and sister, the list of things to do in preparation was endless and required an eight-month head start.

In an attempt to chip away at the list, the three of them had taken off in the middle of what promised to be a slow day at the arena for some dress shopping and, if time allowed, a visit to the wedding supply store.

"Just to check out a few things," Liberty had said.

Right, Cassidy thought. *Define "few."*

Her father, brother and Tatum had volunteered to hold down the fort in their absence. Cassidy had wanted to stay behind, too, but her sister and mother wouldn't hear of it.

She relented after they agreed to include a stop at the party goods store. Benjie was turning six this coming weekend, and Cassidy was planning a party. Tatum's three kids and a half-dozen friends from school were coming. Benjie was beside himself with excitement.

"We're here," Liberty sang out, turning the SUV into the shopping center parking lot.

Cassidy tried to convince herself the sudden rush of nerves she suffered had nothing to do with wedding dress shopping and everything to do with the car that had swerved past them a little too close for comfort. Weddings in general made her uncomfortable. Perhaps because they all too often led to divorce.

They found a parking space right in front of Your-Special-Day.

"Kind of a silly name for a wedding shop." Cassidy slammed shut her door.

"You remember Valerie Kirkshaw's wedding last year?" Liberty marched ahead, speaking over her shoulder. "She bought her dress here. On sale. She swears this is the place to go."

Cassidy did remember the wedding and the dress. Both had been nice.

"She also said they have a huge selection of bridesmaid's dresses."

"Great." Cassidy mustered a smile as they entered the small, tastefully appointed shop. She might not be in the spirit of things, like her mother and sister, but neither would she ruin the day for them.

Thirty minutes sped by surprisingly fast. Liberty stood on a podium in the rear of the store, surrounded by mirrors and wearing her fourth dress. And, for the fourth time, Cassidy gawked in astonishment.

Her cowgirl sister, it seemed, had a penchant for very frilly, very fluffy, very girly wedding dresses, each one more stunning than the last.

Cassidy's mother circled Liberty, alternating between plucking at the voluminous folds and wiping away another tear. "You look beautiful, honey."

Indeed, she did. Cassidy's throat closed with emotion. She'd stopped dreaming of weddings years ago. On the day she'd walked away from Hoyt moments before telling him he was going to be a father. Then and there, she'd decided to dedicate her life to the baby growing inside her.

It wasn't as if guys ignored her. She'd been asked out, now and again. Usually by cowboys attending the rodeos. Less the last couple of years. She supposed, at thirty-five, she appealed less and less to the competitors, who seemed to be getting younger and younger each year. Perhaps her reputation for being standoffish preceded her.

She and Shane were nearly the same age, and he didn't think she was past her prime or standoffish. Not if the way his arms had tightened around her waist or the heat flared in his eyes were any indication.

That was new, she thought. He'd never looked at her like that before. If he had, they might have dated more than a few weeks. Then what?

"Cassidy. Your phone."

"Oh, yeah." At her mother's reminder, Cassidy roused herself and activated her phone's camera. It was her job to take a photo of each dress so Liberty could scrutinize them later. "Smile."

She snapped a picture, checking it to make sure it was in focus before taking a second and third from different angles.

Four more dresses were selected and tried on with the store clerk's help and guidance. Cassidy added notes to each picture, including pertinent details such as price and potential alterations.

"What do you have for bridesmaid dresses in pink?" Liberty asked, running her hand over the plastic garment cover of her favorite-thus-far dress.

"Pink!" Cassidy gasped, imagining the horrors ahead of her. "You said nothing about pink."

"It's a summer wedding. And the groomsmen are wearing dove grey tuxes."

"But pink?" Who was this woman impersonating her sister and where had she hidden Liberty?

"Weren't you listening in the car on the way over?"

No, she hadn't been.

"Might I suggest a pale rose instead?" the clerk said. "It's perfect for August."

Rose had a better ring to it than pink.

The clerk showed them to the racks holding bridesmaid dresses, arranged by style and color.

"Oh, look at this one." Her mother held up a tea-length creation trimmed with a delicate lace.

Liberty rushed forward. "I love it!"

Cassidy let out an expansive sigh.

While Liberty waited, seated on a velveteen upholstered chair with a seashell-shaped back, the clerk fawned over her. Cassidy and her mother ventured into the dressing room, six rose-colored dresses held high so as not to drag on the floor.

Sliding into the first one, Cassidy waited for her mother to zip her up. When that didn't happen, she asked, "Something stuck?"

"No." Her mother sniffed.

Cassidy turned around, holding the narrow straps of the dress to keep them from falling. "What's wrong, Mom?"

"I'm fine. Just a bit emotional." Her mother's smile wobbled. "It's a big deal when your daughter marries."

Cassidy supposed it was. Feeling a little emotional herself, she patted her mother's arm. "Hang in there, Mom."

"I thought you'd be the first."

Cassidy managed an awkward shrug, the dress still gaping in the back. "Hoyt and I never discussed the M word."

"You ever think what might have happened if you'd tracked him down sooner? Before he met his wife."

"Sure. In the beginning. But I doubt I would have married him."

"Because he liked to drink?"

"Drink *and* drive. Let's not forget that."

Growing up with an alcoholic father—former alcoholic, the rest of her family was quick to point out—Cassidy had little tolerance for people who imbibed to excess. She particularly had no tolerance for people who then got behind the wheel of a vehicle, as her father had the night he drove his truck into the well house with Cassidy in the front passenger seat.

Finally, her mother zipped up the dress, enclosing Cassidy inside layers upon layers of rose taffeta. "Shane doesn't drink."

"And why should that matter to me?"

"I've seen him watching you."

Cassidy tugged on the sides of the dress, adjusting the fit. "He's just curious is all. I did once date his brother."

"More than date him. You two had a ch—"

"Mom, not here," Cassidy said in a terse whisper.

"It could explain Shane's curiosity."

"You think he suspects?" Breathing became difficult. The dress's snug bodice could be responsible. More likely it was her constant anxiety.

"Or he likes you. In that way."

Cassidy's anxiety increased.

She stared at herself in the mirror, not quite seeing her reflection. What bothered her most wasn't that Shane might like her. It was that she might like him back. Yes, in that way.

Liberty hailed them from the dressing room entrance. "What's taking so long, you two?"

"Be right there." Cassidy's mother pushed open the double swinging doors after giving Cassidy a final inspection. "You're stunning. No one could blame Shane."

Cassidy walked out to show her sister, a slight unsteadiness to her legs. She'd hardly reached the podium when her sister snapped a picture with her phone.

No decisions were made. Liberty wanted to visit another shop or two first. Cassidy was admittedly relieved and glad when they pulled into the arena driveway two hours later. She alone had packages to unload, having made a haul for Benjie's birthday at the party supply store.

Leaving the bags on the kitchen table, she headed straight for the arena. School had let out thirty minutes ago, and the students participating in the afternoon riding program would arrive any second. While Liberty was in charge, Cassidy frequently helped with the advanced students.

Doc Worthington's familiar truck was parked near the bull pens. He, her father and Shane emerged from behind the chutes. Cassidy's route forced her to either meet up with them or make an obvious and rude detour. Reluctantly, she chose the former.

"Good news." Her father beamed. "Doc here thinks Wasabi's coming along and will be ready to compete in the Jamboree next weekend."

Feeling the intensity of Shane's gaze on her, she

struggled to remain focused on her father. "That is good news."

"Shane's done a right fine job." Doc Worthington's low laugh sounded like an engine rumbling to life on a cold morning. "Who'd've guessed. Massage therapy on a bull. What'll they think of next?"

"Don't know until you try." Shane's tone and smile were both humble. And endearing.

Cassidy was undeniably affected.

Spying several cars pulling into the parking area, she said, "Excuse me. I have a class to teach."

Before she managed a single step, Benjie charged out from behind a parked horse trailer, legs churning and arms swinging.

"Mom! Mom!" He stopped in front of her, red-faced and short of breath. "Did you get the invitations?"

"Yes, sweetie, they're on the kitchen table."

"It's my birthday on Friday," he announced to the group. "But we're having the party Saturday. So more kids can come."

Doc Worthington gave him a pat on his head. "How old will you be?"

"Six."

"Six, huh?" Shane said. "I thought you might be seven. Seeing as how big you are."

Benjie puffed up, adding an extra inch to his height. "I'm the third oldest in my class."

Cassidy fought the surge of panic building inside her. This was exactly the reason she hadn't mentioned Benjie's birthday to Shane earlier. If he bothered to count backward, he might realize she and his brother had been dating at the time she'd gotten pregnant. Though it had been in the last days of their relationship. Right before their big fight. She hadn't noticed her missed period until three weeks after their breakup.

Did guys think about things like when conception occurred? She risked a quick peek at Shane from beneath lowered lids. He didn't appear to be counting backward in his head. Rather, he was smiling pleasantly as Benjie rambled on about the party.

"We're gonna have pony rides and birthday cake and a piñata."

"Sounds like a good time."

"Can Bria come?" Benjie asked.

"I'll see. Thanks for the invitation." He turned to Cassidy. "If your mom doesn't mind."

She could hardly say no. Nor would she. "Of course. Bria's more than welcome."

Doc Worthington made a show of taking out his invoice pad and pen. "Hate to leave, but I've got another appointment."

Cassidy's father got the hint. "Let me get you paid for today."

The two men beelined for the office.

"Grandpa, can I come, too?" Benjie hurried after them, leaving Cassidy and Shane alone.

She could have called her son back, but didn't. When Shane moved closer, and the inevitable hum coursed through her, she reconsidered.

"You don't have to invite Bria," he said. "I can give Benjie some excuse."

"Nonsense. I should have thought of inviting her myself."

"All right." His mouth curved at the corners.

To her chagrin, her defenses crumbled. He did have the sexiest smile she'd ever seen.

"We accept."

We? She blinked at his use of the plural. What had she been thinking? Or not thinking. Naturally, he'd come with his daughter. At least to drop her off and pick her up. Only "we accept" sounded like he intended to stay for the duration of the party.

"Great. I'll, ah, have Benjie leave an invitation at the trailer with the details."

"Looking forward to it."

Cassidy headed to the arena gate to meet her sister, acutely aware of Shane watching her every step of the way.

"You okay?" Liberty asked, concern filling her eyes. "You look a little flushed."

Was that all? Her cheeks felt like they were on fire.

"I don't know, Shane. Seems like a lot of driving for you to do in one day."

"I don't mind."

There was a pause on the phone as Judy considered his request to take Bria for an unscheduled visit tomorrow. "You'd have to be here early in the morning. By seven sharp. My class starts at eight."

"No problem."

"And have her home by six. It's pizza night."

"No problem."

Another pause. Judy wasn't making this easy on him. Their agreement as to when and for how long he had their daughter was literally brand-new and on a trial basis. He didn't want to pressure Judy too much or not keep his word, just on the chance she'd react negatively.

On the other hand, someone had to watch Bria while Judy attended her all-day real estate class. Why not

Shane instead of the sweet, elderly neighbor? Especially when he could take Bria to a birthday party with other children her age. A much better option than her sitting in front of a TV for hours on end. Shane hadn't included that last part when he made his pitch to Judy.

He heard a long, drawn-out sigh. He also heard a man's voice in the background, muffled and indistinguishable. Must be the fiancé, Shane thought, and ground his teeth. Was the man telling her not to give in?

"Fine," Judy finally said. "See you in the morning."

"Thanks. I appreciate it."

Shane was grateful for Judy's understanding, and from what he could tell, her fiancé's cooperation. Perhaps he'd jumped to the wrong conclusion and the three of them *could* effectively parent Bria.

Pocketing his phone, Shane continued walking down Center Avenue, Reckless's main thoroughfare. Normally, he'd be at the arena on a Friday afternoon. Mercer, however, had cut him and several of the bull wranglers loose for the evening.

With the Jamboree Rodeo just next weekend, practicing for events was at an all-time frenzy. A group of calf ropers had reserved the arena tonight, under Cassidy's direction, which meant there would be no bull-riding practices until tomorrow. Shane had decided to take advantage of the unexpected free time by familiarizing himself with the town and, now that he and Bria were officially attending Benjie's birthday party, shop for a gift.

What did one get a six-year-old boy? All Shane and his brother had wanted at Benjie's age were things related to do horses and riding. Living at the Easy Money

Arena, Benjie already had more than Shane could have ever dreamed of owning.

He crossed at the next corner, taking in the sights. Reckless boasted the usual small-town businesses: feed store, gas station, several restaurants, ice cream parlor, convenience market that also rented DVDs and sold bait, a shipping store, two real estate offices, a post office and public library.

In addition, there was a multitude of shops catering to tourists, the town's main industry next to the Easy Money Arena. Those included a bookstore with offerings by local authors in the window, a novelty shop, a photo studio specializing in old-time photographs, two jewelry stores and three antique shops.

Shane was just thinking there was nothing in any of the shops or stores of interest to Benjie, and a trip to nearby Globe was probably in order, when he happened to pass the Silver Dollar Pawn Shop. There in the window was a set of shiny golf clubs. Of course Benjie didn't play golf, but the clubs gave Shane an idea, and he went inside.

"Afternoon." The woman behind the counter flashed him a ready smile that scattered the many wrinkles on her face in different directions. Her gray hair was so tightly permed, it sat upon her head like a knit ski cap. "Holler if you need help."

"Do you by chance carry sports equipment?"

"Some. Over this way." She emerged from behind the counter. It was then Shane noticed she was maybe four-eleven at most, even with her bright pink sneakers. "What kind of equipment did you have in mind?"

"Football. Baseball. Basketball. Something for a young kid."

"Everything I have is right here." She guided him to the last aisle where golf clubs, tennis rackets, ice skates and, Shane was pleased to see, football, baseball and basketball equipment, some of it in decent shape, lined the shelves. "There's a selection of autographed memorabilia in the case over there."

Shane gave the case a cursory once-over. "Not sure memorabilia is what I need."

The woman's smile didn't as much as flicker. "What are you looking for?"

Shane pushed back his cowboy hat and scratched behind his ear. "The thing is, I'm not sure if the kid likes sports. I just figured, he's a boy and most boys do."

"That's a fact. This boy a relation of yours?"

"My boss's grandson. I work for the Becketts."

She snapped her fingers. "You're that new bull manager they hired."

"Guilty as charged." Shane wasn't surprised she'd heard of him, what with Reckless being a typical small town and the Becketts its most prominent residents.

"The boy you're talking about must be Cassidy's youngster, Benjie. My granddaughter's going to his party."

This was promising. "Any suggestions on what might interest him?"

"From what DeAnna tells me, he's quite the class clown."

"I've heard that, too."

"She hasn't mentioned sports, but as you say, he's a boy. And he doesn't have a father around to play any with him."

The woman could be considered by some to be a gossip. Shane thought she was simply making small talk.

He hadn't been at the Easy Money long, yet he, too, had already figured out there was no father in Benjie's life.

"Cassidy does her best," the woman continued as Shane scrutinized the array of sports equipment. "Works her tail off to provide for her son."

Shane had observed the same thing and admired her for it. He might be new to parenthood, but he'd quickly realized raising a child required tremendous sacrifice and dedication.

He selected a Rawlings outfield baseball glove that appeared to be in mint condition. Turning it over in his hands, he noted the logo, size and price tag still attached by a plastic string.

"The man who brought it in claimed it's brand-new," the woman said.

"Seems to be." Shane fingered the dangling price tag.

The glove was probably a little too large for Benjie. Better than too small, Shane reasoned. Room to grow.

Sports had played a large part in Shane's high school days. He'd made the varsity football and baseball teams when he was just a sophomore. During his senior year, he quit school sports to focus exclusively on rodeo. The decision paid off, launching him on a career that would become his life and give him a marketable trade.

"There's a bat by the same manufacturer." The woman indicated a rack at the end of the aisle, the bats in it standing upright, as if at attention.

Shane lifted the solid wood Rawlings bat, testing the weight in his hand. Not too heavy, not too light. Like the glove, it appeared barely used.

While part of him worried he wasn't buying Benjie something brand-new and fresh from the factory, a high-quality glove and bat would make a fine gift. He was actually more worried Benjie wouldn't like them.

"You're going to need a ball to go with those," the woman said. "You take all three, and I'll cut you a deal."

A few minutes later, Shane stood at the counter, removing his bank card from his wallet as the woman bagged his purchases.

"Hard to believe that boy of Cassidy's is six already." The woman passed the bag across the counter, then accepted Shane's card and ran it through the scanner. "I remember when she quit the rodeo circuit and came home to have him. Seems like it was yesterday."

"Time flies." Shane was thinking of his daughter, Bria, and all the years he'd missed with her.

Not a day passed he didn't count his blessings. Had Judy kept Bria from him, he could have wound up like Mercer, going twenty-five years before learning he'd fathered a daughter.

"We all figured at some point her boyfriend would step up and claim the boy. Didn't happen. Guess he's not interested."

"His loss." Again, Shane thought of Bria and the day she came into his life.

The woman escorted him to the door. "Nice to meet you, Shane. Enjoy the party."

"I will. Thanks."

"Be sure and come back."

"Count on it."

He returned to his truck and tossed the bag onto the passenger seat before getting in. He was debating checking out the pizza parlor when something the woman said came back to him. This time, he paid attention.

We all figured at some point her boyfriend would

step up and claim the boy. Didn't happen. Guess he's not interested.

Six years ago. Shane remembered it well. He'd recently won his second world bull-riding championship in December at the National Finals Rodeo. He'd taken the month of January off to recuperate from his injuries. The gal he'd been dating at the time, also a barrel racer, was friends with Cassidy.

The gal had sat on the end of the couch where he was resting, his left ankle elevated atop a stack of pillows, and announced that Cassidy had just given birth to a boy.

"A couple weeks sooner," she had said, "and her baby could've been Hoyt's."

Shane hadn't thought much about it at the time. In part, because his brain was fuzzy due to pain meds. Also, his brother was engaged and soon to be married.

Now, though, Shane did give it consideration. What was the old saying? There were no such things as coincidences.

Was Benjie his brother's son? Did he dare ask Cassidy? More importantly, did he say anything to Hoyt? If Benjie were his son, he'd want to know. He'd *insist* on knowing.

Despite a former lifestyle many people considered wild and impulsive, Shane never moved forward without careful thought and consideration. To that end, he placed a call to Hoyt.

"Hey, buddy!" His brother's greeting was exuberant. "How's it going?"

Shane sat in his truck, out of the cool weather and sheltered from the wind that had kicked up earlier, and chatted with Hoyt for several minutes, filling him in on how things were progressing with the new job.

"I'll be in Payson next month," Hoyt said. "Why don't you drive up to meet me?"

"I just might take you up on that." Shane couldn't think of a way to casually break the ice, so he just went for it. "You know, Cassidy's here in Reckless."

There was the briefest of pauses. Any number of reasons could have accounted for it. Shane didn't jump to conclusions.

"How's she doing?" Hoyt asked.

Prettier than ever, Shane thought. Stubborn, bristly at times, fiercely independent, sexy as hell, infuriating, but in a way that made him want to take her in his arms and kiss her till she melted.

He didn't tell his brother any of those things. "She's good."

"Glad to hear it."

"When was it you two broke up?"

"Jeez, I don't remember. Six, seven years ago. It was right after the Down Home Days Rodeo. Spring, I guess."

Shane had competed in the Down Home Days Rodeo enough times to know it fell in April. If Cassidy had gotten together with another man, it had either been immediately after she'd broken up with Hoyt or she'd cheated on him.

There was a third scenario, and it was making more and more sense by the minute. Hoyt had fathered a son and didn't have the slightest idea.

"Guess I forgot how long it's been," Shane said matter-of-factly. After a few more minutes of catching up with his brother, he ended the call with, "Talk to you next week."

Leaning back against the truck seat, he eyed the bag with the baseball equipment. Without knowing for sure, or, at least having more to go on than an inkling, Shane wouldn't voice his suspicions about Benjie to Hoyt. First, he needed to talk to Cassidy. Then, he'd decide on his next step.

Chapter 5

Benjie, usually a handful, was in rare form for his birthday party. When he wasn't tearing around the backyard, seeing what kind of trouble he could stir up, he was yelling at the top of his lungs and commanding attention. Cassidy bit back another warning and told herself not to stress. This was his birthday, after all. And most of the other children were also being handfuls, though to lesser degrees.

None of the adults seemed to mind too much. His grandparents shamelessly indulged Benjie, accommodating his every wish. His aunt Liberty and future uncle, Deacon, declared he and his little friends were "just being kids." His uncle Ryder filmed the entire party with his digital camcorder, capturing the pony relay races, a rousing game of kick ball and breaking open the candy-filled piñata. Cassidy's best friend,

Tatum, helped out wherever and whenever an extra pair of hands was needed.

Cassidy's mother gleefully finished serving cake and ice cream to the last of the children. Cassidy grimaced. Great, just what they needed. More sugar to fuel their already over-the-top energy levels.

Benjie bounded up to her, cake crumbs and blue frosting smeared over his face. "Can we open presents now?"

"In a bit."

Rather than argue with her, which is what she expected, he ran straight for Shane, his new best buddy. The two of them had been practically inseparable the entire party. Before Benjie caused a collision, Shane scooped up the boy and swung him in a circle.

"Me next," one of the other children shouted, and Shane obliged.

He'd been wonderful the entire party. Arriving early with his daughter, he'd set up the tables and chairs, readied Skittles and the other horses for the relay race and kept Benjie occupied and out from underfoot. The latter might account for their bonding.

Or, Cassidy fretted, was it something intangible? Did they have a connection because they were related, though neither of them knew it?

Since separating them was impossible, she did the next best thing by constantly putting herself in their immediate vicinity. That way, she could monitor them, though hearing their exchanges left her just as rattled as not hearing them.

"Daddy!" Bria dragged a little girl by the hand to where Shane played with the boys. Cassidy recognized the girl as the granddaughter of Mrs. Danelli, the owner of the Silver Dollar Pawn Shop. The little girl was also Benjie's classmate at school. "DeAnna invited me to spend the night at her house."

Shane set down the boy "passenger" he'd been giving an "airplane" ride. "Can't, honey. I told your mom I'd have you home by six tonight."

"No, next weekend, Daddy."

"We have the rodeo."

Cassidy had heard from her father that, because Bria would be at the Easy Money for her regular visit, he was giving Shane more time off than normal during the rodeo. The only thing her father had insisted on was Shane be available during the bull-riding events.

Cassidy didn't know who Shane had recruited to watch his daughter, if anyone. She herself had hired one of her teenaged riding students to babysit Benjie. Should she offer the girl's services to Shane? Cassidy couldn't decide.

"DeAnna's coming to the rodeo, too," Bria told her father.

Her new friend confirmed with a shy nod of her head.

"Well," Shane hedged. "Let me talk to DeAnna's mother when she comes to pick her up."

The girls seemed satisfied for the moment and scampered off, cute as could be.

"Do you know this girl's mother?"

Realizing Shane was speaking to her, Cassidy spun to face him. "A little. We've met at some school functions. She's nice."

"Is she responsible?"

Cassidy almost laughed. In her experience dealing with parents at the arena, the question was one she'd expect from another mother, not a father. "I'd say yes. However, I'm basing that solely on our discussion when I delivered DeAnna's invitation. She made sure the party would be well supervised before accepting. That struck me as responsible."

"Will you talk to her with me? I'm still pretty new at this." Shane looked chagrined.

Cassidy felt herself warming to him. Then again, all he had to do was flash his amazing smile and she warmed from head to toe.

"Why don't you stop by her house first? You'll be able to get a feel for her parenting skills just from looking around."

He hesitated. "Won't she be offended?"

"It's a reasonable request," she assured him. "But if you're uncomfortable with being so forthright, suggest you need to discuss the sleepover first before agreeing. If she refuses, then you have your answer."

"Good idea."

Cassidy met his gaze, and the intensity of it rendered her momentarily mute. He'd had that kind of effect on her ever since his return. What was different now?

"Thanks for helping out today," she finally managed. "I do appreciate it."

"Happy to."

"I know Benjie appreciates it, too."

"He's a great kid. It's a shame his father can't be here."

Cassidy instantly froze. Though this was hardly the first comment about Hoyt she'd had to deflect, this was the first comment from his brother. And, either her imagination was running amok or there was an odd quality in Shane's tone.

Collecting her scattered wits, she said, "He couldn't be here. He lives...out of state."

"Where?"

"I beg your pardon?"

"Where? What state?"

She resisted telling him it was none of his damn business. "Um, last I heard, Ohio. He moves around a lot."

"Because of his work?"

"Yes."

So much for putting herself in Shane's vicinity. Big mistake. She couldn't flee fast enough. "If you'll excuse me, I told Benjie he could open his presents."

Shane didn't let her go two feet before falling into step beside her. "I'll round up the kids."

"You've done so much already."

"I like your family, especially Benjie." His voice lowered and turned a shade huskier. "I like you, too. You can't say you haven't noticed."

Good grief! Had anyone heard him? She swore silently when she caught Liberty's eagle eye zeroing in on them. All hope they'd escaped notice was dashed when Liberty winked, pointed at Shane behind the shield of her hand and mouthed, "I approve."

If her sister knew the truth, that Shane was actually Benjie's uncle, would she still be supportive of the match? Liberty had been denied knowing her real father until she was twenty-four years old. Cassidy was doing much the same thing to her own son.

She doubted Liberty would be supportive or understanding. Especially since Cassidy had lied to everyone except their mother, telling them Benjie's father wanted nothing to do with his son.

In fact, should the truth ever come out, it could tear

the Becketts further apart, undoing all the progress they'd made these past six months.

Her decision had seemed so simple at the time. Not endangering Hoyt's upcoming marriage by dropping a bombshell at the last minute. Avoiding being a home wrecker for the second time. Sparing herself the same heartache her mother had endured should Benjie one day choose to leave Reckless and live with his father.

Except everything hung by a flimsy thread that was threatening to snap any second.

"Benjie," Cassidy called, then said to Shane, "I've got to go."

To her consternation, he followed her to the back porch where the presents lay stacked in the middle of a picnic table. Benjie was already there with his buddies, each of them pushing and shoving for a closer glimpse of his birthday booty. The girls practiced considerably more decorum.

"You sit here, young man," she instructed, giving his shoulder a light nudge.

He obliged, but not before grabbing a present. No sooner was he seated than he attacked the wrapping paper. Ryder was there with the camcorder, filming every minute of her son's greedy antics. The rest of the family gathered around, watching over the heads of the children, each of whom wanted the guest of honor to open their present first.

"Wait," Cassidy admonished. "Read the card first." Did her son not have any manners?

Benjie stopped long enough to discover this gift was from Tatum's children.

"What do you say?"

"Thank you." Benjie barely got the words out before

resuming his assault on the wrapping paper. "Yes!" His eyes lit up. "A remote control car." His second thank-you was considerably more sincere.

It continued like that for several more gifts. Then Benjie grabbed a gunny sack, the contents weighing it down.

"There's no card," he lamented after looking the sack over, his features forming a puzzled frown. "Is this a present?"

"Sorry," Shane apologized. "I'm not much for gift wrapping."

Benjie laughed and untied the sack, then peered inside, his mouth falling open. "It's a baseball bat! And a glove." He gazed at Shane with a mixture of astonishment and pure joy. "Thanks, Mister Shane."

"There's a ball in there, too. It probably fell to the bottom."

Benjie discarded the sack in favor of balancing this newest treasure on his lap. "Look, Mom." His buddies crowded around him, admiring the gift and expressing their envy.

"I see," Cassidy said, a lump in the back of her throat taking her by surprise.

"Just what I wanted."

Did he? She supposed he'd asked for sports equipment before, but she couldn't remember. Or was it that she didn't put much importance on non-horse sports? The kind of sports a father and son might share.

Until six months ago, when Cassidy's father returned to Reckless, her son had had no male figures in his life other than the wranglers at the ranch. Now, besides his grandfather, he had Cassidy's brother, Ryder and, she swallowed in an attempt to dislodge the lump, Shane. His other uncle.

Shane hadn't been here two weeks, and he'd already figured out what her son wanted most. What he needed. Baseball equipment.

"Will you play with me later?" Benjie asked Shane, his features alight with hope.

"You bet."

The rest of the present unwrapping was a blur for Cassidy. She busied herself organizing the cards so Benjie could write thank-you notes. Shane hadn't included a card. Something told her she wouldn't need it to prod her memory.

He stood in front of her as if she'd conjured him with her thoughts. "Let me." Without waiting for an answer, he relieved her of the packages she'd gathered to carry into the house.

She sighed, too physically, emotionally and mentally tired from the long afternoon to object. She'd barely organized a second load when he returned.

"I put the presents in the living room. On the couch."

"Great."

This time when he carried the presents into the house, she accompanied him, bringing a large plastic bag filled with trash. As they entered the kitchen, Benjie and Bria passed them, tripping over their feet in their haste.

"Slow down," Cassidy cautioned.

"Where are you two heading?" Shane asked.

Benjie stopped long enough to wave a package of batteries. "Grandma gave these to me for my remote control car. I'm gonna show Bria how it works."

His cousin, Cassidy just then realized. And they got along as if they'd grown up together.

The door hadn't quite shut when she heard Benjie say to Bria, "You're lucky. I wish I had a dad like yours."

Earlier, when Shane commented on Benjie's father not being at the party, Cassidy had frozen in place. This time, she turned hot all over, as if she was standing in front of a roaring bonfire. Worse, when she dared glance up, she found Shane observing her with unwavering concentration. Awareness flickered in his eyes.

He knows.

She dismissed the notion. He didn't know. He couldn't. She'd been too careful all these years. It had to be something else.

"I suppose we should get back to the party."

Shane didn't move. "Wait, Cassidy. There's something I need to ask you."

"Now?" She steadied herself. "I'm kind of busy."

"This can't wait."

"It'll have to," she said walked away.

His next words stopped her short of the door and nearly knocked her to her knees.

"Is Hoyt Benjie's father?"

Shane had to give Cassidy credit. Once the initial shock wore off, she pulled herself together and acted as though he'd asked about her dinner plans and not if Hoyt was her son's father.

Was he wrong about his suspicions, or was she well practiced in the art of deception? He intended to find out. Leading her outside, he took her to a far corner of the yard.

"Daddy, where you going?" Bria chased after them,

her sweater buttoned crookedly and her purple barrettes coming loose from her hair.

"We'll be right back, honey."

"But DeAnna's mom is coming. You said you'd talk to her."

He hesitated. He had promised to speak to DeAnna's mother about the possible sleepover next weekend.

"I won't be long."

"Can I come with you?"

"We can do this later," Cassidy said, offering a weak smile.

Shane wasn't going to let her get off easily. Their conversation was too important. All of their futures depended on it.

"Wait here, Bria," he told his daughter. "Watch for DeAnna's mother and come get me when she arrives, okay?"

Bria pouted. The next instant, she brightened when her new friend insisted she join in a game of tag.

"You're wasting your time," Cassidy said. "Hoyt's not Benjie's father."

She didn't take her eyes off the group of kids, one of whom was Benjie. He stood out from the rest, because of his height and exuberant nature.

Hoyt was like that. Taller than average and with a gregarious personality.

"Humor me." Shane chose a spot behind the modular play set. Earlier, it had served as an imaginary fort for a trio of boys.

Cassidy faced him calmly, her sole sign of any turmoil a thin layer of perspiration dotting her brow.

"Please don't be angry," he said. "But I need you

to be honest with me. Are you sure Hoyt isn't Benjie's father?"

"*You* need me?"

"For Hoyt's sake."

"Besides the fact it's none of your business, why would you even think that?" She stuffed her hands in her jacket pockets.

"He's turning six. I can count. At least up to eight."

Cassidy glared at him. Clearly, his joke about how long a competitor needed to remain on a bull in order to qualify didn't strike her as funny.

"You have to admit, the timing is right."

"Don't you think if he was Hoyt's son, I'd have told him?"

"To be honest, I'm not sure."

"What reason would I have to lie?"

Another non-answer. She was good at giving them.

"Are you willing to let Benjie take a DNA test?"

The color drained from her face. "I'm not subjecting him to any test."

"Because you're afraid of the results?"

"We're done talking about this." She spoke through gritted teeth. "Don't ever bring it up again."

"How about I bring it up with Hoyt?" He reached for his cell phone in the front pocket of his vest. "Right now."

She gasped. "You wouldn't."

Shane hated being so hard on her, but he'd gone four years having no idea he was a father. He couldn't stand idly by and let the same thing happen to his brother. Especially when Hoyt wanted children and would be a good father. Cassidy had no right to deny him. And putting off questioning her would give her time to throw up more barriers. Possibly leave town with Benjie.

"I'm sorry, Cassidy. But unless you give me the name of Benjie's father, I refuse to drop this."

"I repeat, this is none of your business."

"It's very much my business if Benjie is my nephew."

"I'm not giving you the name of his father. So you can do what? Call and confront him?"

"You said he knows about Benjie and doesn't want any part of him."

"If you don't quit badgering me this instant, I'm going to talk to my parents."

Nothing she said or did would change Shane's mind. This was a mother fiercely protecting her child from what she perceived as a threat. If Hoyt weren't Benjie's father, she'd have no reason to react so defensively.

"And tell them what?" He met her angry glare head-on, not the least bit intimidated. "You're upset because I'm asking a reasonable question? Your father didn't know about Liberty until six months ago. Do you seriously think he'll support you hiding Benjie from my brother?"

"Stop staying that!" Her glance darted wildly about. "Someone might hear you."

"No one can hear." Indeed, the party had thinned considerably. Most of the children were gone and, with the exception of Sunny and Mercer, all of the adult family members, too. Luckily for Shane, DeAnna's mother was late. He still had time to call Cassidy's bluff and dialed Hoyt's number.

"Please." She closed her eyes. "Don't do this."

Shane thought of demanding the name of Benjie's

father again. Her fragile state stopped him. Instead, he softened his voice and attempted to explain.

"Five years ago, I was a different person. Unsettled. A bit crazy. Okay, a lot crazy," he amended when she sent him a look. "Some folks said I was hell-bent on killing myself, and, well, I almost did. I can understand why Judy assumed I wouldn't make a good father. That didn't, however, justify her hiding her pregnancy. I had a right to be part of Bria's life. To help raise her if I wanted. Who's to say how I would have reacted if I'd known? I might have quit rodeoing then and there."

"Do you truly believe that? You wouldn't have won your last world championship title."

"The thing is, we'll never know for sure."

Tears welled in Cassidy's eyes. "It's different for you. Judy and Bria live in Mesa. Not far from Reckless."

"Because I moved here. When I retired from the circuit, I searched for a job that would put me close to them. It was my good fortune your father happened to be looking for a bull manager."

"Benjie's father lives in another state."

Right. What had she told him? Ohio? "That's still no reason. He could relocate." Would Hoyt move? He and his wife had just bought a new house. "Or visit. And Benjie could visit him."

Her angry reaction took him aback. "Not happening," she bit out. "Not ever."

"Cassidy. There's more than you to consider here. There's the father *and* Benjie."

She shook her head. "My brother left when he was fourteen to live with our father. We hardly saw him after that. Broke my mother's heart and mine."

"The reasons were different. Ryder and your mother were at odds."

"You don't know about my family."

"I know a little. Ryder told me the circumstances. How you and he also fought about your father."

She stiffened.

"He also told me he regrets not spending more time with you and Liberty. Is that what you want for Benjie? To miss out on having a father in his life?"

"It didn't hurt me any."

Shane laid a hand on Cassidy's shoulder. "I disagree. You're hurting right now."

The slight tremors he felt beneath his hand confirmed it. As did the shaky breath she drew.

"I won't lose Benjie. He's all I have."

"Who's to say you will lose him?"

"What if he tries to take him away?"

He. For the first time, she hadn't used the ambiguous term *Benjie's father*. Not exactly an admission, but close.

"He won't. You're a good mother, Cassidy. A great mother. The most he'll get is visitation."

"I could lose Benjie all summer."

"Think of what he gets in return. A father who can contribute financially. Improve the quality of his life."

She bristled. "I support my son just fine."

"No one's saying you don't. But think of how much more he can have with Hoyt contributing." Shane continued to press. "My brother's not a bad guy. He'll be good to Benjie. Spend time with him. Teach him. Introduce him to our family. Our parents."

Several seconds passed without Cassidy saying a word. Shane was mentally patting himself on the back for getting through to her when she turned the tables on him.

"I'm asking you to respect my wishes and not say anything to Hoyt."

"What if I don't?"

"It's not your place." She enunciated each word.

"I can help you tell him, if you want."

"You don't understand."

"Make me understand."

"You're thinking only of Hoyt. What about Benjie? His entire life could be changed. Disrupted. He may not be ready."

Shane shook his head. "You're making excuses. He wants a father. You heard him."

"How dare you spring this on me? At my son's birthday party of all places. You threaten me and expect me to go along simply because you happen to think you're right based solely on your own experience."

Had he threatened her? He could see how she might feel that way. He had come on strong.

Against his better judgment, he relented. "Okay."

She stared at him with tear-filled eyes. "Okay what?"

"I won't tell Hoyt."

"Thank you." Her breath left her body in a rush.

"Don't thank me yet. I won't tell Hoyt because you're the one who will."

"I just said I won't."

"I'm going to convince you otherwise, Cassidy. And to warn you, I'll be relentless."

Bria came running, shouting that DeAnna's mother had arrived, which spared Cassidy from having to respond.

Shane was too smart to think she didn't have more to

say on the subject. Once she recovered from the shock, he was no doubt in for an earful. From what he knew about Ms. Beckett, she could be every bit as relentless as he was. Possibly more.

Chapter 6

Cassidy slipped into the tack room on the pretense of fetching a replacement brow band for one of the barrel racer's bridles. The truth was, she desperately needed a few minutes alone to get herself under control. This past week, she'd staved off the beginnings of a panic attack at least a dozen times. Three times just today, including now. Rather than risk someone noticing her usual behavior and asking questions, she'd ducked into the tack room.

The one problem was her odd behavior had been noticed. Especially by Shane, who, not an hour ago, inquired if she was all right.

Slumping against the wall, she inhaled slowly and deeply, the familiar scent of leather and oil filling her nostrils and easing her tension. Marginally. Every moment she didn't completely immerse herself in a task, she was recalling her conversation with Shane. He'd promised not to tell Hoyt about Benjie and, so far, he'd kept his promise.

He'd also kept his promise about attempting to change her mind, and their constant conversations were draining her emotionally and mentally.

Another wave of anxiety struck. Cassidy couldn't be more afraid if she was pinned in the path of an oncoming vehicle.

She'd suffered similar bouts when she was ten, after the accident when her father had driven the truck carrying them both into the well house. Rather than disappearing after he left, they'd worsened. So much so, her mother had finally taken Cassidy to see a doctor.

Eventually, and with the help of counseling, the anxiety disappeared. Until this past week.

Cassidy buried her face in her hands. She couldn't go on like this. Not for much longer. Complaining to her parents would do no good. If they fired Shane and sent him away, he might, and probably would, tell Hoyt about Benjie.

What if she went to Shane? Pleaded with him again not to reveal her secret. She scoffed. He wouldn't agree. She could still hear him talking about Bria and how the girl's mother had kept her from him all those years.

Her only choice was to tell Hoyt and pray he'd be one of those loser fathers who didn't give a flying fig about their offspring. Instinct told her that wasn't going to be the case. Hoyt wanted children. According to Shane, he and his wife were actively trying for one of their own and having no luck.

They would probably jump all over the chance at

seeing Benjie. Getting to know him. Taking him for visits. Seeking custody.

Cassidy's heart twisted inside her chest, pressing painfully into her sternum. The next instant, a bright light flashed in her face, causing her to flinch and shield her face.

"Hey, what are you doing in here?"

The voice belonged to Tatum.

Cassidy blinked, bringing her friend into focus. "Just needed a few minutes alone."

"In the dark?"

"I thought the bulb was burned out."

Tatum moved closer, concern written over her lovely oval face. "What's wrong?"

For days—actually since the moment she'd heard her father had hired Shane for the bull manager position—Cassidy had been carrying a heavy weight. Like an anvil hanging from a chain around her neck. She wanted nothing more than to unburden herself.

"Where do I start?" With that, Cassidy broke into sobs.

Immediately, her friend engulfed her in a soothing embrace. "Oh, honey. How can I help you?"

Cassidy allowed herself a good cry and, when it was over, admitted she felt better. Fortunately, no one had come looking for either her or Tatum.

"Let's get out of here," her friend suggested, and led Cassidy across the barn aisle to the empty office. "Your mom's busy setting up the registration booth for tomorrow morning. We have the place to ourselves." Just to be sure, she put the Be Back Soon sign in the window and locked both doors.

Cassidy helped herself to a cup of water from the

cooler then dropped into a visitor chair. Tatum wheeled her chair from behind her desk and positioned it next to Cassidy's, then folded Cassidy's hand in hers.

"Tell me," she coaxed.

The two of them had been friends since elementary school. It was easy for Cassidy to pour her heart out.

"Shane's figured out who Benjie's father is and has threatened to tell him."

Tatum drew back. "Why would he do that?"

"Because…" It was more difficult for Cassidy to admit than she'd imagined. "Because he's Benjie's uncle."

Tatum slumped in her chair. When she spoke, there was no judgment or censure in her voice. "I assumed as much."

In all these years, Cassidy hadn't told a soul other than her mother about Hoyt being Benjie's father. The fewer people who knew, the less chance of her secret getting out.

She'd suspected Tatum had guessed. How could she not? They were close, after all. But for right or wrong, Cassidy had chosen to remain mute.

Tatum had respected Cassidy's wishes and never pressed her to reveal the father's name, proving just what a good friend she was.

"What are you going to do?"

"I'm not sure yet." Cassidy shrugged. "For the moment, Shane has agreed not to tell Hoyt. But he won't be put off forever. He believes Hoyt has the right to know and wants me to tell him."

"Would it be all that terrible?"

Cassidy gaped at her friend. "What if he tries to take Benjie away?"

"He can't. There's no cause."

"I lied to him."

"Still not reason enough. You're a good mother."

"He can get visitation. And shared custody if he were to move here."

"Which he probably won't."

"I don't know for sure."

"All right. Let's say he does move to Arizona and gets shared custody of Benjie. What's the worst that could happen?"

Leave it to her friend to be practical.

"Benjie could decide he'd rather live with his father." Her voice shook.

"What's to say that wouldn't happen anyway? You've been lucky so far. Benjie hasn't shown much interest in his father. But chances are he will one day. Perhaps soon. Better you tell him while you're still able to control the circumstances. At least, to a degree."

Cassidy couldn't feel more out of control.

"Break the news to Hoyt," Tatum continued, "but wait until you're ready. Get your ducks in a row first. Talk to Deacon. If he can't help you, he'll recommend someone who can."

Cassidy saw the logic in her friend's suggestion. Her future brother-in-law was an attorney, and Cassidy would need one to advise her of her rights. Also inform her of Hoyt's rights and Benjie's, too. Then she could put together an informed plan of action.

"You're right." She sighed. "Thanks."

"It might not be all bad, you know. Telling Hoyt. There'll be child support. Someone who can help with other expenses, if not pay for them, like braces and college."

"I can find a way."

"No doubt. But why do everything on your own if you don't have to?" She stopped Cassidy before she could answer. "Right, right. To keep Benjie with you. Well, let's face it. Single motherhood isn't all it's cracked up to be. I, for one, am incredibly grateful for Ryder's help. He's great with the kids, and they love him. Hoyt's a nice guy. He could be just as great with Benjie."

"He drinks and drives. I don't want him putting Benjie in the same position he did me."

"That happened once, a lot of years ago."

"What if Hoyt hasn't changed?"

"Talk to him. Establish ground rules."

"Mom tried with Dad. He didn't listen."

Tatum studied Cassidy's face. "What's the real reason you haven't told Hoyt? Your father's alcoholism?"

"Please don't give me the speech about how he's sober now."

"I'm not talking about his drinking. I'm talking about the fact that, after six months, you two still can't seem to patch things up."

"One has nothing to do with the other." Cassidy sounded defensive, even to her own ears.

"You don't have a good relationship with your father. Can you honestly say he has no effect on your feelings about Benjie's potential relationship with Hoyt?"

"Hoyt's married. You don't think his wife will be upset he has a child with another woman?"

"I think you're making up excuses." Though Tatum's tone was gentle, her words were harsh. "Plenty of spouses deal with children from a previous relationship. Your brother, for instance. We're getting married, and I have three children."

"Hoyt's going to be furious with me."

"Or he'll be like Shane and your dad, overjoyed to learn he has a child."

After a moment, Cassidy admitted, "I'm afraid. Of a lot more than Benjie possibly leaving when he's older."

Tatum smiled. "Now we're getting somewhere."

"What if I tell Hoyt and it tears the family apart?"

"Your family? Why would it?"

"I've been lying. Like my mother."

"They overcame that." Tatum squeezed Cassidy's hand. "They will this, too."

As much as she appreciated her friend's support, Cassidy wasn't convinced. "I'm just not sure."

"What does Benjie want? Have you asked him?"

She shook her head and, sniffing, wiped at her nose.

"Cassidy, honey, don't you think it's time you did? After all, this is his father."

"He'll say yes. He wants to meet Hoyt."

"Maybe. Probably. But if you introduce them now, he'll be thrilled you did. If you deny him, he'll likely come to resent you."

Confusion muddled her thinking, and she rubbed her temples.

"There's Shane, too," Tatum mused. "And your relationship with him."

"That was a long time ago and nothing special."

"I'm talking about now." Tatum gave her a knowing look. "Anyone can see you two like each other."

"We do." There was no one she could admit her feelings for Shane to other than Tatum. "Which is why him pressuring me to talk to Hoyt feels a little like betrayal."

"Talk to Deacon," Tatum urged.

Cassidy nodded, feeling caught between a rock and a hard place. Whichever direction she took, she was going to collide with something sharp, and the resulting injury would be painful and possibly permanent.

The Jamboree Rodeo didn't technically begin for another four hours, though registration opened early in the morning. Trucks and trailers were arriving in a steady stream. Already the overflow parking area in the back pasture was half-full. Food and merchandise vendors were busy readying their wares for sale. Horses had been washed and brushed, tack cleaned and polished, clothes laundered and pressed.

At this moment, all Beckett hands were on deck. Each family member and employee had been assigned a specific job. Even Benjie was helping the maintenance crew ready the arena, though, truth be told, he was riding along on the tractor with Kenny while the teenager graded the deep dirt.

Cassidy kept watch on her son from the announcer's booth. She'd originally gone up there to run an equipment test. With everything in working order, she had no reason to remain, other than the booth also enabled her to observe Shane.

Just the sight of him caused her chest to tighten. She'd stopped trying to decipher her emotions days ago. There were simply too many to separate.

He'd remained true. To her knowledge, he hadn't told Hoyt about Benjie. At least, she hadn't received a phone call from Hoyt, angry or otherwise.

Trusting people. It was a new experience for Cassidy. Other than her mother, sister and Tatum, there was no one else she relied on implicitly to put her best interests first. She certainly didn't trust her father or, to a lesser degree, her brother. Ryder had abandoned her when she was just twelve. Yes, they'd come a long way in recent months, but inside she was still a lost little girl, deserted by the ones she loved.

She ignored the chronic throb in her head, the one that had started last weekend during Benjie's birthday party and had plagued her all this week. Instead, she continued watching Shane, wondering what it might be like if they didn't have these issues between them. She might well be dating him again. Part of her wanted that. A large part.

At the moment, he was herding specialized livestock, acquired just for the rodeo, into temporary pens which had been set up near the practice ring. Sheep, to be specific, for use in the Mutton Bustin' competition. The miniaturized version of bull riding—children six and under got to ride a sheep—was a popular event at the Becketts' rodeos. The child who stayed seated the longest won first place, though every participant received a token prize.

Shane's daughter, Bria, followed him around like a second shadow. She seemed to exhibit both a fascination with and fear of the sheep, who were a noisy, active and smelly lot. Cassidy had overheard Shane earlier, trying to convince Bria to enter the Mutton Bustin' competition. From the vehement shake of the little girl's head, he hadn't succeeded.

The two of them were quite sweet together. Shane certainly had a way with her. He had a way with all children, apparently, as Benjie adored him. The baseball glove, bat and ball had strengthened the growing bond between the two of them. Most days, Shane and Benjie practiced pitching and hitting in the backyard before dinner.

Shane knew he was playing ball with his nephew. Knew now that his daughter's cousin was a mere fifty feet away, hitching a ride on the tractor in the arena. How, Cassidy wondered, did he feel? Was his chest as tight as hers?

Following Tatum's advice, she'd called Deacon. He'd given her the name of an attorney in east Mesa who practiced family law. During their phone call, the woman had put some of Cassidy's concerns to rest, but raised others. They'd scheduled an appointment for next week. Cassidy had wanted to meet sooner, as she wasn't sure how long she could put off Shane. Unfortunately, the attorney didn't have an opening.

Another week with her chest perpetually tight and this damn headache plaguing her 24/7. The stress had long since begun to show, increasing the number of times each day someone commented on her drawn expression and lack of focus.

She was about to leave the booth when she saw Shane kneel in the dirt in front of Bria. Had something happened? From this distance, Cassidy couldn't tell. Shane was clasping both of Bria's shoulders as if to comfort her, then kissed her forehead.

Last night during practice, Cassidy had watched him tangle with one of the horses. After dumping its rider, the horse had circled the arena at a full gallop. Shane finally cornered the horse and narrowly avoided being struck by a flailing hoof when it reared.

Cassidy had choked back a cry. Only when he had the horse under control had she released her death grip on the arena railing. She hadn't run over and hugged him like before, though the idea had crossed her mind. How could it not? The sensation of his arms around her invaded her thoughts continually.

No denying it. He was strong and capable and confident. All traits she admired...and happened to find attractive. They weren't half as attractive as the traits he displayed with his daughter. Gentleness, compassion, kindness. They drew her to him and made her think about him in ways she hadn't thought of a man in...she couldn't remember when.

He stood, a hand remaining on Bria's shoulder. Perhaps sensing Cassidy, his gaze lifted to the announcer's booth. A small shock wave reverberated through her, but she didn't look away. Smiling, he tugged on the brim of his cowboy hat. She returned the acknowledgment with a nod before leaving the booth, closing the door behind her and descending the narrow stairs.

An hour later, clipboard nestled in the crook of her arm, hand-held radio clipped to her belt, Cassidy navigated the growing crowd. Her mother and sister could probably use some assistance in the registration booth, and she considered going. The line snaked halfway to the office. Mostly, she was killing time until she was needed at the arena.

Benjie was with Tatum's three children, all of them under the care of the nanny Cassidy had hired for the weekend. The expense was a bit beyond her budget, despite Tatum chipping in for half, but she needed assurance her son was well supervised while she worked.

Her mother's and Tatum's words replayed in her head. Cassidy didn't disagree. Child support payments from Hoyt would definitely ease the tight pinch of her finances. The question was, would they be worth the cost?

An overwhelming need for a moment alone—this was becoming a habit—prompted her to change course. There was bound to be less activity behind the barn.

There was also Shane's trailer. How could she forget?

He opened the door and emerged, spotting her before she could get away.

"Hey." He grinned, not a single trace of the tension she'd been battling all week evident in his carefree expression.

Her mind promptly shut down at the sight of him. He looked good. Better than good. Dressed in a clean Western-cut shirt, fitted jeans, black leather vest and matching black Stetson, he could have easily graced the pages of the hot cowboy calendars her sister used to keep before meeting Deacon.

"Whatcha up to?" He stepped down onto the ground and made straight for her, no hesitation in his stride.

"I was, um..." The excuse she'd been prepared to give died on her lips as his proximity breached her defenses. "Frankly, I needed a break."

"I understand. It's been rough lately."

She closed her eyes, bone weary. "That's an understatement."

"Want to come in for a cup of coffee or a cold drink?" He gestured at the trailer's still open door. "I could use a pick-me-up."

"Where's Bria?"

"With DeAnna and her family. Your mom was generous enough to give them free passes. The sleepover's set for tomorrow."

"I'm guessing her mom checked out."

"A real nice lady. I took your advice and paid her a visit the other day. I'm sure Bria will be fine. If not, I'm ten minutes away."

"I'm glad."

"I was serious about having coffee."

Cassidy knew she should decline. Until she decided what to do about Hoyt, it was best she maintain strict boundaries with Shane. But she didn't decline. As one of the four people who were aware of her situation, she could be herself with him. There was something liberating about that.

"Okay."

He moved aside and she entered the trailer ahead of him. The steps creaked as she ascended them. Creaked louder when Shane did. Was it a warning? Had she made a mistake by accepting his invitation?

Shane crowded behind her. Even if she wanted to escape, it was too late now. She was committed to seeing this harebrained idea through to the end.

Chapter 7

The trailer was more cramped than that first day, Shane has settled in, but Bria's things were also everywhere. A doll on the table. Her overnight bag in the corner by the closet. Sneakers on the rug in front of the kitchen sink.

Signs of Shane abounded, as well. He obviously wasn't the best housekeeper. Neither was he the worst. A canvas laundry bag hung from the bathroom door knob, a shirt sleeve poking out. A towel lay crumpled on the floor beneath the laundry bag. Through the doorway to the sleeping area, Cassidy saw the haphazardly made bed.

He must have read her thoughts for he apologized. "Excuse the mess. No time to clean up today."

Cassidy found herself smiling. "I have a six-year-old boy. I've seen much worse than this. Trust me."

"I do. Trust you."

He studied her intently, and a familiar, warm sensation bloomed in her middle. She didn't resist it.

"Funny," she said. "I was thinking the same thing myself. That maybe I could trust *you*."

"Maybe?" Humor tinged his tone.

"It isn't easy. I've been hurt in the past."

"By Hoyt?"

She shook her head. "Not hurt so much as other things."

"Such as?" Shane removed his vest and cowboy hat, hung both on a peg, then selected two coffee mugs dangling from hooks beneath the cupboard. Filling them with water from the tap, he added instant coffee and heated the mugs in the tiny microwave.

"He disappointed me," she said. "Angered me. But, in hindsight, I think the relationship was already circling the drain. I was probably looking for an excuse to end things."

"What happened?"

"Hoyt never told you?"

"I'm interested in your version."

"He liked to party a lot. It was after the Down Home Days Rodeo. He'd won three events and was celebrating with his buddies. I wanted to go back to the hotel room and told him I'd catch a ride with a friend. He insisted on driving me, but I knew he'd been drinking. I wouldn't go with him and accused him of not caring."

"That wasn't like him."

"I agree. But like I said, we were all but broken up." She shrugged. "He knew I was raised by an alcoholic father and had a low tolerance for any kind of dangerous behavior. He could have been testing me. Or picking a fight."

"I'm sorry, Cassidy." Shane moved Bria's doll from the table and set down the coffee mugs. He reached into the narrow pantry. "You take creamer and sugar?"

"If you have it." She sat, laying her clipboard and radio on the seat beside her.

Shane slid in across from her, his manner unhurried. Apparently, he was going to let her tell the rest of the story at her pace.

"I didn't know I was pregnant when we broke up."

"Why didn't you tell him when you found out?"

She stirred creamer and sugar into her coffee. "I thought if he cared so little for me that he'd willingly put me in danger, how would he be with our child? I realize now I was scared. My life was completely turned upside down. I had no clue what I was going to do. I didn't want to marry Hoyt and worried he might insist on it. I wanted less to come home, single and pregnant. My mother had sacrificed everything for me, and I was at the peak of my rodeo career. A shoo-in for state champion. I'd have to give that up in order to raise my baby. Something I knew nothing about."

"Things seemed to have worked out for the best."

"They have. Benjie's a happy, well-adjusted kid."

"Then why haven't you told Hoyt?"

She sipped at her mug, letting the warm coffee soothe her frazzled nerves.

"I almost did." Strange, but telling Shane her story wasn't nearly as difficult as she'd anticipated. In fact, it was surprisingly easy. "I went to Topeka to see him when I was eight months pregnant. I changed my mind at the last minute, and came immediately home."

"Why?"

"I learned he was engaged. Another barrel racer told

me." She met Shane's gaze across the table. "I didn't want to be responsible for ruining his marriage."

"What makes you think you would have?"

"Seriously?" She almost laughed. "You think Cheryl would have been okay with a pregnant ex-girlfriend showing up on their doorstep? And besides, she'd already lost a husband. I couldn't be the cause of her losing a second. She didn't deserve that."

"Hoyt's Benjie's father," Shane said. "He has a responsibility. He also has a right."

Cassidy could sense the conversation going in a direction she didn't want. "Doesn't change the fact it would have been an unexpected blow. One impossible to rebound from."

"If Cheryl called off the wedding because Hoyt fathered a child before he met her, then maybe she wasn't the wife for him."

"I disagree. That's a lot to deal with, literally two weeks before your wedding."

"Okay. Let's agree to disagree. For the moment," he added without anger or rancor. "That still doesn't explain why you haven't told Hoyt since then."

She took a deep breath, then admitted, "Lack of nerve."

"Because of your brother and your fear Benjie will leave like he did?"

"That's not the only reason."

Shane waited, again giving her the chance to explain in her own time.

"I didn't want to be responsible for breaking up a second marriage," she confessed.

"Second?" He looked at her with interest. "You have another old boyfriend?"

"No." Cassidy hesitated. Twenty-five years later, and it still pained her to think about it. "My parents' marriage."

"The way I heard it, your dad's drinking caused their divorce."

"It did."

"I don't understand. How are you responsible for his drinking?"

"I'm not. I'm responsible for my mother not sticking by him and not giving him the chance to get sober."

"I'm still confused. You were just a kid."

She drained her coffee, hoping the caffeine would bolster her courage and enable her to finish revealing this very difficult part of her past.

"One night, my dad picked me up from a friend's house. He'd come straight from the bar and had no business driving. Mom would never have let him if she'd known about it. I didn't want to go with him, but neither did I want to make a scene in front of my friend. On the way home, he misjudged the distance, or wasn't paying attention, and plowed the truck into the well house."

"Were you hurt?"

"No, neither of us was. But it scared the hell out of me and afterward I had a meltdown."

"It's understandable."

"I demanded my mom send him away. Threw fits when she tried to reason with me. A couple weeks later, she did just that. Dad packed his bags and moved to Kingman."

"You didn't break up their marriage. It was already on the rocks."

"What if I hadn't insisted?" Difficult as it was for her, Cassidy met Shane's gaze head-on. "Everything, and I mean *everything*, would be different. Liberty would have known our father her entire life and not grown up confused and hurt, believing herself unlovable. Ryder wouldn't have left, breaking my mom's heart. My parents might still be married and not spent years being apart and miserable."

"Or your mom would have divorced him anyway."

"Ryder begged her not to. It was as if she chose which one of her children she loved more. I don't think he forgave me until recently."

"Cassidy, don't take this wrong, because it's a sad story and I can see you and your family are still coping with the fallout, but what does it have to do with Hoyt and you?"

She bit back a sob, refusing to let Shane see her cry. "I couldn't take the chance of causing him and Cheryl the same kind of misery I did my parents. Neither could I have lived with the guilt. I already have enough of that."

The confession left her oddly empty. And relieved. At the touch of Shane's hand covering hers, she looked down. His fingers, though calloused, were warm and comforting. She didn't resist. A moment later, she turned her hand over to clasp his.

It should have been surreal, her sitting here holding Shane's hand. Instead, it felt natural. As if they'd been holding hands all their lives.

In retrospect, her rushing to his side and his kissing her cheek when Wasabi went on a rampage had also been natural. She hadn't stopped to think, and she didn't now. She just savored the moment.

"Your mother made her choice," he said. "She sent your father away because she wanted him gone."

"I think she was on the fence, and I pushed her over onto the side of divorce. They love each other to this day. He came back to Reckless for Liberty, but also to marry Mom again, which makes me feel guiltier."

"Is that what she wants, too?"

"Not at first. He's made a lot of progress lately convincing her otherwise."

"You're not to blame, Cassidy. She and your dad were adults. He could have chosen to get help with his addiction sooner than he did. She could have arranged an intervention. Gotten him into rehab. Leaving was hardly his only option."

"But what if I hadn't insisted she send Dad away? *Everything* might have turned out differently."

"Or your dad wouldn't have gotten sober when he did, and the next time he crashed the truck he might've wound up in the hospital."

She withdrew her hand from his. "That's a pessimistic outlook."

"I don't like to play the what-if game. I did it a lot after finding out about Bria and drove myself crazy with anger and regrets. None of us can change the past. The best we can do is move forward."

His cavalier attitude rankled Cassidy, but the more she considered his words, the more she saw the logic behind them.

"I have been driving myself crazy."

"You don't know what Hoyt and Cheryl would have done. Called off the wedding, postponed it, gone through with it. Just like you don't know what they'll do now when you tell them about Benjie. But after six years of solid marriage, I can't see her walking out on him."

She noticed he used the word *when*, not *if*.

"They're trying for a child," she said. "Cheryl could resent me and Benjie because Hoyt and I accomplished what the two of them haven't."

"Haven't yet. They've just recently started seeing a specialist."

"What if she takes out her resentment on Benjie?"

"You're doing it again. Playing what-if."

Cassidy's shoulders sagged. "I can't help myself."

"First off, Cheryl's not a resentful person. She's as nice as they come. Secondly, Hoyt isn't the same person you knew six years ago. He's grown up a lot. We both have."

She definitely agreed with the second part. Shane was nothing like the wild young man she'd gone out with. Never in million years would she have imagined herself revealing her deepest, darkest secret to him.

"I'm seeing an attorney next week," she abruptly blurted. "About custody of Benjie."

"Good."

"You're not mad?"

"Why would I be? It's a smart move on your part. Your first priority is Benjie."

He probably felt that way because of Bria. "I'll call Hoyt. After I've figured things out with the attorney."

Shane nodded. "Fair enough."

"You'll still wait? Not say anything to him until I do?"

"Of course. I could also be with you when you make the call." He took her hand again and squeezed. "If you want. For moral support."

Cassidy opened her mouth to say no, though that wasn't what came out. "All right."

She half expected him to gloat. Flash her an I-was-right-all-along smile. Instead, he caressed the back of her hand with his thumb, sending tiny arrows of heat along the length of her arm. Heavens, she was susceptible to him.

"What you're doing takes a lot of courage. If Hoyt doesn't realize that, I'll make sure he does."

"Thanks." She checked the clock on the microwave. "I'd better get going. Mom and Liberty are probably wondering where I am."

"Me, too. Don't want your dad to fire me for being late before my first rodeo."

They stood simultaneously. Shane grabbed his vest and hat and waited for her to enter the cramped space between the table and the door.

Hand on the knob, she hesitated.

"Something wrong?" he asked from behind her.

"I just want to thank you."

"Anytime. We're friends, Cassidy."

Friends. An interesting description, considering the sparks flaring between them since his first day at the arena and their brief, but romantic, past. She pivoted—and confronted the broad expanse of Shane's chest mere inches from her.

"Oops."

She should have moved. Turned back around and hurried outside. She didn't. It was as if finding him so close rendered her immobile. He didn't appear in a hurry to move, either.

Seconds ticked by. She struggled to slow her rapid breathing.

Lord have mercy, he smelled incredible. Masculine but not overpowering. She remembered thinking the same thing that first day in the trailer.

What might it be like to rise on her tiptoes and press her lips to his? She had half a mind to find out. Fortunately, she resisted the impulse.

"See you later," she said, and reached again for the door.

She didn't get far. Shane's arm snaked around her waist, stopping her. The next instant, he pulled her snug against him and lowered his head. Her eyes widened and her mouth opened in shock. He was going to kiss her!

I can't let him was her first thought. *I can't not let him* was her second. Suddenly she didn't want to go the rest of her life regretting this missed opportunity.

Cassidy Beckett. In his embrace. And she wasn't resisting. Shane almost didn't believe it.

He increased his hold on her, assuring himself this was completely real and not his imagination. Were he honest with himself, he'd admit to thinking of exactly this for weeks. He was human, after all, and a man, and he intended to take every advantage of this unexpected windfall.

He lowered his head and, burying his face in her neck, inhaled deeply. "You smell great."

She laughed nervously.

"That's funny?" He nuzzled the sensitive spot beneath her ear.

"Kind of. I happen to think the same thing about you." She angled her head to give him greater access to her silky skin. "That you smell great."

Did she now? He licked the same spot he'd been nuzzling, then sucked gently. Clinging to him, she gave a soft shudder. Shane was immediately hooked, on her and her incredible responsiveness.

He inhaled again, then withdrew to look at her, convinced he would never smell anything as wonderful again in his life, hold anyone as desirable. "You don't know how hard I've had to work at resisting you."

The laughter left her eyes. "I beg to differ," she said somberly. "I do know."

He had truly never wanted a woman more than he did in that moment. Didn't think he'd ever want another woman again after Cassidy. It wasn't just his lust talking, either. She appealed to him on every level, emotionally, spiritually and physically.

How had he not realized this before? Granted, they'd dated a short time and never gone much beyond kissing, but still…

Without pausing to ponder the importance of these new feelings for her, he dipped his head and captured her mouth with his. She gasped in surprise. He groaned, low. The combination of lips and tongues and hands roaming bodies was electric. And it only got better.

Cassidy arched against him, sending a spear of desire slicing though him. She was soft where a woman should be soft, firm everywhere else. Temptation in its purest form.

Good thing they'd waited before. At nineteen, he wouldn't have been ready for this. For her.

Convinced he might lose control, he fought to hold back. It proved impossible. Just as it would be impossible to ever forget her.

He couldn't get enough. Pressing his palm into the small of her back, he waited, not certain he could stop there. At the touch of her fingers sliding into the hair at the base of his neck, his thinly held control threatened to snap.

Deepening the kiss, he explored every delicious corner of her mouth. She might be letting him take the lead, but that didn't mean she wasn't a willing participant with an arsenal of moves designed to drive a man over the edge.

And it was working. Perfectly. Shane lost all track of time and place. Hell, he could barely remember his name. There was nothing and no one but Cassidy and him, wrapped together in this small trailer at the very center of the universe.

If not for the chug-chug of the tractor driving practically beneath the trailer's window, they might have gone on kissing indefinitely. Cassidy stiffened and pulled away.

"Sorry." He wasn't, but he felt obliged to apologize. "I got a little carried away."

"You weren't acting alone."

Thank goodness. "It was some kiss." Kisses, as in many, each and every one seared in Shane's memory.

She brushed a lock of disheveled hair from her face, the gesture self-conscious, yet incredibly sexy. When she lifted her face, she wore a tentative smile.

His relief didn't last long.

"I don't regret kissing you," she said. "That doesn't mean I think it should happen again."

"I disagree."

"Shane, getting involved isn't a good idea. Not now. Not until this situation with Benjie and your brother is resolved."

"I don't see what difference it makes."

She shook her head. "Things are complicated enough."

He inhaled and took an emotional step back. "I agree. They are. But we're entitled to be happy."

"Hoyt may not like me getting involved with you. I can't have him adding challenges to our custody negotiations because he resents my relationship with his brother."

"He isn't a shallow person."

"This is brand-new territory. None of us knows how the others will react. I can't take the chance."

She had a point. "Okay."

"Really?" She studied him skeptically.

Shane was smart enough to realize if he pushed Cassidy she'd dig in her heels and he'd lose all the ground he'd gained. Best to agree with her for the moment then, when the dust settled with Hoyt, make his next move. He could wait. She was worth it.

Reaching behind her for the knob, he opened the door. "Really. Now let's both get back to work before the boss catches us goofing off."

She laughed and exited the trailer, Shane right behind her. Once outside, she paused. He did, too, and she placed a hand on the center of his chest.

"For the record, I enjoyed the kiss."

Did she feel his thundering heart? "Me, too."

"It was never like that before."

"Not even close."

Lifting her hand to his face, she cupped his cheek, her fingers lingering before she turned and left.

Shane stood, watching, until Kenny emerged from the outdoor stalls, leading a pair of arena horses used for steer wrestling. He nodded at Shane, a silly grin on his face.

Had he seen Shane and Cassidy together? Shane wasn't sure—the teenager often wore a silly grin for no reason. He promptly put Kenny from his mind. What had there been to see, other than her cupping his cheek? Nothing inappropriate there.

At the arena, he got straight to work, though his and Cassidy's recent kiss wreaked havoc with his concentration. Bull riding was traditionally the last event of the day, being one of the most exciting and crowd pleasing. That didn't give Shane leeway to sit around, doing nothing. The care and condition of the bulls was his main concern. Especially Wasabi, who had been cleared to compete. However, this decision made no difference to Shane. He intended to check over every inch of the bull before letting him in the arena.

In addition to the eighteen bucking bulls the Becketts owned, they'd leased an additional twenty for the weekend from their competitor, the Lost Dutchman Rodeo Company. Shane had spent the entire day yesterday involved in transporting the bulls from nearby Apache Junction.

It was Mercer Beckett's ambition to purchase more bulls over the next several years. A high-earning bull could bring in tens of thousands of dollars a year, if not into the hundreds of thousands. There were several potential contenders in the Becketts' current stock.

The future also looked bright for another reason. Just prior to hiring Shane, Mercer had purchased a number of champion-producing cows. Breeding would begin shortly and become the next phase of Shane's new job.

"Is Wasabi ready?"

Shane glanced over his shoulder at the sound of Mercer's voice and stepped away from the larger of the two bull pens. "In my opinion, yes."

"We're counting on him."

Something in his boss's tone gave Shane pause. Was this a simple question or his make-it-or-break-it moment? Did his future at the Easy Money depend on Wasabi's performance? If so, he was ready for it.

He squared his shoulders. "I don't think you have anything to worry about."

"I hope so." Mercer took a place at the fence alongside Shane, resting his forearms on the top railing. Inside the pen, the bulls milled restlessly, lowing and swinging their large heads from side to side. They instinctively sensed this was no normal day. In every direction, people bustled about. Cowboys readying to compete. Fans eager for a close-up of the rodeo stock and exhibitors. The Verde Vaqueros equestrian drill team practicing for the opening ceremony.

"Kenny noticed Cassidy coming out of your trailer earlier," Mercer said, his tone flat. "He said the two of you were pretty cozy."

Not what Shane had been expecting, and he steadied himself before answering.

"We're old friends."

"Not just friends. She dated your brother. My grandson is your nephew."

Startled, Shane turned his head. Had Cassidy kept her secret only from Hoyt and the Westcotts? "How long have you known?"

"Always. Leastwise, I suspected. Most people did, I reckon."

Not Shane and Hoyt. Were they idiots? Maybe not. If one wasn't looking, he supposed, then one didn't see.

"I don't want Cassidy hurt. Or Benjie," Mercer said. "I care about both of them. And Benjie's family."

"Take it from me, family can hurt a person worse than any stranger."

"I won't lie. I did ask her on a date."

Mercer muttered a response under his breath. "What about your brother?"

"Doesn't matter. She declined. For the time being," Shane clarified. "She wants to speak to Hoyt first."

"And after that?"

"We'll see what happens."

"Look, son. I'm not judging." Mercer adjusted his hat, shielding his eyes from the bright midday sun. "Lord knows, I have my own complicated family situation. But you need to tread carefully. My grandson has taken quite a shine to you. Cassidy, too. I can see it. If not, she wouldn't be hesitating, waiting to talk to Hoyt first. She's cautious when it comes to men. I reckon I'm the one to blame."

Shane didn't like to think of Cassidy struggling. He did like to think her fondness for him was strong enough to be evident to others.

"I won't hurt her."

"You can't promise that."

"I assure you, my intentions are honorable."

"What about your daughter?"

"What about her?"

"You haven't had custody long. She might resent you dating Cassidy."

"She adores Benjie. I think she'd be thrilled to learn she has a cousin."

"You could be right." Mercer pushed off from the fence. Clapping a hand to Shane's shoulder, he squeezed. "I'm glad our family is increasing in size. And that your daughter's a part of it. You, too, as long as Cassidy's happy." The pressure of his grip increased, almost to the point of painful. He stopped just short. "If for any reason things change, you'll have me to deal with. And there'll be a lot more at stake than your job."

Shane didn't flinch. Didn't blink an eye. "Understood, sir."

"Do you mind telling me what's going on here?" Cassidy stood facing them, her laser stare taking aim at Mercer.

Shane gave the older man credit, who reacted by letting his hand drop and shrugging unconcernedly. "Just having a talk. Man to man."

"You're butting into a matter that doesn't concern you."

Shane had been prepared to stay out of the argument. Cassidy wasn't one to trifle with when riled. Neither was Mercer. They were more alike than they probably realized. He changed his mind when he noticed the attention the three of them were garnering.

"The opening ceremony starts in an hour," he said. "Maybe we should move along."

"Good idea." Mercer approached Cassidy. Rather than walk past her, he stopped and bent his head, kissing her on the cheek. She stiffened but, otherwise, didn't move. "We'll talk later, sweetheart."

"Count on it."

Shane thought it best he, too, leave. He'd have liked to kiss Cassidy, as well. Common sense prevailed.

"I'm sorry about that," she said, catching up with him.

Well, this was a day full of surprises. "Your dad loves you."

"It's too little, too late."

"Only if you let it be."

"There's still a lot you don't know."

Shane stopped abruptly. "This is a conversation you need to have with him. Not me."

She stiffened. A moment later, she was gone, disappearing into the crowd.

Mercer didn't have any reason to worry about Cassidy getting hurt, Shane thought with disappointment. Judging by her brusque departure he doubted they were going on a date, now or in the foreseeable future.

Chapter 8

"Thanks for everything. I'll be in touch." Cassidy tucked the representation agreement she'd signed into her purse and shook the woman lawyer's hand.

"I can't recommend contacting the father strongly enough. If he finds out about Benjie before you've told him, he could, and likely will, use that against you. He already has a lot of ammunition, what with you holding out this long."

"I'll call. This week."

"Today, if possible," the attorney insisted. "His brother may have promised to remain silent, but there's no guarantee he will."

"I trust him."

"Don't. In my experience, there are two times when loyalties are tested and family members choose sides. When someone dies and when there's a custody battle over the children."

Cassidy could think of another time. When one member was an alcoholic.

"That's rather dismal."

"But unfortunately true." The attorney offered a warm and supportive smile. Her first one of their entire meeting.

Cassidy braced a hand on the corner of the desk to steady herself. Was she ready to talk to Hoyt? No, but then, would she ever be? Getting it over with quickly might be the best approach. Then, hopefully, she could go back to sleeping soundly at night.

On the drive home from Globe, she mentally reviewed her meeting with the attorney. She'd liked the middle-aged woman's assertive manner and had hired her on the spot. The advice she'd offered, and her no-punches-pulled honesty, hard as it had been to hear, resonated with Cassidy. She'd be a strong advocate for Cassidy and Benjie when it came to dealing with Hoyt's attorney, as he was sure to hire one.

Shane had offered to be with her when she called Hoyt. The attorney had visibly recoiled when Cassidy had told her and insisted he be excluded. At first, Cassidy had agreed. Now she was having second thoughts. Shane was fiercely loyal to his brother, but he also cared for her, of that she was certain, and wanted what was best for her.

She recalled their steamy kiss from last Friday—something she'd done often during the past five days. It was one of those mistakes a person would make all over again given the opportunity. If she concentrated, she could feel the tingles cascading up and down her spine. The warmth pooling in her middle. The desire weakening her limbs.

Tingles and warmth aside, she wasn't planning on

any more kissing. Not before she and Hoyt reached an agreement. Possibly not after that. The situation was too tricky, and she had her son to think of.

Shane also cared a great deal about Benjie. If he wasn't present when she spoke to Hoyt, she'd for sure have him there when she told Benjie. Her son already felt a strong bond with Shane. If Benjie wound up reacting negatively, Shane would be a good person to calm him and ease his fears.

Unless Hoyt objected. What if he didn't like his brother interfering with his nephew? She hadn't considered that before.

Because her mind was spinning a hundred miles an hour, she opted to delay deciding until later. Upon entering Reckless, she spontaneously turned into the Dawn to Dusk Coffee Shop for a caramel latte. Her favorite. After a day like this one, she deserved to indulge herself in some comfort food. Or a comfort beverage, as it happened to be.

She was next in line to be served when someone came up behind her and cut in.

"Excuse me," said an irritated customer. "I was here first."

Cassidy whirled to find Shane standing there, cheeks ruddy from the wind and smelling of the outdoors.

He moved closer and tipped his hat to the woman customer. "Sorry, she was saving me a place."

Caught off guard, Cassidy had no choice but to allow him in line with her. She gave the woman customer her nicest smile and was rewarded with an agitated huff.

They reached the counter and placed their orders. "I'll buy," Shane said and removed his wallet from his jeans. "Hers, too." He indicated the woman behind him.

"Oh, thank you!" she said.

Cassidy wasn't so easily mollified. She still hadn't forgiven him for cutting in line. "Fine," she told the cashier, "I'll have a tall."

"Where were you today?" Shane asked as they waited for their coffees. "You left and didn't tell anyone."

"I wasn't aware I had to report in with you."

Not the first time she'd been short with him this week, and it was wrong of her. Truthfully, she was mad at herself and taking it out on him. Hardly Shane's fault that she'd practically ravished him in the trailer, then argued with her father in front of him.

"You don't, but we were worried."

"I told Deacon."

"He wasn't anyone we thought of asking."

Shane's repeated use of the word "we" puzzled her. Was he including himself with her family?

"I went to see an attorney in Globe. I didn't want to tell anyone until I saw how it went."

"And?"

Shane didn't have a right to ask her. This was none of his business. And the attorney had soundly advised her against including him. On the other hand, she'd included him earlier by discussing Benjie and her plans for telling Hoyt. She supposed he felt he had the right.

"It went okay."

The barista called their names. Shane retrieved the steaming cups.

"Let's sit outside." He all but hustled her to the shop's exterior seating area.

She went along. She didn't want to talk in the noisy and crowded shop. It seemed more people than usual were free for coffee at one o'clock on a Thursday afternoon. Shane being one of them.

"Wait," she said. "You didn't tell me what you're doing here."

"I was headed to the feed store for some supplements. I saw your SUV parked out front."

Just her luck, or bad luck depending on one's point of view.

They found an empty table for two under the awning. It wasn't warm. In fact, the temperature had dropped this week to the upper fifties. But it was bright out, and Cassidy's tired eyes were grateful for the awning's shade.

"So, what did the attorney say?"

She chose her words carefully, not intending to reveal everything to Shane in case the attorney was right about choosing sides.

"She told me what I can realistically expect to happen. What I can reasonably ask for from Hoyt. And what the worst case scenarios are. We also discussed strategies and options."

"I think you just said a lot of nothing."

Cassidy sipped her coffee, relishing the taste and warmth. "I'm not going to discuss details with you. Not until I speak to Hoyt."

"Is that what the attorney suggested?"

"It's what I want. What I'm comfortable with."

"How much of you shutting me out has to do with our kiss the other day?"

She tightened her grip on her cup. "We agreed not getting personally involved was for the best."

"We did. But when did not getting personally involved include stop being friends?"

"Hoyt's your brother. Your loyalties are understandably with him."

"Believe it or not, the person I'm most loyal to is Benjie."

Damn. He *would* have to say the right thing.

"For various reasons, the attorney recommended that I call Hoyt as soon as possible. Today, specifically."

Shane rubbed his chin, considering her remark. After a moment, he said, "There's no time like the present."

"I'm not calling him now." Cassidy glanced around nervously, which was silly. None of the nearby patrons were the least bit interested in them.

"It's as good a time as any. I'm here. You're here. I know for a fact Hoyt's off this week."

She shook her head vehemently. "The attorney was clear. She said I shouldn't call Hoyt with you present."

"I won't sabotage you."

She believed him, mostly because of the remark he'd made about Benjie. She didn't want to call Hoyt alone. With an audience, she'd be more inclined to keep a level head. Not lose her temper or her courage.

"I need some paper," she blurted. "For notes." And for something to do with her hands that didn't involve biting her nails to the quick.

Shane pulled a small notepad from the pocket of his jacket. On the top sheet was a list for the feed store in small, blocky printing. Why she would notice now, she had no idea.

"Here." He set the pad in front of her, then reached inside his jacket. The next instant a ballpoint pen lay atop the notepad.

He had everything at the tips of his fingers. *How convenient*, she silently groused.

Pulling her phone from her purse, she stared at it, her nerves deserting her at an astounding rate. Eyes closed, she willed them back.

"I'll dial for you."

"What?" Her eyes snapped open.

"Hoyt's number. I'll dial it for you."

She passed him the phone, grateful he wouldn't see the tremors in her fingers making dialing impossible.

God, it was here. The day she'd been dreading and avoiding for over six years. She resisted the urge to flee to her SUV and drive far, far away. That wouldn't solve anything. But, oh, how she wished differently.

"Here." Shane handed her the phone.

The device felt heavy in her palm. She almost couldn't lift it to her ear. At the sound of ringing on the line, everything and everyone faded into the background, and she was left alone, standing on the edge of a steep cliff.

More ringing. Maybe she'd catch a break and Hoyt wouldn't answer. Then what? Should she hang up and call back later? Leave a message? God, what would she say?

The choice was taken from her when the call connected, and life as she knew it, the world she'd carefully constructed for herself and Benjie, entirely and irrevocably changed.

"Hello. This is Hoyt Westcott."

Cassidy couldn't speak. Her mouth, it seemed, had gone completely dry. Her lips refused to work properly. Her mind had emptied all coherent thought.

"Ah...ah..."

She couldn't do it. Regardless of what her attorney

said, she'd wait until next week when she was more prepared. Next month. Next—

Shane whipped the phone away from her. "Hoyt," he said, "it's me." There was a pause. "Yeah, well, I'm calling you from Cassidy's phone." The next pause seemed to go on forever. At the same time, it was over much too soon. "She has something to tell you."

And, again, the incredibly heavy device was placed in her hands and pressed to her ear. How could that have happened without her remembering?

"H-Hoyt. How are you?"

"I'm good. How 'bout yourself?"

He sounded the same, if a little hesitant. Then again, what had she expected? Passing years and being married would change his voice?

A small glimmer of hope sparked inside her. He'd always been easygoing and jovial. If he was still the same, then maybe he'd be reasonable and cooperative about Benjie. Not mad as hell and determined to get back at her for lying.

Cassidy went numb all over. Please, she silently prayed, don't make this hard.

Aloud, she said, "Um, I'm all right. Is this a good time to talk?" Maybe he would say no.

"It's great. We just got back from taking Cheryl to the doctor. She's resting now."

"Is she all right?"

"Fine. A routine exam. We're hoping for a big family," he added haltingly.

"Oh. Yes." How could she have forgotten?

What if Cheryl didn't conceive and the fertility treatments failed? How would that affect custody of Benjie? Because of the distance, Cassidy's attorney had recommended allowing Hoyt to visit frequently. But, for the time being, he only take Benjie to Jackson Hole twice a year: four weeks over the summer and either Thanksgiving or Christmas.

Cassidy considered that doable, though the idea of Benjie being away for nearly half the summer left her with an empty ache in her heart. She simply couldn't live with him being gone any longer.

"I don't want to disturb you," she told Hoyt. "I'll call back next week."

Across the table, Shane gave her a look. "It won't be any better next week," he said in a low voice. "And it might be worse."

At first, she was angry. Who was he to tell her what to do? Then she realized the remark was meant to be encouraging. And, much as she hated to admit it, he was right. There was no going back now. She must tell Hoyt. Better to get it over with.

"This is as good a time as any," Hoyt insisted, closely echoing Shane's earlier comment. "What's up?"

"There's something I need to tell you. Haven't told you," she amended, still stalling.

He waited. And waited. "Cassidy?"

"When we broke up... I was..." *Breathe. Breathe. It's going to be okay.* "I was pregnant."

"You were?" He sounded startled. And confused. "Why didn't you tell me?"

"I didn't know it. Not for a few weeks."

His voice grew increasingly strained. "What happened? To the baby?"

"I had a son. His name is Benjamin. Benjie, for short."

"A son." Dead silence followed.

Cassidy spoke in a rush to fill it. "He's six. Just had a birthday. That's how Shane figured it out."

Hoyt went from sounding startled and confused to accusatory. "Is that why you're telling me now? Because Shane got wise?"

Technically, she was telling him because her attorney had recommended it. Better not to mention legal representation just yet. That could create a problem where there wasn't any.

"I was planning on telling you. Shane's discovery did speed things up."

"Planning on it? The kid is six years old."

Here came the anger Cassidy had been anticipating and fearing.

She glanced at Shane. Like that day in the trailer, right before they kissed, he reached across the table and took her free hand in his. His kind smile said she could do this. He was with her every step of the way, and she could depend on him.

Returning her attention to the phone, she continued, "What matters is I'm telling you now."

"Sorry," Hoyt said. "I don't buy that. You don't do anything without a reason."

"All right. I'm telling you because I'm backed into a corner." More silence. Was she wrong to have been completely honest? "Hoyt?"

"This is a lot to assimilate," he finally said. "I need a minute."

"Take your time."

"Why not tell me before?" he repeated, with less animosity this time.

She supplied him with a boiled-down version.

"I was scared. Of a lot of things. Mostly, I thought

you'd pressure me into marrying you, and I wasn't ready for that. Later, I changed my mind. I flew to Topeka to tell you and learned you and Cheryl were getting married. It didn't seem like the right time to spring the news on you that I was eight months pregnant."

"I'd have taken care of you and our son."

Our son. She always referred to Benjie as *her* son.

A very large, very painful lump formed in Cassidy's throat. Dammit. She didn't want to get emotional. If she wasn't careful, she'd fall apart, and she desperately needed to remain in control. Hoyt's next words, however, snapped her tenuous hold in two.

"I want to see him. Soon."

The attorney's advice resounded in Cassidy's head, warning her not to refuse any reasonable requests. Pick your battles, she'd said. Compromise on the small stuff. Stand strong only on the big stuff.

"All right. We can arrange a visit. Benjie has Monday off school next week—"

"Tomorrow."

Air rushed out of her lungs. "No. Impossible!"

"You've kept him from me for six years. I won't wait, Cassidy."

The threat was subtle but there. Would a judge say, because she'd hidden Benjie from him for six years, Hoyt could have him for the next six?

She refused to let him steamroll her. Back when they were dating, Hoyt had believed he could win every argument simply with a show of force. That, along with his immaturity, had caused their relationship to deteriorate.

"Next weekend," she insisted. "You can come out Friday morning and spend the long weekend in Reckless. That'll give me time to tell him about you and that you're coming for a visit. Also give you time to tell Cheryl about him."

"He doesn't know about me?"

"No."

"What *did* you tell him?"

His earlier anger had returned. She had to proceed cautiously. "His father was a cowboy I had dated and cared about greatly, but things didn't work out."

"A father who didn't want him?"

"It's not like that, Hoyt." She tried to keep the strain from her voice. Shane squeezing her fingers helped calm her and keep her focused. "I told him when he was ready, he could meet you."

She didn't add that, thus far, Benjie hadn't shown interest in meeting his father. Hurting Hoyt's feelings wouldn't gain her anything. Besides, it was unkind.

"What does he like? To play with, I mean." The change in Hoyt's tone was abrupt. "I want to bring him something."

"Well, recently, he's gotten into baseball." She looked at Shane, who responded with a nod.

"A glove?" Hoyt suggested.

"He has one already."

"A bat, then."

Why hadn't she suggested something else? "Lately, he's been building model cars and planes. The simpler ones."

"I did, too, when I was his age."

She could hear the smile in Hoyt's voice. It tore at her heart much more than she would have expected and gave her pause.

Hoyt wasn't the enemy. She'd been wrong to label

him that way for all these years. He'd been young and made a stupid mistake, insisting she come with him when he'd been drinking. That wasn't reason enough to hide his son from him. Nor was the possibility of ruining his upcoming marriage. It was an excuse Cassidy had latched onto rather than face the real reason.

No maybe about it. Her mother had hit the nail on the head when she'd said Cassidy's refusal to tell Hoyt was connected to her unresolved issues with her father.

Did everything have to keep going back to her parents and their divorce? How could one event impact so many people and completely change the course of their lives? Cassidy was tired of coping with the aftereffects.

Collecting herself, she said, "Why don't you call me back when you've worked out the details of your trip? Then we can make plans." And Cassidy could arrange another appointment with her attorney. Just to get more of those concerns laid to rest.

"Can you email me some pictures of him?"

Cassidy blinked, taken aback, though she shouldn't have been. "Of course."

"Shane has my email address."

She might have said goodbye, she couldn't be sure. The last seconds of the phone call had become a blur. Tears filled her eyes and she laid the phone down on the table.

"You did good." Shane hadn't moved. He continued to sit across from her, his hand squeezing hers.

Cassidy had occasionally imagined telling Hoyt about Benjie. In none of those versions was Shane there, comforting and consoling her. She liked reality better. He was making this difficult day a tiny bit more bearable.

"If you want, I can help you tell Benjie."

She wiped at her cheeks. Already, her tears were drying. "I do."

Possibly, she was making a huge mistake by allowing Shane to get closer. Then again, he might be the one person she needed most to survive the weeks ahead.

Chapter 9

Benjie wriggled and tugged at the collar of the shirt Cassidy was attempting to button up.

"Please, sweetie," she coaxed. "Settle down."

"I don't like the shirt."

"But you picked it out." Wanting him to look his best for this first meeting with Hoyt, she'd driven him into Globe yesterday specifically to buy him a new outfit. Benjie had chosen a pair of Wranglers—go figure— and a Western-cut shirt that looked a lot like the ones his uncle Shane wore. Cassidy didn't think it was a coincidence.

"This is itchy," he complained and tugged again on the collar.

She doubted that. More likely, her son was nervous. They both were. Cassidy had been in a constant state of agitation since her conversation with Hoyt—which intensified a few days ago when he called to advise her of his travel plans.

Telling Benjie that his father and his father's wife were coming to meet him had gone surprisingly well. Since his birthday, and especially since meeting Shane and Bria, Benjie had been fixated on the idea of a father. All of a sudden he had one, and he couldn't be more excited.

All week he'd pestered Cassidy with questions. What was his father's name? Where did he live? What was he like? Was he a champion bull rider like Uncle Shane? Did he look like Uncle Shane? Did he play baseball like Uncle Shane?

Sometimes, Cassidy thought he was more excited about Shane being his uncle than Hoyt being his father.

Then, yesterday, the questions began to change, as did Benjie's mood. He became untypically reserved and quiet.

"What if he doesn't like me?" he asked her again.

Cassidy bent and fed his belt through the loops on his jeans. "He likes you already and can't wait to meet you."

"Do I have to go see him in Wyoming?"

She had tried to explain the possible visitation schedule and now regretted it. "Jackson Hole is nice. Very different from Arizona."

"But what if I hate it there? I won't know anybody."

"Nothing's been decided yet." She gave Benjie a hug before straightening.

"What do I call my stepmom?"

She'd also tried to explain the whole stepfamily concept. It was a lot for a six-year-old to comprehend.

"She and your father will tell you when they get here."

Cheryl. Cassidy had been pondering her a lot lately. Was she friendly and personable? Patient and even tempered? Would she resent Benjie because of her own difficulty conceiving? Worse, what if he liked her? Would Cassidy be jealous?

Benjie crossed his arms and stuck out his lower lip. "I don't want him to take me away like Grandpa took Uncle Ryder away."

"Oh, sweetie." She smoothed his hair, then kissed the top of his head. She should have been more careful and not let him overhear her conversations with her family. "Grandpa didn't take Uncle Ryder away. It wasn't like that."

"But Uncle Ryder left."

"Because he wanted to."

"Well, I don't want to leave." The lip extended farther.

"Then you don't have to."

They finished dressing soon after that, and Cassidy told Benjie he could watch TV while they waited. She'd purposely gotten him ready early in order to give herself plenty of time to shower and change before Hoyt and Cheryl's arrival.

She was just buttoning up her own shirt when a soft knock sounded on her bedroom door.

"It's me," came her mother's voice from the other side.

"Come on in."

"How are you holding up?"

"Not bad, I guess."

"Tell me the truth." Her mother perched on the edge of Cassidy's bed. "You're white as snow."

"Am I?" She caught a glimpse of herself in the

dresser mirror. Good grief, she was pale. "It's been a tough week."

"I'm proud of you, honey. What you're doing takes courage."

People, including Shane, kept telling her that. Cassidy didn't feel courageous. She felt scared out of her wits.

"I can't lose him, Mom."

"You won't."

"But what about Ryder? He left." The assurances she'd given Benjie were all for show. Deep down, she dreaded the possibility.

"It's not the same. Benjie doesn't resent you."

"He might. When he's older, he could figure out I prevented him from seeing his father for the first six years of his life and resent the heck out of me. Hoyt could poison his thinking. Cheryl could be the wonderful, fun stepmother who overindulges him while I'm the mom who makes him do his homework and clean his room."

"You're letting yourself get carried away. For all you know, Benjie and Hoyt won't get along."

"That's not what I want."

"Of course you don't. My point is, we can't foresee the future. The best we can do is take each day as it comes."

Cassidy plunked down on the bed beside her mother, who put a comforting arm around her shoulders.

"We're here for you if you need us."

We, Cassidy surmised, meant her mother *and* father. "You and dad are getting pretty cozy lately."

Her mother gave Cassidy a squeeze before releasing her. "I won't deny it."

"You didn't come home last night."

"I'm a grown woman." There was a cheerfulness in her mother's voice Cassidy had been hearing more often lately.

"If you're happy, then I'm happy."

"I am. More than I thought possible."

"What if he regresses? Alcoholism doesn't go away."

"I doubt he'll regress. He hasn't touched a drop for over twenty years."

"You've made quite a turnaround. When Dad first returned to Reckless, you fought him tooth and nail at every step."

"Things are different. You children are grown, for one."

"Yeah, but you have a young grandson living here. Let's just say, for the sake of argument, that Dad—"

Her mother cut her off. "Take every day as it comes, remember?"

It was a bad habit of hers, anticipating the worst. Also a difficult one to break.

A glance at the bedside clock made Cassidy jump to her feet, heart racing. "They'll be here soon."

Her mother also stood, though considerably more slowly. "I'd really like for you and your dad to patch things up. He wants it, too."

Cassidy pushed her hair off her face, breathing deeply in an effort to relax. "Can we talk about this later? Please. I have enough to worry about right now."

"I understand." At the door, her mother paused. "Just give it some consideration, okay? It would mean a lot to both of us. Your brother and sister, too."

"Sure."

Why, for heaven's sake, was her mother pushing a reconciliation now, of all days? Had something changed? Cassidy was too rushed to give the matter more than a passing consideration. Benjie's voice carried from the other end of the house, followed by thundering footsteps.

"Uncle Shane!"

He'd slipped so easily into calling Shane "uncle." She should be pleased. Shane certainly was. His booming voice also carried down the hall.

"How are you, buddy? Ready for the big day?"

Walking toward the kitchen, Cassidy could imagine Shane lifting her son into his arms as he often did. She stopped just before the entryway and silently observed them.

They were exactly as she'd pictured them in her mind, both grinning broadly. Cassidy marveled at the slight resemblance she hadn't noticed before. It was more mannerisms than anything physical. "Is my dad like you?" Benjie was clearly still bursting with questions.

"In some ways. He's also different than me."

"How?"

"He's taller. I'm a better bull rider."

"Is that true?"

"Would I lie?"

Benjie giggled, and Shane lowered him to the floor, ruffling the hair Cassidy had meticulously smoothed not thirty minutes ago. "Actually, you're a lot like him. Funny. Smart. Gregarious."

"What's gregorus?"

"Outgoing. Enough energy for two kids."

"Mom's always telling me to calm down and go slow."

Shane glanced at Cassidy and gave her a wink. "She was always saying that to your dad, too."

Had she? Cassidy couldn't recall. Then again, she had surprisingly few memories about her relationship with Hoyt. Had she purposely tried to forget? Pushing him from her mind with the same diligence she'd pushed him from their lives?

She berated herself for being selfish. Regardless of how her relationship with Hoyt had ended, she should have preserved their memories for the day when their child would ask. Certainly the good ones, and there had been some happy times.

"I wish you were my dad." Benjie's proclamation caused both Cassidy and Shane to stare at him, Cassidy with her mouth open.

"Sweetie, no." She had no idea how to respond. "Don't say that."

"But it's true." He pouted, all trace of her charming little boy gone.

Shane went down on one knee in front of Benjie. "Hey, look at me, buddy."

Benjie did. Reluctantly.

"It's scary. Meeting your dad for the first time. I know because Bria had to go through the same thing when she met me. But I'll tell you a secret."

"What?"

"This is just as scary for your dad."

Benjie shrugged.

"I don't know what kind of dad he'll be, but I can tell you he was a pretty great big brother. Stuck up for me when I got in trouble or was picked on. Helped me with my homework. Played with me. Took care of me.

He'll do the same for you. All you have to do is give him a chance. Okay?"

"Okay."

Shane stood and pulled Benjie to his side. "That's my boy."

Tears gathered in Cassidy's eyes, undoubtedly the first of many today. Clearing her throat, she edged closer.

"Hoyt and Cheryl should be here any minute."

"They're probably pulling in the driveway now," Shane said. "Hoyt called a few minutes ago."

"So soon!" Alarm filled Cassidy—and might have overtaken her if not for Shane's steadying hand on her arm.

"Relax. Everything's going to be all right."

She believed him—for exactly three seconds. Then, the front doorbell rang.

Shane sat in the far corner of the living room couch, watching the goings-on and keeping his mouth shut. The situation was hard enough on everyone without him making comments.

But, if he was to speak, he'd tell his brother to dial it down a notch. Overwhelming the poor kid with a big personality and a bright, shiny gift wasn't going to win him over. He should just take it easy and be himself. Then, maybe, Benjie would stop clinging to his mother and squeezing into the slim space between her and the arm of the wingback chair where she sat.

Shane would also tell Sunny that being the perfect hostess wasn't necessary. Once the tray of lemonade was delivered and the glasses filled, she should have skedaddled out of there. An audience wasn't helping.

Shane would be gone, too, if Hoyt hadn't insisted he stay and Cassidy didn't look as though she was ready to splinter into a dozen pieces.

Of all of them, he felt the worst for Cheryl. This was what she wanted. A child. The longing in her eyes was heartbreaking. She attempted to cover it with a forced smile, sickeningly pleasant small talk and a chin-up attitude.

Maybe she, Sunny and Shane should leave. Let Benjie and his parents figure things out on their own. How to suggest that? He was interrupted by Benjie's first real contribution to the conversation.

"Uncle Shane plays baseball with me every day."

Hoyt looked over, his expression difficult to read. "He does?"

"More like catch," Shane clarified.

"And we go horseback riding," Benjie said.

"Only a couple times."

"Shane's been very good to Benjie." Cassidy placed her hand on Benjie's head. The gesture could be interpreted as motherly...or protective. "They've become close."

Whatever was going on, Shane didn't want to be a part of it. Regardless of his feelings for Cassidy, he had no intention of usurping Hoyt's place in Benjie's life. "I've been telling him a lot about you and stories from when we were kids."

"Do you like to fish?" Hoyt asked Benjie.

"Never been."

The gift he'd brought was a new youth-size rod and reel. A good idea, considering Roosevelt Lake was a mere thirty minutes away and the fishing there some of the best in the state.

"Maybe you should go while you're here," Shane suggested. "Your dad's a pretty good angler."

"What's that?" Benjie asked.

"A fisherman."

Benjie peered at Hoyt with new interest, then twisted in the chair to look at Cassidy. "Can I, Mom?"

"We can certainly talk about it."

The tension in the room, already high, increased.

"Cookies anyone?" Sunny rose. "I have homemade chocolate chip."

Shane considered chasing after Sunny and waylaying her in the kitchen, just to give the rest of them some privacy. Unfortunately, she was too fast for him, so he did the next best thing.

"Hey, Benjie. Why don't you take your dad to the barn and show him Skittles?" When Cassidy nearly exploded from her chair, he added, "Your mom, too. We'll have cookies when you get back."

"Okay." Benjie was suddenly all smiles. "You come, too."

"I'm going to wait here. Keep Cheryl and your grandmother company."

His sister-in-law looked almost relieved. Not Benjie, who fixed a stubborn scowl on his face.

Shane was trying to think of what to say next when his brother surprised him.

"Skittles, huh? I've ridden that horse. Years ago. I was competing in the Wild West Days Rodeo. Calf roping. My horse threw a shoe. Your grandmother let me borrow Skittles." Hoyt smiled and exchanged glances with Cassidy. "I came in second place. You remember?"

"I do. You beat out Shane."

Her voice had softened, and a tiny smile touched

her lips. Shane was completely enamored and, for just a second, forgot where they were and why.

Benjie giggled, his interest in his father at last genuine. "You beat Uncle Shane?"

"He barely qualified, as I recall."

In calf roping. But Shane had taken home the gold buckle for bull riding. "Your dad was always a better roper than me."

"I can't believe Skittles is still around." Hoyt slapped his thigh. "I'd like to see him. If you'll take me."

"We have to hurry." Benjie jumped up and grabbed Cassidy's hand, pulling her out of the chair and across the room to where Hoyt sat. "Grandpa feeds at five o'clock. We're not allowed in the barn then."

Hoyt stood and patted his son on the back. "We'd best get after it, then."

Benjie forgot all about including Shane, for which he was glad. He wouldn't trade his relationship with Bria for anything in the world and wished the same for his brother.

At the entryway from the living room to the kitchen, Cassidy paused and glanced over her shoulder. He nodded encouragingly, trying to let her know she was doing just fine, and he'd be right here when she returned.

"Thanks for helping," Cheryl said to him after the others had left. "This has been a strange and strained day."

"Where did everyone go?" Sunny appeared holding the tray of cookies and wearing a perplexed expression.

"They needed some time alone." Shane snatched a cookie off the tray and took a bite. "Good," he muttered.

"Hmm." Sunny set the tray on the table and motioned to a chair. "Would you two like to join me?"

"Thank you." With a what-else-can-I-do attitude, Cheryl sat.

She was making the best of a difficult situation, a quality Shane admired. He liked his sister-in-law and had always thought her a good match for Hoyt. More serious than her husband, she grounded him without dragging him down or smothering his outgoing nature.

Cassidy was also serious, but with a razor-sharp intensity that, when ignited with just the right match, turned into a fiery passion. Shane liked igniting that passion. When the time was right, he'd do it again.

"I'll take a rain check," he told Sunny and grabbed another cookie on his way out the door. "The bull riding jackpot starts at six."

Two weekends every month, when there wasn't a rodeo, the Easy Money hosted bucking stock events. For a reasonable fee, participants entered a nonsanctioned competition. A portion of the entry fees were set aside, with the top three scores for the evening splitting the pot. The popular event had increased in recent months with the addition of new, championship-quality bulls like Wasabi.

Shane assumed his brother would come looking for him when he finished with Cassidy and Benjie. He wasn't worried when he stopped at the trailer for a quick bite of supper before the jackpot. He wasn't worried an hour later when the jackpot got underway. An hour after that, he was having trouble concentrating. Every few minutes, his gaze wandered toward the barn or the house.

Where were they? How was it going? Had something happened? Should he call Hoyt?

Shane was ready to dispatch one of the hands to look

for them when he spotted Cassidy sitting alone in the last row of the bleachers.

"Kenny," he hollered to the teenager. "Cover for me. I'll be right back."

Spectators' heads turned as he bounded up the bleacher steps two at a time. Cassidy's wasn't one of them. She was so lost in thought, she didn't glance up until the vibration of his boots hitting the floorboard roused her. Even then, she didn't appear to recognize him for several seconds. When she did, she turned her head.

Catching his breath, he lowered himself onto the seat next to her. "How'd it go?"

Her answer was to cover her eyes with her hands. It was then Shane realized she'd been crying.

"Hey. Don't do that."

Without thinking, he nestled her in the crook of his arm. At first, she tensed. The next moment, she slumped and leaned her head against his shoulder. Shane didn't disturb her, even when his arm fell asleep.

Chapter 10

Cassidy suppressed a groan. How had this happened? Once again, she'd let Shane breach her defenses. Why was he the one who evoked feelings in her she'd rather keep buried? The one who knew without being told what she needed? Today, it was unconditional support without questions.

"I'm not a crier," she said at last, lifting her head from his shoulder and wiping her damp cheeks with a tissue procured from her jacket pocket.

"You cry. You just don't let people see you."

How true. Figures he'd see right through her pretenses. "Sorry." She straightened, putting a few inches between them. His arm slipped from around her shoulders.

Much better, she thought. The distance, slight as it was, lessened her vulnerability to him.

"Did Hoyt and Cheryl leave?"

"A while ago. Mom's watching Benjie for me."

Cassidy had attempted to calm her son after his father left—*his father* still sounded so strange to her—without much success. Benjie was over the moon. Once the ice had been broken and common ground discovered, thanks mostly to Skittles, he and Hoyt had talked nonstop. Cassidy had barely gotten a word in until the end of the visit. For all she knew, Benjie was still talking.

When her mother had offered to forego the bull riding jackpot and take over Benjie's nighttime routine, Cassidy had jumped at the chance, desperately needing to get away and recover emotionally and mentally from a trying afternoon.

Out of habit, she'd wandered to the arena. Any other evening, she, too, would have been working the bull riding jackpot. No one had been sitting in the uppermost row of the bleachers until Shane had joined her. Before she could tell him to go, he had sat down. At the time, accepting the comfort he'd offered seemed natural. Lord knows she could use a friend.

Now she was less sure. What if he jumped to the wrong conclusion? She was already having a hard enough time keeping him at arm's length. Sitting with her head on his shoulder, for twenty minutes according to the clock on the electronic scoreboard, sent the wrong message.

"Am I wrong to assume things didn't go well?" he asked. "I wondered when Hoyt didn't find me to say goodbye."

"Things went great."

"They did?"

She summarized Benjie and Hoyt's successful visit.

"Is that what has you upset? The visit going well?"

"I am so shallow." She sniffed and rubbed her nose.

"You're scared. Which is perfectly normal."

"I don't want to lose Benjie." Her chest hurt as if every bit of air was being squeezed from her lungs. "I can't."

"Hoyt won't do that to you."

Cassidy wanted to believe him, but there were too many variables. "You know what upsets me the most?" She couldn't believe she was about to confide in Shane.

"What?"

"Seeing Benjie with Hoyt. It was…sweet. And kind of endearing."

He chuckled. "That's not so terrible."

"Maybe." She'd had the same reaction when she saw her son and Shane together. Then, she hadn't felt as threatened.

"Did Hoyt mention visitation?"

"We didn't go into details. That's for the attorneys to hash out. But he swears he'll be reasonable. He also asked me to bring Benjie to Payson next month while he's there working."

"Okay. That's not asking too much."

She sighed. "No, it's not."

"I could go with you. Bring Bria. Before Hoyt learned about Benjie, we agreed I would drive up and meet him for the day."

They could hardly sit next to each other without touching. A two-hour road trip would stretch their willpower to its limit. Then again…

"I'll think about it. Thanks for the offer," she added. They watched the bull riding for several minutes in silence. Then, Cassidy surprised herself by saying, "I would like you to come with us tomorrow."

"What's happening?"

"Hoyt suggested a trail ride with a picnic lunch. I'm not comfortable letting him and Cheryl take Benjie alone. When I expressed my concern, he said that, naturally, I could come along."

Which had irked her. As if *Hoyt* got to invite *her* along on an outing with *her* son.

"Maybe you should stick to the four of you."

"I already told him I was inviting Ryder, Tatum and her three kids." Safety in numbers, as far as she was concerned. "I think Benjie will be more comfortable that way."

"Okay," Shane mused aloud. "If Hoyt doesn't mind."

She wanted to say the hell with how Hoyt felt. Instead, she simply nodded. "We're leaving at eleven."

"I'll need to be back by three. Doc Worthington is stopping by."

"We all need to be back by then." Saturdays were always busy at the Easy Money.

Another several minutes of silence passed, after which Shane said, "Hard as it is, you're doing the right thing."

"Yeah." Her voice cracked.

"You're not going to cry again, are you?" His tone was teasing. The look in his green eyes was mesmerizing.

She couldn't bring herself to look away. "No, I'm not."

He touched her cheek, wiping away a tear with the pad of his thumb. "Too late."

Damn it. She hated him seeing her like this.

Before she could stop him, he brushed his lips across hers. The kiss was tender and comforting. Night and day from the smoldering one they'd shared in his trailer. Yet desire pulled at her, stronger than ever.

How could he do that with the merest of touches? She blamed the fact she hadn't been kissed by another man in a long, long time. Also, she'd been an emotional wreck this past week.

The truth was, she wanted Shane. With a desire that terrified her as much as it thrilled.

"You should know," he said, his voice low and husky and raw with need. "I'm going to kiss you."

Hadn't he just done that?

"If you don't want me to, you'd better get up and leave right now."

She should have thanked him for the warning and run for the hills as fast as her legs could carry her. Instead, she remained seated, willing him to make good on his promise.

"There's no going back after this, Cassidy."

Back to what? Her lonely life?

This had been one of the hardest days she could ever remember. She wanted Shane to take her to heaven and make her forget, if only for a minute. Or, two. Maybe three.

"What are you waiting for?" She tilted her head and parted her lips. "Kiss me."

Shane didn't hesitate and covered her mouth with his.

She let him take control, abandoning all resistance. It was wonderful. Freeing, actually.

Her hand sought his jaw and stroked it. The stubble from his five o'clock shadow tickled her fingertips. She liked the sensation so much, she went in search of others, finding the silky texture of the fine hairs at the base of his neck and the strong muscles of his neck and shoulders.

A groan emanating from deep inside his chest distracted her. He withdrew long enough to whisper against her lips. "You are incredible."

Was she? Shane made her feel that way. Incredible and sexy and desirable. It was a heady combination, and an addictive one.

"Tell me to stop," he said.

"And if I don't? Will you kiss me again?"

His answer was to make her every romantic dream come true. She clutched the fabric of his vest in her fists, pulling him close and sealing their lips together. He, in turn, wrapped his arms around her. Never had they been closer. Had more intimate contact. Been more attuned to each other.

Too far!

The words exploded inside her head and caused her to abruptly pull back. "Wait."

"What's wrong?"

"Slower." She expelled a long breath. "I need to go slower."

"I can kiss you as slow as you want." One corner of his mouth quirked in his trademark disarming grin.

"No more." She placed a restraining hand on him. "Not tonight." And not in front of all these people.

"All right. As long as it's not for good. It's not for good, is it, Cassidy?"

"I need some time." She had to stop letting him kiss her. Stop kissing him back.

"You're right. I'm sorry. I took advantage of you." He eased away.

"No more than I took of you," she admitted.

He smiled. "Feel free to do that anytime the mood strikes you."

"Shane." Her pleading eyes searched his.

"I get it." Patting her leg, he stood. "I'll see you tomorrow. At the trail ride."

"Tomorrow," she repeated.

The next instant, he was gone.

She should be thinking about Benjie and Hoyt, the trail ride and the changes coming at her like a freight train traveling full steam ahead. Instead, she missed the warmth of Shane's body. The scent of his skin. The taste of his lips.

It was scary how quickly she'd gotten used to him. Scarier how miserable she'd be if he left.

The weather held. Cassidy had worried up until the moment they set out on the trail ride that they might be rained out. Slowly, the clouds transformed from dark and gloomy to a washed-out gray. Other than the periodic gust of wind, it wasn't a bad day. Weather-wise or otherwise.

Hoyt and Cheryl hadn't expected it, but along with Ryder and Tatum's children, *all* the Becketts accompanied them, including Cassidy's parents, and her siblings and their respective future spouses. When ascending the first hill in single file, the line of horses they rode stretched better than thirty yards from first head to last tail.

Liberty brought up the rear, leading a coal-black mare she was training for a client. The young horse carried a pack saddle. Inside was the light picnic lunch Sunny and Cassidy had quickly assembled. Cheese spread, crackers, beef jerky, individual cups of applesauce and leftover chocolate chip cookies comprised their fare.

Ryder rode double with Tatum's youngest son seated in front of him. Other than that, everyone had their own mount. Shane, Cassidy couldn't help observing, stayed close to her. Perhaps because Benjie stayed close to Hoyt. Either way, she appreciated his presence.

Her hands ached from constantly gripping the reins too tightly, and she forced her fingers to relax. A moment later, they strained again. *Stop it*, she told herself. All was going well. Nothing bad had happened. There was no reason for her angst. Yet there it was. By the end of their first hour she was exhausted.

When they reached a long flat area on the south ridge and her father announced this was probably as good a place as any to break for lunch, she was more than ready. Hopefully, stretching her legs for a bit would relax her. Calm her. Distract her.

While the four children darted to and fro, burning off excess energy, the men tethered the horses to any available low-slung branch. Sunny and Cheryl distributed the food. Cassidy should have helped. Her mind, however, refused to settle down, and she wandered aimlessly.

Finding a large rock to use as a stool, she sat, took a long pull from the bottled water she'd brought in her saddlebag and watched the children play. Benjie, younger than Tatum's oldest by a year, was still taller. He had inherited his height from Hoyt, as well as his outgoing personality and his sense of humor, which, in Benjie's case, often manifested itself in class clown behavior.

What had he inherited from her other than his looks?

Cassidy didn't think of herself as timid. More like guarded. And cautious. She wasn't one to leap without first looking. Funny, at Benjie's age, she'd been just as adventurous. Just as carefree. Her father's drinking had changed her. After the accident and her parents' divorce, she'd become a whole different person.

Speak of the devil...

Her father approached. "You doing okay?"

"Fine," she automatically replied. No one ever wanted to hear the truth.

"Mind if I join you?" He lowered himself onto the rock beside her.

"Not at all." Did she mind? Cassidy wasn't sure.

That in itself was interesting and new. She'd spent the last six months being angry at her father and making every effort *not* to be alone with him. Now, all of a sudden, she didn't care?

"You okay?" he asked. "You seem preoccupied."

"It's been a rough week. A strange week."

"I can relate."

He probably could, no doubt to Hoyt.

For the first time, Cassidy was curious about her father's reunion with her younger sister. "What was it like, meeting Liberty after all those years?"

"Weird." He gave a low chuckle.

"Seriously."

"I am serious. Took me weeks, months really, to get used to the idea. Not that I didn't love her right away. But she was a stranger to me, and me to her. I wanted us to instantly click. Instead, it took time."

"Benjie and Hoyt are clicking."

He followed her gaze to where Hoyt and his wife sat

with Benjie, eating their lunch. "It does look that way on the surface."

Cassidy wasn't sure what to make of his remark. "You think they aren't?"

"Hoyt's trying hard. Too hard. Though I understand his motives. But he needs to rein it in a bit. I did the same with your sister. Rushed the connection before either of us was ready, and it backfired."

"Benjie's excited to have a father."

"Sure he is. But watch him closely. The initial thrill is wearing off, and even if he doesn't realize it, he's starting to wonder what impact this new dad is going to have on his life and if all the changes will be good ones."

She hadn't realized her father was so perceptive, or so deep. He was noting the same subtle differences in Benjie she'd observed these last two days.

The man apparently had sides to him she'd yet to see. Sides, she admitted, were intriguing to her.

"What makes you say that?"

"He asked me before the ride if Hoyt planned on taking him to Wyoming."

Cassidy sighed heavily. "My fault. He's heard me telling the story of when Ryder left. I should talk to him again."

"You and Hoyt should *both* talk to him. Assure him he has nothing to fear."

Why hadn't she thought of that? She was the worst mother in the world, concerned only with herself.

"I will. We will," she amended. "After the ride."

Several moments passed in silence. The three older children, having finished their meals, were pleading with Shane to join in their antics. Why not Hoyt?

Perhaps because Shane wasn't trying too hard the way Hoyt was, at least, according to her father. Shane was also someone the children knew better. Visiting only periodically, Hoyt might never be someone Benjie knew well.

She turned to her father. "Would you have come back more often if you'd known Liberty was your daughter?"

"Absolutely. Regardless of the grief your mom gave me." He removed a pack of gum from his shirt pocket. She accepted when he offered her a piece. "Not sure I'd have moved back permanently, but visited, yes. Frequently."

"Was it hard on you, being so far away from me?" Cassidy hadn't realized how desperately she wanted to learn the answer to that question until she'd asked it.

"It was terrible. I missed you something awful," he said earnestly. "I'd have visited more often if you hadn't hated me like you did. Still do, at times."

"I was angry," she defended herself. "With good reason. And I didn't...don't hate you."

"Sometimes it's hard to tell the difference between the two. Anger and hate."

Guilt consumed her. If she hadn't treated her father in such a cold manner, her parents might still be married and Ryder wouldn't have left. "I'm responsible for the rift in our family."

"Not at all, baby girl." He brushed a knuckle along her cheek. "That's my fault entirely. I'm the one who drank away the arena's profits. The one who drove while intoxicated, with you in the passenger seat, and ran the truck into the well house. I'm the one who let your mother down time and again and divided our family."

Baby girl? He'd called her that endearment when she was little.

Memories from years ago promptly assaulted Cassidy. Unlike before, these weren't painful or hurtful. They were lovely and sentimental.

She could see the two of them walking across the back pasture, her small hand enclosed in his larger one. Four, maybe five years old, she'd begged him to take her to pick the wild hollyhocks, their large, delicate white blossoms in stark contrast to their coarse stalks. Another time, he'd found her in the haystacks, sobbing after the family dog died unexpectedly from an infection, and comforted her with a story of dog heaven.

It hadn't always been bad between them. Mostly it had been good. Ryder had tried to tell her, but she wouldn't listen. Shame on her.

"If I could do it over again," her father said, "I would. Fight harder for you. Truthfully, I'm not sure what I regret more. Losing out on knowing your sister for the first twenty-four years of her life or the night of the accident."

The moment had come for Cassidy to atone. Six months ago when her father returned—heck, last month before Shane showed up—she wouldn't have said that. How things had changed. And how incredibly quickly.

"I'm the reason Mom divorced you."

He chuckled again. "I hardly think so."

"No, it's true. After the accident, I was scared. I insisted she make you leave. I forced her to choose, and she picked Ryder and me over you."

Her father sat back and scratched his whiskered jaw, a bemused expression on his face. "Your mother isn't that easily manipulated. Believe you me, she wanted me gone."

"Because I insisted."

"Because of my drinking and its effect on our lives."

"I ruined your marriage."

"While I'd like nothing better than to lay the blame at someone else's doorstep, if there's one thing I've learned in twenty-plus years of AA meetings it's no one's responsible for my marriage hitting the skids other than me. I had choices, and I made one wrong one after the other."

Cassidy looked for Hoyt. He'd taken Shane's place with the children. Benjie beamed up at him, obviously hanging on his every word.

Had she made a mistake not telling Hoyt the truth all those years ago?

Her father, mother and Shane, they were each of them right. She couldn't alter the past. The best she could do was affect the future.

"Thanks, Dad." She squeezed his hand, feeling the walls between them slowly crumble. It was a shame they hadn't had this talk before, though Cassidy wouldn't have been receptive.

He beamed at her with the same joy her son showed Hoyt. "You have no idea how long I've waited to hear you say that."

"Say what?" She smiled.

"*Dad*, with just that tone."

She glanced away, afraid her face would reveal the depth of her emotions. "I can be stubborn. And difficult."

"You're your mother's child." He tucked his finger

beneath her chin and lifted her face to his. "Makes me love you all the more."

Impulsively, she threw her arms around his neck and hugged him close. Not the same as saying she loved him in return. Still too many walls between them. But it was close. And enough for now. The rest, she was suddenly confident, would come.

"Well, well, well," he said, his voice gruff. "That's the nicest thing to happen to me in quite a while."

She released him slowly and said softly, "Same here."

Neither of them moved from the rock. Rather, they enjoyed their newfound closeness in mutually agreeable silence. It lasted until Benjie came running up to Cassidy.

"Can I have another cookie?"

"Sure." Why not? she thought. Nothing said celebration like a chocolate chip cookie, and she had reason to celebrate today.

Benjie scrambled back to Hoyt, carrying not one but two cookies.

"He'll do right by Benjie," her father said, referring to Hoyt.

"You think? I've kept my distance from him for six years. I have no idea what kind of person he's become."

"Give him a chance."

"I will." Before, she'd felt cornered. Pressure coming at her from all sides. Today, the pressure had been lifted. "Shane's a great dad. I never saw that coming. He was every bit as wild as Hoyt back in the day."

"Shane's been through a lot. Nothing like staring your future in the face to mature a person."

"Are you talking about his fall from Wasabi last year?"

"No, his daughter."

Cassidy was staring her future in the face, too, and it wasn't easy.

"I know you got mad at me the other day for interfering in your relationship with him."

"You were out of line," she agreed.

"Only because I care about you."

She now knew that to be the real reason, whereas she hadn't before.

"I approve of him for you. He's got backbone and strength of character, which he'll need plenty of."

Cassidy narrowed her gaze at her father. "Because I'm stubborn and difficult."

"Because you stand up for your convictions," he said, with a fondness in his voice that made her smile. "And if Shane isn't bursting with admiration for you like I am, he's not the man for you."

She shook her head. "I'm not ready for a relationship."

"No one ever thinks they are. That's what makes it wonderful when it happens."

"You're talking about you and Mom."

"Mark my word, I'm going to marry her."

He'd been saying as much all along. But until today, Cassidy hadn't supported the match. Funny how one's perspective could be suddenly altered.

"Mom's a long ways from being convinced."

"She'll get there." He winked at her, then pushed to his feet. "I'd better check on the kids' horses. Benjie's saddle looked a little loose during the ride. Girth probably needs adjusting."

After giving her shoulder an affectionate pat, he left, stopping first to talk to Cassidy's mother. She could see the love and devotion in his face. What would it be like to have a man look at her like that? She searched out Shane, finding him engrossed in conversation with her brother. Probably about arena business.

She supposed she should get after it, too. Help with the cleanup and run herd on the children. The last person she expected to come over and give her a hand was Cheryl.

"Here, let me," she said and bent to collect the empty juice boxes strewn on the ground.

"Thanks." Cassidy held open the trash bag.

"It's absolutely beautiful up here."

"I've always loved this spot."

What an incredible day, Cassidy mused. Benjie playing with Hoyt. She and her father having their long overdue reconciliation. Working together with Cheryl and casually conversing.

"Hey." Shane appeared beside her, his green eyes alight with curiosity. "Your day must be improving."

"Very much so."

"I'm intrigued."

She took in his rugged, handsome features and the easy grin that always started her heart fluttering, and smiled in return. No reason the day couldn't continue to improve. All she need do was open herself to the possibilities.

Chapter 11

By the time they returned from the trail ride, the arena was in full swing. Tom Pratt had scheduled his popular calf roping clinic. This was the renowned expert's third such event at the Easy Money and, with each one, attendance increased.

"Hey, sis." Ryder sidled up to Cassidy, his voice dripping honey. "You mind taking care of our horses? Deacon and I are heading over to watch Tom."

"No problem. Have fun."

"You sure?"

"Get out of here."

"Our horses" turned out to be Ryder's, Deacon's, Tatum's and the two her children had been riding. Cassidy shrugged off the inconvenience, glad to have something to keep her busy.

"I owe you," Tatum said when she discovered that Cassidy had been burdened with the job.

"It's okay." She smiled at her friend, who would have helped but was taking care of her youngest. The toddler had complained of an upset stomach during the ride home. "You can do me a favor sometime."

"Count on it."

Benjie wasn't so lucky. Rather than getting off the hook, he had to unsaddle, brush and put away Skittles. The task went from being a chore to something fun when Hoyt stepped in to help. Cheryl had mentioned during the cleanup that she and Hoyt were having dinner in Mesa with a local rodeo promoter and his wife. They would return in the morning to spend the day with Benjie and again on Monday for a last visit before flying home.

One at a time, Cassidy led the horses down the barn aisle to the hitching post outside the tack room where she unhurriedly tended them. When she was done, she returned them to their stalls and went back for the next horse.

She was just finishing with the last horse when Hoyt strolled down the barn aisle.

"Mind some company?" he asked when he neared.

"Not at all." She peered behind him. "Where's Benjie?"

"With Cheryl and your mother."

"Oh." That was unexpected. Hoyt hadn't ventured three feet from Benjie all day. "How is Cheryl handling all this?" For some, the question might be none of their business. Cassidy felt she had a right to know.

"She's doing okay," Hoyt said.

"It must be hard on her, you having a child when you've both been trying for quite a while without success."

"She's glad for me."

Cassidy didn't doubt it. But neither was Cheryl made of stone. She must be hurting to some degree. Would it get worse during the summer when Benjie visited?

"Tell her she can call me anytime. If she has questions about Benjie."

"She doesn't need parenting advice from you, Cassidy."

Her defenses rose. "Benjie's my son."

"Mine, too."

So much for things going well. Cassidy had enough of this mild sparring. Hoyt's next words let her know they weren't done, not by a long shot.

"Cheryl and I have been talking. I want to be an active father."

"Of course." A spark of nervous energy traveled through Cassidy. Was he leading up to a demand for additional visitation? Custody?

"Not just when I visit, either," Hoyt said. "I'd like to be included in any major decisions. Like new schools or medical procedures."

"Okay. Sure." What was going on here?

"It's important to me."

"I promise, Hoyt. I'll call. We'll talk."

He seemed satisfied. "I realize we need to take things slow. For Benjie's sake, as well as ours. I won't push you into anything you aren't ready for or threaten a custody battle if you don't agree."

"I appreciate that."

"We're a team, and Benjie isn't a battleground."

He was saying all the right things, though his speech sounded a bit rehearsed. She wished she felt more confident.

A nudge in the arm from the horse reminded her she'd been shirking her duties. Dropping the brush in the nearby plastic caddy, she wiped her hands on her jeans.

"We have to leave soon for dinner," she said. "See you in the morning?"

"Wait. There's one more thing."

His tone gave her pause. More than that, it alarmed her. "What?"

"Is something going on with you and Shane?"

"I don't understand."

"I'm not blind, Cassidy. Or stupid."

"What did he say?"

"Nothing yet. I'm asking you first. Are you dating?"

Cassidy tried not to panic. "We're friends."

"Good friends?"

"Hoyt, nothing and no one is more important to me than Benjie. You don't need to worry."

"Relax. I'm not angry, Cassidy."

She stared at him. "You're not?"

"If any man other than me is going to be involved with my son, I'd rather it be Shane."

Wow. Did Hoyt just say he approved of her and Shane dating, or was this a test?

"Nothing's decided yet."

"I'd better get back. Told Benjie I'd watch the roping clinic with him."

After Hoyt left, Cassidy walked the horse to the row of outdoor stalls behind the main barn. The thirsty gelding buried his face in the automatic waterer and drank lustily. Cassidy rested her arms on the stall railing and watched, not quite ready to return to the arena.

Hoyt seemed to be saying he wouldn't fight her when

it came to custody of Benjie. That might not stop Benjie from choosing to live with Hoyt when he was older like Ryder had. Her brother claimed he'd left because of loyalty to their dad. Was there another reason? Their mother, specifically, and her controlling nature?

Cassidy had always sided with their mother, in large part to justify the guilt she felt. Ryder, however, didn't know about her guilt. What if he'd left because of their mother's constant and chronic negativity toward their father?

That would *not* happen to her, Cassidy vowed. She'd try her hardest to speak well of Hoyt in front of Benjie and never put her son in a situation where he felt he had to pick one parent over the other.

While far from completely relieved, some of the tension left her.

"What's that? Another smile? This is becoming a habit."

Shane. He was here. Perhaps he'd come looking for her.

She faced him. "Thought you'd be at the roping clinic."

It was good to see him, and not just because of their mutual attraction. He'd also become her friend. Advising her and supporting her with Hoyt and Benjie and, in a small way, her father.

No man had done that for her. Not that she'd have let them. Only Shane. What, if any, significance did that have?

"Just came from the bulls," he said. "Your dad and I decided on a breeding schedule."

"You're making progress."

"And it gives me the rest of the day off."

"I was also thinking of taking a little time for myself." In truth, she'd been considering a long, hot bath.

"Why don't we spend it together? We could have dinner."

A date. She should have seen this coming.

It was on the tip of her tongue to refuse. She'd insisted there could be nothing between them until her personal life was sorted and settled. Then again, wasn't it? More or less, anyway.

All of a sudden, she wanted to forget her worries and enjoy herself for one night. What would be the harm? None. She and Shane were both single. Benjie adored him, and her family liked him. If Hoyt was bothered for any reason, he'd simply have to get over it.

"Sure."

Shane drew back, studying her intently. "Did you actually accept?"

"I did." She laughed.

"And here I was prepared to twist your arm."

"Life is full of surprises."

"It most certainly is." His gaze locked with hers and held.

Cassidy broke away first. "Where are we going? I'll have to change clothes first." She tugged on the hem of her denim jacket.

"The Hole in the Wall has never-ending shrimp baskets on Saturday evenings."

While known more for its live bands and dancing than its cuisine, the honky-tonk did serve up decent specials.

"I haven't been there in ages." She honestly couldn't remember the last time.

"Pick you up at six?"

It was nearly four. She had plenty of time to get ready and...take a bath. Heavens, wouldn't that be a treat?

"Let me find Tatum. See if she can babysit Benjie tonight."

Cassidy hadn't planned on calling in her favor this soon. Hopefully, her friend was available.

Shane nodded. "See you at six."

She half expected him to kiss her. She fully expected him to give her a quick hug. He did neither before heading to his trailer, leaving her more than a little anxious about what to expect tonight.

The nerves Cassidy had been fighting to control were back with a vengeance. This time she wasn't afraid of what the future held. She was ready to embrace it.

Shane wasn't much of a dancer. Or maybe he was, and the bodies bumping and jostling them from all sides affected his skills. Cassidy couldn't have cared less. She was enjoying herself simply being held snug in his arms.

Talk was impossible over the noise, and they'd all but given up trying. Of the three saloons in town, the Hole in the Wall was typically the place to be on weekends, due in large part to the band and food. While Cassidy and Shane were waiting for their orders to arrive, he'd asked her to dance. She'd accepted, acutely self-conscious about her own lack of skill when it came to tripping the light fantastic.

Too soon the music came to a stop, and Shane guided her through the throng of patrons to their table.

"Come here much?" he asked. From someone else, the question might have been a cheesy pickup line.

"Not really." Cassidy had to practically shout to

be heard. "Once in a while Liberty used to drag me. Thanks to Deacon, those days are over."

"You don't sound sorry."

"The bar scene isn't exactly my thing."

"It goes with the territory."

That was true. Cowboys liked to whoop it up at the local hangouts almost as much as they did rodeoing. She was lucky to avoid the Hole in the Wall at all.

Tonight, it seemed, she didn't mind the noise and the crowd and the carrying on. Not with Shane for company.

"You must have been in your share of bars." She flashed him a smile, then caught herself. Had she just insulted him by implying he spent a lot of time partying?

"More than I care to count." He didn't appear offended, but with all the commotion surrounding them, it was hard to tell. "Like you, those days are over. Bria keeps me on the straight and narrow."

"Same for me. Because of Benjie."

He raised his long-neck bottle of beer. "First one of these I've had in a while. And it'll be my last one tonight."

She appreciated his concern for her feelings regarding drinking and driving. "Me, too."

"Then here's to living it up." He clinked his bottle against hers.

A few minutes later, the waitress arrived with their food. Before the woman could set down the shrimp baskets, Shane stopped her.

"Any chance we could take these outside?"

"Absolutely. There's plenty of seating."

"It'll be quieter," he told Cassidy as they followed the waitress through the patio entrance.

And colder, she thought, slipping into her jacket. What was Shane thinking?

Turned out, his idea was a perfect one. Besides being quieter and cozier than inside, the patio's freestanding gas heaters kept the area toasty warm. No sooner were they seated and the waitress gone than Cassidy removed her jacket.

"You were right to suggest this." She looked around. The tables were close, but not so close she worried their nearest neighbors would overhear their conversation.

"Better than inside. Though, I kind of liked the dancing."

"Me, too."

Shane grinned and dug into his basket, drowning a plump shrimp in cocktail sauce before popping it into his mouth.

She followed suit and tried to remember her last meal out that wasn't fast food or pizza. The shrimp practically melted in her mouth.

"Thank you," she said, a satisfied sigh escaping.

"I'm free tomorrow night, too."

She hesitated. "Maybe we should take this one step at a time."

"Whatever you're comfortable with."

Cassidy wouldn't agree to a second date until she saw how this one ended. She and Shane faced a lot of twists and curves in their relationship.

Strains of music floated through the partially open door, adding a delightful ambiance to their dinner. Conversation flowed. Cassidy couldn't recall talking this much ever. She regaled Shane with tales of Benjie growing up, wanting him to get to know his nephew better.

She stopped cold when he said, "Hoyt would love to hear that story. You should tell him."

Hoyt probably would love it, but she didn't enjoy the same sense of ease with him she did Shane. Perhaps she eventually would, with time and practice.

"Did he mention anything about us going out?" she asked.

"Earlier."

"And?"

"We talked more about how our lives are the same. Both of us having children we didn't know about."

"I suppose it is strange."

Shane smiled. "He's okay with us dating."

She gave a small shrug.

"You don't believe him?"

"If we were to…continue seeing each other, you'd be spending more time with Benjie than he would."

"I'm already spending more time with Benjie than Hoyt."

"As his uncle. Not as his mother's…"

"Boyfriend?" Shane finished for her, amusement lighting his features.

"Well, yes." And if things between them were to develop into more—not that she'd considered it, they'd barely had one date—the situation could become more complex.

"Guess we'll find out for sure soon enough." He sent her a look that warmed her inside and out, far more than the nearby gas heaters.

"One step at a time," she reminded him.

The band broke into a new number, this one a slow

and romantic favorite of Cassidy's. Shane stood and reached out his hand to her.

"Dance with me."

She wasn't ready to leave the patio. "I like it out here."

"Who says we're going inside?"

He led her to an open area near the low stucco wall. She noticed the smiles and glances of the other diners. One woman jabbed her companion in the side and pointed at them as if to say, "Look at him. Now there's a guy with swagger."

A dozen steps into the dance, Cassidy realized she'd been wrong about Shane. With room to move, he proved to be a good dancer and expertly executed turns as they swayed to the music.

What else was he good at? Her mind wandered, venturing into territory she was hesitant to consider. With his palm pressed firmly into the small of her back and his lips brushing the hair at her temple, her mind wandered further.

When the song ended, she was tempted to ask him for another. The band announcing a short break put a stop to her plans.

"Another round of beer?" the waitress asked when she came to clear their table.

"Not for me," Cassidy said. "Thanks."

"Coffee?" Shane asked.

If she had a cup this late, she'd be up half the night. On the plus side, she could spend more time with Shane.

"Yes, please."

"Make it two," he told the waitress.

When they finally left forty minutes later, Cassidy was practically walking on air. For an entire evening, she'd forgotten all about her problems and simply enjoyed herself. Who'd have thought it possible? And why hadn't she done it sooner?

Hands clasped, they crossed the parking lot. The glow of the lights alternately cast Shane's face in shadows and light. The effect was intriguing. Halfway to his truck, he put his arm around her waist and pulled her snug against him.

"Cold?"

She hadn't been. Then again, she didn't want to give him reason to release her. "A little."

His arm stayed firmly in place.

"Thanks again for dinner," she said. "It was wonderful. The food and getting away."

"My pleasure."

His low, silky tone let her know the evening had indeed been pleasurable for him. At his truck, he opened the passenger door for her and waited as she climbed in. She was a bit disappointed he didn't try to kiss her. Her second strikeout that day. She tried telling herself it was for the best. She'd been the one, after all, to remind him repeatedly she wanted to proceed slowly.

"We could stop for dessert," he suggested as they drove past the Flat Iron, the town's iconic restaurant.

"I'm stuffed. But if you want to." Another excuse to prolong the date.

"Let's save that for next time."

Darn it. They were going home, a fact becoming increasingly apparent when he took the road leading to the arena.

"You okay?"

She glanced at him across the front seat. "Fine."

"You seem awfully quiet."

"Am I? Sorry."

She hadn't spoken for the last five minutes. Anxiety was getting the best of her. How was the date going to end? Was she wrong to put the brakes on earlier? Up until now, Shane had had no reservations about initiating their kisses.

"I had a great time." Even his smile wasn't its usual one-thousand-watt brightness.

"Me, too."

He pulled to a stop in front of her house and reached for his door handle. "I'll walk you to the door."

Then what? A kiss good-night? At that precise moment, the back porch light turned on. Her mother must have heard the truck engine. No way could Cassidy kiss Shane with her mother twenty feet away on the other side of the wall. If he intended to kiss her at all, considering how strangely he was acting.

"Wait!" she blurted.

His hand paused on the handle.

"Um." Had she lost her senses? "Can we..." Oh, jeez. She was insane. Or a fool. Both, in all likelihood.

"What, Cassidy?"

She wished she could see his face. Read his expression. Then, she'd know what to say next. But the interior of the truck was too dark.

"Can we go to your trailer? Just to talk," she clarified. "For a while. I'm not ready to call it a night." Was this what one beer and a basket of fried shrimp did to her? Turned her into someone who invited themselves inside a man's home? "Unless you're tired."

"I'm not tired." He threw the truck into Reverse.

As they passed beneath the arena's security light high atop a post, she saw his wide, satisfied grin.

Dammit! She'd been played. He'd wanted her to be the one to ask.

Cassidy squared her shoulders, not bemoaning the loss of her pride. Played or not, she wanted to be alone with Shane.

He unlocked the trailer door and waited for her to enter first. She hesitated before climbing the steps, remembering the last time she'd been here and their smoking hot kiss, rivaled only by the one on the bleachers. She was, she admitted, ready for another.

Wow, she barely recognized herself. This wasn't how she behaved. Shane had completely changed not just her life but *her*. He'd given her courage. Filled the large empty void surrounding her heart. Taught her to let go of what wasn't important while still holding on to what was.

It was on the tip of her tongue to tell him how much he'd come to mean to her, but she couldn't.

"Cassidy?" Shane switched on the dim kitchen light. "Is something wrong?"

"Yes," she whispered and raised her hand to cup his strong jaw. "We're not doing this." Standing on tiptoes, she pressed her lips to his.

The kiss was sweet. Chaste. And all too brief. On a scale of one to ten, his response was maybe a one-point-five.

What an idiot she'd been, thinking he wanted her. Well, she wouldn't make that mistake again.

"Sorry," she muttered and spun, ready to flee.

"Don't go."

"I've made a terrible mistake."

"If you think that, then go ahead. Leave right now.

Because if you don't, I'm going to kiss you again. *Really* kiss you this time."

Cassidy didn't move, except to part her lips in anticipation.

"Exactly what I thought," he said and wrapped her in his arms. When his mouth crashed down on hers, she was ready. And willing.

Chapter 12

More than once, Shane had cursed the trailer's cramped bedroom. He stubbed his toes on the corner of the dresser. Banged his elbows into the wall. Repeatedly walked into the closet door, which never quite closed all the way.

Tonight, he was grateful for the tight quarters, which put him close to Cassidy, and for the wall lamp with its low-energy bulb that emitted just the right amount of minimal light.

It hadn't been easy breaking down her defenses. Finally, with a lot of effort and double the patience, he'd succeeded. His reward was the passionate, sexy woman he'd glimpsed hidden beneath the surface.

She returned his kisses with a fervor matched by his own. It had been she who entered the trailer first, peeling off her jacket as she did. Then, when he'd unzipped his vest, she'd insisted on divesting him of it. Now, she tackled the buttons on his shirt.

"Whoa, sweetheart." He stayed her hands by taking them in his.

"Sorry," she murmured, her cheeks blushing a lovely pink.

"Don't be." Tucking a lock of hair behind her ear, he lifted her face to his. "I liked your enthusiasm. More than you can imagine. But I'd also like the night to last."

She smiled shyly, which was a charming contrast to her earlier unabashed eagerness. "I'm probably woefully out of practice. Which, I'm sure, the last five minutes demonstrated."

He bent his head and skimmed his lips along the side of her neck, paying special attention to the delicate skin beneath her jaw. She shuddered when he nibbled on her earlobe.

"Follow your instincts," he whispered, his voice rough with desire, "and we'll both be just fine."

She grabbed the front of her shirt and tugged, popping open the snaps in quick succession. Shane's eyes widened, at her lack of restraint and at the glorious sight before him. Beneath the lacy peach bra were a pair of beautifully rounded breasts, the loveliest he'd ever seen.

"Aw, hell," he said and scooped her up, one arm behind her knees, the other supporting her back. Walking to the bed, he deposited her in the middle. "Going slow has always been overrated."

With a low, sexy chuckle, she fell back onto the mattress. Shane swallowed, his throat sudden dry, and he lowered himself on top of her. The next instant, they were right where he wanted them to be, amid a tangle of arms and legs.

"My boots," she protested and toed them off. With a hollow thud, they fell to the trailer floor.

Shane did the same with his, then removed his shirt, nearly shredding the fabric in his haste. His white T-shirt came next.

"Oh, my." Cassidy stared at his bare chest with a look akin to wonder, then trailed her fingertips down the length of him, from collarbone to belt buckle. He hissed, his muscles clenching in response as her nails lightly scraped his skin.

"Sweetheart." He groaned when she unfastened his belt buckle. "I thought it was my turn to undress you."

She slid down his zipper. "Or you can watch me undress myself when I'm done here."

No man in his right mind could pass up an offer like that.

He wound up having to help her with his jeans, and was happy to oblige. She sat back on her calves while he removed his socks. Hooking his thumbs into the waistband of his briefs, he started to tug.

"No, let me," she said with relish and took over the task, easing the briefs over his hips. Her heated gaze lingered.

Shane was no Adonis, not in his opinion, anyway. But, thanks to years of hard, demanding labor, he knew he could hold his own in the physically fit department.

"My turn." He sat up and reached for her.

She withdrew. "That's not what we agreed on."

No, it wasn't. She'd promised to make all his dreams a reality.

Standing, she removed her shirt, fully exposing her peach bra and all her lovely bare skin. Next, she shimmied out of her jeans and tossed them onto the floor. In the pale light of the wall lamp, wearing no more than her underwear, she resembled a golden goddess. Shane had never been more enamored.

"You're incredible."

Her gaze softened. "You make me feel that way."

He fitted his hands to her waist and pulled her forward until she stood between his knees. Next, he skimmed his hands up her rib cage, stopping just shy of her breasts.

She slipped the bra straps off her shoulders. A moment later, the flimsy piece of lingerie lay on the floor beside her jeans.

Shane could only stare, unable to remember ever seeing, much less holding, such beauty. His hands were on the verge of shaking as he raised them to her breasts. The nipples instantly beaded at his touch. What would they taste like? He couldn't wait to find out.

He brought his mouth to first one breast, then the other, sucking greedily. Her breathing quickened. His was coming in great, loud rasps that filled his ears.

Oh, yeah. He'd been right, she tasted as delicious as she looked.

She threaded her fingers into his hair and kissed him soundly. "Make love to me, Shane."

"Count on it."

"Now."

He tugged on her bikini panties, sliding them down the length of her long, shapely legs. Once she stepped out of the skimpy garment, he ran his hands back up the same path. Her skin was like silk. He didn't want to stop.

Circling her waist with one arm, he pressed his

splayed fingers to her belly. Like her breasts, the skin there was smooth as satin. Did it, too, taste delicious?

Shane found out for himself. She inhaled sharply as his mouth replaced his fingers. Trembled when his tongue circled her belly button. Not stopping there, he dipped his tongue inside, causing her to shudder.

"That tickles." She attempted to wriggle away from him.

He held fast, his arm circling her waist. "What about this?" He slipped his hand between her thighs and nearly lost it when he encountered her moist folds.

Her answer was a low, desperate moan.

She wanted him. As much as he wanted her. The knowledge excited him further.

Growing bolder, he slid a finger inside her. Then a second.

"Oh, Shane." Her limbs trembled, and she swayed unsteadily. "This is…"

"Incredible?"

She braced her hands on his shoulders and rocked her hips in rhythm with his thrusting fingers. "I was thinking indecent."

"Want me to stop?" He rubbed his thumb over her most sensitive spot.

Her eyes drifted closed.

"Yes?" He increased the pressure. "Or no?"

"Don't…stop." Her grip tightened, her nails digging into his flesh. "Please."

Taking his cues from her, he stroked and fondled and caressed her. She was incredible to watch, unbelievably responsive. He couldn't take his eyes from her expressive face. A moment later, she rewarded him, her body quivering as a stunning climax claimed her.

"Shane!" She threw back her head and gave herself over to the sensations.

He steadied her, not removing his hand until the tremors subsided and her legs grew stronger.

She exhaled a long, uneven breath. "Wow."

"My sentiments exactly."

"I don't usually... I haven't ever let a man..." She smiled shyly down at him, brushing the hair off his forehead. "I'm glad it was you."

The sincerity in her voice and the warmth in her eyes caused his chest to swell. She wasn't playing to his ego or feeding him a line. Her enjoyment had been genuine and real and, for him, just the beginning.

"Cassidy, this isn't a casual hookup. I care about you. A lot. I hope you know that."

When her gaze met his, he saw understanding blaze in her dark eyes. "I do."

"Our date tonight, it's the first of many."

"Maybe we can take the kids along with us sometime."

She was truly out to win his heart. "Sounds great."

Assuming she needed a few minutes to recoup, he was surprised—and delighted—when she pushed him down onto the bed and straddled his hips.

"Wait." He grabbed her hips and anchored her in place. "We can't yet. Not without protection."

"You're right." She nodded thoughtfully. "Do you have any?"

Shane almost laughed. She'd asked the question with the same nonchalance she might have when inquiring about the weather or his day at work. Would she ever cease to amaze him?

"There's some in the drawer." He reached for the built-in night stand.

She eyed him wryly. "You planned this?"

"No, no. Not at all." He faltered, realizing nothing he said would make him sound less of a heel. "They're left over from…" He was making this worse by the second.

"It's okay." She bent over him until their foreheads were touching. "I'm not upset." She kissed him, slow and sweet and thoroughly. It quickly escalated to fire and heat. "Now, Shane," she whispered when they broke apart, their former sensual mood restored. "I'm not sure I can wait any longer."

Damned if she wasn't the most extraordinary woman. Quickly donning the condom, he positioned her above him and drove inside. Incredible. Smooth. Slick. Tight. His body bucked involuntarily as sensations overpowered him.

Her moan of pure delight incited him to thrust deeper and harder. Within seconds, sweat broke out on his skin, as much from forcing himself to hold back as the physical exertion.

She shifted, the new position allowing him to go deeper, feel more, give her greater pleasure. He ground his teeth together, unable to take much more. Filling his hands with her breasts, he squeezed and fondled.

After that, there was no going back and no stopping. His release came with all the force of a thundering stampede. He was aware of calling out her name. Of holding on to her as if he didn't dare let her go. Of needing her with a desperation exceeding all others. Ever.

When their breathing returned to a semblance of normal, she fell onto his chest, limp as a rag doll and completely spent. He, too, had yet to recover and might never.

"That was…pretty great," she said at last, dropping light kisses on his face and neck.

"Pretty?" Shane might have laughed if he wasn't exhausted. "Speaking for myself, I'll never be the same again."

She rose, her smile conveying just how aware she was of her effect on him. "I think we did okay for two people out of practice."

"We did great." He was already imagining the next time. Possibly later tonight.

When she went to roll off him, he pulled her down onto the mattress beside him.

"I should go," she murmured.

"Why?" He stroked the length of her back, familiarizing himself with the exquisite contours of her body. Round, lush hips. Narrow waist. Flat belly. Full breasts. She might not realize it, but she was made for a man's touch. His touch. "Isn't Benjie staying at Tatum's tonight?"

"My mom will notice I'm gone."

"Your mom's busy with your dad. He told me earlier they were having dinner together. He's at the house now."

"Ah." She made a wry face. "Now I understand the porch light."

"Didn't you see his truck?"

"I guess not."

"You okay with that? Your dad staying over?"

He felt her relax. "I'm better these days than I was."

"Good."

"Yeah." She stretched and sighed contentedly. "It is."

Shane had heard from Mercer that he and Cassidy had a heart-to-heart talk earlier today. His boss was of the opinion he and his daughter had rebuilt all their burned bridges. She seemed to share that opinion, to a degree anyway.

Shane was much more interested in the two of them than in Cassidy's parents.

"Stay with me tonight." He propped himself up on one elbow in order to gaze down at her. "I can't let you go."

"Can't?" she asked playfully.

"I'm serious. You're necessary to me and what we just had together, well, it doesn't happen often. Never to me. And I don't want it to end."

"If I stay here, my family will find out."

"I'll speak to them. Let them know my intentions are honorable."

"Honorable, huh?" She grinned and nestled closer.

"I'd like to see where this leads. I have a chance to make a real life for myself and Bria here in Reckless. I'm thinking I'd like that life to include you and Benjie."

Her expression softened. "I'd like to see where this leads, too. But I should warn you. I'm not the easiest person to get along with, even on my good days."

"Sweetheart, I wouldn't have you any other way."

Shane kissed her then. A moment later, when the smoldering embers between them had been stoked into a fiery blaze, he pressed her onto her back and covered her body with his.

She was spending the night with him. He wouldn't take no for an answer. And in the morning, they'd make plans for the day, and the next day and the one after that.

***

"Do tell." Liberty's eyes lit up.

"There's nothing to tell." Cassidy dismissed her sister with a nonchalant wave. Inside, she was still tingling from Shane's good morning kisses.

"You spent the night with him!"

"Technically, two nights."

Liberty gasped with delight. "Details. I demand details."

Cassidy obliged her sister by summarizing the first night with Shane after the trail ride. Luckily, Benjie had yet to wake, giving the sisters some time alone.

"It's been incredible. Yesterday, while Hoyt took Benjie to the Phoenix Zoo, Shane and I went on a drive in the mountains. On the way home, we stopped in Punkin Center for dinner. I haven't been there in years."

"That's all?"

Cassidy grinned slyly. "All I'm telling."

Parting from Shane last night had been hard. Which was why, after Benjie had gone to bed, Cassidy had slipped out to his trailer, then hurried back to the house before anyone was awake. Liberty, at the arena earlier than usual, had caught sight of Cassidy and confronted her in the kitchen a few minutes ago.

"Not one juicy tidbit?" Liberty implored. "You're mean."

At that moment, their mother stumbled into the kitchen, took one look at Cassidy and announced, "Didn't you sleep? You look terrible."

"Me?"

With her hair in complete disarray, her robe hanging off her left shoulder and dark shadows beneath her eyes, her mother wasn't one to talk.

"Dad spent the night," Liberty said.

"Again?" Cassidy raised an eyebrow.

Her mother huffed defensively. "People in glass houses have no right to judge."

Cassidy rolled her eyes. "That's not how the saying goes, Mom." She grabbed a mug from the cupboard. After pouring herself some coffee, she joined her mother and sister at the table. "Fine. I'm seeing Shane. You care to comment?"

Liberty beamed at their mother. "I totally saw this coming."

Cassidy refrained from commenting. Her younger sister was head over heels in love and soon to be married. As a result, she imagined all sorts of romantic pairings, some with the most unlikely of couples.

"I'm happy for you, darling." Her mother patted Cassidy's hand.

The reassuring gesture didn't fool Cassidy. She knew her mother well enough to detect "the tone."

"What's wrong, Mom?"

"Nothing."

"Come on. Tell me."

"I simply think you should be careful."

"Are you kidding?" Liberty gaped at their mother, clearly appalled. "Shane's a great guy. He's settled, a family man, ready to make his home in Reckless and the best bull manager in six states. Not to mention gorgeous. She could do a whole lot worse."

"His brother is also Benjie's father."

"Don't think we haven't considered that." Cassidy and Shane had done more than while away the hours snuggled under the covers. They'd talked at great length about all sorts of things, including Shane's relationship with Benjie and the trials they faced. "We understand it's complicated, and we're treading carefully."

"Spending every night with him isn't treading carefully."

"Two nights." Cassidy's hackles rose. She wanted her mother to be glad for her. Not deliver her a lecture.

"Besides," Liberty added, "it's not like you and Dad have an uncomplicated relationship."

"And you're suddenly an expert?" Their mother glowered at her.

Liberty frowned. "It's true. You divorced him years ago, lied to him, refused to allow him in our lives. Then, he returns, practically forces you to accept him as your business partner—"

"No practically about it," Cassidy interjected.

"Right. And now he's courting you, telling everyone you're getting married again." Liberty snorted. "Cassidy and Shane don't even compare."

"We're not getting married." Their mother turned away to reknot her bathrobe belt.

The sisters exchanged glances. Something was amiss.

"What happened?" Liberty asked.

"Nothing." Their mother's answer rang false.

"Did you and dad have another fight?" Liberty persisted.

"No."

"Is he drinking again?" Cassidy asked.

"Jeez, Cassidy, why do you always assume the worst?" Her mother made a visible effort to control her emotions.

Okay, maybe she wasn't being fair. She tended to jump to conclusions where her father was concerned. "You're right. I shouldn't have said that. Old habits are hard to break."

"He loves you so much, honey. Both of his girls." Their mother's gaze traveled from Cassidy to her sister. "And he wants what's best for you."

"We have the best," Liberty said. "Deacon and Shane."

Cassidy agreed wholeheartedly.

Was this what it was like to be in love? Believe one had the best? Truthfully, Cassidy didn't know the answer. She hadn't been in love before. Not really. Not the way her sister was in love. Cassidy had had a small taste with Hoyt. She'd cared greatly for him, but not enough to try harder when, after six months, their relationship deteriorated.

In hindsight, she probably should have broken up with him sooner. But then she wouldn't have Benjie.

"So what's wrong?" Liberty demanded.

Their mother tiredly swirled her coffee. "We were up late talking is all."

"About getting married?"

"I'm just not ready."

The kitchen door swinging open made the three of them simultaneously turn their heads. Ryder strode in, looking recently showered and shaved. He was wearing a freshly pressed Western shirt.

Their mother instantly brightened. "Good morning. You must have a meeting today."

Like the rest of them, he went straight for the coffeemaker on the counter and poured himself a cup. "Actually, Tatum and I have an appointment with Pastor Douglas at the Guiding Light Community Church."

Their mother jumped up from her chair. "You're changing the wedding date?"

"Well, it depends on whether or not the church is booked. We're looking at April."

"That's two months away!" Her hand flew to her heart. "How can we possibly plan a second wedding in such a short amount of a time? Liberty's getting married in August."

"Don't worry, Mom. It's going to be a small, intimate service. Family and a few close friends." He gave Liberty's shoulders a squeeze. "As long as you and Deacon are okay with it. We don't want to steal your thunder."

Cassidy resisted rolling her eyes. Liberty was planning a wedding the likes of which Reckless had never seen.

"Are you kidding?" Liberty returned the hug. "I'm thrilled. Tatum's a wonderful woman, and she has three of the cutest kids."

All at once, everything fell into place, and Cassidy blurted, "Tatum's pregnant."

Their mother grabbed Ryder and shook him, her feet dancing in place. "Is that true?"

He grinned sheepishly. "She took the home pregnancy test yesterday."

"Oh, my God! I'm so excited for you both." She pulled him into a fierce bear hug. "Another grandchild." Tears filled her eyes.

Cassidy wanted to cry a little herself. Only a short time ago, the rift in her family had seemed too wide to ever bridge. Now, they were growing by yet another member.

"Tatum wanted to tell you herself," Ryder said to Cassidy after their mother finally released him. "I owe you an apology for letting the cat out of the bag."

"It's all right. You deserve to be excited."

"I am."

She could tell. Her brother wore the look of a man completely over the moon. Her own heart was ready to burst.

More hugs were exchanged and tears of joy wiped away. Cassidy, unfortunately, was jarred out of the sentimental moment by her cell phone ringing down the hall.

"Excuse me." Thinking it might be Tatum about the pregnancy news, or Shane checking on her, she dashed to her bedroom. It was neither of them. Instead, Hoyt's number appeared on the display. Had he and Cheryl changed their minds about visiting this morning to say goodbye to Benjie? Had Shane told Hoyt about their last two nights together?

No, impossible. She and Shane had decided to wait until after Hoyt and Cheryl left. Why potentially rock the boat?

She answered the call with a breathless and slightly anxious, "Hello."

"Morning. Did I wake you?"

"No, I'm always up early." Very early this morning. "Are you still coming by?"

"We're on our way now."

"Um, Benjie's still asleep. I'll wake him and get him fed and dressed."

"No hurry."

That was odd. Hoyt and Cheryl didn't have long before they needed to leave for the airport.

"I'd like to talk to you," Hoyt said.

"What about?"

There was a long pause during which Cassidy imagined the worst. Finally, when she could stand no more, Hoyt said, "I want more time with Benjie."

Her pulse instantly raced. "This coming summer?"

"No. Starting right now. Today."

"Wait. You're leaving in a few hours."

"We postponed our flight and are taking the red-eye tonight."

"Why?" Something more was going on, and her panic escalated.

"I've been talking to Cheryl and Shane. They're both in agreement."

"Shane? What does he have to do with this?"

"It was his idea, actually. He suggested we stay another day in Reckless and that I talk to Benjie about additional visitation. Possibly taking him for the entire summer."

Cassidy swayed, feeling as if she'd been shoved from behind. This couldn't be happening to her. Benjie was slipping through her fingers, and Shane was the one responsible.

Chapter 13

"I can't let you do you that." Cassidy shook her head.

"You're not in sole charge of Benjie. Not anymore." Hoyt spoke tersely through clenched teeth.

They'd been bickering nonstop for the past fifteen minutes, and he was clearly losing patience with her.

"I don't mind you wanting to take Benjie fishing before you leave." The truth was, she did mind, but she was trying her best to be accommodating. "What I do mind is you and him scheduling additional visitation without me present."

"He'll respond better if you're not there."

"You mean you can manipulate him more easily."

"Don't make me out to be the bad guy, Cassidy. I'm the one who went six years with no idea I had a son."

Okay, she had hit a little below the belt. "I'm sorry. That was uncalled-for."

Hoyt didn't acknowledge her apology. "I'm his father. I have rights."

"You do, but those rights don't include you getting to come here and make outrageous demands."

"Seeing Benjie isn't outrageous."

"He's too young to understand and far too young to make his own decisions. Of course he'll agree to additional visitation. He's excited to have a father."

"No more excited than I am to have a son."

"Enough with laying on the guilt."

She and Hoyt sat at the picnic table in the backyard, not far from where she and Shane had argued at Benjie's birthday party. Funny how things came full circle.

Cheryl waited inside the house with Benjie and Sunny, who'd volunteered to keep Cheryl company and oversee Benjie's breakfast so Cassidy and Hoyt could talk in private.

Cassidy rubbed her temples. "We agreed to let the attorneys hammer out the schedule."

"Actually, *you* told me how it was going to be, and I didn't object." Hoyt sat opposite her, his crossed arms propped on the table. Everything about his demeanor and posture was confrontational. "Now, I've had time to think and process."

And talk to Shane. Cassidy was still in a state of shock from hearing the news. Whatever he'd said had caused his brother to change overnight.

She'd yet to confront Shane. There'd been no time, plus she was too angry and hurt. Mostly hurt. They'd spent the weekend together, for crying out loud. Made love. Discussed the future. Held each other for endless hours. Laughed, teased and simply sat in contented silence.

That he would influence Hoyt against her was like a betrayal of the worst kind. She simply didn't know what to make of it.

"Please, Hoyt. You can't spring this on me with no warning and expect me to go along."

"I'm taking Benjie fishing at the lake. Along with sports and school and whatever other subject comes up, we're going to discuss him coming to live with me for part of the year. I want to get a gauge for how he feels before meeting with my attorney."

Her heart stopped beating. "One minute ago it was the entire summer. Now, you want him for part of the year. What's next?"

"The more you fight me," Hoyt said, "the more time with Benjie I'm going to demand. And when our attorneys get together, it'll be to discuss a custody suit."

"You promised not to threaten me."

"New terms, Cassidy."

Her head pounded, and her stomach roiled. *Please, Lord, let this all be some sort of awful, horrible mistake.*

"What do you want, Hoyt?" The scratchy voice was barely recognizable to her ears.

"What I've been telling you since I called. To take Benjie fishing."

When Hoyt had originally made the request, Cassidy deemed it completely out of the question. In light of this last demand, for shared custody, a drive to the lake was nothing.

"I need to make a call," she said feebly.

"Now?"

"Five minutes."

He grunted his consent, and Cassidy struggled to escape the picnic table that had become a trap. Going to stand by the modular play set, she removed her phone from her pocket and dialed her attorney. When the call went straight to voice mail, she hung up and dialed Deacon. Thankfully, he answered on the first ring.

"Hoyt wants to take Benjie fishing," Cassidy said, then filled him in on the specifics.

"What's the problem?"

"He plans on discussing additional visitation with Benjie. Naturally, Benjie will agree."

"Okay."

"Okay!" Cassidy squeaked, her anxiety rising by degrees. Sensing Hoyt's eyes on her, she turned her back to him. "He threatened me with a custody suit."

"Cassidy, calm down, will you?"

"I can't let him take Benjie from me."

"All I'm hearing is a fishing trip."

"To discuss visitation. Without me there."

"As long as it's not immoral or illegal, you can't dictate what he and Benjie talk about."

Her resolve to stay strong waned, and she swallowed a sob. "I'm scared. Benjie's young. And impressionable."

Deacon softened his voice. "Trust me when I say, don't fight Hoyt on this. His request isn't out of line."

"Custody! It's crazy. Insane."

"Taking Benjie fishing. The rest, at this point anyway, is Hoyt's temper getting the best of him. I wouldn't put a lot of stock in what he says."

"He seems pretty serious."

"This could be his way of testing you. To see how far he can push you. Your best defense is to remain calm."

"It's hard," she whispered.

"I know." Deacon stopped talking to her like an attorney and consoled her like a friend. "Hoyt's leaving today. He's emotional. Once he gets home, he may change his mind."

She glanced at Hoyt and was confronted by his implacable stare. "Somehow I doubt that."

"Hang in there, Cassidy, and save your strength. This is only the beginning."

After a few more words of encouragement, she and Deacon disconnected, and she returned to Hoyt.

"Well?" he demanded.

"Fine. Take Benjie for the morning." The painful lump in her throat made speaking difficult. "But swear to me you'll have him home by noon."

Hoyt didn't exactly smile, though the lines around his face become less rigid. "One o'clock at the latest."

It was, she supposed, the best she could hope for.

The back door banged open, and Benjie charged out. Breakfast was obviously over, and he could no longer be contained.

"Daddy." He ran straight for Hoyt. "Cheryl says we're going fishing."

Cassidy suppressed a scream of frustration. What business did Cheryl have telling Benjie before the decision was made?

In the span of an hour, her perfect world had spun out of control. First, Shane went behind her back to Hoyt. All right, maybe not behind her back, but he should have told her about his conversation with Hoyt. Then Hoyt showed up making demands and threatening her. Now, Cheryl had overstepped her bounds. It was too much all at once.

Hoyt lifted Benjie into his arms and held him against

his chest. "You ready to give that new rod and reel of yours a trial run?"

"Yes!" Benjie cranked his head sideways to ask Cassidy, "Can I, Mom?"

"She's already agreed," Hoyt cut in before Cassidy could reply.

"Yes, you can." She wasn't about to let him speak for her. Or let Benjie think he could pit one parent against the other. "For a few hours. Remember, you have school tomorrow."

Just when she thought things couldn't get worse, Shane approached from the direction of the arena, not looking at all surprised to see his brother. Then again, as far as Cassidy knew, this entire trip to the lake was his idea. He'd mentioned taking Bria one day soon.

"Hi." He smiled warmly and dipped his head for a kiss.

She deftly sidestepped him and, frowning, cut her glance to Benjie.

Shane must have figured out this wasn't the time or place for a discussion because he said nothing. Fortunately, both Hoyt and Benjie appeared oblivious.

"Hi, Uncle Shane."

"Hey, partner." Shane waited until Hoyt set Benjie down, then ruffled the boy's hair, after which the two brothers clapped each other on the back. "You heading to the airport soon?"

Airport? Hadn't Shane heard?

"Cheryl called and booked us a later flight," Hoyt said. "I took your advice. She, Benjie and I are heading to the lake first for a little fishing."

"You are?"

"Last-minute decision."

"I see."

Either Shane didn't know about the trip or he was a great actor. What, then, was the advice he'd given his brother?

"Come with us," Hoyt invited.

Hold on a minute. He got to tag along and not Cassidy?

"Thanks." Shane caught her glance. "But I have plenty to do here."

Whatever he was planning wouldn't include her. Not after she told him how she felt about his interference.

"Speaking of which," Hoyt said, "we need to get going. It's already eight." He took Benjie's hand. "Where'd you put your new fishing pole?"

The two of them walked toward the house, Cassidy following—except she didn't get far. Shane stopped her by blocking her path.

"What's wrong?"

She gaped at him. "You have to ask?"

"Frankly, yes. A few hours ago, I was holding you naked in my bed and we were deciding whether you, me and Benjie were going out for pizza tonight or staying home and grilling hot dogs."

"Did you tell Hoyt to challenge me for custody?"

"Why would I do that?" He frowned in confusion. "He lives in Wyoming."

"Well, he's threatening to take me to court if I don't cooperate."

"Cooperate how?"

"Allow more visitation. Let him take Benjie for part of the year."

"Did you say no?"

She suppressed a groan. "It's not the visitation I object to. It's his methods. He insists on talking to Benjie alone. Without me. He *says* Benjie will be more receptive, but what he's doing is pitting Benjie against me."

"That doesn't sound like Hoyt."

"It's exactly like Hoyt. He bullied me when we were dating."

"Bullied is a pretty strong word."

"I'm not making this up."

"I admit, he can be overbearing."

"He said you and he talked and the fishing trip was your suggestion."

Shane shook his head. "That's not true."

"You suggested Hoyt take Benjie fishing on Saturday when he gave Benjie the rod and reel."

"Hoyt did call me this morning right after you left the trailer and asked about my custody arrangement with Judy."

"What did you tell him?"

"I said I value each moment I spend with my daughter and regret the missed years. I suggested he take advantage of every opportunity to see Benjie. All the rest, the fishing trip, visitation, the custody suit, is entirely his doing."

Cassidy supposed it was possible for Hoyt to have taken Shane's words and put his own twist on them. Or maybe Cheryl had influenced him.

"Look," Shane continued. "Hoyt is single-minded when he wants something. The more you dig in your heels, the more he'll push. Give a little, and he'll give, too. Possibly back off entirely."

Deacon had said pretty much the same to Cassidy during their call.

"Do you really think that?"

Shane nodded. "I'll call him later. Talk some sense into him."

"Thank you." Hoyt did listen to Shane.

He put his arm around her, and she leaned into him rather than resist. He was looking out for her, after all. And, were she honest, she'd admit how good it felt to have someone special in her life to count on.

"This has me rattled," she said. "Hoyt keeps saying one thing and doing another."

"He's always been impetuous."

Benjie was a lot like that, too. Hardly began one task, and he was off to another.

Worst case, the lake wasn't far. If needed, she could drive there and get Benjie. Though, she was probably getting ahead of herself. Hoyt had promised they'd be home by one o'clock.

A terrifying thought occurred to her. "He won't be drinking, will he?" A lot of people imbibed while fishing. For some, the two were inseparable.

"No. Absolutely not."

"How can you be sure? He drank and drove when we were dating."

"He and Cheryl gave up alcohol when they started fertility treatments."

"They did?" She was relieved and impressed.

Shane pulled her into a warm hug. "I don't agree with the arm-twisting tactics he pulled on you. And while I did encourage him to spend more time with Benjie, it wasn't to hurt you."

"I know." She hugged him back.

"Come on." He pulled her along with him.

"Where?"

"The Dawn to Dusk Coffee Shop."

"I should get to work. I'm scheduled to teach a riding class in an hour."

"We have time for a caramel latte to go."

When it came to arm twisting, Hoyt had nothing on Shane.

He stopped and, cupping her cheek, bent to brush his lips across hers. "The next few hours are going to be rough for you. Coffee will help."

Her mouth dissolved into a smile. "Is this your idea of a bribe?"

He flashed her that sexy grin she'd grown to love. "It's my idea of what a boyfriend does for his girlfriend."

Coffee did hit the spot. Cassidy sailed through her first riding class. The second one, however, dragged. At eleven forty-five she concocted an excuse to leave the arena in order to be at the house when Benjie returned.

On the way, she ran into Shane. It pleased her to think he might be watching for her.

"You won't mind if I come by later?" he asked, giving her a quick kiss.

"Not at all." She lingered for a moment, enjoying the sensation of laying her head on his shoulder.

On the walk to the house, Cassidy dialed Hoyt's cell phone, assuming they were on their way, if not nearly home. It rang six times before going to voice mail. Frustrated, she shoved her phone back into her jacket pocket. Maybe they were out of range. Nearby Pinnacle Peak was notorious for interfering with reception.

Inside the house, she tackled their never lessening mountain of laundry. Every ten to fifteen minutes, she paused to call Hoyt. Each time he didn't answer, her frustration and anger increased, as did her worry. Why hadn't she asked for Cheryl's number, as well?

By one thirty, she'd abandoned the laundry and paced the house. Was it too soon to call the sheriff's department and report her son missing?

Finally, at two-fourteen exactly, and after a dozen attempted calls, Hoyt answered his phone.

Cassidy instantly laid into him. "Where the hell are you?"

"We're still at the marina."

"Is Benjie all right?"

"He's fine."

"I want to talk to him. Put him on the phone."

"Cassidy, for God's sake, will you calm down?"

"You swore you'd have him home by noon. One at the latest. Am I wrong, or don't you have a plane to catch?"

"There's been a change of plans," he said slowly.

"Another one?"

"Listen to me."

"Whatever it is, the answer's no." She would not allow him to do this to her a second time. They were establishing ground rules, and the first one was that he didn't get to run the show. "Benjie has homework to do for school tomorrow. He needs to come home."

Hoyt cleared his throat. "I've rented a boat. We're staying overnight on the lake. We won't be back until later tomorrow."

An incessant pounding on his trailer door had Shane leaving the water running in the sink to see who the heck was in such a hurry. He hoped there wasn't a problem with one of the bulls. Come to think of it, Wasabi had been hobbling a bit yesterday.

He'd barely turned the knob when the door was literally yanked from his hand. Cassidy stood there, jacketless, windblown and flushed.

"Hi, sweetheart."

Not waiting for an invitation, she climbed the steps and pushed past him into the trailer. "Your brother took Benjie."

"What!" Shock coursed through Shane. "You're kidding."

"He did." She faced him across the small space. Tears had left telltale smudges beneath her red, swollen eyes.

He quickly shut off the water, then took her in his arms, wishing he could erase her pain. "I'm sorry. I can see you're upset."

"With good reason." She pushed away from him and paced the small space.

"I agree. We'll straighten this out. Get Benjie back."

Frankly, Shane couldn't believe his ears. What was his brother thinking? Fishing was one thing, but leaving Reckless with Benjie, before he and Cassidy had reached a formal custody agreement...it was heartless and cruel. It would also hurt his case when the time came to appear before the judge.

Shane reached for his phone on the table, intending to call Hoyt. "They probably haven't boarded the plane yet. Their flight's not for another hour."

She stared at him, confusion clouding her features. "Plane? What are you talking about?"

"You said Hoyt took Benjie."

"He did."

"Aren't they on their way to the airport?"

"They're still at the lake." Cassidy's voice broke. "Hoyt rented a boat. They're staying overnight."

"At the lake." Shane let the information sink in. "Not the airport."

"Yes!" Cassidy resumed pacing. "Hoyt promised to have Benjie home by noon. I called and called and *called*. He didn't answer until after two. Then it was to tell me he was keeping Benjie. Whether I liked it or not."

"Look, I'm not defending Hoyt's tactics, so don't misunderstand me."

She halted midstep. "Don't say you're siding with him."

"Of course I'm not siding with him."

"Then why would I misunderstand you?"

"Calm down, and let's put this in perspective, okay? Benjie's all right." Shane paused. "He is all right, yes? You did talk to him?"

"Not at first. Hoyt wouldn't let me. We had a big fight, and then he finally put Benjie on."

"He shouldn't have done that. No question. But again, Benjie's fine, you know where he is and he'll be home tomorrow. Concentrate on those things."

"Hoyt *swore* he'd have Benjie home today. What guarantee do I have he won't pull the same stunt tomorrow?"

"He has a rodeo this coming weekend. And Cheryl works. They have to get home."

"And Benjie has school tomorrow, which he's going to miss."

"It's one day."

"That's not the point!"

"I understand you're angry, Cassidy. Hoyt was out of line. He put you through a lot of needless worry. But Benjie is also his son. A son he hardly knows. Wanting to spend more time with him is understandable. You could cut him some slack."

"Did you know he was planning on taking Benjie?"

Shane didn't like the accusation in her tone. "If I did, I'd have insisted he tell you."

"I'm sorry. I'm taking my frustration out on you." She buried her face in her hands. "I was just so worried. I still am."

"Hoyt won't let anything happen to Benjie."

"I just wish you hadn't encouraged him."

"Wait a minute." Shane straightened. "This isn't my fault."

"Hoyt was ready to leave today. Then, he talked to you."

"Benjie had a choice, too. Did you ask him if he wanted to spend the night with his father?"

"No."

"Was that because you didn't want to hear the answer?"

Her eyes widened, then narrowed. "The problem here is Hoyt," she snapped. "Not me or Benjie."

"There are two sides to every story."

"Implying what, exactly?"

"It's possible you're hanging on too tight to Benjie. Being too controlling."

She recoiled as if struck. "I'm no such thing."

"You're used to dictating Benjie's every action without having to consider anyone else. Now, there's Hoyt. It's a big change and will take some getting used to. Judy's going through the same growing pains with Bria and me."

"Have you ever taken Bria without Judy's permission?"

"We've already agreed Hoyt was wrong. Rehashing it won't solve the problem."

"What will?" She stabbed her chest with her thumb. "Me admitting I'm a control freak?"

He didn't react to her anger. "If you are, you come by it naturally. Didn't you tell me last night how, when your father first came back to Reckless, he strong-armed your mother and forced her to accept him as her business partner?"

"I am *nothing* like my father."

"You do like to be in charge."

"Hoyt broke his promise."

Shane swore he could see steam pouring from her ears. "Maybe he wouldn't have if he'd thought you'd listen to reason."

"I let him take Benjie. That was reasonable."

"Let him? Benjie isn't a possession."

As if collapsing from the inside, she stacked her hands on the table and laid her head down.

Shane could have kicked himself. In trying to get through to her, he'd been too harsh.

"You're choosing Hoyt over me," she said in a small, defeated voice.

"I'm not." Given the choice, he'd have sat next to her. Since there was no room, he slid into the other side of the table. "You've been holding on to Benjie so long and so fiercely, you don't know how to let go. Even a little."

"I don't want to let go. I'm afraid of what will happen."

Right. Her brother. "Did your mother ever let Ryder visit your dad?"

"Of course not." Her head shot up. "Dad was an alcoholic."

"Say he wasn't. Would your mom have let Ryder, and you, too, go to Kingman?"

"I...don't know. Maybe. But what difference does it make?"

"If you were to give Benjie a little freedom, he might not abandon you like Ryder did."

"There's a big difference between me giving Benjie freedom and Hoyt taking him," she snapped.

"I don't disagree. Simply making a suggestion."

"I could drive to the lake." Cassidy looked at him expectantly. "You could come with me."

Shane sat back. "Don't do that. You showing up unannounced will make matters worse."

"I just want to check on Benjie. Take him some things. He needs pajamas and a toothbrush and clean clothes for tomorrow."

"It won't hurt him to sleep in his clothes one night." Shane had done much worse during his rodeo days. "And I'm sure the marina store sells toothbrushes."

Cassidy wrung her hands. "Benjie's never been away from home before, except for spending the night at Tatum's."

"Let it go, Cassidy."

She stared out the tiny trailer window into the darkness.

"How about I fix dinner here?" he said. "We'll go to bed early and start fresh in the morning after a good night's sleep."

She looked at him. "*You* could drive out there."

"I'm not." Seriously, enough was enough.

At his sharp reply, Cassidy sprang from the seat. "I thought you cared about me."

"I do. Which is why I've spent the last twenty minutes listening to you rant."

"Rant!"

"Sorry, wrong choice of words."

Her features crumbled. "I trusted you."

"I haven't let you down."

"You won't drive out to the lake."

"I would if there was a reason. But Benjie's fine."

"You're the first man I've let get close to me since Hoyt." She stiffened. "I thought you were different."

Shane's temper snapped. He'd been making allowances for her because she was under enormous stress. No more. "That's unfair and uncalled-for."

She narrowed her gaze. "Caring for someone means unconditional support."

"I do support you. And I'll talk to Hoyt. But I'm not going out to the lake like some crazed person and searching for them. Especially when I don't feel Hoyt's entirely at fault."

"And you think I am?"

He sighed. "This is arguing for the sake of arguing."

She whirled and headed for the door.

Well, she'd warned him about her stubborn streak. "Cassidy, don't go. Not like this."

"We're done."

Good idea. A cooling-off period might benefit them both.

"I'll call you later," he said. "Better yet, I'll come by the house."

"Don't bother." She stopped at the door. "I won't see you."

He didn't like the finality in her voice and crossed the small room in two steps. "Today? Or again?"

She refused to turn around.

"Cassidy."

"You're breaking my heart, Shane." She left without a backward glance.

He thought of going after her, but didn't, telling himself she was just being Cassidy. Instead, he returned to work, his way of coping with stress when climbing on the back of a bull wasn't available.

Despite her warning not to bother, Shane dropped by the house later to see Cassidy—twice. Once right before supper and once about eight o'clock. Both times, Sunny politely but coolly informed him Cassidy wasn't available.

He took the first rejection in stride. She was mad and needed some solitude and space. The second rejection annoyed him. He accepted that people occasionally fought. But in order to compromise, learn and coexist harmoniously, there had to be communication. His parents, happily married for nearly forty years, had taught him that.

During his second attempt to see her, he'd tried to enlist Sunny's aid, until she rebuffed him. Probably for the best. Who knew how much Cassidy had told Sunny, or how willing she was to be drawn into an argument that, as far as he was concerned, didn't involve her?

And, really, did he want her help? She'd treated Mercer poorly in the past. Shane would rather not receive the same treatment himself, thank you very much.

Face it, the Becketts were complicated people with a complicated past and who complicated their relationships as much as possible.

He should wise up and take warning from what had happened with Cassidy today. If every difference of opinion ended up like this one, with the boxing gloves out and her storming off, refusing to speak to him, they didn't have a snowball's chance in hell of making it to next week, much less long term.

Chapter 14

After a final pass by the bull pens, something Shane did more to burn off excess energy than any real concern that the stock wasn't quietly settled in for the night, he wandered back to his trailer. It was nearing ten and sleep beckoned. The crack of dawn came early, and he had a full day tomorrow.

Instead of hitting the shower as was his habit, he grabbed a soda from the fridge and, sitting at the table, powered up his laptop. He and Bria had recently taken up a new daily routine of emailing each other pictures and jokes and sometimes a short note. It was a way of maintaining constant contact. It was good for both of them. Of course, the emails were sent to and from Judy's account, who read them to Bria and composed the ones from her to Shane.

He was pleased to find a new email from Bria in his inbox including the link to a humorous YouTube video.

Smiling, he watched the video in the semidarkness before firing off a quick reply. The smile promptly dimmed as thoughts of Cassidy and their disagreement intruded.

She was an amazing person. A loving and devoted mother, a hard worker with an incredibly passionate nature that, when ignited by the right spark, was a wonder to behold. That same passion, unfortunately, could also take the form of anger, obstinacy and tunnel vision.

Life with her would never be boring. It would also be a challenge, and Shane had begun asking himself if he was up to the task.

It was possible they'd rushed into their relationship before either of them was ready. They were both still putting their lives in order. Shane had a new daughter and a new job. Cassidy had recently reconciled with her estranged brother and father. Wasn't tonight proof enough they were ill-prepared for the challenges facing them? One fight and Cassidy was ready to call it quits.

His chest tightened. She *had* called it quits. This was no cooling-off period. Two visits, four phone calls and three texts, all unanswered, couldn't be denied. The realization left him hollow inside.

Closing his laptop, he began getting ready for a shower and bed. His steps were slow, his spirits low. Foolishly, he'd hoped he and Cassidy could beat the odds. He should probably be glad to get out early before they hurt each other worse than they already had. Hadn't history shown them they didn't have what it took for the long haul? Heck, this time they hadn't even lasted a month.

Tired as he was, sleep eluded Shane. Quite a difference from the last two nights he'd spent with Cassidy. He hadn't slept then, but for entirely different reasons.

His ringing cell phone made Shane bolt upright in bed. He glanced at the alarm clock on the night stand, momentarily confused. Twenty past eleven? Apparently, he'd fallen asleep, after all.

The distinctive ring identified the caller as Hoyt.

"Hey," Shane cleared the sleep from his voice. "What's up?"

"It's Benjie." His brother didn't return the greeting. "He won't stop crying."

Shane didn't need to be told. He could hear Benjie's wails in the background. "Is he hurt?"

"No. I don't think so. He was fine up until a couple hours ago. We fished all afternoon, then had sandwiches from the marina store for dinner. I have no idea what's wrong."

"He could be sick."

"Cheryl felt his forehead. She doesn't think he has a temperature. And he's not throwing up."

"What did he eat besides sandwiches?"

"Fast food chicken at lunch with the usual fixings," Hoyt said.

"What else?"

"Chips and dip. Cupcakes. I bought him an ice cream bar at the marina store."

Not the healthiest of snacks. And consumed on a rocking boat. "You sure he doesn't have a stomachache?"

"He didn't say."

Shane felt like he was leading a toddler by the hand. Was he once that naive? "Ask him."

There was a rustling on the line while Hoyt put the phone down. He came back a minute later.

"No stomachache."

"What does he say is wrong?"

There was a long hesitation before his brother answered. "Something about being scared."

"Of what?" Shane heard it then, loud and crystal clear. Benjie cried out over and over that he wanted to go home and wanted his mother. "Want my advice? Take him home."

"You sure he won't quit and fall asleep?"

"Probably, but is that the kind of good time you want to show him? He'll refuse to go anywhere with you again."

"I guess you're right."

"Why are you hesitating?"

"We rented the boat for the entire night."

"You've got to be kidding." Shane tried to be sympathetic. He'd been in Hoyt's shoes himself not very long ago, completely inexperienced with kids and having to be taught. Luckily, Judy had been, and still was, patient with him. "Look, Benjie hardly knows you."

"I'm his father."

"Doesn't change the fact, until this weekend, you were a complete stranger."

"Yeah, well whose fault is that?"

Shane ignored the dig at Cassidy. "Look, she told me Benjie's never spent the night away from home except at her friend's house. This is all brand-new for him."

He heard Cheryl in the background seconding his suggestion. At least his sister-in-law was showing some sense.

"I don't want to take him home yet," Hoyt said firmly. "If I do, Cassidy will win."

"This isn't a contest."

"She'll deny me visitation."

What was with these people? Shane was ready to pull his hair out.

"Quit being selfish and bring your son home. Accept it's too soon for an overnight trip. Plan your next visit. Make peace with Cassidy."

He waited while Hoyt spoke to Cheryl, straining to decipher their murmured conversation. He made out nothing other than a word here and there.

"Okay," Hoyt finally said. "We're on our way."

"Good. I'll see you in the morning." Shane figured his brother and Cheryl would come around sometime before their flight left.

"Actually, we're going to head straight to the airport. It's been a tiring trip."

"What about Cassidy? Aren't you going to talk to her?"

"The less said the better."

"You're making a mistake."

"I'll see you in Payson next month."

"Benjie, come back here." Cheryl's voice rang out. "We're going home, but first we have to pack."

Where was the boy going? Weren't they still anchored at the marina? Shane jumped out of bed, wanting to do something and feeling helpless.

"Wait," Hoyt said. "Benjie wants to talk to you."

The next instant, his nephew's trembling voice said, "Uncle Shane?"

"Yeah, pal. How you doing?"

"I want to come home."

"You are. Your dad's promised. As soon as you're packed."

"He wouldn't let me call Mommy."

Poor decision on Hoyt's part. Had Benjie talked to Cassidy, he might not have had a meltdown, or as big a one. Hopefully, Hoyt had learned his lesson.

Benjie audibly swallowed a sob. "He doesn't like me."

"That's not true, pal. He loves you."

"He doesn't."

Shane's shoulders sagged. He'd badly wanted this initial meeting between Hoyt and Benjie to go as well as it had with his own daughter. And the frustrating part was it could have been great. Hoyt, as usual, allowed his excitement to overrule his good judgment.

"I want you to do me a favor," Shane told Benjie. "It's important."

"What?"

"I want you to give your dad another chance. Just because you didn't have fun this time, doesn't mean you won't the next. He's learning to be a dad, and you're learning to be his son."

"I guess."

"Good boy. Now, go on, help Cheryl pack so you can come home."

"Will you be there?"

The hope in Benjie's voice tore at Shane, and he regretted his answer. "Not tonight. But you can bet I'll see you tomorrow."

Cassidy, he was sure, wouldn't appreciate him being there. Plus, he didn't want to interfere in Hoyt's relationship with Benjie. Now that he thought about it, he and his nephew really should have a talk soon about how they could be the best of friends, but Hoyt was still Benjie's dad.

His brother took back the phone when Shane and Benjie were done. "Thanks for your help."

Unlike earlier, Hoyt sounded truly appreciative. Good. Maybe he was slowly coming around.

"Anytime."

After knocking around the trailer for the next ten minutes, Shane fell into bed, utterly spent—only to toss and turn. Wound up tighter than a spring, he grabbed a magazine and read until barking dogs, the low hum of an engine and distant voices alerted him that Hoyt and Cheryl had returned with Benjie.

Rising, he threw on some clothes and a warm jacket and ventured outside. His plan wasn't to barge in on the family, merely observe them from a distance.

From the corner of the barn, he watched Hoyt and Cassidy talking, their forms clearly illuminated in the beam of his brother's rental vehicle's headlights. Shane couldn't make out what they were saying, which he supposed was for the best. So far, they weren't yelling at each other. Benjie must have already gone inside. The poor kid was probably a wreck. Hell, they were all wrecks.

The minutes passed. If Shane had the sense of a gnat, he'd haul himself back to bed. He was further motivated when Cassidy turned to go inside the house. The discussion, whichever way it had gone, was over, and no one seemed any worse for it.

Shane started down the long barn aisle. He'd just

reached the other end when a dark but distinctive figure emerged from the shadows.

"Mercer." Shane froze. "What are you doing out here in the middle of the night?"

"Same as you." Mercer stepped closer. There was no warmth in either his voice or manner. "Sunny called me."

"I'm glad Benjie's all right."

"That brother of yours, he doesn't know how lucky he is. If he ever tries anything like this again, I'll personally deck him."

Shane wasn't in the emotional frame of mind to debate his brother's behavior with Mercer. Not at two o'clock in the morning when they were both tired.

"He did the right thing in the end and brought Benjie home."

"He'd have been sorry if he hadn't."

"If you don't mind." Shane took a step. "I've got to be up in a few hours."

"One more thing." Mercer planted a hand in the center of Shane's chest.

"What?" He immediately went on the defensive and shook off the offending hand.

"I also heard about you and Cassidy. She's pretty distraught."

"Frankly, Mercer, it's none of your business."

"If it concerns my daughter, it is."

Before learning about Bria, Shane would have disagreed. Now, he understood and marginally lowered his guard.

"We had a misunderstanding."

"More like a knock down and drag out fight." Mercer's face hardened. "I warned you weeks ago you weren't to hurt her and, if you did, you wouldn't be working here anymore."

"Are you firing me?"

"I'm considering it."

Shane tensed. He needed this job. The chances were slim he'd find another one so well suited to him and close to Bria. But he wouldn't beg. He wasn't in the wrong.

"I hope you'll consider carefully. I'm a good bull manager."

"You've got one week to make it right."

With that, Mercer strode off in the direction of the house.

Make it right? Shane wasn't sure how to interpret his boss's remark. Did he want Shane and Cassidy to reconcile or did he want Shane to end things with her on good terms?

How could he decide when he wasn't sure himself what he wanted? Cassidy had changed, going from someone he thought he could possibly love to someone he barely knew.

Tatum's two oldest children bailed out of Cassidy's vehicle the moment she came to a full stop in front of the elementary school.

"See you later," Drew called. He was a year behind Benjie, and the pair were practically inseparable. "You coming?" He waited for Benjie, who remained rooted in the middle back seat.

Cassidy studied her son's glum expression in the rearview mirror. "Give him a minute, will you, Drew?"

"Okay." The kindergartener hesitated, then, adjusting

his backpack, joined his sister in the stream of students walking from the drop-off point to the school entrance.

"Want to tell me what's wrong?" Cassidy asked, though she had an inkling. Benjie had been out of sorts for most of the week, ever since the fishing trip fiasco.

"Uncle Shane says he and Bria aren't coming with us to Payson."

"He does, huh?"

Originally, Shane and his daughter were to accompany them on their visit to Hoyt at the Payson rodeo in March, turning the excursion into a family trip. But she and Shane had argued and barely spoken all week, ruining the plans.

He must have assumed he and Bria were no longer invited and told Benjie they was driving separately. Well, he'd assumed correctly. She wasn't ready to spend two days with him. She may never be ready.

"Why, Mommy?" Benjie asked.

She sighed, unsure how to answer.

Behind them, a horn beeped. Cassidy automatically checked her side mirror, noting the long line of vehicles waiting impatiently for their turn at the curb.

"I want him and Bria to go with us," Benjie whined.

"You can see her another time."

"You're being mean."

In his eyes, she probably was. Cassidy hadn't explained her argument with Shane to Benjie. She was, stupidly, hoping it wouldn't affect their relationship. Wrong, yes. She should practice what she preached and do what was best for her son. Except Shane had hurt her, and she wasn't ready to let bygones be bygones.

More than hurt her, he'd disappointed her and betrayed her, though the latter was a bit of a stretch. Still, she'd trusted him, which wasn't easy for her, and he'd let her down. He knew her fears. She'd told him during their most intimate moments, and he'd shown her he didn't care. Just because he felt a certain way, she was supposed to feel the same. Well, she didn't.

Five weeks ago, her life had been ordered and simple and routine. Now, she didn't know what was happening one minute to the next. And Shane was responsible. Like a tornado, he'd appeared and wreaked havoc, picking up the different pieces of her life, tossing them around and then dropping them. She had yet to stop reeling.

"I'm sorry, sweetie. I know it doesn't seem fair." She was about to say how parents sometimes had to make difficult decisions. Benjie's disappointed face had her reconsidering. "Maybe we can all drive up together. Let me see."

"Yay!" Benjie grabbed his backpack off the seat.

"No promises," she said, her words drowned out by the sound of the slamming rear door.

Benjie was gone in a flash.

Another sigh escaped. She would have continued to sit there, the engine idling, if a horn blast hadn't roused her.

"All right, already, I'm leaving." She threw the truck into gear.

Thanks to traffic letting up, the drive home was considerably quicker than the one to school, leaving Cassidy with less time to ponder her current dilemma than she'd have preferred.

How to approach Shane about the trip to Payson

without him getting the wrong idea? Economics, she supposed. Why take two vehicles on the four-hour round trip when one would suffice? And with the children for company, she and Shane could avoid each other.

But wait. If they drove together, they'd have to stay at the same hotel overnight. Had he already made reservations? Damn, she should have thought this through more carefully before mentioning it to Benjie.

At the arena, she went straight to the office and found Tatum alone.

"How'd it go?" her friend asked. "The minions behave themselves?"

"They were fine." Cassidy sank into the visitor chair across from Tatum's desk, already exhausted and the day had hardly begun. "It's Shane. Well, not him. Benjie wanted to know why the four of us aren't driving together to Payson to see Hoyt."

Tatum laid down the monthly newsletter she'd been proofreading. "What did you tell him?"

"I'd talk to Shane about it."

"Good." She went back to reading.

"That's your only comment?"

"You two need to sort things out. You're both miserable, and this is a great icebreaker."

"I'm not miserable."

"Humph. Could've fooled me."

Cassidy sulked silently, fiddling with the buttons on her jacket.

After a moment, Tatum glanced up from the newsletter. "I'm not suggesting you make up. Actually, I am. But, at the least, you and Shane have to get along. Your children are cousins and friends."

"Is he really miserable?"

"And then some."

Cassidy sunk farther into the chair. "I don't care. It doesn't matter."

"You know, your father put him on probation."

"What?" She jerked upright.

"I overheard him telling your mom. Don't say anything to them."

"Forget it. I'm confronting Dad." Cassidy groaned. "The man knows no bounds, I swear."

"He's worried about you."

"Which is no reason for him to put Shane on probation. What happened between us has nothing to do with work." Mad as she was at Shane, she hadn't wanted this. Did he blame her? Probably. "I bet Mom gave Dad an earful."

"No. She agreed with him."

"I don't believe it." Cassidy pushed on the chair's arm rests, ready to hunt down her parents.

"Wait," Tatum said. "Before you go, I think you ought to ask yourself a question." She gave Cassidy a stern look. "Why are you so upset?"

"Why? Because I don't want him to lose his job, of course."

"And why don't you want him to lose his job?" Tatum persisted.

"Don't be ridiculous. He needs to work. He has a daughter to support. And living in Reckless puts him near Bria."

Tatum smiled with satisfaction. "How is it you can be so understanding of Shane and not Hoyt? He has a son and wants to be near him as much as possible."

"It's different with him."

"Not so different."

A tiny crack formed in Cassidy's defenses. Tatum had voiced aloud what Cassidy had been refusing to admit for days.

She sighed. "Okay, I get it. Hoyt just wanted to spend more time with Benjie. But he shouldn't have taken him without talking to me first."

"No one's arguing that." Tatum again put down the newsletter. "Speaking of which, how are the visitation negotiations going?"

"Hoyt had his attorney submit a schedule. I'm reviewing it now."

"And…"

"It's not unreasonable."

"You don't say."

"We are asking for a few adjustments."

Tatum's smile broadened. "Will wonders never cease? Two adults communicating and coming to a sensible, mutual agreement."

"Somehow I get the feeling you're not talking about me and Hoyt."

"Oh, I am. I just wish I was talking about you and Shane."

"I confess. Hoyt and I both acted badly. We allowed our emotions to get the better of us."

"You think?"

"But, Shane…" Cassidy couldn't go on. The pain had yet to lessen.

"The man is plumb crazy for you."

"Then why did he side with Hoyt against me?"

"Good grief!" Tatum clamped a hand to her forehead

in frustration. "You think because he didn't completely, one-hundred-percent agree with you, he disagreed."

"Excuse me, but isn't that the definition of disagreeing?"

"Not at all. Nothing is ever black and white. Shane saw both sides, yours and Hoyt's, and understood them. He tried to be the mediator, encouraged you both to compromise, which, according to you, was a huge mistake."

"I was a little hard on him," Cassidy conceded.

"A little?"

"I was scared, all right?"

"I know, honey." Tatum's tone softened. "The last few weeks have been rough on you and a big adjustment. But the world hasn't ended. The thing you feared the most came and went, and you're still standing. Granted, with a few expected cuts and bruises. But you survived intact, other than losing a great guy you're head over heels in love with."

"Who said I was in love?" Cassidy asked in a small voice.

"You didn't have to. Anyone with half an eye can see it."

"It's too late for us," she said.

Tatum waved her off. "It's only too late if you let him leave."

"Leave?" Cassidy panicked. "Has he taken a new job?"

"If your dad fires him, he will."

Cassidy had made enough mistakes. She refused to be responsible for Shane losing his job. "Where are they?"

"If you're talking about your parents, they're at the livestock pens behind the arena. The team penning jackpot is tonight."

Cassidy didn't hear whatever else Tatum had to say. In the blink of an eye, she was out the office door and charging across the open area to the arena. Her parents must have sensed her coming for they turned in her direction well before she reached them. One look at their faces, at her father's arm around her mother's waist, and Cassidy instantly knew something was up.

"I'm glad you're here," her mother said after casting Cassidy's father a shy glance. "We have news."

Cassidy ground to a stop in front of them. "You finally said yes. You're getting married." It was, she supposed, inevitable.

"What!" Her mother blinked in surprise. "No, no."

"She's keeps stalling me," her father grumbled, then gave her mother a resounding peck on the cheek. "I'm moving into the house. This weekend."

"We thought you should be the first to know," her mother said.

Cassidy waited, expecting to be flooded with doubts and, possibly, anger. It didn't happen. Quite the opposite, in fact. She was overcome with—was this even possible?—contentment. "I'm glad for you."

"Are you sure?"

"Yes. In fact, I think it's great. As much as you fight, you're happier together than you are apart."

"That's how it usually is when you're in love."

Cassidy heard her father as if from a distance. The past weeks replayed in her mind. Shane's arrival at the Easy Money. Their building attraction and fervent kisses. The night he took her to dinner at the Hole in the Wall.

He'd pushed her, it was true. Made her face her fears and do right by her son. He'd also been her friend, her lover and her confidant.

Tatum was right. This had been the hardest time of her life. It had also been the happiest she could remember. Because of Shane.

Cassidy did love him. Tatum was right about that, too. She loved him with all her heart.

Yet, she'd driven him away. Made them both miserable. Possibly cost him his job.

"I'm so pleased you're okay with it." Her mother beamed. "We were worried."

"Yeah, fine, whatever." She turned toward her father. "About Shane. You are not firing him, do you hear me?"

"Hell's bells, I'm not firing him. Where would I find a better bull manager?"

"I heard he was on probation."

Her father grimaced guiltily. "He might have been."

"But no longer?"

"I suppose I should tell him. The man's suffered long enough."

"You haven't!" Cassidy was appalled.

"When did you change your mind?" her mother asked, evidently not in the loop.

"A few days ago. After Benjie told me about the phone call."

"What call?" Cassidy and her mother asked simultaneously.

"According to Benjie, it was Shane who convinced

Hoyt to bring him home last weekend. Hoyt wasn't going to at first."

"Shane did?" Cassidy's jaw dropped. "He never said a word."

"Did you give him the chance?"

No, she hadn't. "That doesn't explain why he wouldn't take the credit."

"You aren't the easiest person to approach."

From the time she was ten, she'd diligently kept people at a distance. What had it gotten her? She might have safeguarded her heart, but it had turned stone cold. She didn't want to live her life alone.

Tears blurred her vision. "I've spent years being afraid of nothing."

Her mother put an arm around her. "That seems to be the curse of this family."

"I've been awfully unfair to him."

"Tell him."

"He doesn't want anything to do with me." She struggled to bring her crying jag under control.

"I doubt it. He's still here."

Rather than drain her, Cassidy's outburst envigorated her. Was it possible for her perspective to change so quickly? Or had it been changing all along, day by day with Shane?

"Is he here?" She glanced around expectantly.

"Took the day off," her father said. "Mentioned some errands and picking up Bria."

His daughter. Shane was such a good father. The best. He would have been a good stepdad to Benjie, too. She and Shane had talked about it the mornings they'd woken up together. They could have had that every morning if she didn't mess up.

"He'll be back later this afternoon for the team penning jackpot."

Could Cassidy wait until then? Then again, what choice did she have?

Just her luck. She finally came to her senses, and Shane wasn't around for her to first apologize and then ask him to forgive her fit of temper.

What if he refused? She had all day ahead of her to worry about it.

Chapter 15

Shane automatically looked for Cassidy as he and Bria drove onto the arena grounds. It was a habit he'd gotten into well before they'd spent last weekend together. Probably from his first day at the Easy Money when he found her tidying his trailer.

"Can I go riding, Daddy?" Bria asked from the rear passenger seat, the doll she always brought with her lying across her lap.

"Sure. After we put your suitcase away."

Benjie wouldn't mind if she borrowed Skittles. The two children were close as, well, cousins. He'd be home from school soon. Maybe he'd join them. Shane decided to saddle up Rusty the mule just in case.

He'd have to check with Cassidy first, of course, fully aware he was manufacturing an excuse for them to talk. He'd been doing that a lot lately without much success. When she got mad at someone, she evidently stayed mad a good long time.

Damned if she wasn't infuriating. *And* addictive. When he wasn't wanting to rail at her, he wanted to kiss her till she begged him to stop. Never had he felt this strongly for a woman. She would be impossible to get over. Harder still when every night she visited his dreams and every day she invaded his thoughts.

He and Bria pulled up to the trailer and parked. He studied his temporary home while Bria scrambled from her car seat and ran inside. He'd need a new place soon. Real soon. A trailer was no place to raise a little girl. For a while, he'd thought maybe he, Cassidy and Benjie could find a house in Reckless. One with an extra room for Bria. That idea had gone up in smoke, and he had no one to fault but himself.

He'd told Cassidy he understood her fears and concerns and sympathized with them. The truth was, he hadn't. Not until it was too late. She and Hoyt weren't him and Judy. They were two different people with different histories and an entirely different relationship. He'd been wrong to assume Cassidy would feel and act like Judy or Hoyt like him, simply because their circumstances were similar. In hindsight, he should have done exactly what Cassidy needed and asked for: supported her unconditionally and gone to the marina, insisting Hoyt return Benjie home.

The mistake had cost him dearly.

Grabbing Bria's small suitcase and backpack from the floor of the truck, he carried both inside. At least he'd kept his job. Mercer had called earlier today to let Shane know he wasn't on probation anymore. Thank God for that much. Mercer hadn't offered an explanation, other than to say he'd spoken to Cassidy and all was well.

What did he mean? Shane would probably never find out.

Suitcase and backpack stowed in their usual place, Shane and Bria headed outside. She skipped along beside him to the stalls where Skittles and Rusty greeted them with lusty snorts and eager pawing.

"Up you go." Shane hoisted Bria onto Skittles's bare back.

She clutched the old horse's mane in her small hands as he led the mounts to the main barn for brushing, saddling and bridling.

He was just finishing when Benjie came bounding down the aisle. Did the kid ever walk?

"No running, son," Shane called, not that he expected either Skittles or Rusty to react with anything more than a docile swishing of their tails.

"Can I go with you?" Benjie asked, grabbing Shane around the waist for a hug.

That was one quality Shane found appealing about his nephew. He always greeted Shane as if they hadn't seen each other for months instead of hours.

Two days ago, Shane had found a chance to speak with Benjie about their relationship, clarifying his role as uncle. Benjie had seemed to understand, which relieved Shane. He didn't want to confuse the boy further.

"I was planning on you coming along," he told Benjie, "but you'll have to ask your mom first."

"It's okay with me."

Shane swung around at the sound of Cassidy's voice. She was here! Within a few feet of him. Every cell in his body jumped to high alert. God, he'd missed her.

"Hey," he croaked, his throat having gone bone-dry.

She looked incredible, and not just because she was perpetually on his mind. There was something different about her. A glint in her eyes. A lightness to her step. A softness to her mouth that was in stark contrast to the thin, hard line of late.

What, he was desperate to know, accounted for the change? He had to find out.

"Can I talk to you?"

She smiled. Smiled! "I was about to ask you the same thing."

Shane didn't wait. He lifted Bria onto Skittles and settled her into the youth-size saddle. Benjie was already climbing onto Rusty.

"Come on," Benjie said to Bria once he was seated, and nudged the mule into a trot. "Race you."

Bria followed in hot pursuit before Shane could warn the boy to go slow.

"She takes after you," Cassidy said, watching the two children.

"They shouldn't run the horses down the barn aisle."

"Actually, they're trotting, not running. And I find it difficult to believe you never did anything like that at their age. I did."

"I plead the fifth."

This comfortable, casual banter was the kind of interaction Shane had been hoping for with Cassidy. The kind they'd once shared. He'd rather there be more, but he'd accept friendship.

"What happened?" he asked when they reached the end of the aisle and stepped into the open area. "You're not mad anymore."

"I'm not sure where to begin."

"Try."

"An epiphany, I guess." She laughed quietly. "Or a severe reprimand from Tatum and my parents. They told me what I already knew."

"Sometimes we need to hear it from someone else."

She gazed up at him with those incredible, luminous dark eyes. "You're right."

All around them, the arena buzzed with activity. Students arriving for the afternoon riding classes. Vehicles and trailers hauling horses and participants for the team penning event. The Becketts, Mercer, Sunny, Ryder and Liberty, all hard at work. Benjie and Bria rode in the round pen, joined now by Tatum and her children who begged to ride double.

Home. Shane couldn't get the word out of his head. He'd felt as if the Easy Money was the right place for him and Bria from the day he'd arrived. Sooner, in fact. From the moment he'd driven across the town line into Reckless. Cassidy had been a large part of that.

"Is there any chance we can start over?" he asked.

"We should probably talk first."

Hope blazed inside him. She hadn't said no.

Before he could respond, she cradled his cheeks in her hands and drew him down for a full-blown, mouths-fused-together kiss. And, like each time before, she rocked his world.

A blank stare was all he could muster when she released him.

"You okay?" she asked.

"Uh, yeah." Was he? "What was that for?"

"Added insurance. In case you don't accept my apology."

"You have nothing to apologize for."

"I do. You've always been there for me. I was wrong to accuse you differently."

"I forced you to tell Hoyt about Benjie."

"I needed forcing. My family's a mess. *Was* a mess. I didn't want the same for Benjie and convinced myself that hiding him from Hoyt was the solution. It wasn't. Isn't."

The future Shane had thought lost to him appeared again on the horizon. "Things will work out with Hoyt."

"They will. Sooner or later. I'm committed. Hoyt is, too. We spoke last Thursday. Cleared the air. Set some ground rules we can both live with."

"I'm glad."

"Thank you." The glint was back in her eyes. "You've been a good friend and a good uncle to Benjie."

"I'd like to be more."

"I know. I wouldn't be here if I didn't."

He had to be sure he understood correctly, that she wanted what he did.

"Are you saying what I think you are?"

Her cheeks blushed a pretty pink Shane found sexy as all get-out. "I'd like for us to date."

He grinned. This was what he'd been waiting for. Praying for. "No."

"No?" She stumbled backward. "My mistake."

He captured her hand in his. "The only thing you're mistaken about is dating. I won't settle for that."

"I'm confused." She looked it, too.

He hauled her around the corner where they were out of sight.

"What about the kids?" she protested.

"Tatum's with them. They'll be all right for a minute, which is all the time I need."

"For what?"

"Cassidy." He dipped his head and nuzzled her ear. "I love you."

"It's too soon." She closed her eyes and trembled when he planted tiny kisses along the side of her neck.

"Are you saying you don't love me, too?"

"I…oh!"

"Yes?" He moved toward her mouth, ready to kiss a confession out of her. He didn't have to.

"I do," she whispered against his lips. "Love you—"

He cut her off with a searing hot kiss that went on and on. This was the missing piece, he thought through the haze surrounding his brain. The last one he needed to make his home, his life complete.

"Marry me," he said when they finally broke apart.

"You're crazy, you know." She laughed, the sound lovely and bright.

Shane lifted her by the waist and hauled her against him. "Is that a yes?"

"We can't."

"No?"

She became more serious. "What about your brother? How will he feel?"

Shane set her down, but he didn't let her go. "We'll figure it out."

"And Benjie and Bria. They're already confused. They'd go from being cousins to stepbrother and stepsister."

"Sweetheart, we can do this. Look at what your parents overcame. If they can work through their differences, we can, too."

She relaxed in his arms and he took heart. "I love

you, and I'm committed to you and the family we'll have."

"We need to go slow," Cassidy insisted.

"Sounds reasonable. A month or two should do it."

"You're joking, naturally."

"A little." Shane kissed her again, this time a quick brush of his lips. He'd save the real celebration until later when they were alone. "I haven't met a woman yet I wanted to put a ring on her finger. Until you."

"Shane."

He could grow used to her saying his name like that. "Marry me, Cassidy. Soon. This summer. Next year. I don't care. As long as you do."

"Ah..." She kept him waiting another grueling few seconds before ending his agony. "Yes. But I do want to date awhile first."

Shane pulled her to him. "I'm going to make you happy. I swear it."

"You already have. You've given me the family I've always wanted and never thought was possible."

She'd taken the words right out of his mouth.

Epilogue

Three months later...

Cassidy flitted from one spot to the next, mentally checking off items. Cold hors d'oeuvres were laid out on trays, hot ones warmed in chafing dishes. The caterers were busy in the kitchen, putting the finishing touches on the barbecue dinner. A four-tier cake sat on a table by the window, the top adorned with a miniature cowboy groom and cowgirl bride. A three-piece band was setting up in the backyard and tuning their instruments.

The wedding, the biggest one ever hosted at the Easy Money, had gone off without a hitch. The newly married couple was outside, finishing up with the reception line. They'd be here soon, and the reception would begin.

"There you are."

Cassidy felt Shane's arms come from behind to circle her waist.

"Hi." She leaned into him, weak in the knees from loving him so much and being loved in return.

He'd been her biggest helper in putting on this wedding. Cassidy didn't know if she had the strength for the next one. The Becketts were getting hitched right and left. That was one of the reasons she'd decided to take her time becoming Mrs. Shane Westcott. Plus, they were still developing their unique blended family.

Benjie and Hoyt had made considerable progress since the fishing trip. Their visit in Payson two months ago had gone well and there was a second one in the works for May.

Bria accepted Cassidy as her father's girlfriend, and the two were becoming close. For now, she called Cassidy "Auntie," which made sense to her because Benjie was her cousin. Cassidy was fine with that and didn't care if it ever changed.

Make no mistake, however, she would marry Shane. Their time together had shown her what life could be like, spent side by side with the man of her dreams.

They'd finally found a house this week. The purchase would be finalized next month, and then they'd move in. She, Benjie, Shane and, on every other weekend, Bria. They were a family, happy and close-knit.

"Here they come," someone shouted, and the crowd separated to make a path for the bride and groom. "Mr. and Mrs. Beckett."

Cassidy's parents, all smiles and radiating joy, entered through the door, their arms linked and the photographer snapping pictures.

"Mr. and Mrs. Beckett again!" someone else said.

Her parents laughed unabashedly.

Cassidy laughed, too. More than accepting her parents' spur-of-the-moment nuptials, she was delighted. They'd come full circle, all of them. What had started nearly a year ago as Liberty seeking her biological father had ended with the Becketts becoming complete. Whole. Healed. A family in the truest sense of the word.

It was the greatest gift Cassidy could have hoped to receive.

"Liberty and Deacon are next," Shane said.

"Three months from now."

Ryder and Tatum had exchanged their vows last month in a small, quiet service. Today, with her pregnancy clearly showing, she'd sat beside Ryder, along with the rest of the family, during the ceremony.

"Can I talk you into finally setting a date?" Shane turned Cassidy inside the circle of his arms, then gave her a light kiss. "The kids are getting anxious."

"The kids couldn't care less."

Benjie and Bria were at that moment playing with Tatum's brood under the watchful eye of the sitter Cassidy had hired.

"Don't make me wait too long."

"Or what?" Cassidy smiled up at Shane. What had she done to deserve this man?

"Ever hear of a shotgun wedding?"

"I think you have it backward. A shotgun wedding is when the groom is forced to marry the bride."

"A technicality."

She'd been determined to wait, at least until this summer, to decide. Suddenly, she wanted nothing more than to have her future set. It must be the mood of the day.

"I've always thought a June wedding would be nice."

Shane's head snapped up. "Next month? Really!" He broke into a grin. "All right."

"No, no. A year from next month."

"Too long," he insisted.

"I'll make the wait worth it."

"I'm holding you to that." He reached into his pocket. "Guess I can give this to you now. Been carrying it around for weeks."

He took her left hand and slipped the diamond and ruby ring onto her finger.

She blinked back tears. "It's beautiful." More beautiful than she could have imagined. "I love it."

"And I love you."

While everyone surrounded the newlyweds, Shane swept Cassidy away to a secluded corner of the house, where they sealed their brand-new engagement with kisses promising a lifetime of happiness.

* * * * *

A former innkeeper and radio talk show host, **Heidi Hormel** has always been a writer. She spent years as a small-town newspaper reporter and as a PR flunky before settling happily into penning romances.

A small-town girl from the Snack Food Capital of the World, Heidi has trotted over a good portion of the globe, from forays into Death Valley to stops at Loch Ness in Scotland.

Visit Heidi at heidihormel.net, Facebook.com/authorheidihormel, Twitter.com/heidihormel and Pinterest.com/hhormel.

Books by Heidi Hormel

Harlequin Western Romance

The Surgeon and the Cowgirl
The Convenient Cowboy
The Accidental Cowboy
The Kentucky Cowboy's Baby

Visit the Author Profile page at Harlequin.com for more titles.

THE BULL RIDER'S REDEMPTION

Heidi Hormel

To my hometown for giving me too much inspiration—I'll never have the time to write all these books!

Chapter 1

Just like riding a bike, my aunt Fanny. The weighted edge of Clover Van Camp's sequined, tailored gown and her three-inch stilettos were parts of a life she'd left years ago, when she'd gone to college and finally convinced her mother that statistics class would get her further in the fashion industry than pageants. This was a one-night only return to the stage as a beauty queen. Her mother had promised.

Clover handed the award to the man in the cowboy hat and Western tuxedo with buttons straining over his middle. She stood behind him as he spoke about his philanthropy to the crowded Phoenix ballroom. Her smile was pleasant, masking a desperate desire to move her pinned and sprayed head of "naturally tousled" red hair. *La-di-da and fiddly dee*, she said to herself, the joys of being a vice president of events for her mother's fashion house. The clapping prompted her to step forward to direct the winner to the spot for his photo with the Junior League's president. As she maneuvered him into position, his hand squeezed her sequined, Spanxed butt.

"What the hell?" she yelped, pushing him and knocking him off balance and into the Junior League president. Clover watched as the pinwheeling man and woman sprawled onto the wooden floor, as Grabby Hands' white Stetson rolled off the stage. Crap. What was it with her and cowboys, gowns and trophies? That was exactly how she'd "fallen" for tall, blond, blue-eyed Danny Leigh years ago. She'd handed him the Junior Championship Bull Rider trophy and, in trying to get herself close to him for the picture, she'd stepped on his cowboy boot with the thin heel of her stiletto, skewering his foot and sending him into a jig that had them both tumbling from the platform.

Now in the Phoenix ballroom more than a decade later, this audience laughed politely, and Clover went on as if nothing had happened. She'd learned how to tape her breasts for the best cleavage and how to smile through anything on the pageant circuit. Good thing, too. She figured tonight's spectacular cleavage (thanks to her taping skills) might make the cowboy forget she'd knocked him to the ground.

Two hours later and on the way to the airport for a redeye flight back to Austin, Texas, Clover finally read the text from her mother: WTH. U punched award winner?

No punch. Accident. Will explain at office.

By then Clover would have a better, and more PR-friendly, explanation than that Grabby Hands should have kept his mitts off her. She'd already salvaged the situation to the best advantage for her mother's brand—Cowgirl's Blues. In two days, everyone would be talking about the new jeans that lifted butts and flattened tummies, not Clover's stumble. Oh, the glamour of working in the fashion industry.

Was this what she'd pictured when she'd smiled for the camera with her new MBA diploma in hand? She was no closer to a position of real responsibility than a polecat with a ten-foot pole. Of anyone, her mother should be able to understand Clover's ambition to be more than a clothes hanger with breasts. Clover wanted to be the kind of businesswoman her mother was, one who made her mark on an industry.

Why did she have to explain anything to her mother? Clover shouldn't have been forced into the gown and into a position that should have been filled by an intern. The jet flew through the darkened sky and Clover made a decision she'd been working up to since her father had tempted her with a dream job: CFO of Van Camp Worldwide. She'd be second only to her father in power. But it wasn't just the power that mattered—it was also the fact that the position as chief financial officer would allow her to finally use her crazy fast and nearly supernatural ability to look at numbers and see where the problems were. She was done with fashion and more than done trying to please her mother and her Texas-sized ego. Why had she ever imagined that her mother would loosen her grasp on the reins of Cowgirl's Blues?

Clover shoved her foot hard into the stiff boots she hadn't worn since...well, since that summer, the one where she'd met Danny Leigh, lost her virginity and had her heart broken all in the space of a few weeks. Ahh, youth was wasted on youth. She grinned until she remembered her mission. She'd accepted her father's challenge, after two weeks' notice to her mother, who told her to leave immediately and not let the door hit her on the way out. Clover's job over the next few months for her father was to prove her worth by convincing property owners and the town council that creating a resort out of Angel Crossing was the best way to save the Arizona town.

She checked over the packed luggage—jeans, cowgirl shirts and plain white undergarments. She needed to dress her part from her skin to her hat. Sure, the town would know her and her purpose. After all, Danny was the mayor now. She wondered if her father had sent her here because he remembered her relationship with the junior champion bull rider. Maybe. Her genius with numbers was matched by her father's photographic memory.

Clover didn't care. She was on her way, and if she needed to use an old relationship to get what she wanted? So be it.

"Hey, bidder, bidder." The auctioneer started his patter as the sun beat down on Danny's cowboy hat. He was waiting for someone to start the bidding. Then when it looked like the property was ready to sell, he'd jump in. The buildings at the very end of Miner's Gulch, Angel Crossing's main thoroughfare, were perfect for his plans because they were cheap, on large lots.

The crowd was sparse. Good. Probably meant the price would be even lower than he'd hoped. Finally the auctioneer accepted a bid. Danny held his number at his side. He didn't want to jump into the bidding too early. Someone behind him and to the left upped the price by $2,000. The auctioneer looked pained.

"Come on, folks," he said. "These properties are worth a whole lot more than that."

That little push got another person to up the price. Then Danny nearly bid when the auctioneer looked like he was going to call everything done.

"You're making me work for my money, aren't you? I see John back there. Are you bidding?" Silence. Danny saw the auctioneer lifting the gavel to start the count down.

Danny held up his number and nodded. He was sure he'd be the winning bidder now... Then a feminine voice said, "$155,000."

That put the properties near the top of his price range. He and the all-male crowd looked around for the woman in their midst. Though he was tall, all he saw were hats. The high desert where his town sat might not get boiling temperatures—except in the dead of summer—but the sun was just as fierce as anywhere else in the Grand Canyon State.

"Mayor?" the auctioneer asked. Danny nodded and gestured that he'd match the bid and add $1,000. The bidder's voice sounded familiar but wasn't an Angelite.

"It's back to you, Mayor. The little lady does seem determined."

Danny nodded and added $2,000 to her bid of $166,000. He'd already gone beyond what he had to spend. She must have nodded because the auctioneer pointed at Danny again. Damn. If he begged friends and family he might be able to cover the check. He did more calculations in his head. Could he still come out with a little bit of profit after converting the properties? He had to shake his head no. Converting the old warehouses into homes might put money in his pocket in the long term and make Angel Crossing a better place, but he'd be in the red on the project for longer than he could afford. Maybe if he was still bringing in the big purses from his bull rides. But not now.

"Sold," the auctioneer said. "To the lady in the pink hat." Now Danny saw her. About the same height as the men around her, although she'd still be shorter than him. He had to know who'd just bought a chunk of his town. He quickly moved toward her as she walked to the legal eagles ready to sign over the properties as is.

"Pardon, ma'am," Danny said, raising his voice a little to catch her attention. She turned and he stopped. Hells no. "Clover?"

She smiled, her perpetually red lips looking as lush and kissable as they had been during that rodeo summer. The one where he'd won his buckle, lassoed a beauty queen and lost his virginity.

"Hello, Danny," she said, a light drawl in her voice. "I heard you were mayor here. Congratulations." She smiled again. Not the real one he'd come to love, but the staged one that stretched her lips, lifting her cheeks but never reaching her bluebonnet eyes.

"Why?" he asked, not exactly sure what he meant.

"Good investment." She turned back to the paperwork.

Danny wouldn't be dismissed this time. He'd let her take the lead when they'd been teens because she was older than him by two years. He'd seen her as a woman of the world. Not now. Not all of these years later. He wasn't a horny sixteen-year-old with more hormones than brains.

"What exactly do you plan to do with the properties?"

She continued to sign where the official from the county tax sale office pointed but didn't answer.

"I'm mayor and chair of the revitalization committee," he added. True, though the "revitalization committee" was just him. He wanted Angel Crossing to thrive and he had plans that built on some of the changes that were already taking place. He didn't want any of that to be ruined.

Clover nodded but didn't turn. He was starting to get annoyed. He didn't expect her to fall all over herself for an old boyfriend or even because he was mayor. He did expect her to be courteous enough to answer his very legitimate questions. He wasn't moving until she did. Folding his arms over his chest, he stared at her... hat—not her jean-clad rear and long legs. It didn't look like she starved herself anymore. Her mother had been big on her daughter becoming a model for her clothing line, so Clover had watched every morsel that passed her lips. He remembered her almost drooling while he'd eaten a greasy, powdered-sugar-covered funnel cake. It had taken the enjoyment out of eating it.

Slowly, deliberately, he thought, she put down the pen and took the papers before turning to him. Her expression was pleasant even without her wide smile. "What did you need, Danny?"

"I don't *need* anything. I would like to know your plans for the properties, strictly as an official of the town."

"I don't think so." She looked him in the eye, nearly

his height in her impractical pink cowgirl boots, matched to her cowgirl shirt—probably one of her mother's designs. She looked the same, yet different. A woman grown into and comfortable with her blue-blood nose and creamy Southern-belle skin.

"There must be some reason you won't share your plans."

"It's business, Danny. That's all. You were bidding against me. You must have your own plans." There was a question in there somewhere.

"I'm mayor. Of course I have plans. But you work for a clothing designer, don't you?"

"I understood you only became mayor because you lost a card game."

That damned story. It had gotten picked up by a bunch of papers and repeated on a ton of websites. "Not exactly."

She smiled politely. Waiting.

"The vote for mayor was a tie and we drew cards to decide the winner." He didn't need to tell her that he'd been a write-in candidate as a joke. He could have turned it down, but by then he'd decided to step away from bull riding while he was at the top of the profession—he'd just won his champion buckle. That was what he'd told the reporters. It was true enough. He'd had his place in Angel Crossing and the town seemed as good as any to put down roots after years on the road. Anyway, who wouldn't want to be mayor, he'd thought at the time, imagining all kinds of cool things he could do.

"Drawing cards. That's very Wild West, isn't it?"

"I guess. But I'm still mayor."

"Well, it was nice to see you, Danny." She turned

from him before he could say anything else. Damn. What was he going to do now? He watched Clover walk away. A beautiful sight, as it always had been. Tall, curvier than she'd been at eighteen and proud. He knew she worked for her mother. A friend of a rodeo friend had told him that years ago, thinking he'd be interested. He hadn't been.

Now, though, what she was up to was important to Angel Crossing. He wasn't the big dumb cowboy who was led around by his gonads anymore. He was a responsible adult who had a town to look after.

Clover kept her head high and her steps confident as she walked away from Danny. She could feel his eyes on her. She refused to acknowledge that she knew he was watching. She definitely didn't want him to know that the corner of her heart still ruled by her teenage self liked his denim-blue gaze on her.

Clover disciplined her thoughts by going over the numbers and how these properties fit in with the ones that Van Camp Worldwide already owned. The buildings were slated for demolition, despite their sturdy brick walls. Most places in Angel Crossing were made of wood or adobe, but not these. What had Danny planned for them? Didn't matter. They were hers... well, VCW's.

She walked to the small, fully furnished house she'd rented—simpler than staying at the hotel nearly half an hour away or in Tucson. There used to be an old grand dame of a hotel in Angel Crossing, but it had closed years ago and sat empty, beginning to sag and rot. The town had little future on its current path. It would end up like the other Arizona ghost towns, a place on the map that tourists visited hoping to see spirits of the Wild West.

Next on her to-do list was finding the owners of six other key properties. She had done what she could from New York, but she needed to go to the courthouse in Tucson to start pulling records. She got in her rental car and fired up the GPS, telling her phone to call her brother, Knox, so she could speak with him about the purchase and any other issues he might know about, having worked for their father for years.

It took extra rings for her brother to answer, but he was willing to talk.

"Make sure the attorneys go through the deeds and the town's regulations with a fine-tooth comb," Knox said around a yawn. It was early, early in Hong Kong. "They'll assume they're a bunch of yahoos and blow off a full review."

"I'm on my way to Tucson to check on the ownership of the other properties. I should be able to straighten that out by the end of the day. I think the purchases will be completed faster than we'd calculated. Good thing because this town is definitely on a downward slide."

"What about the mayor?" Knox asked. She could picture her dark-haired brother squinting at his phone because he'd left his glasses somewhere.

There was more to the question than what sat on the surface.

"You mean, what's it like catching up with an old boyfriend? We were kids. He's just a retired bull rider and accidental mayor of a dying town."

"You might be interested to know that he's been buying properties along the main street—Miner's Gulch."

"That explains why he was bidding against us today."

"Interesting. Do you think he's a front man for another company?"

Clover was getting used to the suspicion and worry that ran through VCW. "I doubt it. I don't see Danny Leigh allowing himself to be used that way, but I'll have New York check into it if you think it's important." Maybe she should meet with Danny to figure out why he'd wanted the properties. All business. Clover was no longer the beauty-queen cowgirl looking for her one and only cowboy. She had plans, including turning Angel Crossing into Rico Pueblo. With that accomplished, her father would make her CFO. It might feel good, too, knowing that she'd fix something Knox had messed up—for the first time in their lives, maybe.

"If you have any other questions, just give me a call," Knox said. Why was he being so nice? "It's great having you with the company."

"Thanks," Clover said before she hung up. She didn't really believe Knox wished her well. They had always been in competition, especially for their parents' attention. He'd agreed to help her now, even though their father had sent him to Hong Kong. She knew there was more to his banishment to the China office than he was letting on.

She shook her head, wondering if siblings ever got past being ten-year-olds with each other.

Outdoing Knox wasn't childish, though. It would get her the job she'd trained for at the Wharton business school and really start her life as an adult. No more picking out tablecloth colors or deciding whether roses or lilies were better in the centerpieces, as she'd done for Cowgirl's Blues. She would be reshaping a town and leading VCW into an entirely new business venture. First, though, she needed to find the owners of the next properties on her list, then make offers. That would provide VCW with enough land to begin the process of rezoning.

Clover turned onto Miner's Gulch—the name of the street would need to be changed. Picturesque for a ghost town, but not so much for a fun, yet sophisticated village and resort that would be Rico Pueblo. She reached for her phone on the passenger seat to record a reminder about the street name. Where was it? She turned to look and saw that it had slid out of reach. She glanced back to the road. "Oh, no!" she said, seeing a dog cowering in her path. She slammed on her brakes and swerved just as the dog unfroze and ran toward her turning car. The thud of car into dog made Clover wince and cry out.

She couldn't see the animal. Her heart beat in her ears. She put the vehicle in Park, her hands shaking as she turned off the engine and hurried out of the car. She didn't want to look. She didn't want to see the animal's mangled body. But it might be alive. She walked toward the side that would have hit the dog. No body, but there were drops of blood. She'd definitely hit the dog. She left the car and followed the trail of red dots toward an alley. Should she call someone for help? Her first thought was Danny. No. She'd deal with whatever she found when she reached the end of the blood trail.

Chapter 2

A howl lifted the hairs on the back of Danny's neck. Not a coyote, though they did creep into town. Definitely a dog, and one in distress. Danny stopped for a moment, listening to figure out where it was. His own hound had died just after he'd stopped riding bulls. He hadn't been able to make himself adopt another.

He moved as a whine echoed off the wooden facades of the buildings. The animal was definitely in pain. He stopped again, squinting down the sidewalk for the dog or someone looking for it. Whimpering drifted to him from his left, down a short alley that led to a parking lot. He hurried as the whimper scaled back up to a howl.

"Doggie," a female voice said as he rushed down the narrow passage and toward the lot. He scanned the empty area until he noticed a woman standing near a Dumpster. The whimper changed to a growl. Didn't she know what that meant? That was more than a warning.

"Hey," he yelled. She whipped around as a dirty dog darted away despite a heavy limp.

"Darn it," Clover said because, of course, it had to be Clover. "I finally had him cornered."

"You're lucky you didn't get bitten."

"I have on gloves and I have a coat to cover him," she said, moving past Danny. "He won't have gone far. Could you call the police for help?"

"I'll help." They walked toward a narrow space between the buildings, too small for a vehicle but large enough for a dog or a person.

Clover pulled a tiny light from her huge purse. She shone it into the darkness. The dog's eyes glowed, its teeth bared as he growled long and low.

Danny put his hand on Clover's arm. "Wait. I don't want either of us to get bitten. Give me the coat. You go around to the other end to keep him from getting away. But don't go near him."

"This is all my fault. He came out of nowhere. I couldn't stop—"

He didn't want to hear her confession now. "Have you ever had a dog?" She didn't answer. "I didn't think so. I grew up around dogs and cattle and every other ornery animal there is. We have to be careful."

She handed him her coat and jogged around the building. He waited for her to appear at the other end of the narrow passageway. The dog was whimpering again in a way that made Danny want to rush to him. Finally, he saw Clover and the dog did, too. It turned to her, and Danny moved slowly forward with the coat in front of him. By the time the dog looked his way, Danny was close enough to drop the Pendleton-patterned jacket over him. Clover hurried from her end of the lane. In the dimness, she whispered over the dog's low growls and whimpers, "What do we do now?"

"Wait until he calms down. Then we're going to use the strap on your purse to lead him out of here."

"This is an Alexander McQueen," Clover said.

"Do you want to save this dog?"

She didn't reply, instead taking the strap off her purse, and two minutes later he lifted the brightly colored coat off the dog enough to reveal a dirty collar—thank God. He hadn't been sure how else he would have gotten the lead on the animal. He clicked on the "leash" and the dog froze. Then Danny lifted the coat at the same time he pulled up on the lead to keep control of its head. After a few feeble attempts to snap, the fight went out of the creature. Its medium-length matted fur was mostly white with brownish-red patches and ears that drooped. Danny could see the gleam of blood on its flank.

There wasn't a vet in town and the nearest was an hour away. But he knew who could help. Angel Crossing's physician's assistant Pepper Bourne treated humans; she could care for dogs, too. He hoped. "Clover, can you get to your phone?"

"Are you going to call the dog catcher?" she accused.

"I want you to phone Angel Crossing Medical Clinic and speak with Pepper Bourne. I bet she can fix him up."

"Oh." Clover sounded both confused and a little sorry. He gently led the limping and whimpering dog from the lane. He only half listened to Clover's side of the phone conversation.

"Pepper says she can't work on him at the clinic. Can you take him out to the ranch?"

"Tell her we'll be there in twenty minutes."

"Thank you," Clover said. She stepped forward. He moved his head a fraction of an inch, from habit, from want, and the peck she'd been ready to land on his cheek found its home on his lips. Like biting into the ripest peach, the taste of her exploded in his mouth. He pulled her close with his free arm. She didn't protest. Her mouth opened under his and the peaches became spicy with need. This was not the kiss of fumbling, horny teens. This had nothing to do with their past at all. This was its own connection. One that Danny hadn't known before. He deepened the kiss, explored her mouth and her amazing curves. None of it was enough because of this suddenly huge feeling between them.

The dog yanked on its leash and he stepped away. The ache and the need were not what he wanted. He hadn't kissed her for that. He had kissed her because—

"Let's go," he said, knowing his voice growled like the dog's. He didn't care. He was only helping her now because he couldn't let this dog suffer.

"You're lucky I keep a kit here at the house," Pepper said as she stitched. At least Clover assumed the other woman with a honey-colored ponytail was stitching, since Clover had stopped watching.

"We need a vet closer than Tucson," Danny commented.

"I know. It costs us a fortune when we bring someone here for Faye's walking yarn balls, aka my mother's alpacas and llamas," she said to Clover. "Hang on. This might be a problem."

"What?" Danny asked anxiously. She remembered

the dog he'd had when they'd first met. It'd had only one eye.

"She's pregnant."

"She? Puppies?" Danny sounded both stunned and aggrieved. "Who would dump her?"

Clover's stomach lurched. She'd hit a pregnant dog? Jeez. If there was ever a reason to go to hell, that had to be it. "Do you think they'll be okay?"

"I can feel them moving, so I guess they're good. Since I can feel them, I would also say that she's fairly far along. You'll have to take her to the vet to know for certain. The wound wasn't as bad as it looked. I'd keep her quiet for the next couple of days and come back in a week for me to take the stitches out, if you can't get to the vet or her owner doesn't come forward. Definitely keep a bandage on it in the meantime."

If Clover hadn't felt so bad for the dog, she would have laughed at Danny's stunned face. "Thanks. What do we owe you?" she asked.

"No charge," Pepper said. "Faye wouldn't let me. This is Angel Crossing."

Clover didn't know what that comment meant. Danny lifted the dog carefully and carried it…her to the truck. Puppies. This had gotten complicated quick.

"What was the name of your dog?" Clover asked when they were on the road with the dog's head on Danny's lap, where she was snoring softly. The rest of her limp body draped across the old-fashioned bench seat of his pickup and half onto Clover's lap.

"Which one?"

"The one you had when we met. He only had one eye."

"That was Jack because of the eye."

"I don't get it," she said after a moment of trying to make the connection.

"Like the card. The one-eyed Jack."

A laugh leaked out. "You never told me that."

"We weren't big on talking."

She couldn't deny that. Most of their conversations had been about how to fool around and make sure no one found out. What a summer that had been. So exciting and happy and sad and scary, especially looking back and knowing that she'd nearly ditched college to be with Danny. And the kiss they'd just shared? The one neither of them seemed willing to acknowledge now. The dog whimpered, and she reached out to soothe her.

Danny spoke again. "We had a good time."

She smiled because that was what she'd been more or less thinking. They'd been like that, finishing each other's sentences, or he'd call her just as she got her phone out to call him. "It was a long time ago, and we were very young."

"Not you. You were eighteen. A woman of experience."

"That just meant I'd been somewhere other than a ranch or a rodeo. You know I was a—" She stopped herself because what she would say next sounded so silly and juvenile. They'd both been virgins when they'd finally been able to sneak off for a few hours one night. They'd done the deed. She'd refused to admit it to him or anyone else at the time, but it had been a huge disappointment.

"Two virgins do not a good night make," he said. "It's not polite to talk about other ladies, but I'll just say I've learned a bit since then."

"This is where I should say 'me, too,' but ladies definitely don't say that sort of thing, as my grandmother Van Camp would remind me. My Texas grandmother... She'd say, 'Thank God you're only a heifer once.'" They both laughed. The dog yipped, and Clover rubbed her fur. The poor animal.

"What are we going to do with her?" he asked as he turned onto the main road to town. "I'll check for an owner, but I'm sure she was abandoned."

"I'm not staying here long and my New York condo forbids pets, even goldfish," she said.

"I've got a no-pets sort of place, too."

"You don't have a dog? You said that a cowboy isn't a cowboy without a dog."

"I was sixteen."

Teenagers were allowed to make pronouncements like that before they learned how the world really worked.

"You're the mayor. Can't you make a rule to allow you to keep the dog at your place?"

He laughed. "I wish it worked that way. Maybe Chief Rudy knows someone. The police know everyone."

"You've really settled in here, haven't you? I assumed you wouldn't retire until you couldn't walk anymore."

"Not much choice when I became mayor."

"How could you get written in for mayor? You weren't actually living here if you were still competing."

"Since Gene was here. Do you remember him? He kept AJ and me in line and helped us figure out the bulls. Anyway, Gene had a ranch here, so I decided this would be as good a place as any to call home. I gave this as my address. The next thing I know, I'm mayor. It all happened kind of quick." He didn't look at her, but she saw that he had his signature half smile. The one that had made her heart flutter—hers and every other girl in the arena.

"That still doesn't explain how you wound up retired."

"A story for another time," he said. "What are we going to do with mama dog?"

Clover had grown up a lot since that summer. Danny's charm—his kisses, too—didn't make her brain short-circuit anymore. "She can't come with me. You have to know someone who will look after her. I'd be willing to pay."

His smile disappeared. "Money doesn't solve everything, you know. That's not how things work here in Angel Crossing. Don't worry about Mama. I'll figure something out."

How could she have forgotten his pride? Prickly and strong. Maybe that was why he fit so well in Arizona. He had the personality of a cactus. "What I meant was that I would stop at the store and get food and anything else the dog needs. I want to help, even if she can't stay with me."

"We'd better hurry. Lem will be closing up shop, and he doesn't care if it's an emergency. He doesn't reopen for anyone."

"Sounds like you tried?"

"We were having a poker game and ran out of beer. Lem was at the game, so we asked him to restock us. We were going to pay. He wouldn't even reopen for himself."

"Hurry up, then." She'd buy the food and then go back to her rental and go over which property owners her brother had indicated were highly motivated to sell.

"You go in," Danny said. "I'll wait here with Mama.

Might need to come up with a better name." He stroked the dog's silky red-brown ears, her fur in crimped-looking waves. The animal sighed in pleasure. Clover could understand that. She'd made nearly the same noise when Danny had used his hands to—

"I'll be back." She did not hurry into the store. She had more dignity than that, and their shared summer was a long time ago. She wasn't that girl anymore.

She came back to the truck with three bags filled with dog paraphernalia, which she was pretty sure she'd been overcharged for. She opened the door to put the loot in the truck.

"My God, woman, did you buy the whole store?" Danny asked as she shoved the bags in.

She stiffened. "I wanted to make sure she had everything she needed."

He rooted in the bags. "A pink rhinestone collar? Lem carries these?"

"Obviously he carries them. Where else would I have gotten it?"

"Well, take it back. I'm not walking a dog with that kind of collar. The one she has just needs to be cleaned up."

"Excuse me?" She couldn't believe what he'd just said. He'd insulted her... She was pretty sure he had.

"I am not putting this collar," he said as he dived into the bags again, "or this leash on Mama. It's not right. She's a ranch dog."

"A ranch dog? You live in a tiny apartment, in a tiny town, not on a ranch."

"I'm not using these." He got out of the truck, lifted down the dog and tied her to the door handle so she was in the shade. Then he strode toward the store. She followed him.

"Danny, the collar and leash are fine. She's a girl."

"She's a ranch dog, and she doesn't need rhinestones." He didn't slow down. She continued after him and back into the store.

"Lem," Danny yelled. "What the hell are you selling? I want a real collar and leash."

"You know the rules," the tall, skinny and stooped Lem said. "No returns."

"That's BS. There are returns when you're selling us crap." Danny glared at the man.

Clover had already guessed she'd been taken advantage of. But she felt it only fair since she was guilty of hitting the dog. Somehow getting gouged made her feel better about that. Like she was paying her dues. "I like the leash and collar." There was that, too.

"Of course you do. You're from New York City," Danny said, as if she'd come from Sodom or Gomorrah.

"They're girlie. And I've spent more of life in Texas than New York."

"They're ridiculous."

"Not man enough to walk a dog sporting a few rhinestones?" she jeered, smiling at the image of him. He was not going to return the darned leash and collar.

"I was man enough for you, darlin'." His tone said exactly what that implied.

She blushed, wanting to smack him because she could see the speculation in Lem's eyes. She did not want to be one of Danny Leigh's women. "That was when you were a bull rider. What are you now? Mayor of a dying town, living off your fading fame." She'd gone too far. She knew it even as the mean words came out. She opened her mouth to apologize or maybe to suck the words back in.

The dog woofed as she came waddling and limping in. She went over to Danny, stretched up and grabbed the leash and collar from his hands, which had fallen to his sides with her ugly words.

Danny seemed to awaken and tried to pull them back. "No," he said. The dog growled and yanked the collar and leash to her, showing teeth.

"Hell's bells, Mayor. That your dog?"

"Just a stray," Danny said. "A bitch who doesn't know what she wants, apparently."

Clover sucked in her breath. Even in their worst teenage fights, Danny had never called her that.

Chapter 3

A call to his sister Jessie had gotten Danny no help and no sympathy for mama dog. His sister had her own child to deal with, her horse therapy program and a husband adjusting to a new job and baby. Jessie had a lot of choice words. Next he tried Lavonda, the sister closest to his age. She said that Cat, her cat, had nixed the idea. Danny told her that he didn't see how a property could function with just a cat to keep the stock in line. Lavonda reminded him who Cat was—an overweight Siamese mix who had a miniature donkey at her beck and call. When she asked him about Clover, he ignored the question.

Mama had made herself at home in a pile of not-so-clean clothes that had missed the hamper. So far she'd been quiet, probably tuckered out. He'd find her a new home soon because even if the original owners came forward, he wasn't giving her up to them. It was obvious they didn't care. His landlord would eventually hear what Danny had in his rooms, and the lease had been clear. No animals. One of those rules he'd figured wouldn't matter because Danny had never planned to stay. It had just been a place to put his gear between competitions. After becoming mayor and retiring from bull riding, he hadn't had time to find a better place. On the other hand, his tiny apartment was convenient to the diner and the rooms were easy for him to clean with his meager housekeeping skills. The rent was cheap, too, freeing up money for his business.

He'd bought properties, purchased more or less as favors to the owners who couldn't keep up with the repairs. The buildings had been sliding toward neglect, so he'd fixed them up, rented them back to the owners at a reasonable price and come up with a grander scheme than just living off rental income and handyman work.

Danny had wanted to buy warehouse properties near to the depot, some of them already broken up into small apartments. He'd also been able to purchase a half dozen buildings on and just behind Miner's Gulch that needed TLC. He'd transform some of them into good housing at a good price. With his ties to bull riding, sisters nearby and friends in Tucson, he'd entice new families to move to Angel Crossing. The town was literally dying, the population aging every day. His homes wouldn't be fancy, but they'd be affordable for couples just starting out. He'd mix in a few more expensive options so that the town didn't get segregated into the haves and have-nots, as he'd seen in many places. After all was said and done, he'd make a little money and the town would be better.

He looked at Mama sleeping peacefully. Maybe he should see about recruiting a vet.

Losing the auction had been a blow to his long-term strategy. He couldn't understand what Clover, or rather her father, wanted to do with the property. He'd searched online for her and found out that she was working for her dad now. He needed to do more checking. He had a vague memory of someone, somewhere in town saying that a New York City company had bought other properties.

He couldn't find anything on Van Camp Worldwide's website about a plan for Arizona. "Why would she buy those old warehouses by the tracks?" he asked the sleeping dog. "They'll have to tear them down. That's what I wanted to do. It was the only way to build anything that would appeal to first-time home buyers. I might have been able to reuse bits and pieces of the interior. Or if I could have found a group of artists, I thought about studios and living spaces. Guess I won't get to do either."

Mama sighed heavily and wiggled her brows before burrowing further into the clothing.

"I'm going to Jim's," he told the dog. He deserved a beer for the day he'd had. A little uncomplicated loving and attention would have been nice, too. Not happening as long as he lived in Angel Crossing. The downside of a small town was that if he made a move on anyone and it didn't work out, he'd have to see her day after day. It had definitely put a damper on his love life.

"Do you really do karaoke on Tuesdays?" Danny asked. He couldn't believe the wood-paneled, domestic-beer-serving tavern ran anything that appealed to someone under the age of 70. He'd seen the sign before but hadn't wanted to ask.

"Country-western only," said Anita, the owner, who'd gotten the place from a former husband.

"Anyone any good?"

"Nah, but that don't stop them." She stared hard at Danny before going on. "Hear your high school sweetheart's in Angel Crossing."

The gossip nearly had it right. He didn't even wonder about the speed of the stories that flew around town. "She and I dated over a summer when I was with the junior rodeo."

"Makes sense. Couldn't imagine how someone like her went to your high school. She was the rodeo queen or something?"

"Miss Steer Princess," he corrected automatically.

"Huh," Anita said before strolling off.

Danny wondered exactly what of that conversation would be shared. By the time he heard about him and Clover next week, they would have run away as teens to get married in Vegas only to be stopped by a gun-toting daddy. He smiled into his beer. Maybe the story wouldn't be quite that clichéd.

"Mayor," Irvin Miller said as he clapped Danny on the back and sat on the bar stool next to him.

"Mayor," echoed his wife, Loretta. The two dressed alike and even the gray in their hair matched. If you saw one, you always saw the other. Anita served the couple without asking for their order. They always got the same drink: Coors Light draft in a mug that had not been stored in the freezer.

Irvin turned again to Danny after a sip of beer. "We

heard that a big company out of New York City is buying up the town."

"The old warehouse buildings by the depot. They were falling down and behind on taxes. It'll be good to see it taken care of."

"It's not just that property. They've bought others and got plans."

"I thought I remembered someone saying that a New York buyer had gotten a couple of places. And what's wrong with having a plan? Angel Crossing could use a little revitalizing," Danny said.

Loretta broke in. "I was at the town hall talking with Pru and she showed me what those Easterners want to do—turn our little metropolis into a resort called Rico Pueblo."

"Resort?" Danny asked. "What the heck is Rico Pueblo?"

Irvin went on. "This VCW company owns a good third of the town already, according to Pru. The plans, though, came in with your lady friend."

"Lady friend? Clover?"

"Yep," Loretta said. "Her. She brought them in and told Pru that her daddy's company wanted to improve Angel Crossing. Pru said your lady friend is asking the town council—" of which Loretta and Irvin were longtime members "—to rezone everything within two blocks of Miner's Gulch into something she's calling an entertainment zone. Everything will have to look a certain way, so they'll tear down almost everything there and rebuild it. Businesses only, though, and that fit into 'an integrated theme highlighting the Western ethos.' We had to look it up and we still don't understand what it means."

"How are they going to get that many businesses? What about everyone already living here or the shops already there?"

Irvin took up the conversation. "Seems that they want to make something like Tombstone or Disneyland but fancier. No showdowns at noon and no saloon girls."

"You'd mention the girls," Loretta said.

Danny couldn't imagine any company wanting to do that with Angel Crossing, but...the land was cheap, and it was within easy driving distance of Tucson and its airport. Was that really why Clover was here?

Irvin added after another sip of beer, "Pru said it'll mean businesses and people will have to move. Not so sure about that."

Maybe the Millers had it wrong about the company taking over the town and driving everyone out. It wouldn't be the first time the couple had gotten only half of a story. "See you, folks," Danny said as he quickly finished his beer and left. He'd just go and see Clover. Find out firsthand what she and VCW meant to do with Angel Crossing.

Clover sat on her front porch, looking out over the mountains as the sun made its finale. The streaks of purple tonight were a shade she should tell her mother about—not that her mother would care to hear from her. Still, it'd make a beautiful basis for a line of clothing. She sipped at her icy-cold glass of victory beer. She'd gotten another property they needed for this phase and submitted the concept plan to the clerk at the town hall. She'd wanted to wait, preferring not to tip the company's hand for fear of driving up the other properties' prices, but the timeline was tight. To get everything approved by the town, the county and the state in time, the process needed to start now. Actually, it should have started two months ago, but her brother had dropped the ball on that one.

The Rico Pueblo concept of "culturally appropriate" entertainment and retail mixed with residences would transform the town and its economy. There would be jobs and money coming in. It would change Angel Crossing, and for the better—obviously—because right now there wasn't much to recommend the place. Faded facades, uneven sidewalks, potholes on the main street and homes with peeling paint and sagging roofs. She could see the revitalized "downtown" with meandering side streets radiating out to climb into the rugged terrain of the mountains. The residential area would be a combination of time-share rentals and housing managed by VCW. Then in additional phases there would be homes owned by individuals. This was the first project of its kind the company had tried. If they could iron out the kinks, this type of planned community could be used throughout the country. She already had ideas for at least six more venues. She just needed to make the numbers work here.

She nodded to a man walking a dog, which made her think of Mama and her own part in that sad story. Then Danny strolled up the road, stopping to talk with the dog walker. Of course. Because her evening had been going too well. She studied the changes between sixteen-year-old Danny and nearly thirty-year-old Danny—none of which were bad. He'd grown into his height, his shoulders filling out and his gait gaining confidence. Unlike many bull riders she'd seen over the years, he didn't have any hitch in his step or even a visible scar. How had he ridden and won all of those years and come out unscathed? Because he was Danny Leigh.

He turned his head to her almost as if she'd called his name. He smiled. Her heart beat a little faster, just as it always had. Darn it. She was a grown woman, not a naive girl. More important, she had only one reason for being here and that was Rico Pueblo, not reliving a summer love affair.

Her eyes hadn't left Danny, though. He lifted his hat in greeting and stumbled on an uneven bit of street. He righted himself easily, his smile never wavering. If she'd been her vain, beauty-queen self, she would have imagined that she'd made him stumble. Ha!

"Hello, Clover. I heard you were renting Dead Man's Cottage."

"That's very funny."

He came closer. "Really. That's what it's called. The first four owners were hung—one by mistake, the other three for stealing horses or silver."

"Colorful," Clover said, hoping alone at night she wouldn't imagine feeling or seeing the ghosts of the men. "How's Mama?"

"She's settling in. I've got feelers out for a new home for her. It won't be long until my landlord figures out that I've got a dog. But that's not why I'm here."

"Oh?" He was on the narrow porch now, standing over her. She was not intimidated nor interested. She was an MBA-toting businesswoman on her way to running an international corporation.

"I was speaking to Loretta and Irvin Miller. They're on town council, and they told me something intriguing."

"Did they?" She'd hoped her plans would be ignored

a little longer, but she was prepared for this situation. She'd studied the town and her father's venture, laying out every scenario and contingency.

"What are you up to? They said you want to tear down the town and rebuild it but restrict what and who can go where."

"Is that what *I'm* doing?"

"Fine. What Van Camp Worldwide is doing. Since your last name is Van Camp, I'd say it was you, too."

"I submitted a concept plan." She didn't need to tell him anything until she was ready.

"Are you trying to ruin my town because I dumped you?"

She couldn't stop the laugh. "I have an MBA from one of the best business schools in the US. I'm in line to become CFO of VCW. Why would I care about a teenage fling?" He stared at her, as if he was expecting her to really answer his question. "You actually believe that? That you dumped me? You must have very different memories than I do."

He crossed his arms over his chest and didn't blink. "I know I didn't call you after that last show. I know you asked about me."

He sounded triumphant. She checked his denim-blue eyes for mischief. Not an iota of levity. He was dead serious. "I was eighteen when we parted ways and on my way to Milan then college," she said, not adding that she'd nearly given up on college to stay with him. She'd been a stupid-in-love girl then. "I never thought about you until I was assigned to come to Angel Crossing."

"I know the 'first time' for a girl is a big deal."

Dear Lord. She definitely remembered their first time. It hadn't been a magical moment and was a memory she'd rather forget. They both had been nervous and inexperienced. The disappointment had been epic. "It must have been a big deal for you, too, since you told anyone who would listen." She sounded snippier than she'd planned. She must still feel a little resentment. Who would have known?

"I apologize for that. My mama taught me better," he said, dropping his arms and dipping his head.

She'd accept his meager apology. "Thank you. It's a little late, though."

"I'd have said it sooner, but my buddies kept ragging on me that a college girl who'd been to Italy wouldn't be interested in a cowboy who was still in high school."

She shrugged and took a sip of beer. He might be right but she still would have liked to have heard from him. To know that she wasn't just some stupid, macho, cowboy conquest. "Would you like a beer?"

Danny hesitated, his blue eyes darkening to something akin to the brightening of a morning sky. "Thank you."

She indicated that he should sit and went in to get him a beer from her limited stock. She'd invited him to have a drink because it was polite. There might be a little bit of the old chemistry. The tingly spark was just an echo of what they'd felt, that intense connection that happened only with a first love. He'd been her first love before he'd been her first lover. She smiled as she thought of their first and only time. His hands had been shaking so badly she'd had to unzip her own jeans.

"Here you are," she said as she handed him the beer and pushed away the old memories. She had a job now. Get the properties VCW needed and convince the town to agree to their rezoning requests and restrictions, which would make Rico Pueblo possible. She couldn't worry about what she'd heard about Danny. That he was starting a rehab and contracting business by buying properties in the same area VCW had slated for its entertainment zone.

He looked at the bottle carefully. "I never pegged you for a beer drinker."

She shrugged. "The label has a horse's head on it."

He took a sip and then said, "You went to Wharton business school? I remember you saying that you wanted to be a designer."

"I thought I wanted to follow in my mother's footsteps. But my talent was more about the numbers and less about creating the perfect hemline. I switched gears partway through my undergrad program. What about you? Weren't you going to go to your mom's alma mater?"

"That was my mom's idea anyway and I tried, but you know what I thought about school. When I started winning big at the bulls and bringing in a decent living, I knew if I went full-time I'd make it."

"I can't imagine your parents were thrilled you quit college." She could imagine her own parents' reaction, if she'd done something like that.

"They just wanted me to be happy. I can always go back to school, with all of the online classes."

She nodded. "I heard you've become a builder or something?"

He talked about his work, then about his family, including his nearly new niece. "Jessie and Payson were so excited when she got pregnant, and now that little Gertie is here, they're awful. Jessie has taken thousands of pictures and sends me all of them. See," he said, passing along his phone with the picture album app open. Clover could hear and see the love he had for the baby. She would never have imagined that of the swaggering cowboy he'd been. Perhaps he really had changed. After all, she had. Being the prettiest girl in the room had stopped being important to her.

"So when are you going to settle down and have babies yourself?" she asked—because it seemed like what she should ask, not because she was dying to know.

"Would need to find the right woman."

Clover refused to think about why she was relieved to hear that.

Danny went on. "What about you or your brother? Any little Van Camps?"

"Knox, well... He's Knox. I'm focused on my career and working with VCW."

"No boyfriend? No fiancé?"

She shook her head. "What about you?"

"Between my business and being mayor, I just don't have the time."

"That doesn't sound like you. You said you could always make time for the ladies."

"I said that in an interview when I was twenty-one and just won a buckle. You kept up with me?"

She may have followed his career...a little. Anyone's first real boyfriend would hold a special spot in their heart. "I lived in Texas. I didn't have much choice but to follow you and everyone else I knew from bull riding."

"Good recovery." He laughed, his blue eyes bright with humor. "I'd better get going. I don't want Mama piddling in the apartment." He unfolded himself from the chair and she stood, too.

"It was good to visit," she said like the Texas beauty queen she'd been.

"Same here." He didn't move and his gaze remained on her.

Clover's breath quickened just a little. That old flush of heat and desire worked its way through her. How could this be, more than ten years after *that* summer? Danny smiled slowly as he put out his hand to shake hers. She grasped it, exquisitely aware of the calluses scraping her palm, making her stomach dance with desire. She pulled her arm a little toward herself, feeling the passion that simmered between them. Danny didn't hesitate but stepped into her, keeping their hands firmly clasped and placing his mouth over hers. Her neck arched and her lips eagerly sought his.

Chapter 4

Cotton candy and popcorn. Clover. The taste of her hadn't changed, taking him back to that summer. The heat and passion, the fear and uncertainty. His hand moved along her familiar and new curves. Every one of them fit into his palm just right, despite the frequent numbness that made the grip in his right hand uncertain. He took one more deep taste of her, then pulled away.

"I've got to go," he said, turning and walking down the hill toward his apartment, where he'd find beer in the fridge and a dog waiting for him.

"Danny Leigh," Clover yelled at him, losing her beauty-queen coolness. "Sticking your tongue down my throat doesn't change anything."

He waved his arm at her without turning.

"Way to go, Mayor," a man standing in his front garden said, giving Danny a thumbs-up.

Danny hadn't meant to kiss Clover. Maybe it was the

past sneaking up on him. That was happening a lot since she'd come to town. Even when his friend and riding buddy AJ McCreary had moved to town, Danny's time on the back of a bull had felt far away. He'd been able to put all of that behind him. Between being mayor, rehabbing houses and doing handyman work, he'd been content. He'd been busy—too busy to worry that he didn't have much of a social life. Who needed that when he was so industrious, just like a worker bee. The ladies would always be there, he told himself.

Even better—with his sister Jessie and her husband, Payson, having produced the first grandchild, he was under less pressure to settle down. He could take his time and help his town be its best. Pepper and AJ had started changing Angel Crossing for the better with their community garden and farmers' market. Stylish and affordable housing like he planned would encourage new residents to give the town a try.

Danny walked up the stairs to his small apartment, hoping that he wouldn't find a mess. He ran through people who might want a dog and puppies. He was coming up with a zero. Mama wasn't really big enough to be much of a threat to wild animals or intruders but was too big to be a lapdog. She was an awkward size and who knew what the puppies were.

Mama waddled to him as soon as he got in the door. The apartment looked as neat as it ever did. He put a blanket over her to hide what he was carrying in case someone squealed to his landlord. He carried the wiggling animal down the stairs and through the back lot, past the restaurant's Dumpster. Once they reached a patch of low scrub, he put her down. The grass nearly hid her and her rhinestone collar and leash. She sniffed and quickly got down to business. He'd brought along a bag and would throw away what he had to in the Dumpster. She sat down, tired out from the very short walk. She couldn't be too long from delivery, he thought. He vaguely recollected one of their dogs having puppies as a kid, but he only remembered how cute they were, not the lead up or the process of them being born. He'd call his folks for advice. Maybe they would want a dog to go with them on their travels. Plus, they had a ton of friends. One or more of them might want a puppy.

He carried the dog back to the apartment, where he fed her and gave her clean water. Then he dialed his parents and left a message.

He took a beer from his fridge and sat in his tiny living room with his laptop open and the TV on the Bull Riding Network. He rubbed at his numb fingers, the ones the doctor told him might regain feeling or not. Sometimes he was sure they were better. Then he'd go to pick up a glass and drop it. Still, he'd retired. He'd refused to regret that it had been an "injury" that took him out, not that he'd told anyone that. When he'd said he was retiring because he wanted to go out on top, none of his friends had questioned him.

"Friends in Low Places" sang out from his phone. It was an old riding buddy who was watching the same competition on TV. They were both sitting this one out—Danny because he was retired and Frank because he'd reinjured his foot. Danny was on beer three when they said goodbye. He considered going to bed and taking Mama out for her final potty break before the long night. Maybe one more beer then bed? Good idea.

He finished his longneck and went to get himself another, liking this slightly floating feeling. He was completely relaxed, not worrying about the dog—who really needed a new name—about his town or about Clover. Dang it. Her taste and curves popped back into his mind, and he tried to focus on the TV.

By the time the contest and another beer were done, he was ready for bed. First he'd take the dog out one last time. He didn't want any accidents. Dang, it was a pain having a dog in a second-floor apartment. Fortunately, because it was dark and late, he didn't need to bundle her up and carry her down the stairs. He could lead her with her sparkly leash. He went down the steps, the floating feeling continuing as he stumbled over a stone or two. Definitely time for this cowboy to hit the hay. Mama did her business fast. Danny started back to the apartment.

He got to the bottom of the stairs and Mama scrabbled toward the top, pulling on the leash. Danny meant to let go but his numb fingers didn't work as well as they should and she jerked on his arm as he stepped up, pulling him off balance. Danny face-planted on the stairs and saw stars. He cursed as the dog darted to the top and barked at him.

He lay sprawled on the stairs, glad no one was nearby. He needed to catch his breath and check for damage. Not much. More pride than anything. He pushed himself up and Mama barked.

"Jutht a minute." *What the hell?* He used his tongue to explore the hole at the front of his mouth. Son of a— The fall had knocked out the fake tooth he'd gotten as a kid after a spectacular crash on his minibike. Great. Nothing he could do tonight. He walked slowly up the stairs, the pain from the fall and the throbbing in his mouth telling him tomorrow morning would not be fun.

Hell. He was a bull rider. *Retired* bull rider. Still, he'd lived through worse.

"Inthide, Mama," he said and opened the door. She scooted past him and sat on the floor, fluffy tail wagging, waiting for her treat and the leash to come off. "Proud of yourthelf?" The dog barked. Wait till she had to eat generic food because he had to spend all of his money on a new tooth.

Maybe Clover would buy some of the expensive brand she'd bought at Lem's—but, no, he wasn't asking her for anything. They'd been a summer-lovin' teen thing. They were adults and she'd already messed with his plans, just like she had that summer. He wasn't getting stupid over her again. He'd learned a lot since their time together. He wouldn't be showing her exactly what he'd learned, though. At best they were Angel Crossing–style neighbors. At worst, they were businesspeople on opposite sides of the fence.

He gave Mama a treat, took an aspirin and lay down in his sagging bed that nearly filled the room. He really needed to move. As soon as he got more properties sold and had a little cash, he'd find his own place and redo it the way he wanted. What he had now was good enough. The bed dipped under Mama's weight and she dug at the covers as he moved his legs to accommodate her. He shouldn't let her on the bed, but he was too tired to make her get down.

"Don't have puppyth," he told her as he settled into his pillow, "pleathe."

She sighed deeply and scooted to take up more of the bed.

Clover used her confident pageant walk to get her across the threshold and into Jim's Tavern, the only bar in town. She wanted to check it out and determine if it was the kind of kitschy business that would appeal to the Rico Pueblo clientele. Her father had said he'd prefer buying up everything and starting over. Clover, however, had outlined an approach that would purchase properties and work with current business owners so VCW could best leverage its investment—that was what she'd told her father, anyway.

Few patrons glanced Clover's way. Instead, they were glued to the stage and the two women laughing their way through a country duet. Neither could sing but they didn't care. The crowd was with them, laughing along and clapping. Actually, most of the crowd was women... Not most. *All* of the patrons were women and there was a woman behind the bar. Now, this was interesting. Not what Clover had expected. That seemed to be the case again and again in Angel Crossing.

"Whoa! Clover," said the tall light-haired woman with the karaoke microphone in her hand. "Come up here. You can sing a lot better than us. Sing that song you did when you were named Miss Steer Princess? 'God Bless the USA.'"

Clover looked harder at the cowgirl who was motioning her forward and the short dark-haired woman beside her. Danny's sisters. The two women had been on the road with their brother back when Clover had been the princess. She'd had an okay voice because her mother insisted she take lessons.

Lavonda chimed in, "Or you could sing 'It's Raining Men.'"

She'd sung that song during a rain delay at a rodeo. Of course Lavonda would remember that. Clover didn't want to humiliate herself but she could go along with the suggestion to get a few brownie points from the women of Angel Crossing. She'd need allies. Clover walked with purpose and grace to the open area set aside for the singing.

"Whoop, whoop," Jessie said. "This'll be a treat."

"Anything's better than the two of you," a woman heckled. Jessie and Lavonda laughed.

Clover smiled at the audience of women. They actually looked friendly.

"We cued up the song," Lavonda said, her dark eyes and hair so different from her light-haired older sister's. "Good to see you again." Then the smaller woman leaned forward and whispered quietly, "Heard you've been visiting with Danny. What's that about, huh?"

Clover just smiled. The speed at which gossip zipped through a small town shouldn't be a surprise. Who needed newspapers or TV when there was such an efficient way to pass along information?

Jessie and Lavonda went back to their bar stools, and Clover sang. She'd forgotten how much fun it was to perform. She hammed it up for the audience and got talked into singing another two songs before giving up the mic. She was parched. The Leigh sisters motioned for her to join them. She wanted to say no, but there was no polite way to bow out. Plus, the two of them might give her more insight into the town and what the mayor had planned.

"What do you want? We're buying," Lavonda said. Jessie stayed silent. She'd always been the quiet one.

"A beer."

"Anita, a beer for the best performer of the night."

Jessie took a drink. "You in town to buy it?"

"Something like that," Clover said. There was no use

lying. Everyone had heard about her buying the warehouses at the end of Miner's Gulch, plus other properties. When Rico Pueblo opened, she would rename the street Torro Boulevard.

"My husband, Jones, and I are curious about your plans," Lavonda said with a pleasant smile. "We own a guide company and more people visiting here would certainly be great for our finances. But this area is ecologically fragile. There are archaeological sites nearby that need to be protected, too."

Clover hadn't known about any sites. There hadn't been any noted on any of the surveys or maps. "There are?" she asked noncommittally.

"Jones has been exploring. He's an archaeologist."

Clover nodded, waiting for more from Lavonda.

"Talk about that another time," Jessie said. "I want to hear what Clover's been up to, besides being a business mogul."

Clover tried to understand what Jessie was really asking and decided to take her at face value. She gave them the short version. "What about you?" she asked Jessie when she'd finished her short bio. "Still riding, even with the baby?"

"Not the trick riding," Jessie said. "Gave that up, but I have a therapeutic horse-riding program for youngsters. Kids with physical and emotional challenges."

Lavonda added, "Don't get her started on Gertie. We're out so that she can live it up and act like a normal human being."

Jessie gave her sister a dirty look, the kind of sibling communication Clover always wanted to have with Knox and didn't.

Lavonda said, "This is the first time Jessie has gone

out on her own since Gertie made her grand entrance. That girl already has the flair for the dramatic."

"She does?"

"Yes," Lavonda said, shushing her sister. "Jessie's husband is a pediatric surgeon, operated on thousands of kids, probably. When Gertie made her appearance at their ranch—Jessie kept saying the pain wasn't bad enough to go to the hospital—he fainted. Smacked down on the floor. The three of them shared an ambulance."

"Stop telling that story. That's not the way it happened," Jessie said. "Payson didn't faint. He tripped."

"He tripped because he was faint."

"Faint because he hadn't eaten or slept."

The sisters bantered back and forth for a few minutes before returning to their interrogation.

"Bet you were surprised that Danny is mayor, huh?" Lavonda asked.

"He was a popular rider," Clover said flatly.

"Popular with you," Jessie mumbled, sounding suddenly unfriendly.

"We were very young."

"You're older by a couple of years, aren't you?" Jessie asked without a hint of humor.

"I don't remember," Clover lied.

"Really?" Jessie's sage-green gaze locked on to Clover. "Never knew a woman who forgot her first—"

"Danny is our baby brother," Lavonda broke in. "We might feel a little protective."

"He's a grown man," Clover reminded them. "I don't think he'd appreciate you discussing his…private life."

"Sorry about that. Like Lavonda said, he's our baby brother."

"He's lucky to have you two," she said, meaning it. Nothing like her and Knox. They had shuttled between their separated parents until Knox settled with their dad in New York and she chased tiaras with her mother in Texas.

Lavonda smiled and said, "He'll probably disown us…again…if you tell him we talked to you. So could we just keep this between us hens?" Jessie nodded agreement.

"Sure," Clover said. "One thing, though. Why did Danny agree to be mayor? He won't tell me."

"That's his story," Jessie said, "and it's time I head back to my baby. Come on, Lavonda."

"I'm proud of you. I expected us to leave at least an hour ago."

Clover watched the sisters stand and said, "It was good seeing you, and your secret is safe with me."

"Wait—one more thing," Lavonda said as Jessie gave her an impatient look. "This isn't a warning or anything. Danny is different than when he was a teen, but one thing that hasn't changed is how much he…cared for you when you were young."

Before Clover could respond, the women walked away. What did they mean by that? Danny had some torch for her? But they said to leave him alone? The bonds between siblings made her envious and confused. She didn't understand exactly how it all worked.

Time to finish her beer and head home. The chat with Danny's sisters hadn't been anything more than a little girl talk. A lot of water and everything else had passed under the bridge since Danny and she had been a couple. He might be a better kisser and had aged well. That didn't mean anything more than that she'd been working too hard and neglecting her social life. She'd take care of that as soon as this project got off the ground.

She'd spend her time reworking her numbers and tweaking her presentation for the council. She planned to win over this town and prove to her father she was the kind of executive he needed. Not much at all riding on this upcoming meeting, where she'd be laying it on the line in front of an old boyfriend who could still make her forget her name when they kissed.

Chapter 5

As he waited for the town-council meeting to start, Danny's tongue pushed at the empty space between his teeth. The dentist required payment up front and Danny was a little short. He'd been desperate enough to look on the ground around the stairs for the knocked-out tooth but he hadn't found it. He'd been nodding along to the conversation, not opening his mouth and holding his lip down over the gap. He'd never thought of himself as vain, but a big old hole in his mouth made him want to hide.

Of course, Clover, in a professional but formfitting suit, sat front and center in the audience at the council meeting. Her proposal was number two on the agenda, after the Pledge of Allegiance. He looked around at the four other members of the board. They'd called Angel Crossing home all of their lives, and like a lot of the old-timers, they didn't want their town to change. But they also understood that without change their children and grandchildren would never stay. He had a vague idea of how they might view Van Camp Worldwide's proposal. He'd been explaining his own ideas, but they were long-term solutions, not the quick one that Clover would be presenting.

The president of the board looked at his watch and hammered down the gavel. "Let's get this show on the road. I want to be home before that dancing program starts. Everyone stand for the Pledge."

Danny stood, turned to the flag and caught the gleam of Clover's auburn hair out of the corner of his eye. He would not be distracted by her or the memories of their recent kiss.

"Miss Van Camp," said Bobby Ames, the president of the board and Angel Crossing's lone attorney and taxidermist. "Your presentation, please. You have ten minutes."

Clover stood and picked up a stack of printouts. She quickly went down the table handing out the colorful and slick paper. Danny would not feel bad that he hoped her big-city presentation raised the hackles on his fellow board members.

"I am here on behalf of Van Camp Worldwide," Clover started.

"We know that, missy. Get to the point. What do you want us to do for you?"

She looked a little flustered, but her smile seemed genuine. "It's more what we can do for you all," she said, a Texas twang suddenly entering her voice, making her sound more like the girl he'd met on the junior rodeo circuit.

"Give everyone a job and a thousand dollars," Loretta Miller said.

"I wish I could help y'all out."

Boy, she was laying it on thick. Didn't she know that Arizona wasn't Texas?

"Seven minutes," Bobby said.

Clover took in a long breath and stood with regal, beauty-queen posture. "Van Camp Worldwide can provide the town with a viable plan to transform it into a new style of resort that will bring both jobs and tax revenue."

"That's what they all say," Loretta muttered to Irvin.

"The materials I've provided outline in detail our proposal." She went on before Bobby could interrupt her with another time check. "We will and have purchased properties at fair market price, but I'm before this body because we need to secure permission to rezone the Miner's Gulch corridor and demolish the properties from just north of the town hall to the railroad."

"Wait," Danny interrupted. He had properties along Miner's Gulch. He needed the zoning to remain as is for his own plan to work. He'd already sunk a chunk of his savings into his own revitalization project. She'd messed up part of his plan when she'd purchased the warehouse properties. "I talked with everyone about what I wanted to do. I'll use local labor and end up with affordable housing for residents—a mix of senior, family and singles. It's just what we need."

"When you have your plan ready to present formally, bring it in," Bobby said. "You really shouldn't even comment on Rico Pueblo."

"But I'm mayor," Danny said, not looking at Clover. "I live here and I care about Angel Crossing. I won't come in and cut out its heart, pull out my profits and move along."

"That's not how the law works," Clover said, her drawl disappearing again. "I can have a lawyer come with me next time, if need be."

"No need for that," Bobby said. "I'm a lawyer and I know what we're mucking into. Mayor, we can't make a decision that favors you because you're 'local.'"

"Why the hell not?" Loretta asked.

"President Ames," Clover said, her drawl rounding out her words. "Thank you for being so fair-minded about the concept plan. If you turn to page eight, you'll see our projections for tax revenue going forward. I believe that sort of influx will be essential for the smooth operation of—"

Danny interrupted, "But it'll cost us in police and maintenance. Think of all of the people here to party. Chief Rudy and his team are stretched to breaking just keeping up with the current population."

"Mayor," Bobby warned.

Clover went on, speaking directly to him. "The additional revenue from taxes plus the private and state-of-the art security measures will not put any more strain on the town's finances than the current situation. That is outlined on page thirty-six."

When they were teens all Clover had talked about was her hair and the sorority she'd pledge when she went to college. Where had she hidden this Clover? He scanned quickly through her material. "Wait a minute," he said. "What's this about tax forgiveness and stepped-down assessment and an amusement-tax abatement?"

"Thank you, Mayor—a very insightful question," she said sweetly, like doubly sweet sweet tea. "This front-end investment by the community will match that of Van Camp Worldwide's, making Rico Pueblo a public-private partnership."

"I thought you said you'd be giving us revenue," one of the other council members said, followed by similar questions.

There. He'd gotten her. They'd have to say no to her, which would be a yes for him when he gave his plan. Not that he really had any doubt. He'd been living in Angel Crossing and had settled in for the long haul.

The council members moved from asking about revenue on to how they would deal with the snow...if they got any this year. At this elevation, they did get the white stuff, but they were also in the high desert, so they didn't get a lot of precipitation, period.

"Mr. President," Clover said, her voice easily carrying over the continued discussions. "I hate to be pushy about this, but you see, we have deadlines to meet with the state."

"We won't be bullied," Danny said, sounding self-righteous and thinking that was just the right tone.

"I'm not trying to put the pressure on, Mayor Leigh. It's just that those are our deadlines. If we don't make them, then we'll have to pull the project. There's another location just a few miles closer to Tucson that actually might work better. I told the board at VCW, though, that Angel Crossing had the heart to be the kind of community we want. Plus, there were hardworking men and women who would be proud to be our employees."

Danny saw the faces of his fellow council members. They were eating it up. Couldn't they see she was playing them? "Really. Another town but we were the top pick. Isn't that a convenient detail to bring out now?

We don't need your kind of attention. I already have a plan to put Angel Crossing on the map. A charity bull-riding event featuring all the top cowboys. I'll even come out of retirement for this one." There. See if she could top that.

Her blue eyes narrowed and bright pink stained her cheeks. "You just came up with that. You don't have a competition organized," she said, hanging on to her twang but glaring at him.

"Are you calling me a liar?" He kept his gaze locked on her. She wasn't going to win this. It was his town and his future.

"Hot damn," Bobby said. "A bull-riding competition. You shouldn't keep events like that under your hat, Mayor. Wish we could get into all of the details tonight. We'll talk about it at our next meeting."

"What about me?" Clover asked, her smile a little less bright.

"Next month for you, too."

"That puts us awfully close to our deadline. We'd certainly be willing to underwrite the cost of a special meeting, if need be."

Bobby looked at the wall clock pointedly. "Our next meeting. We should be able to give you an answer then. Anyone else?"

Irvin piped up. "This rodeo is going to be bigger than that time the governor's car broke down and I gave him a ride back to Tucson."

"Is AJ helping?" asked Claudette, the fourth council member and receptionist at the town's clinic.

Danny stalled. "He's so busy with Santa Faye Ranch." His friend and fellow retired bull rider would probably help, when Danny asked. Of course, that would mean actually organizing the event, which he'd never done before. Why had he let Clover get to him like that?

"We expect a full report next month, Mayor," Bobby said sternly with his *Law & Order* lawyer voice.

Danny felt nothing but relief when Bobby moved along on the agenda. What was he doing? He'd always been focused, always been able to make a list of what he wanted to accomplish and then check off each item. Not now. Not since he'd really understood his retirement was permanent.

"We're adjourned." Bobby slammed the gavel. Clover shot across the room, trying to talk to Bobby, who waved her off. He was nearly running from the building, intent on his dancing show. The other council members listened to Clover. Danny didn't move, not sure if he wanted to speak with her or not.

Clover knew she was intelligently answering the council members who came up to speak with her. At the same time, she was aware of Danny standing to her left. Watching with his blue gaze and arms crossed over his chest. He looked just like a cowboy waiting to confront the black-hatted bad guy in a Western. In classes at Wharton, they hadn't discussed how to face a former lover/boyfriend during business negotiations. Maybe she should call the dean of the school and suggest that class.

"I understand your concerns," she said to Irvin. "I will take that into consideration."

"See that you do," the older man said just before he was led away by the woman who was obviously his wife.

"Mayor," the woman named Claudette said as she

walked toward the door, "we're going over to Jim's. You coming?"

Clover kept her gaze on her large professional rolling case packed with papers.

"Not tonight," he said. Clover moved, but not quite fast enough. Danny reached out and took her arm. "Need to ask you a few questions, Ms. Van Camp." His voice would easily carry to the leaving council members and she wondered if anyone else had noticed that he'd suddenly developed a lisp.

She stopped, not afraid or worried, but tell that to the quiver in the pit of her stomach. "Certainly, Mayor Leigh. I'm happy to answer any of your questions, though you might want to wait until my next presentation."

"Since you're trying to run me out of business and change my town, I think I'll ask you now."

"Certainly." She used her polite smile. She'd dealt with caterers and venue owners for her mother. Danny would be much easier than them. She knew him, or had known him. Wouldn't that give her an advantage?

His gaze stayed stern and locked on her even as he uncrossed his arms. "I'm going to ask you again—why Angel Crossing?"

He still thought this was about revenge for a teenage affair she'd forgotten long before she'd graduated from college. "VCW did a survey of properties and locations in a radius of major airports with appropriate transportation connections and with land at favorable pricing. Angel Crossing met the criteria."

"Really?"

"Really. Danny, my brother headed the project initially."

"Then you stepped in."

"Yes, I did. Knox hadn't—" She stopped herself, calculating how much she should say. "He was called to another project." That wasn't a lie. He was on another project but because he'd messed this one up.

"How, with all of the tax breaks and waiving of fees, can this provide revenue for Angel Crossing?" Danny asked, obviously changing tack.

"I explained it in the presentation. This may require short-term pain for all of us with the opportunity for long-term gain."

"Seems like we're the only ones in for 'short-term pain.'"

"VCW will be investing in land and improvements before any money comes in." He snorted. "What?" she asked, beginning to get annoyed.

"Your daddy's company doesn't do anything for nothing."

"Of course not. We wouldn't be in business if we didn't make money."

"Exactly. There's something you're not telling us in these papers." He waved his copy of her presentation.

"I'm not lying," she said. That accusation really hurt.

"Everybody lies. Didn't you lie to me?"

"What are you talking about?"

"You said it didn't matter that I was just a bull rider from a family who followed the rodeo. It mattered all right. I was just a notch in your sorority belt." His arms crossed his chest again and his eyes had gone an icy blue.

None of this should matter. They'd been teens. It'd been years ago, and had they really made any promises to each other? "What about you? Telling all of your friends? Bragging that you'd...well, you know."

His shoulders drooped a little. "I do apologize for that. What can I say? I was young."

They had been young, so young. "You didn't email or call."

He dropped his arms and shoved his hands into his pockets. Her heart clenched. He did that when he was embarrassed or uncomfortable. She was transported right back to the first time he'd asked her out.

"My friends told me that you'd moved on, you know. You were going to Italy, then on to college."

Her mother had dragged her to Milan for a crash course in fashion because Clover was expected to work on her degree and spend time at Cowgirl's Blues. "My mom and school kept me busy. You said you had no fear or something like that."

"That was about getting onto the back of a bull." He pushed his hands harder into his pockets. "Going after an older woman was something else. When you didn't even send me a postcard, I figured you'd met some sophisticated Italian guy. Probably a prince or duke or something."

She laughed loudly. "The men in Milan told me—the two or three who actually spoke English—that I was an unsophisticated girl. Beauty-pageant pretty was nothing to them. Talk about a wake-up call." She should be embarrassed to reveal such a failure on her part, but it felt comfortable with Danny, in an odd way.

"Those guys were blind," he said, taking his hands out of his pockets.

"It's fine. They were right. I was unsophisticated, and I thought I was *Vogue* pretty. I'm not."

"You're better. You're *real* pretty." His gaze locked on hers and she saw he was sincere.

"Thank you," she said with difficulty. It had taken her years to learn to take a compliment without pointing out all of her flaws. "You were really a nice boy then."

"Then?"

"I don't know you now."

"You could," he said.

"Stop. I don't want Danny, champion bull rider who all of the women love. I'm good with Danforth Leigh," she said and meant it.

"What about you? Are you still Clover Anastasia Van Camp?"

"Yes, a part of me. But a bigger part is plain old Clover, the woman with an MBA and a way with numbers."

"Good to meet you, plain old Clover."

She smiled at him, thinking that she was glad they'd cleared the air of the past. It had been silly to hang on to that hurt. "So what happened to you? How did you lose the tooth? I couldn't figure out why you were lisping until just now."

His hands went back into his pockets. "Fell." He barely moved his lips.

"Must have been some fall to knock out a tooth."

"It was a fake tooth. I knocked it out the first time when I was a kid."

"Riding?"

"Kind of. I had a minibike and thought I'd try jumping over two dogs and a goat. It didn't go as well as I'd planned." His smile looked odd because he still didn't show the empty space where the tooth had been.

A bit of silence stretched between them. "Guess I'll see you around."

"Guess so. This doesn't mean that I don't think your plan is bad."

"I've got a month to convince you otherwise."

"You ready to leave? I'll escort you out."

She felt the whiplash of being thrown back to those faraway days when Danny acted like a "pardon me, ma'am" cowboy. He was back and it still made her heart flutter. She needed to stop that right in its tracks. "I'm a grown woman with pepper spray and big-city experience. I'll be fine."

He just looked at her and waited for her to precede him. She wouldn't allow him to follow her home. She needed to wrest back control. She didn't want to feel like the helpless little woman. She'd given up that role years ago.

"My car is there." She pointed. "I know you want to meet up with your friends."

"They'll wait." He didn't move. Again, she was older, wiser. She would not cause a scene. She walked with purpose to her car, started it up and waved as she pulled out. Danny stood watching her drive away. She couldn't decide how that made her feel. Then she told herself the only feeling she had was satisfaction from settling their ancient and very personal hurts—no matter the recent kiss. Now she could move forward on strictly professional footing.

Chapter 6

Danny amazed himself. Maybe he should give up on being a builder and become a charity ride event promoter or organizer or whatever because he'd organized the hell out of the first annual Save Angel Crossing (SAC) Bull-Riding Extravaganza. He had the date booked at the community college's arena, he'd gotten two of his old sponsors to put up cash to help with advertising costs and prizes, and he'd called ten of his former riding buddies and all ten had said hell yes. He'd roped (he was getting good at puns) AJ into talking to a stock contractor. The goal was to get the animals for free or, at worst, a huge discount. Of course, Danny had had to tell everyone he would be competing. They said that would draw the crowds. "A 'champeen' back in the saddle."

"You sure about this, buddy?" AJ asked during another call for this damned charity ride that had taken over every one of Danny's waking hours—not spent working on properties or dealing with Maggie May—as he'd decided to call Mama—or fantasizing about Clover.

"Why wouldn't I be sure? Two years isn't long. Plus, you're getting easy bulls, right?"

"Ha. Dave said he wants to try out new stock, ones that he's sure will be in the money. He figures this is a way to get them a name, reputation."

"What the—"

"Cowboys who want things for free can't be choosy," AJ said.

"Yeah, well, *farmers* and their significant others who will benefit from a charity bull ride should look out for the guy who is making it happen." Danny had decided once he got the event rolling that any money they made (which was still not a sure thing) would go to the community garden project and the rehab of the old theater into an under-roof farmers' market.

"You offered," AJ said. "Besides, you'll draw in more riders and spectators with challenging bulls. You know that."

He did know that. He also knew that his hand and sometimes part of his arm went from sort-of to totally numb without warning. "Since you're so excited about these bulls, I'll expect you to talk the two new champs into coming."

There was a long silence and finally AJ said, "I'll do it, but it's for Pepper. Gotta go. I've got llama training."

"What?"

"The yarn from the llamas isn't as popular, so we're

going to train them to carry packs and rent them out for hikes."

"That's just wrong in so many ways."

"They've got to earn their keep," AJ said and hung up.

So, Danny had no choice. He'd have to get back to bull-rider training and do it fast. Until he could be sure about his arm, he didn't want to ask AJ to help him find a practice bull. Angel Crossing didn't have a gym but that was no excuse for not getting into riding shape.

Best to get on this now. Waiting would mean he might talk himself out of it. Danny searched online for new ideas and workout routines that he could do without special equipment. There was one that used a balance ball—something about working on his core by standing on the unsteady ball. He found a basketball at the back of his closet. He needed to balance for fifteen minutes at a time to get the maximum benefit.

He found a rerun of one of his PBR championship rides to watch. Perfect. He should analyze what he would need to do to compete against his friends—friendly competition or not.

"Time to get in shape," he told the empty living room. He put one foot on the ball. Good. Then he transferred his weight to the leg on the ball and everything went south faster than a Texas two-step. His arms pinwheeled as the ball slid from under his foot. He overcorrected, flew forward, twisting his body until his head connected solidly with the edge of the TV stand. He yelled.

On his back on the floor, Danny noticed that more than a few flies had gone to the great beyond in the ceiling's light fixture. Maggie May whined and nudged his ear with her cold, wet nose. Ugh. His head hurt but he didn't have a concussion. He knew about those. He needed to get up and ice his head to keep the throbbing from turning into a goose egg.

Why couldn't he have just done old-fashioned sit-ups to strengthen his core? What the hell kind of idea was it to stand on a damned ball? He sat up. No dizziness, so he stood. Blood dripped onto his jeans. Damn. He ached in other places now that he was upright. He pulled up his T-shirt and held it against his head. He'd better not need stitches. He couldn't afford that on top of the tooth that needed to be repaired. The butterfly bandages in the cabinet would have to do.

In the bathroom mirror, he saw the cut, high on his head, was a mess of bloody hair and ragged skin. Dang it. Good thing it was Saturday and he didn't have any work. He looked at the cut again. He needed his hair trimmed or he'd never get the butterfly bandages to stick. He considered using his razor, but even he knew dragging a sharp blade along the open ends of the wound would be a dumb move. Plus, he'd have to do it backward in the mirror.

AJ. His friend would have clippers. They had to use something like that on the llamas and alpacas at the ranch. AJ would also keep his mouth shut if Danny asked. Probably. Before he could talk himself out of it, he called.

"What do you want now? Bulls that have been broke to a saddle?" AJ asked instead of saying "Hey."

"Can you get away and come into town?"

"I told you I'm working with the llamas."

"Right. Well—" Hell. What would he do now?

"What's wrong?"

"I fell."

"From a bull?"

"Sure. I dragged a bull up to my apartment."

"If you fell, call 911 or drive to the ER in Tucson."

"No way," Danny said. "This isn't worth their time. I just need you to clip away the hair. Scissors won't get close enough and I can't shave it."

"Fine. Come on out to the ranch. You owe me, though, especially since I'm guessing you don't want to involve Pepper."

Danny was proud that he'd come up with such an easy and cheap solution. AJ would clip his hair so the cut could be bandaged. He looked down at his blood-stained T-shirt and picked up another almost clean shirt from a pile. Now he needed ice to keep the pounding to a bongo-drum level.

He walked into his little kitchen and heard whimpering from Maggie May, who'd wedged herself into the small closet where he kept cleaning supplies, including rags—which had become her nest—along with discarded shoes she'd pushed out of her way. The dog was licking at…a puppy. He looked down at Maggie May, who seemed proud of her accomplishment. The pup was coal black except for a pink nose, a white toe on the left front paw and a spot of white on one ear. Cute little critter. It squeaked and squawked as Maggie May nudged and cleaned him. Danny couldn't leave the dog. He called AJ and told him about the puppies. His friend agreed to drive into town with his clippers.

Danny sat against the fridge watching the dog. Enough time passed that he had refilled his towel with ice. His skin was nice and numb but a headache was building. He hoped AJ got here soon because the wound just wouldn't stop bleeding. Maggie May yipped loudly and he scooted back to her. The first puppy lay close to his mother and Danny expected to see another little wiggling body. Nothing. Maggie May's sides heaved and she whined. He had no idea if this was normal or not. He reached out to pet her and she snapped at him. She must be in pain. She yipped loudly and then barked. He looked—no puppy. And no sign of a puppy.

Should he call Clover? They'd taken care of the dog together and it seemed like something bad was happening. The dog's side rippled with what he assumed was a contraction. His head was throbbing in time with the movement.

"Maggie May," he murmured, slowly reaching out his hand to see if she would allow him to touch her. She raised her lip over her teeth but didn't growl. Laying his hand on her side, he could feel the contractions. He petted her slowly until his hand was on her hindquarters so he could move her tail out of the way.

Dang. It looked bad, her legs smeared with blood and gummy pink wetness. Could Pepper help with this? He moved as Maggie May barked loudly and the door shook with a knock. Good. That was AJ. He'd owned dogs. Maybe he'd have an idea of what they should do.

Danny got to his feet, the pain in his head peaking as Maggie M whimpered. "We'll get you help, sweetheart," he said, hurrying to the door, the nearly melted ice still clutched to his head.

"AJ," Danny said before the door was fully open.

"Jeez, Danny. Are you trying to reenact *The Texas Chainsaw Massacre*?" Pepper asked as she entered the apartment.

Before Danny could say anything, AJ broke in. "She caught me with clippers and bandages. She knew I was lying when I said it was nothing."

The dog yowled.

"What the heck is that?" Pepper asked.

"Maggie May. She's having her puppies and I think one's stuck. Can you check her first?" Danny asked, relieved that Pepper was there.

"You," she said, pointing to Danny, "sit down. AJ, take one of the pads from my bag and press it hard on his thick skull."

"Hey—" Danny started.

"No use arguing when she's got that tone. That's her 'physician's assistant Pepper in charge' look, too. Don't fight it, man."

"Let's have a look... Lordy be," Pepper said.

"What?" Danny asked, surging to his feet. Had the dog died? Had the puppy died?

"Sit down before you fall down," Pepper said with authority. "Everything is fine. While we were talking Maggie May here got down to business. There are three puppies."

"Three? Wow."

"I don't think we're done. I feel one more."

"Four puppies. Oh, crap. How are we going to find homes for all of them?"

"Sit so I can push this really hard on the cut," AJ said. "You know that our daughter is on a girls' weekend with her Grana and Grammy C. Pepper and I had planned a whole weekend alone together. You're lucky I answered the phone."

"Sorry, man," Danny mumbled. His bull-riding buddy had settled nicely into family life with his daughter and Pepper. The two hadn't announced when the wedding was but it couldn't be far off.

"This looks like it's going to need more than butterflies. How did you do it?"

Danny tried to think of a lie but his brain felt mushy between the ache of the cut and his worry for Maggie May. "I should probably have called Clover."

"Really?" AJ asked as he pressed the bandage back on the wound.

Danny saw stars as the pain went from throb to spike. "She helped rescue her," he rasped.

"Ahh," AJ said.

"What?"

"Nothing."

"It's something."

"Nah. Just remembering the two of you from back when. Attached at the hip—and lips—that whole summer."

"We were young," Danny said. "She's got a New York life now." He hoped that would end the conversation.

"Four puppies," Pepper said, ending AJ's unwelcome comments. "Three boys and one girl. Now I'll check you. AJ, get the suture kit."

Danny might be a big bad bull rider, but he'd never liked getting stitches. He wiggled in the chair, trying to get his brave on. "How many do you think?"

"A few," Pepper said. "I'll numb it up." She patted his shoulder as she looked at the wound. "Get the clippers, too, AJ. I'm going to have to shear him before I start."

Clover stood on the wooden steps at the back of the diner that led up to Danny's small apartment. She hesitated even though she had a very valid reason for stopping by. She'd heard about the puppies and his stitches. She was only interested in the canines. She felt responsible for Mama. If she hadn't hit her with the car, though, the creature would probably have given birth out in the open. *What a way to justify hitting a dog, Clover.*

She moved before she had a chance to talk herself out of the visit. She knocked. A "woof" came from inside. She didn't hear any movement that sounded human. She waited. She knocked again. More barking. What if Danny had passed out? What if he'd landed on Mama and she and her puppies were trapped under him? No, that wasn't likely since the dog was barking.

Clover tried the door. Most people in Angel Crossing didn't lock up during the day. The handle turned. She opened it, yelling out for Danny as she walked in. Nobody other than Mama and the puppies.

The mother dog raced past Clover and outside. Nuts. The puppies mewled and cried. Clover took in their fat, wriggling bodies, then turned to look out the door. Mama was at the bottom of the stairs sniffing around the small parking lot. She probably just needed to go potty, but Clover wasn't going to take a chance on the dog staying away from car wheels. How would she explain it to Danny? *I broke into your apartment, let your dog out and she got hit...again.* She went down the stairs and stood by Mama as she took care of business. Back inside, the dog quickly settled back into her box with her puppies.

Clover was surprised by the number of little animals. They were all so different looking. Brown, black, white, spotted. Their coats went from smooth to rough to curly to long and silky. She couldn't imagine what sort of dog had fathered them. Clover leaned over the box, reaching out to touch the white one, who looked to be the smallest.

"What the hell are you doing?" Danny asked with fierce anger.

"Oh," Clover said, snatching back her hand and whirling to face him. "Jeez Louise," she gasped, trying to take in his half-shaved head and raw wound. And he was sunburned.

He closed the door to the bedroom and took two large steps toward her. "I should call the police. Breaking and entering."

"The door was open. I heard about your head—" she gestured to his sore-looking scalp "—and when you didn't answer I got worried."

"I was working. I'm here for lunch and a little aloe."

She wanted to leave but her feet didn't move. "The puppies look good." That was a safe topic. She knew how to make small talk. She'd been taught the art by her mother and Grandmother Van Camp. Both women prided themselves on being able to start a conversation with anyone.

"I only have half an hour break. Was there anything else?"

"I guess not. Sorry about walking in." Her feet still didn't move. "I have sunscreen if you need it." She rummaged in her purse.

He stared at her. "Can't wear my hat," he finally said, turning toward his kitchen.

His stitches would make a hat uncomfortable. "What about a visor? Like you wear on a golf course?"

He snorted. "No." He dug in the refrigerator. He didn't tell her to go.

"Sit," she said. "I'll make you something. Least I can do for breaking into your place and for you taking such good care of Mama. Why don't you go slather yourself with aloe. You might want to get a bandanna to cover your—" She gestured to his red scalp.

"Her name's Maggie May," he said and left.

"Maggie May? Like that woman in that song. She was an older woman, too." She wouldn't think too hard on what that might or might not mean. Talking to the dog, Clover said, "I would never have believed it, but Danny Leigh can actually look ugly." She found fixings for a sandwich and soup in the fridge. She poured him a glass of iced tea and told herself she'd leave as soon as he got back from the bathroom…and she had a chance to visit with the puppies. Could she take one for herself? How would that work in a New York apartment and with her crazy hours? When her father finally named her CFO, her life would never be the same. She'd happily put in the twelve-hour days, the weekends and holidays. She really wanted to sink her teeth into the numbers.

While Danny was still doing whatever, Clover strolled to the pile of puppies. The fluffy white baby dog gnawed on her finger as the others fought over positions for the best milk.

"You'd better get back in there or you'll be hungry," she said softly as she nudged the puppy toward its mother.

"Hulk is the littlest. His brothers and sister push him out of the way," Danny said from behind her.

"He's very cute. I'm sure he'll be the first to be adopted." She turned around to tell Danny his lunch was ready and burst out laughing. His face and head were covered in green aloe vera gel. He looked like a swamp monster who'd been in the sun too long.

In addition to his scalp and nose, Danny's cheeks reddened. "I don't have any of the clear stuff."

She really did try to not laugh. "Now I know why they sell the clear stuff. You're sporting a facial-gone-wrong vibe now." She laughed again as a blob of the gel fell to his shirt and he frowned.

"Great. I'm going to have to change." He stomped off.

A well-timed retreat was called for. "I'm going, Danny. Food's on the table and let me know about the puppies."

"Wait," he yelled from his bedroom, which was just a few feet from the kitchen. Actually, everything in the apartment was just a few feet away.

He came back pulling on a T-shirt, his body revealed from his taut abs to his well-muscled chest and arms. That was certainly different from when they'd been young. He'd been teen-boy skinny. No more.

"The puppies and Maggie May will need to go to the vet. I can't take time away from my projects. Would you be able to take them?"

"Absolutely. Just let me know when. My schedule is fairly flexible."

"Other than when you're outbidding legitimate businessmen."

"My offer was legitimate and so is VCW's proposal."

"The town council will decide that," he said. Looking down at her, his gaze was stern and stubborn.

"You're right. I want the same thing for Angel Crossing as you do. It's just that VCW and I are going about it from a different avenue."

"More like a major highway."

There was no use going over the argument. "The food is on the table. You said you didn't have a lot of time."

"Crap. Maggie May needs to go out."

"I already did that. She did her business and everything."

"Thanks," he said, and it sounded like he meant it. Why did that little word start a glow in her? This stubborn cowboy—who currently looked like an extra in a horror film—could make her hot one second and mad as anything the next.

"Happy to help. Let me know about the appointment." She fled the apartment, not liking that she no longer wanted to laugh or hit him. Instead, she wanted to kiss him. The spark between them was still there.

Clover might have learned early on how to put on a good face for the world, but she'd also learned over the years how to be completely honest with herself. The honest-to-God truth was that she had the hots for Danforth Clayton Leigh. Wasn't that just a kick in the head?

Chapter 7

Of course Clover was at Jim's. Danny just wanted to sit on a bar stool, enjoy his brew and stumble home. But, no, Miss Steer Princess had to be in his bar. To be fair, there was only one bar in Angel Crossing, but she could have gone to Tucson. In fact, she was the kind of woman who looked like she'd never stepped foot outside of a big city.

He ordered his beer and glared at Clover and Pepper. They were probably plotting the downfall of every man in town.

"What's got you in a mood, Mayor?" asked Rita, Anita's twin sister. "That woman here to buy up the whole town? Would think you'd like that, seeing as how you own properties that she just might want to buy."

"Maybe I'm not selling. I've got plans."

"Yep?"

He took a gulp of beer. "She wants to change everything. She and her father and Van Camp Worldwide. What kind of name is that?"

Rita shrugged. "Heard council might say yes to her proposition."

"They're still deciding. Irvin and Loretta are fighting about it. It might mean a lot of people will end up being bought out or pushed out. I read through what was submitted by Clo... Van Camp Worldwide. The community gardens will go, which is why I can't imagine why Pepper is over there talking with her."

"Keep your enemies closer," Rita said cryptically.

He'd like to get close with this particular enemy. Although he was pretty sure that was his lackluster love life talking. Look at his friend Darren. He'd gotten married two years ago, just as Danny "retired," and now his first baby was on the way. The numbness in Danny's hand and arm had been why he'd quit, but could it be he left bull riding for another reason, like one having to do with settling down?

Except he was spending all of his time and money buying properties and fixing them up for other people. Exactly how was any of that getting him closer to being a family man? The pressure from his mom had even eased now that she had a grandbaby. He was sure Lavonda would soon announce that she and Jones, her Scotsman, were expecting. Lavonda had even told him Clover's plan might be good for her fledgling trail and guide business, appealing to people looking for the treasure that her archaeologist husband insisted was still out there.

He signaled for a refill. He had thinking to do. He couldn't believe he hadn't been accosted by a resident.

Usually when he was out, people stopped by to say hi, complain or pass along tidbits of gossip.

"Looks like that lady is stealing your thunder," Rita said as she gave him the refilled mug.

He shrugged.

"Are the two of you an item?"

"When we were teenagers."

"Heard you were canoodling on her porch."

"I wouldn't call it canoodling." What the hell did that even mean?

Rita pushed at her 1970s bleached blond hair. "Necking, then? Swapping spit? Playing tonsil hockey?"

He hoped the bar's dimness hid his blush. He tried a nonchalant shrug.

"She'd have to have a lot of intestinal fortitude to neck with you now. No offense, Mayor, but you're missing a tooth, half of your hair is gone and your face is peeling like a molting snake."

Danny wasn't vain. At least he hadn't thought he was until he'd looked in the mirror the last two mornings. "All temporary."

Rita nodded. "She looks high maintenance. Check out the purse and those boots. Still, she does drink beer and even ate deep-fried jalapeños."

"Her mama's a Texan. Daddy's from New York City."

"Really? Now, that's interesting." Rita turned from Danny. "Hold on. I'm coming," she said to someone over her shoulder. "You were too pretty before. You're finally starting to look like a real man. Clover seems like a woman who can appreciate that."

Clover's auburn hair tumbled down her back in big snaky curls and he could imagine the curve of her hips and breasts, just what a man would want next to him in bed. Soft enough for comfort, but strong, too. Clover turned suddenly, like she'd read his thoughts, and smiled with a devilish curl that heated him up. Pepper turned to see where Clover was looking. Damn. Pepper waved him over.

"Hey," he said to Pepper. "Clover." He tipped his head, missing his hat, which was still too heavy to rest on the stitches.

"We were just talking about you," Pepper said with a gleam.

"You were?"

"I explained to Clover how you helped me and AJ and that you worked miracles with those state agencies. I think you're wasting your talent here in Angel Crossing. You could run for state office. Maybe not now, but when you get your tooth fixed and your hair grows back."

"I like Angel Crossing," he said automatically.

"I know you do," Pepper said, "but you're still young. You don't want to be stuck here."

"You're no older than I am." He tried to not notice how well Clover's shirt fit. "I think going back to bull riding would be better for me than politics."

Pepper laughed. Clover looked both surprised and like she cared.

"I'd say the majority of people coming to SAC are coming to see you ride," Pepper said. "I bet if you ran for office, you'd win because everyone would remember your name and your bull riding."

"Is that why you're opposing my plan? Because it'll look good when you run for office?" Clover asked.

Was she serious? "I told you that I was a write-in for mayor and only won after a card draw. I don't have any political ambitions."

"Whether you do or not," Pepper said, "you should think about it. You could make a difference. Now that Clover has company, I'm heading home before my daughter and husband think I've gotten lost."

Neither he nor Clover had a chance to stop her. Danny stood for a moment, not sure what he should do. He sat. Clover took a sip of beer. "You want another one?" he asked.

"Not yet," she said, giving him a look he couldn't read. "Why wouldn't you want to run for state office?"

"Because I have a business here and a commitment. I take both of those seriously." Now, of course, he might not have much of a business if Van Camp Worldwide got its way. Under Clover's plan, his properties couldn't be converted into homes or even apartments. Even if he got out of his project, he doubted he could go back on the road with bull riding. He couldn't do what he'd done for years with an arm and hand that weren't 100 percent.

"So why did you retire from bull riding? You still haven't told me."

And I won't, he thought to himself, although it would be easy to tell Clover the whole story. He'd always been able to talk to her. "It was time."

"That's what you said to the reporters. But what was the real reason? Your sister Lavonda is a PR genius. I bet she told you to say that."

"I didn't talk to Lavonda or anyone in the family about it." He took a long drink. "I'm getting another. You sure I can't get you a refill?" She shook her head.

He was supposed to be here to forget everything, not to examine his life choices. He pushed his mug forward for Rita. Why was he beginning to feel like he was at another crossroads, like the night he'd flipped the card and become mayor? He shook his head. He was getting as fanciful as Pepper's mother, Faye, who believed in astrological signs and energy vortices.

Rita started to draw his draft and talked over her shoulder to him. "I see you're getting reacquainted. You two look real good together, you know."

"That so. She's a good-looking woman."

"More than that," Rita said. "She's got more than cotton candy between her ears."

"She's got an MBA." That little fact still stunned him. The Clover he'd known had been all about the clothes and the hair.

Rita set down his mug but didn't let it go. "You're not the kind of cowboy who should be alone."

"Not much choice in Angel Crossing."

"Seems like you've got a good chance right there." She nodded to the table. "She watched you walk up here. You know women like to look, too. Why she'd want you now, who knows?" Rita pushed the beer at him.

Should he be taking dating advice from the woman who served him drinks? Why the hell not? Ending his dry spell with an old lover just made sense now that he thought about it. He might not be the smartest cowboy, but even he knew that she'd enjoyed kissing him. She'd not be staying in Angel Crossing for very long. That would mean no chance of a messy breakup where he had to see her every day like he would with anyone else in town. He smiled without showing off his missing tooth. Dang. Why couldn't he have come to this decision before his disasters or a week from now when they'd all be healed or replaced?

"Danny, I know you just got a drink," Clover said

as he sat down and took his first sip, "but let's go back to my place."

He dropped the mug to the table, splashing himself with beer. "Damn it."

Clover swallowed her laughter and nervousness. It wasn't that she was a shy, retiring wallflower. She was a grown woman who'd traveled the world and was the next in line to run her father's business. She'd decided that she wanted closure on her relationship with Danny. For her, that meant sleeping with him again and proving she was good at it. She might have been older than Danny when they'd first hooked up, but he'd had a lot of make-out experience.

Danny looked down at his wet crotch. She laughed. He gave her the half smile that had always gotten her hot and bothered. "Go back to your house to talk about Angel Crossing?" he asked.

"Maybe." The longer he took to leave with her, the more nerve she lost. If they didn't leave in the next five minutes, she'd totally chicken out.

"What else could be between us?" he asked, his gaze steady on hers.

She stood and moved closer so the entire bar wouldn't hear her. There'd be enough talk when they left together. "Bad sex."

"Bad?"

"Really bad. The worst. Is that how you want me to remember you?" She'd play to his ego, not that her own didn't need stroking. She smiled at her double entendre. She must really be losing it if that amused her.

"I have learned a lot since then," he said softly, leaning into her so his lips just brushed her ear. "And I'm still the Boy Scout and I always make sure I'm 'prepared.'"

She shivered. *Oh, my.* "Me, too," she said, turning her head to brush her lips along the cords of his neck, where she could feel the quiver that raced through him. Good to know she wasn't the only one who was affected. She was doing this. She would prove to him she'd grown up and was a woman through and through. More important, she'd prove to herself that she could get over this old flame. "So, what are we waiting for?"

His blue gaze stayed locked on hers, searching. Then he smiled, covering his missing tooth but still looking sexy, dangerous and strangely familiar. "Ladies first—as it always should be."

"Can't argue with that, can I?" she asked softly, starting out of the bar, knowing that Danny would follow her. She turned off the numbers part of her brain, the part that would tell her being with Danny might be a mistake. This wasn't about her brain. This was about getting emotional closure.

The night was cool at this elevation, even if the days were warm. Danny wrapped his arm around her and she snuggled into his warmth, drinking in the comfort of his nearness. An awful lot for one hug.

"You haven't seen any ghosts?" he asked as they walked along the quiet streets.

"Not even an odd noise."

"Disappointed?"

"A little. Who wouldn't want to see at least one ghost in her life?"

"I almost thought that's what you were when I saw you again."

"Not very flattering." She wasn't sure where this was going or how it was making her feel.

"I'd been thinking about that summer recently, and then there you were. Maybe *surreal* is the better word."

"What about now? What does this feel like?"

"This," he said into her hair as she felt his light kiss, "is where I need to be."

"I agree. Come on—let's get moving." She rolled out of his hug, took his hand and tugged him toward her house. No more thinking, no more worrying.

She pulled him inside, closed the door and pushed him up against it so she could kiss him with everything that had been pent up inside her. She slipped her tongue into his mouth. He opened to her, allowing her to explore before he delved into her mouth. Then his hands cupped her buttocks, pulling her up against him. She dug her fingers into his shoulders to hold herself steady and to make sure that he stayed right where he was. They fit together even better than she remembered. She started to melt. She wanted him, but she also wanted this to last, wanted to drag out the pleasure to make sure he wouldn't forget her and walk away.

She paused. This was supposed to be about closure, not convincing him to stick around. She kissed him long and deep, forcing herself not to think, losing herself in the pleasure of his calloused fingers caressing her sides and slipping into the top of her jeans.

"This way," she finally said. They would be doing more than necking, and they weren't going to do it against the front door. She made it three steps before he pulled her back to him, snuggling her butt into his crotch and wrapping her in his arms so he could gently cup her breasts. Her head fell back onto his shoulder with pleasure. He took advantage of her vulnerable neck, nibbling at the sensitive skin. From the tips of her breasts to the place just behind her ear, Clover had become one exposed nerve ending. She wrenched away to lead him to the bedroom. She wanted him, but in her own way. He followed, taking time to stroke her shoulder, his breath coming in deep gusts.

The bedroom was tiny with just a double bed. She hadn't had much choice and hadn't planned to share it. At least it would mean getting close. "Come here," she said. "I want to undress you."

"Undress me?" Danny asked, his hands loose at his sides. The rest of his body was as a taut as a bow.

She didn't say more, but approached him and started with the snaps on his shirt, opening one, kissing him and then putting her hands under the fabric to feel every inch of his skin. She stopped on the ridge of a scar.

He turned his darkened gaze on her. "Few stitches when I got pinned while moving cattle for a friend." She nodded. Another button, more skin. Warm with the tough muscle underneath that made her feel at once protected and on edge. He was so strong. She had to give him her complete trust. This man who was nearly a stranger, except he wasn't.

"I would never hurt you," he said, reading her thoughts through her skin.

She shivered for a moment, but shook her head. "You still have on too many clothes." She tugged at his jeans. He stopped her, his hand grappling for his wallet. She knew what he wanted and didn't let him search for the protection. With a knowing grin, she pulled out the condom, tossed the wallet and shimmied down his underwear. He sprang free, proving he was more than interested in what she'd started. She pushed against him until he lay on the bed.

"You," he rasped. "Your clothes."

She took off her shirt.

"The bra," he said. "Undo it slowly."

She complied, trying to think about the sexy striptease she'd seen in movies, except things didn't go exactly as planned when she couldn't get the hooks to unhook. Danny helped, placing a kiss on her shoulder.

"Out of those jeans, princess," he commanded.

She stood so he could watch and slowly peeled out of her pants. She stood naked, vulnerable and not feeling as powerful as she'd hoped. He sat up and reached out his hands to grab her hips and pull her toward him, placing a kiss on her belly, making her shiver with delight.

When she was on the bed with him, he took the condom from her and...they were going to do this. He entered her and she raised herself to him. Their hips slapped together in an out-of-sync rhythm. Then she leaned forward, moved and their foreheads knocked. Oh, no, not again. It was like the first time—awkward, uncoordinated and unsatisfying.

Danny held himself still until Clover relaxed. "Princess," he whispered in her ear as he pulled her onto her side with him. So they could face each other. So they were equals. "I want to be with you more than I've ever wanted anything. But I want us to both want this. Tell me what to do."

"Kiss me," Clover said. So he did, softly tasting her lips while his fingers skimmed her back. She heated and softened again. He moved. She moaned into his mouth.

"Better?" he asked.

Clover used her legs to pull him close, his body and hands loving her. She didn't want it to end and was afraid she couldn't take more.

"Clover, I'm going to take you to the moon and back." And he did.

Chapter 8

Danny stood over Clover, watching her sleep. The moonlight from the window highlighted the creamy perfection of her skin. Her lips were red and puffy. They'd proved more than once they were no longer awkward teens. He hoped this one night would be enough. But what if it wasn't?

He'd faced his fears more than once; he could do it again. First, he needed to get out of Dead Man's Cottage. There were the puppies and Maggie May to care for and his apartment was probably a mess. He looked down at Clover again. One last time. He leaned forward, but, no, not one more kiss. She mumbled in her sleep and turned under the sheets. He held his breath. She snuggled into the pillow. Turning away, he slipped out of the house, stopping his shout when he stubbed his toe hard on the front porch chair. He sat on the steps to pull his boot on over his now aching foot. What was it about Clover being back in his life and his quotient of accidents hitting an all-time high? At this rate, he'd collect more injuries than he had in all the time he'd been a bull rider.

The streets of Angel Crossing were quiet and dark as he made his way across town. He heard Maggie May whining from his landing and hurried to open the door. She rushed past to take care of business. He checked on the puppies. All fine. Moments later Maggie May came up for a pet before climbing back in with her babies. He went to bed, but he couldn't sleep.

Clover wasn't for him. She wanted to ruin his town by turning it into a place where people like her and her family would be comfortable. And where people like him and the rest of the town would be the employees. Angel Crossing was a workingman's town—Ford pickups, Wrangler jeans and Spam. He'd read in her proposal that there would be Michelin restaurants and spas behind the wooden facades. That would just take the heart out of the town. Lem's general store and Jim's would be gone. Maybe not right away but how could they compete? Those kinds of businesses, along with the people who patronized them, were what made Angel Crossing Angel Crossing. Take that away and what did you have? Some cardboard town.

He shouldn't have been surprised by the type of plan she'd presented. Clover had been a princess in more ways than one. He always figured she'd gone after him because he wasn't from her world and would upset her parents. He wondered if, years later, things were much different. Maybe not, but he wasn't the same. He needed to worry about Angel Crossing.

He turned onto his side, closing his eyes and telling himself to go to sleep. He had a job tomorrow, and he needed to talk to and convince another property owner that Danny's plan for the town was better than Clover's. He also needed to get back to training so he didn't disgrace himself at the charity bull-riding extravaganza. His life was too full to worry about what he may or may not want to do with Clover, Miss Steer Princess.

Danny's leg jittered as he waited for the council to get to the only item on the agenda that mattered: Van Camp Worldwide's requests...blah, blah, blah. The legalese Bobby Ames had used couldn't hide the fact that the company's—Clover's—request would change his town. Instead of using his powers of persuasion to talk business, he'd gone to bed with Clover. Stupid. Stupid. Stupid. A week and a half later, more and more Angelites seemed to be on her side.

Bobby said in his best *Law & Order* voice, "We will now consider Van Camp Worldwide's Rico Pueblo proposal. Is there a representative from the company here?"

Of course there was. She was sitting in the front row, looking like a cross between a Texas beauty queen and a corporate tight ass. How did she do that and look sexy on top of all of it? Her lush lips...the bright color of her clothes making her skin look like silk and her hair like a flame. Dear Lord.

Clover stood. "Thank you, Mr. President."

"Call me Bobby."

She smiled and Danny refused to be jealous. Bobby was old enough to be her daddy.

"Bobby, then," Clover said. "I've spoken with all of you as well as many members of the business community. Everyone has been very welcoming. They've understood the advantages of VCW's plan to transform your community and provide economic viability. For those looking for work and those looking to start or grow their businesses, I can see a range of possibilities."

"What about the cost of living?" Danny asked.

"Taxes will decrease with the influx of business. Plus, there will be opportunities for increased services for residents," she said, giving him a look that was all business.

"Hey, Bobby, I've got a question." Anita from Jim's spoke up. Her twin, Rita, sat next to her looking stern and unhappy. Good. At least two people were on his side. "What about those of us who already got a good business? I didn't see anything on your plan about that."

"If you look at page—"

"You're bringing in competition," said Lem, the owner of the general store.

"We'll also be bringing renewed interest in Angel Crossing," she said before being interrupted by a number of angry voices.

Finally Bobby cracked down his gavel. "That's enough. I will have order, and if I have to call the chief to arrest the disrupters, I will." The crowd quieted but not happily. Danny kept silent. It looked like he might have more support than he'd hoped.

Clover started again. "VCW is well aware of the worries and challenges of a project of this scope and importance. For that reason, even after we receive approval, we will continue to have open discussions with residents and property owners."

Loretta spoke up from her council seat. "I like you and your plan. Angel Crossing has been dying for years.

Sure, we got that farmers' market, but that's not going to save us."

"She's right," Irvin, her husband, said, "and you offered our neighbor a fair price for his property."

Just like Danny had been able to read the shift of muscle that told him exactly how the bull he was sitting on would twist or turn, he felt the crowd starting to sway to a different direction. Dang. How had she done that and what could he say to get them back to opposing the plan?

"I also believe with these changes, your children and grandchildren will want to call Angel Crossing—Rico Pueblo—home," Clover said.

That was exactly what the older residents wanted to hear. They'd been complaining that their families were being split apart because there were no jobs or much of anything else for the young people.

"Wait," Danny said, but Anita talked over him.

"I saw that New York City snoot nose—" she pointed at Clover "—hit a dog with her car and not even stop." The audience gasped and glared in unison.

"I didn't—"

"I've seen the mayor caring for the dog and the puppies," Rita added.

"You hit a mama dog?" someone else in the audience said.

Danny felt the shift again, just like a bull ready to move from a right-to a left-footed spin. He could keep the bull on its current path or have it switch feet for a new turn. He'd guessed at the truth of the dog's injury and Clover's part in it, even though she hadn't fully confessed what had happened to him or anyone else, as far as he knew. He wanted to win this vote for the Angel

Crossing he could imagine. If he won because he didn't stand up and explain the whole story, would he really have won? Hells yes. But he'd still feel guilty about it.

"Wait a minute," he said into the grumbling. "That's not exactly the way it happened."

"Are you calling me a liar?" Anita asked with a glare.

"No, ma'am." He gave her his sweetest smile, now back to normal since his tooth had been replaced. "It's just that you didn't have a chance to see what happened then or what Ms. Van Camp has done since the accident."

He couldn't decide if he saw relief, surprise or something warmer in Clover's bluebonnet eyes.

"Let the mayor speak," Bobby said.

"Miss Clover did hit the dog—" Danny started.

"See?" Rita and Anita said together.

"But—" Danny talked over them "—it was an accident. The dog came out of nowhere. That's happened to everyone at some time. A critter just ends up in your path." The bull was going into a spin and he'd hold on till the bell. "She stopped and tracked down the dog with my help. Then we took her out to Pepper, who patched her up. Miss Clover bought Maggie May a collar, food and everything else she needed. She's done what she could for her. She didn't mean to hit her. She might be here to change Angel Crossing, but she understands one thing about us. We look after our own and those less able to care for themselves. We help those who need it and don't ask for anything in return."

Hell, damnation and fire ants. How was she supposed to handle him being nice to her? Clover had been sure he'd let the bus driven by the twins from Jim's run her over. Instead, he'd defended her, even though he had been fighting hard against her plan. He didn't look at her now, keeping his gaze on the crowd. She couldn't say her presentation had gone well, but it hadn't gone badly either. She'd been trying everything she could think of to help the town understand what an opportunity VCW was offering them, their children and even their children's children.

"I think we've heard enough for tonight," Bobby said, looking at the audience and then at his fellow council members. "But I don't believe we're ready for a vote. I want to have our state representative go over your numbers, Miss Van Camp. There's also that section about options I'd like to review." The other council members bobbed their heads. She couldn't look at anyone because she didn't want them to see her disappointment and worry.

She smiled politely, as her Texas mama and grandmama had taught her. "I understand completely, but if you have any questions or concerns, I would love to address them now." Clover waited but no one said anything. She pressed on. "I understand the due diligence the council must have to ensure that Angel Crossing's interests are best met. However, I do want to point out that this plan is time sensitive and delaying a decision could negatively impact our project." She didn't need to let them know that it might also mean her father showing up. Something she didn't want. The entire reason she was here was to prove she could do the job better than her brother. Good enough to become the next CFO.

"We don't work on big-city time," said council member Marie Carmichael with a stern tone.

"I understand, ma'am," she answered. "Maybe the

council could call a special meeting in two weeks for residents to ask questions before the decision is made?" That would help with the timing, although they were still cutting it close.

"That'll cost us for an advertisement and it isn't enough time," Bobby said. "Do I have a motion to table the proposal?" Before Clover could protest again, the plan was tabled and the meeting adjourned. Even as the council members left, she tried to convince them of the wisdom of calling a special meeting. Then she got pinned down in the hallway by the twins, who accused her of lying to the mayor about what had happened to the dog.

"Rita, Anita." Danny's voice came from behind her and she tried not to feel relieved. "I told you it was an accident that couldn't be avoided. She did the right thing by helping the animal. If you're so worried, how about you agree to take two of the puppies. One for each of you." Suddenly the fierce twins were backpedaling and nearly ran out of the town hall.

"Thanks," Clover said.

"I might be many things, but I'm not a liar and I'm not going to let lies hurt someone else."

She nodded her head. "I guess I'll see you next month."

"Speaking of Maggie May and her offspring…would you like to see them? They've grown a lot since you saw them."

She hesitated, not sure that she wanted to be in his apartment and alone. No. She'd gotten closure. She didn't need closure a second time. "Absolutely. How long until they can be adopted?" she asked as they left the building.

"Good night, Mayor," one of the police officers said.

Danny gave him a wave of acknowledgment. For some reason, a flush of embarrassment heated her face. They weren't doing anything wrong.

"My sister's brother-in-law's sister-in-law is a vet tech and she said another three weeks and they'll be ready. The other problem is getting them to the vet in Tucson for their shots. I want to make sure that they're good to go for adoption."

"That's nice of you." There were times when Danny had surprised her with how thoughtful and caring he could be. He'd always had a particularly soft heart. She was glad to see that hadn't changed. Just glad in the abstract, though, not because she cared or expected the two of them to get any closer. Hadn't they already been as close as two people could get? That had just been closure. Nothing more.

"Jolene, the vet tech and my sister's...relative by marriage, should move here. I bet she could open a pet store or something and clean up. I wonder if she could open a clinic? I should check on that."

She didn't mention that soon Rico Pueblo would provide everything residents needed.

The walk to the apartment had been quick and almost furtive. Even so, they were noticed by more people than she would have imagined, each one taking time to say hello and make note of some problem or issue. Danny always smiled and answered politely but kept moving.

"You're good at that," she said as they climbed the steps to his apartment.

"At what?"

"Being mayor."

"You think so?"

"Absolutely. Consummate politician. You answered each person without promising anything."

He looked at her oddly before opening the door. "My landlord said I can keep the dogs for another six weeks. Then they've got to go."

"That gives you some time to get rid of them."

He flicked on the light and turned to her. "I'm not getting *rid* of them. I'll find good homes. They're not trash to throw away."

Wow. She'd hit a nerve. "I didn't choose my words well. I don't think they're trash."

Puppy yips and scrambling nails silenced them. Maggie May raced past them and out the door. The puppies struggled after her. "Catch them," Danny said as he moved to the furred horde. "We have to carry them down the stairs."

She picked up the little white puppy and another who looked like a cross between a shepherd and a beagle. She followed Danny into the back lot, putting down the little animals and laughing with him at their antics. Maggie May made sure they didn't wander too far. When all business was done, they carried the puppies back up the stairs with Maggie May at their heels.

In the apartment, Clover put down her two puppies in a corner that had been barricaded and lined with newspapers.

"They're getting better, but still have accidents if I leave it too long between potty breaks," Danny explained. "Would you like a beer?"

What exactly did he mean by his invitation? Was he just being polite? He was a cowboy, after all, raised by a mama who expected a certain level of behavior. She'd learned that when they'd been a couple. Or did his invite mean something more? In either case, she was a big girl and could say yes or no as she pleased.

"Thanks. That would be nice." He smiled his patented Leigh smile of conquest. She nearly changed her mind. Then remembered that she was immune, inoculated by years of sophistication and a little kernel of hurt that remained from his rejection of her all of those years ago. Maybe the closure hadn't quite finished off that chapter.

"Here you go," he said, handing her a bottle and motioning for her to take a seat in the recliner as he pulled up a kitchen chair.

"I guess you don't have many visitors." He shook his head. "Do you have any leads on adopters?" Suddenly the room felt small, hot and full of promise. Had she really followed him out of her interest in the puppies? She looked over at the blocked-off area. When she turned back, Danny was right there beside her, looming over her. She shivered. Slowly he leaned down, pushing back the chair as his lips touched hers. She sighed in delight. He lay across her, holding himself up so that he didn't crush her but molded to her tightly enough that she felt every heated inch of him.

"I didn't come here for this," she gasped between his kisses.

"I didn't ask you here for this," he whispered across her cheek. "But you are the sweetest, sexiest woman I've ever met, and I just can't resist tasting you."

And taste her he did, until they were both breathless, and then he took her to his bed. She urged him to go faster. He wouldn't listen, dragging out each touch, each brush of his lips, until she was begging him. When they did finally come together, she couldn't think, only feel.

She mumbled into his sweaty shoulder as she kissed him, "We can't keep meeting like this."

"Why not? Seems like the best nights I've spent in a Rocky Raccoon's age. Go to sleep before I'm tempted to show you again why we should keep meeting like this."

"Promises, promises, promises," she teased. And show her he did.

The next morning as Danny slept, she woke with Maggie May and the puppies, making her way down the stairs in one of Danny's oversize cowboy shirts. Of course, the white puppy, the runt yet the most adventuresome, hustled around the building. Clover yelled after him, fearful he would get to the street. She heard Danny coming down the steps, saying something to her as she went around the corner of the building.

"Hulk," she called.

"Clover?" her father asked, standing on the sidewalk looking at her with a frown.

"Clover," Danny called just as he came around the corner, "don't go out on the street without your—"

"Daddy," she said, interrupting Danny as she yanked at the shirt to magically make it longer. Maybe this was a nightmare.

Her father's frown deepened. "I sent you here to clean up your brother's mess and what are you doing but taking up with some drifter."

Chapter 9

Danny's hand automatically went to his head to brush down his hair that had grown in but refused to lie down nicely. He stepped in front of Clover and stretched out his hand. "Good to see you, Heyer. I mean, Mr. Van Camp."

The tall man with a thick middle, hair plugs and a pinkie ring didn't take the hand.

"I'm Mayor Danny Leigh," he said, trying not to wince. Not exactly how he wanted to meet the man who had the fate of the town in his hands and was also Clover's daddy. He didn't need the man's approval, but no man wanted to meet a daddy half-dressed, making it clear what he'd just been doing with his daughter. "If you'd like to go on to the diner, we can meet you in a few minutes." Clover poked Danny hard in the back as she moved from behind him, holding the puppy like a shield.

"Daddy, where are you staying? I'll meet you there after I've had my shower and breakfast."

Danny saw the mean squint to the man's eyes and stepped in again. "If you give me two minutes, I can be ready to take you on a tour of the town. You can meet up with Miss Clover later."

"Don't try that 'yes, ma'am' cowboy bull crap on me. I remember you, boy," her daddy said in a blue-blood tone that made him feel about two inches high.

"I'm mayor of Angel Crossing and a lot of things have changed."

"Not everything," the older man said. "Clover, let's go. You can take me to where you're staying. We'll talk there without interference from the *mayor*."

Clover tried again. "I think it would be better for me to meet you later."

"Now, please," her father said in a voice used to command.

Danny couldn't believe the fierce take-no-prisoners Clover turned and hurried up the stairs. Danny wasn't sure whether to stay here and talk with her father or try to comfort Clover. He didn't know exactly what she needed to be comforted for but he knew that she needed it.

"So," the man said, rooting Danny to the spot, "you're after Clover again and you think being mayor makes you worthy of her now, do you?"

"Clover is a grown woman," Danny said. Because what else could he say?

"She may be but she has a lot of her mother in her. A little too much concern about love and not enough about facts. The fact is that Clover has the chance to—"

"I'm ready, Daddy," she said, hurrying up to them

dressed in yesterday's suit and looking great despite the mussed hair, which he vividly remembered helping muss. "The paper in the puppy pen needs to be changed," she told Danny, dismissing him in a way he didn't like and didn't deserve.

He reached for her hand and, before she could stop him, pulled her close for a kiss, just to prove to her that he wasn't someone to be so easily forgotten. Dang. She tasted good and for a second she softened. Then she pushed—okay, shoved—him away.

"Mayor," she said in an icy tone. "We'll see you at the next meeting."

She walked off with her daddy. Danny stood watching and not doing a blasted thing.

To get the puppies used to life in Arizona, Danny took the wriggling animals and their mama for a ride in his pickup with strict orders (to the little ones) that there would be no piddling in the truck. The trip to see AJ had another purpose. Danny would show the pups to AJ's daughter, EllaJayne, who would see the animals and instantly fall in love. It might be a dirty trick but he needed to find good homes for the puppies. AJ's ranch was a perfect place. Could Danny convince him that two were better than one?

"All right, boys and girl," he said to the box of puppies. "It's showtime. Be on your cutest behavior."

Butch, AJ's girlfriend's dog, came running up to him with his friendly tail wagging furiously. Danny looked around for AJ, figuring he wouldn't be far behind. The llamas and alpacas were milling in the corral and the fields of vegetables stretched out in every direction. Here was one of the people Danny wanted to protect by fighting Clover and her daddy's company. It wasn't just his own plans. Others had invested in Angel Crossing, too, including his own sister, who had a tour-guide business. She'd been in PR with big corporations. She understood how all of this worked, so maybe she could help him. On the other hand, he hated running to his big sister for help like a little boy.

Danny heard a yip, a growl and pounding hooves. Dang it. The puppies had escaped. He'd forgotten they were actually mobile now. They had, of course, found their way into the corral with the furballs, as AJ called the alpacas, llamas...and goats? When had he gotten goats? Hairy goats with big horns. Butch and Maggie May ran past Danny and toward the corral. That unfroze Danny and he sprinted for the animals. Crap. Clover would kill him if the animals got hurt.

Butch had one puppy in his mouth and Maggie May another, the two of them coming out of the corral as Danny climbed in. The big animals seemed to be stepping delicately around the racing puppies. Danny caught another quickly and deposited him back outside the corral with Butch. The dog guarded the two puppies. Good. Danny went back in for the last one—Hulk. He might be the runt, but he had the most personality, 100 percent fearsome. Today that meant he was having a growl-off with a large billy goat, who had been tolerating the nonsense. Now he lowered his head, ready to butt the puppy into kingdom come.

Danny hurried forward to scoop up Hulk, who readied himself to leap at the goat. He got the pup into his arms, stumbled forward, just as the goat rammed, hitting Danny solidly in the nose. He fell to the ground and saw stars, moons and rainbows.

"Hey, Norman, get away from him," a woman's voice said, followed by AJ's loud whistle. Danny breathed in carefully, trying to figure out what might or might not be broken. Hulk licked his cheeks.

"Danny?" Pepper asked. He felt more than heard her kneel, and then her fingers were checking him over in a professional manner.

"I'm okay," he managed to say around the pain in the middle of his face. Damn it. Had the goat broken his nose?

"I don't think you're okay. Stay right where you are. AJ, come and get this puppy and give him back to his mama and lock them up in the barn. Don't let EllaJayne see any of them." During all of that, Pepper didn't stop her examination, moving his head and neck. He winced and the movement made his nose shift into a new level of throbbing pain. "I know I took an oath and all, but I'm almost ready to let you lie out here. Bringing puppies—that's low."

"Just taking them for a ride."

"Uh-huh. Right now, though, I'm going to be the bigger person and treat you. You didn't break your nose, but the bruising will sure feel like it. You also strained muscles in your neck. As soon as AJ gets back, we'll help you into the house. I need to get ice on the nose and pack it. You're bleeding everywhere."

"I am?" he asked but it sounded more like "niam nam?"

"You are." She swatted away the hand he'd lifted to feel his nose and wipe away the blood.

Without fuss, AJ and Pepper got him into the Santa Faye Ranch's original homestead. Their own new home wasn't completed…yet. The residents of Angel Crossing were helping them get the house up as fast as possible, but money and time were both in short supply. He sat in the kitchen chair as Pepper, a physician's assistant, worked on him, helped by her mother, who believed fervently in the power of astrology and Summer of Love medicine she'd learned from who knew where. He winced as Pepper found a particularly sore spot in his neck and swallowed a moan when the movement made his packed and iced nose throb.

"Definitely a strain. Faye, get me the aspirin."

"I think he'd do better with willow bark and turmeric."

Through his nearly closed eyes, he saw Pepper get the painkillers. He hoped it would help. His head had started to pound now, too.

"Here," she said, handing him a glass. He reached out with his right hand without thinking and the glass slipped from it. Dang it. "That's it. You're going to the hospital. Faye, call 911."

"No," Danny said, sitting straight up despite the surge of pain. "I'm okay."

"You've done something more to your neck than strain the muscles. Sit still. You don't want to make it worse."

"It's not new," he managed to mumble out. At least that was what he hoped she heard.

"Not new. What have you done to yourself and why haven't you seen me?"

He'd have to confess now. AJ stood in the doorway with his daughter, EllaJayne. Great. Why not just announce it in the paper? But from the determined look on Pepper's face, he had little choice. He worked on speaking as clearly as his aching and stuffed nose would allow. "I have...numbness in my right hand and arm. Doctors said it might be something with my back or with the joints. Told me it might get better with rest."

"Obviously that hasn't happened," Pepper said sternly.

"It's better some days than others. But I've been doing a bit of practice for SAC. It's acting up again."

"You need to have it checked," Pepper said.

AJ stepped forward and laid his hand on her shoulder. "Let him be. He's a bull rider. He knows what he's about."

"Trying to cause permanent damage to himself."

"One little ride won't do that," AJ said. "I thought there was a bit more to the story of you retiring."

Danny nodded. Becoming mayor had happened just as he needed to make a decision about riding.

Pepper stepped away from AJ. "I don't care about your bull-rider code or whatever it is. You can't ride with that numbness."

"I'm teaching myself to use my other hand. It's not a real competition, just for fun."

"Puppies," EllaJayne screamed. Every adult eye turned. A proud Butch sat surrounded by four puppies posed in exactly the same way.

"Oh, my," Faye said. "I didn't know it was the Year of the Dog."

Clover really wanted a drink, but since Rita and Anita at Jim's were dead set against her father, VCW and Rico Pueblo, she'd have to go to the Devil's Food Diner for coffee and pie. Her head might appreciate it in the morning, but her thighs would be hating it when she upped her workout. She'd start by walking to the diner from her house. It would give her time to try to figure out what her father was up to besides proving that she'd made a mess of things. He'd been ignoring her and had even set up a meeting with the council president that she hadn't been invited to.

She sped up her walk to outpace the voice that whispered to her that her father would never respect her and never believe that she could handle anything without him checking on every detail. She made it to the diner in record time.

Danny's sister Lavonda called to her, "Are you by yourself? Come sit with us."

Danny was the reason she was at the diner ready to drown her sorrows in lemon meringue pie. *That* morning two weeks ago was the real reason she and her father had been fighting about everything. Finding her wearing only Danny's shirt had been really, really bad luck. She blushed remembering it.

"Come on," Lavonda urged. "You've got to see the cutest baby in the universe."

Clover walked over, intrigued because she knew the baby wasn't Lavonda's. She had a donkey and a cat and a Scotsman but no baby.

She looked for Jessie, Danny's oldest sister and the baby's mama. There she was, striding from the hallway that led to the bathrooms. "Thanks for watching Gertie," said Jessie when she got to the table. "Hey, Clover, heard you were still in town."

Clover wondered if this was a setup. The women had been very protective of their little brother even as teens. Could she gracefully leave? No, she could not. She sat down and admired the baby with Jessie's smile and, disconcertingly, Danny's blue eyes. Her dark hair was apparently from her surgeon father.

After pie and coffee had been ordered and the baby resettled into her car seat for a nap, the two Leigh girls turned on Clover—as she'd guessed they would.

Lavonda started. "You know I spent years in corporate communications. I'd like to know exactly how you can promise you won't be pushing out current business owners and residents who don't sell."

"I've outlined that in the presentation. We don't control economics, but those businesses that take advantage of the influx of visitors will certainly have the opportunity to thrive. Take your guide business, Lavonda. More people coming to Rico Pueblo must include those interested in exploring the desert or looking for the Scottish treasure, right? We project that within five years the average stay will be two weeks."

"Isn't there a housing component?" Lavonda asked.

"A part of the plan is for condo-style housing that will be managed by VCW. It will allow people to make this their second home or a vacation retreat."

"What about Danny?" Jessie asked, her sage-green eyes fierce. "He wants to help families here afford housing. It sounds like your plans will push them out. There's Pepper, too, and her market."

This was tricky because the approval of Rico Pueblo would be the end to Danny's plans. The properties he'd bought would remain zoned as commercial. "He could shift his project farther from the core of the town, possibly."

Lavonda said firmly, "The point, though, was that the residents could walk to what they needed—the doctor, the market and Lem's store. Moving them farther from town will mean they need to drive, which some don't do or shouldn't do. Having an affordable core was also attractive to younger home buyers. This town definitely needs younger folks and a place for the children of the current Angelites to start off."

"Two things. With the influx of tourists, there could be a public transit system. Second, VCW and Rico Pueblo will provide jobs that will help keep younger people here. There'll be viable career opportunities."

"Huh." Jessie snorted. "I don't see the people here wanting to ride those cute little trolleys like they have in Tucson and Phoenix. And careers? Sweeping up at restaurants and washing dishes?"

Clover wasn't going to argue about the clear economic pluses of the plan. Instead, she said, "It's not up to me, really. The council will make the final decision on whether our project is best for the town. I think that makes it fair all around."

"It would be," Jessie said, "if Danny had your money for slick presentations and throwing around the promise of good prices for land. A couple of property owners told me that you…sorry, your father and VCW… offered them above-market prices for their properties."

Clover scrambled to understand why her father was making offers. She was supposed to be doing that, as they'd decided in New York months ago.

"Plus, you're sleeping with our brother," Jessie said. Her stubborn cowgirl chin thrust out. "What are you trying to do? Convince him of your way of thinking with—"

"Of course not!" She was hurt to her core that these women would think she'd do something like that.

"Good," Lavonda said. "At least you're not using Danny's 'interest' in you to get your own way. We wondered about that."

"I'll be leaving," Clover said with as much Texas beauty queen as she could manage. "Everything I'm doing in Angel Crossing is legal and ethical. I resent that you would imply anything else."

Clover walked out of the diner quickly, not even paying for her pie and coffee. After the grilling, the Leigh sisters could take care of that. Half a block down the sidewalk, Clover had cooled off enough to get back to the biggest surprise in the conversation. Why was her father buying properties and paying above-market price? She needed to confront him about his interference. She was an adult woman and could certainly stand up to her daddy. As long as he didn't bring up Danny and that morning. No. She could face that, too, and hold her head high.

Chapter 10

Danny stood watching with nothing like excitement as AJ helped his former boss unload the bull. They were setting up a little practice ride at the small outdoor stadium near the community college, where the charity bull-riding extravaganza would take place in just over two months.

The bull his friend had found for him had enough pep to give Danny a workout without the full force of the spins and bucks of a competition ride. It would give him a chance to practice riding with his left hand. Right now, the numbness in his right was barely there, but it could be full-on numb at any time, something that would be dangerous if it happened during a ride. If his hand was numb, how could he grip the bull rope? It would be a good chance to get hurt really bad.

"DD here is a good bull," AJ said as they got everything ready in the chute. Danny's guts churned. It felt like a really, really long time since he'd climbed aboard a bull. What the hell had he been thinking? "He'll give you a good ride without thinking he needs to kill you."

"You're the expert." Danny gritted his teeth as he prepped himself. It all felt so wrong. The wrong hand, the wrong bull, the wrong arena. Except he'd promised his town he'd do this. He'd also promised himself that he hadn't quit riding because he had to. He'd prided himself that he'd known when to get out. This event would prove to himself that he could've kept riding if he'd wanted to.

"Dave will be out there to help you off, if you need it. But this old bull is easy. No worries. Dave uses him a lot for his classes and clinics. He knows the drill."

Crap. It sounded like AJ thought he was a rookie. "You know how many buckles I have?"

"Yep. And I also know you haven't ridden for at least two years, and you're using your left hand."

"Always said I could ride with one hand tied behind my back."

"That one of your mama's sayings?"

Anger flared through Danny, making him want to punch his longtime friend. He pulled in a breath to calm himself. He couldn't ride like that. He needed a certain amount of quiet in his brain to ready himself for the ride. He worked to find that place where everything went quiet, calm. He nodded his head that he was ready, but instantly the calm was gone and it was too late to change his mind. AJ had released DD and the bull knew his business. He bolted from the chute and lifted his hindquarters in a mighty buck. Danny stayed centered…barely. He worked to find the rhythm of the animal's stride and buck. It just wasn't there. He could feel the animal bunching its body for a spin, cursed and went flying. The dirt of the arena hadn't gotten any softer. DD stood quietly, tail flicking. He really was a beginner's animal. Crap.

Danny stood and dusted himself off. AJ was looking at him oddly, maybe a little worried. Danny waved his hat and went back to the chute. He would have a bruise on his hip, but otherwise he was good. He'd climb back on board after giving the bull a rest. This was just practice. You fell when you practiced so you didn't when it came time for the big show.

"One more time," he told AJ after another three-second ride.

"Not sure DD wants to."

"He's barely gotten a workout."

"Dave," AJ yelled. "One more?"

The stockman considered the request, then nodded. The bull had let him test his left arm. Though the animal was barely working to unseat him, Danny couldn't figure out exactly why he was having such trouble. Staying on the bull should have been easy. This time he'd do it. He'd clear his mind properly and get his seat settled. Number four was the charm, right?

He could've sworn as he settled himself on DD again the bull gave him the side eye. *You again, fool?* Danny silently told the bull to shut it. He was a two-time champion with multiple picture-perfect rides and more buckles than days of the week. He would ride this old bull and win this time. He nodded to AJ, and in that split second Clover's face popped into his mind. He ate dirt. Damn it.

"What the hell, cowboy?" AJ said.

DD didn't even have the momentum to keep going. He stood by Danny and AJ snorting…laughing before trotting toward Dave, who was holding out the bull's favorite treat: marshmallows.

"Bee flew at me," Danny lied. He wouldn't tell AJ that Clover had distracted him. He'd always said no matter how many women he chased, they'd never come between him and a bull. "I'll do more conditioning. I know what I've got to work on now."

"Like how to ride a bull? You were better your rookie year. What's wrong?" The last was asked with the serious tone of a good friend with worries.

"Been longer than I thought since I climbed aboard. I'll be ready to try again as soon as you can line something up."

"If you say so. Let me help Dave. Then I'll buy you a beer."

"Sorry. I've got to go. Mayor stuff," Danny lied. He didn't want to talk to AJ about his failure and what was at the root of it. He wanted to go home, shower and brood. The best he could do was brood on the drive home because there was a handyman job he'd been promising to finish up and another small project he needed to bid on. Both could probably be put off until tomorrow, but right now he wanted to keep busy.

On the way to the job, he analyzed the rides, as his late friend Gene had taught him and AJ to do. He hadn't been able to get the right rhythm or feel of the bull using his left hand. He couldn't believe that it made such a difference. He couldn't believe he'd never had to ride that way because of a broken bone or a strain. Or maybe being teenager-stupid had made it easier. Next practice, he'd have to use his right hand and hope that it didn't decide to go numb at the wrong time.

AJ and his former boss Dave showed up with another practice bull a few days later. This one was DD's son, fierier than his father but still a good practice animal. He wasn't fond of turning corkscrews or more challenging bucks, making him not-so-popular with the professionals but perfect for training.

Today Danny had prepared himself to use his less reliable right hand in the hope he could find his rhythm again. Waiting for AJ and Dave to get Black Fury into the chute, Danny pictured what he would do for each twist and turn of the bull. He then cleared his mind, focusing on a tuft of hair on the bull's head as he lowered himself on the animal, who twitched at the weight but otherwise didn't move. Danny found his seat and the calm he'd been looking for last time. He nodded and the gate opened. The bull crow-hopped, then threw up its back legs. Danny easily rode out those maneuvers until he heard AJ yell "Eight," and he easily jumped from the bull.

Dave corralled the animal and Danny knew he had his mojo back. He'd be able to ride in the event and not make a fool of himself. It felt right, too. The smell of dust and heated animal. The creak of the leather under him. All of it added up to a weirdly comfortable place.

"Well, hell," AJ said as Danny went back to the chute. "Look who showed up to watch."

Danny squinted into the stands and saw the sun glinting off auburn. Damn. Clover was here. Why was Clover here? He wanted to be 110 percent on his game before anyone saw him riding. He was at 85 or so. Another three weeks of conditioning and practice rides would get him there with plenty of time left over before the event. He wanted to do all of that without an audience. She waved.

"Still draw ladies like bees to a flower, huh?" AJ commented.

Danny didn't answer and didn't wave back to Clover. While he was confident he had his timing back, he wanted to work on his form. He had at least two, probably three more rides on the bull before they needed to call it quits.

Danny blanked out the fact that Clover was there and focused on the bull's tuft of hair again. He mentally went over the last ride and the animal's quirks. He'd go for the tip of the hat, one of his signature moves that audiences loved and expected from him.

He nodded his head to AJ to let the animal out and Black Fury tore out of the chute, racing forward before going into a series of hard bucks and sharp turns. Danny found his rhythm, and as he counted to the six-second mark, he reached for his hat. But Black Fury went into a fast spin—the move he never did. Danny tried to tighten his grip as well as find his center. His hand was numb. He couldn't move his fingers. He let the hat fly as he reached down to loosen the rope so he could get off the bull fast. The animal reversed his spin and Danny went soaring off the animal, landing hard, his deadened right hand and rapidly numbing arm crumpling under him.

Clover's heart stuttered as Danny flew through the air then stopped when his arm collapsed under him and his head smacked onto the dirt. He didn't pop up immediately. She ran from the stands, ignoring the ankle-breaking unevenness of the dirt to reach him. Two other men were already there. "Danny," she yelled. "Danny."

He didn't answer and the men didn't even turn to look at her. This was bad. She searched for her phone in her purse as she ran forward. The men moved and she saw that Danny was sitting up. Thank God. His arm looked odd. Had he broken it?

"I want to go again," Danny said. "Just caught me off guard with that spin."

"His spin is more like a slow turn in a cul-de-sac," AJ said. She remembered him from her days on the junior bull-riding circuit.

"Is your arm broken? How many fingers do you see?" she asked, elbowing past the men.

"What the hell are you doing here?" Danny asked, the new knot on his forehead looking worse with his frown.

"Was looking at some land out this way and wondered what the commotion was," she lied. Danny's frown deepened. "Let me call 911. You probably have a concussion."

"I don't have a damned concussion and my arm is fine."

She could see the arm wasn't fine. It hung at the wrong angle with his fingers clawed inward. She reached out to touch it and he didn't move away. "What's wrong?" She was worried. Had he broken his arm? Put it out of joint?

"Damn it, woman. I'm fine." He pushed himself up

with his good hand and stood. Neither of the other men said anything as he rubbed at his dangling arm. It didn't move or jerk. That had to mean it wasn't broken. He couldn't do that with a broken bone, could he?

The older man said, "That's enough for today."

"That bull's got at least two more rides in him."

AJ put his hand on Danny's shoulder. "If Dave says we're done, then we're done."

Danny stiffened except for that dangling right arm. Had he injured his back? Was he paralyzed? "Danny, I'm taking you to the hospital right now if you won't let me call 911. Or what about Pepper? I'll call her."

He knocked the phone from her hand. "I said no," he shouted. Everyone froze, including the bull.

"What the hell, man?" AJ said. "You need to apologize."

Danny kept his back to her. "Sorry."

"Lame," AJ muttered.

Danny whipped around, his arm swinging and his face dark with anger and fear. "I'm sorry, m'lady. I shouldn't have hit your phone. I shouldn't have yelled." He stomped off.

"Aren't you going after him? He hurt himself," Clover pointed out to the men.

AJ answered, "Bull riders hurt themselves all the time."

She snorted and hurried after Danny. She knew riders hurt themselves, but this was bad. Between his head and arm, he shouldn't be driving. She caught up with him just feet from his pickup.

"Danny." He stopped but didn't turn to her. "At least go see Pepper. Your arm looks bad."

"Enough," he whispered hoarsely. "I don't need you acting like you care."

That hurt. "I care about you, Danny." She tentatively touched his shoulder, approaching him like she would a hurting horse.

"Ha. You're trying to destroy me and my town."

She'd chalk that up to his pain. "Regardless, you're a human being, and it's obvious that something happened to you in that fall."

"Nothing more than usual."

"Turn around and talk to me. I know you're stubborn, but I never knew you to be stupid."

His shoulders dropped a fraction of an inch and he turned. His face was anguished.

"Danny," she whispered, "what's wrong? Let me—"

"It's numb. It may never get better."

"Your arm?"

He nodded. "The doctors said that it's probably a nerve that's inflamed. Probably. When it…well, when it acts up, my arm goes numb. My fingers are numb a lot but that's not so bad. Have to be careful with the saw, though." He laughed hollowly.

Words fled from her and she just wanted to enfold him in her arms. She was woman enough to know he wouldn't allow that. "I hadn't heard. How do you expect to ride?"

"I've ridden with worse. I can do this."

She wouldn't point out that had been stupid. "I know doctors in New York and San Antonio. I could talk to them."

"I've seen enough doctors. I'll do this show because that's what I said I'd do. It's going to raise tens of thousands of dollars for the garden. I can't let Angel Crossing down."

"But you could—"

"I'll be fine. Plus, you and your daddy will be gone by then. Destroyed our town and moved on."

"I never took you for a drama king," Clover said, not sure exactly how much of that was teasing.

"I don't need this crap."

She touched his good arm. "It's my turn to apologize. At least let me drive you home."

"I told you I'm fine."

"Yeah, right. I can see the knot on your forehead. I'll follow you, then."

He didn't say anything but got in his truck. She hurried to her rental to follow him. She wasn't done with convincing him to go see Pepper or head to the emergency room. She knew how bull riders were—as stubborn as the animals they rode.

They had taken the puppies and Maggie May out and rounded them back up and into the apartment without a word between them.

"I've got people adopting all but Hulk and Maggie May," he said when they got back to the apartment.

"You're keeping them? What about your landlord?"

He shook his head and stopped abruptly.

"That's it. Sit and let me look at your head and arm. I see your hair has grown in over the stitches just fine." Thinking of Danny hurt made her stomach clench with fear.

"I'm not a little boy," he said, plopping down in a chair.

She pushed back the blond hair with streaks of near white from being hatless in the sun. The lump had a small bruise in the center. That needed ice. Even she knew that. She reached down for his right arm and he moved his shoulder to keep her from touching him. "I need to make sure you didn't hurt it. You wouldn't know since you can't feel it."

He turned his head away from her but she could see his jaw moving with anger and frustration.

She carefully and slowly took his arm, treating him like a skittish stallion who needed his hooves cleaned. She smiled at that. Danny would like being compared to a stallion over a bull. She worked the plaid sleeve of his shirt up his forearm. The skin looked fine. She ran her hands along it and couldn't feel any lumps or bumps. His hand looked fine, too. Could the odd angle she'd noticed been all because of the numbness? She couldn't push the sleeve beyond the elbow, so she'd have to take off his shirt. His face was still turned away. *Pretend you're Pepper examining a patient.* She started at the button at his neck. Now he turned his head.

"What the hell are you doing?"

"I need to look at your whole arm." She kept her voice steady and unemotional.

"I'll do it." He stood and yanked off the shirt clumsily.

Clover focused on his right arm. She reached deep to touch him without emotion. Her hand started at his shoulder, well muscled and strong. Everything good there. Her hand inched down onto his bicep, which jerked. She glanced up at him, but his face hadn't changed from its stoic cowboy lines. She massaged down the muscle, feeling for anything that shouldn't be there. The skin was warm and taut with a spring that reminded her of their nights together, her fingers digging into those same arms and holding on.

"I've never had an exam like that," Danny said as he looked at where her hands stroked his bicep. His smile was cocky.

She stilled her fingers, even as they ached to sink into his flesh to feel the heated strength of him. "You seem okay, but you should still see Pepper."

"I don't think her exam will be the same."

"Stop being such a jerk." She stepped away from him. The warm bubble that had surrounded them as she'd checked his arm had burst with his stupid comments. Time for her to go.

"I'm sorry," he said suddenly. "My mama taught me better. I appreciate your checking on me."

She nodded, not able to speak because she was so off balance. She was getting whiplash from his shifting mood. "I'm glad you really are fine, except for the numbness." Now they were back to stoic cowboy.

"There is that. I'll be practicing more with my left."

She'd been dismissed again. She'd take the hint this time. "I'm glad to hear that the puppies have homes."

"All but Hulk."

"He's a cutie, though. I can't imagine it will take long."

"Maybe. Except he may be deaf. That's sometimes the case with white dogs. It's hard to say."

"Poor little guy," she said as she looked over at the puppy pen, where everyone was sleeping peacefully.

"Yeah." Danny's shoulders slumped with...weariness, fear, sadness? She couldn't be sure. She was a glutton for punishment because she stepped to him and picked up his bad right hand, giving it a squeeze even if he couldn't feel it. He stiffened for a moment, and then she was in his arms, his lips on hers devouring her and heating her.

Chapter 11

Danny wasn't sure if he'd slept. The evening and night were a haze of loving Clover. Now it was morning and only one beam of the rising sun crept through the crack in the curtain. He couldn't deny that a new day had dawned. Maggie May had yipped twice to be let out. He slid from the bed so he wouldn't wake Clover. Her mass of auburn hair sparked red in the light. He wanted to bury his face again in its softly fragrant length.

He had responsibilities. She would wake soon enough and realize that they had made another mistake, except it didn't feel like a mistake. That aching emptiness he'd been trying to fill with Angel Crossing and its problems had been gone in her arms. Even now that space had a fullness he hadn't felt since…he'd been a teen and trembling with his love and need for her. Dangerous thoughts and imaginings. She was going to destroy what he'd built for himself here.

He kept moving. He'd learned that was the best way to deal with pain, just keep moving and don't think. He got Maggie May and the puppies outside with no accidents. He allowed them to romp longer than usual, telling himself they needed the extra exercise, not that he was hoping Clover would sneak away and he wouldn't have to face her. Now the canine family stood at the bottom of the stairs waiting for him. No more stalling. When he got them all adopted, he'd miss this in the mornings. But it was best for them. They couldn't live in an apartment, especially with his busy schedule. He didn't have the time for training a puppy or a new dog.

He herded them up the stairs. The door opened and Clover appeared in yesterday's clothes, her hair shining in the sun and her expression in shadow. His face felt numb today. He couldn't make it move in any way that made sense. He looked down at the boards of the landing. Better than trying to control his stiff features or seeing the regret in her eyes.

"I wanted to make sure your arm's okay," she said as he brushed by her and inside.

The reason she'd stayed. Pity. "Good enough to take care of myself."

"Don't be so sensitive," she said. "I didn't mean anything."

"Thanks for letting me know what last night was about. Helping the cripple feel better about himself."

He went to the dog food bowls. Why didn't she leave?

"The puppies and Maggie May will be leaving soon?"

"Yes." The dogs crowded him as he put down their food. Time to refill the water.

"You'll miss them?"

That didn't deserve an answer. He didn't have a choice, like he hadn't about his career or about being mayor.

She went on when he didn't answer. "Do you need help paying the vet bills?"

"Just because I'm not riding anymore doesn't mean—"

"Jeez. You're as prickly as a cactus in May."

"What?"

"You used to say that."

He may have. It was one of the many sayings from his mother that made as much sense as a cowboy in heels. "My mama said that. She says a lot of things that don't really make sense."

"I did wonder. But it sounds good, doesn't it? Should I make us coffee?"

Why did the thought of sitting down and having coffee with Clover seem like the absolute best way to start the morning? Because this woman had always made him feel that way. He had never been sure around her, like he was with other women or even around ornery bulls. "Sure," he said. "I don't think I have much for breakfast. I can run down to the diner." How would he explain an order that would probably include yogurt or fruit or something like that? Everyone in the diner would know what he'd been up to.

"Coffee will do for now." She turned from him and went into the kitchen. He stood for a moment, watching her, and the unsteady feeling was gone. This felt right, a morning routine and a little conversation. He'd had a girlfriend or three over the years and this time of day had never felt like this. What was it about Clover?

"Black with sugar, right?" she asked over her shoulder.

He went to her and wrapped his arms around her, burying his face in the crook of her neck because he wanted her right now. He couldn't wait and he didn't want to think about why.

"Oh, my," she said. "Someone doesn't need a cup of coffee to wake up."

He and Clover had spent the past two weeks looking for homes for Maggie May and Hulk. So, of course, that meant spending a lot of time together, both in and out of bed. She'd gone to the arena with him as he continued to work on his riding, not saying anything when he ate dirt regularly. She'd even helped him with his strength training and cardio with jogs through the streets. He knew the town had taken note. He'd gotten looks from Irvin and Loretta that said, *What are you doing, boy?* Bobby Ames had straight-out asked if he believed fraternizing with a VCW representative would get him a better price for his properties. Danny had barely stopped himself from punching the man.

He and Clover stood in the parking lot behind Angel Crossing's main street, which also served as the town's outdoor farmers' market. They'd just sent off another puppy to one of the homes he'd found. The family had two kids and everyone looked so excited. Maggie May and Hulk were still with him. He knew Maggie May would be tough to place and had hoped that AJ would take her as a friend for Butch. Danny knew most people wanted puppies, not full-grown mutts. He'd been working with her, though. Teaching her commands to make her more attractive to a family or even an older person looking for a companion. As smart as she was, he'd bet he could teach her to get the remote and turn on the lights. Hulk, the little runt, was deaf in one ear with only a little bit of hearing in the other. Danny was teaching him hand signals, and like Maggie May, he picked them up quickly.

"I know that she'll be happy, but I'm still—"

Danny pulled Clover into an embrace. She'd cried each time they'd placed one of the pups in a new home. "You can't have a dog and neither can I. The kids looked so excited. She'll do well. I gave them my number in case there's any problems. I told them they could call me and I'd come get her, no questions asked."

She hugged him harder and whispered her thanks. Nearly as good as winning a buckle and the money. Damn. He was getting in deep with Clover. Two more weeks until the big meeting, the final decision on Rico Pueblo having been postponed at the last council meeting. The one he should be preparing for, instead of worrying about puppies and Clover's feelings.

"I knew there was something special about you when we first met."

"It was my butt in my jeans. That's what you told me."

"That was good, too. But I saw the way you treated that ragged dog you had. You never yelled at him, even when he chewed up your new belt."

"Jack was a piece of work. I had that belt specially made and had only worn it once."

She looked up at him, her blue eyes shining with more than tears, and he couldn't imagine how he'd live up to what she thought he was. "You even told your sister Jessie to stop teasing me."

"I knew what it was like to be in her crosshairs," he said lightly.

"Now look at you, trying to save a town and a bunch of puppies." She pulled his head down and kissed him hard. "Why do you have to be so sweet? Why did I think you weren't worth my time back then?"

"I wasn't and I'm not," he said, trying to put a little distance between them. "I was young, innocent when we met. A lot has happened since then."

"To both of us, but you haven't changed that much. You still have a great butt," she said with a laugh. "Even better," she whispered softly into his ear, "you've learned how to… You're a good lover, generous, kind, caring."

"It's you. You make me that way. No one else… Let me just say that it's special." Crap. Why had he confessed that?

She kissed him again, her lips softly nibbling at his as she held him to her. Her curves so familiar that his hand settled into her waist like a chicken coming home to roost. He laughed against her lips. Happy.

"What?" she asked, her blue eyes unfocused.

"Nothing. Let's go home." He didn't think what he meant by that.

"Yes. Maggie May and Hulk are waiting for us."

Their hips bumped companionably against each other as they strolled to his apartment, his arm thrown over her shoulder. No point in thinking too hard about why he could imagine doing the same thing every day for the rest of his life.

Clover stirred as the puppy's whine went from pathetic to a baying howl.

"Shh." She heard Danny and his "stealthy" footsteps. "Don't wake your mama."

Her heart stopped then cracked open. Danny had loved her last night well and truly but that wasn't what made her want him. This early-morning stealth and his comments were what had wormed themselves into her heart. She feared this would make her want to stay in Angel Crossing and give up on her dream. Just like when she'd met him the first time. She'd fallen hard for him and wanted to give up on college to be with him while he competed. He'd been on his way even then. She would have given it all up and gladly. But going back to her "real" life and eventually seeing pictures of Danny with another girl had convinced her that her future lay elsewhere. She had to remember that again. She'd nearly gained the position she'd fought for. The one that she'd gone to Wharton for, the one that her ability with numbers should have gotten her over her brother years ago.

But when she started thinking about the future, she had doubts, worries and fears. That was normal. Then Danny would kiss the nape of her neck, making her shudder all over. Her dreams would shift. She'd see herself with him and with their babies. She'd never imagined herself with children. Her life was going to be all about her work.

A puppy growl reached her as did Danny's attempt to quiet Hulk. She could put off for another day making decisions about the rest of her life. She didn't need to understand statistics to know the likelihood of her and Danny staying together made for a bad bet.

Two hours later, she'd done a week's worth of deep breathing after finding the hole the puppy had chewed in her new Coach bag. Despite her early-morning dreams of a life with Danny, she was on her way to meet with Melvin about a tract of property he owned just outside of town. VCW wanted it as part of Rico Pueblo.

Her father had decided to stay until the next council meeting two weeks from now. He'd set up a satellite office in one of the properties they owned along Miner's Gulch. Danny had even helped fit it out to make it usable.

The different parts of her life were beginning to blur. She hadn't figured out if that was a good or a bad thing...yet. She had two more weeks to make that decision. Well, hell, there was Danny's pickup. What was he doing out here? He'd better be bidding on a rehab job and not talking to the man about his property.

The long, low ranch house had a history to it and amazing views of the surrounding mountains. Well, history for Arizona. In New York, it would be just a pup of a house. A back part of it was old-time adobe. Too bad the house and the barns would be flattened for VCW's plans. Sometimes you had to break a few eggs. Or something like that. Clover knocked on the door as she rubbed each boot against the back of her jeans. Not something her mother or father would approve of, but in dusty Arizona, it was a must to keep her pink cowgirl boots looking decent. Today she'd dressed not to impress or intimidate, but to prove that she wasn't so different from the residents of Angel Crossing—jeans, plaid shirt (one of her mother's designs in pink and purple, highlighted with silver lamé), white hat with a dyed pink snake band and her pink boots. Feminine and Western. She looked good.

"Hello, Melvin, good to see you again," she said to the balding man with the thick waist and short legs. "I hope I'm not disturbing your talk with the mayor." No use pretending she didn't know who was here.

"Seems everyone wants to visit today. Even your daddy is here."

She smiled because otherwise her mouth would have dropped open. What was her father doing here? Had he hidden his car on purpose? She'd told him she'd take care of this. She'd spoken to Melvin at least four times about the property, the price, the contingencies. Today she was going to close the deal and get his name on the sale papers, which would give her plenty of time to finish the transfer before the meeting. She wanted this property to be the cornerstone of the portion of the Rico Peublo single-family home development that mixed history and nature, in the form of world-class views.

"We're out back. Come along. I never would have guessed this dry old ranch would be worth so much."

Crap. The man saw dollar signs, always bad for making the budget work. Clover smiled again. That was what a lady did when she didn't agree and needed to keep her mouth shut. She wanted to figure out exactly what was going on before she said anything more.

They walked around the outside of the house, entering a garden and patio protected by a wooden gate that looked even older than the house and included a crude carving of something that might be an angel.

"Daddy," Clover said.

Her father nodded at her and Danny gave her a blank-eyed stare. What the heck was going on?

"Take a seat," Melvin said as he sat down in a large wooden chair with more angels carved on the arms and back, similar to that on the gate. "Growing up here, I never could have imagined anyone would be so interested in my ranch, and now I have three buyers."

"Two," Clover corrected, settling herself. She would speak calmly with this man who held a lot of the cards right now. "I also work for VCW."

"Yep, but there must be some kind of insider trading or something since there are two of you here." The man was absolutely gleeful.

"I assure you that VCW has a very clear plan for this and the additional properties that we have acquired."

Danny said, "Melvin, you've lived here your entire life, and it was your great-grandfather who built the ranch and founded the town. Do you think a company from New York City will treat you and Angel Crossing right?"

"If they give me the money I want, I'll be treated right."

Clover knew it. This was all about money. She'd found that a lot of life came down to money. At least for her parents it had. They'd never officially divorced because it would cost too much. Each continued to grow their business and ignore that they were still hitched to another human.

"I believe," her father said smoothly, "that we had a very advantageous agreement."

"Probably." Melvin stalled. "But I want to hear what the mayor and your daughter have to offer."

"I'm not bidding against my own company," she said, dismayed that her father had stepped into the fray.

"I'm only out here to make the offer you should have and clean up your mess," her father said to her in a low tone that she hoped Melvin couldn't hear.

She was more than annoyed. She'd been near to completing a deal with Melvin. She'd even been toying with the idea of keeping elements from the old ranch as part of an entrance to the development, hoping it would bring down his price.

"What about you, Mayor? Going to up your price?" Melvin asked.

Danny's expression froze and his fingers drummed against his leg. "You know I don't have anything more to offer and this property is worth less than we offered. At this rate, I'm going to end up back at the rodeo to make money."

"Don't care about you and the bull riding. This property is worth whatever anyone is willing to pay, not what the county has on that piece of paper. Your sister and her archaeologist have said that there could be 'significant historical meaning to the property as well as evidence of presettlement materials.' That should be worth some coin."

Danny stood, his blue eyes cool as his gaze landed on Clover before he spoke to Melvin. "I gave you the offer and explained why your property is important to Angel Crossing. I can't do more than that."

She hesitated for a moment and followed Danny out. "This is just business."

"Dirty business," he countered. He took in a deep breath and blew it out. "Like I said, it might be that I'm not meant to be a developer or a mayor, that my place is on the back of a bull."

"Danny, I—" What could she say? That she didn't want him to ride bulls again because it was too dangerous? She didn't have any right to say that. "Sorry about the property." She turned and walked back into the house.

"We have an agreement, then?" her father asked Melvin.

"Maybe. I'll need to think on it now that I've got so many people interested and know that there might be some ancient artifacts underground."

"The only ancient artifact that you should be looking for is your integrity," Clover said, glaring at her father as she walked out again. She wouldn't think about why she'd been more upset about Danny's crazy idea about bull riding than her father stepping in to take over her project.

Chapter 12

After the meeting with Melvin, Danny couldn't speak with Clover. He couldn't ignore she was in competition with him for his town—even though that sounded pompous and asinine. He didn't have a problem with the company presenting its vision to the council. That was fair. But now her father was using cash to get his way. Danny had seen how much Melvin had been offered—twice the value of the property with extra for resettlement. Losing the ranch, though, would be losing a part of Angel Crossing's heritage. Lavonda's husband would prove that. He'd already poked around and found archaeological evidence of pre-Spanish settlement.

Today he and Clover were supposed to have met potential adopters for Hulk. Clover had texted him twenty minutes before the meeting that she couldn't come. She hadn't even given him an excuse. Even if he didn't want to see her or speak with her, he'd thought she'd cared about the little puppy. Apparently, she'd just been passing the time until she and her father threw around their millions. They'd even been after Pepper to sell them the old theater so it could be torn down and replaced with a state-of-the-art IMAX theater that would take people on virtual tours of the Grand Canyon. They were in Arizona. Just go to the blasted Grand Canyon, if you wanted to see it.

What a day. Hulk's adopters hadn't worked out, he had a lull in his business and his plan was ready to go belly-up. He went to the diner, hoping for a little food but, more important, hoping that he'd see people who had some influence over other Angelites and even the council. It was a long shot that he'd see anyone like that or that they'd want to talk with him. Everyone was getting a little tired of the discussion.

"You just missed your girlfriend," Marlena, the waitress, said as he walked in. Others nodded hello to him.

"She's not my girlfriend."

"Could have fooled me, considering I saw her coming out of your apartment in the morning."

No use denying it. Plus, he had a greater purpose, as they say. "Just here for coffee and pie."

"No pie. Got some of those doughnuts that get delivered."

The doughnuts were awful. "Just coffee." He looked around for someone he could persuade to join his cause.

"Why aren't you at the Hendersons'?" his sister Lavonda asked from behind him, giving him a start.

"Waiting for a tile shipment. Where did you come from?"

Lavonda opened, then closed her mouth, then opened it again. "We're in the back room."

He'd heard about the room and the women, aka the Devil's Food Diner Back Room Mafia. A group of ladies who spun yarn, knit and ran the town (according to them). "Who are you trying to match up now?" The group had convinced Pepper that she should take on AJ and his daughter months ago.

"We're not a matchmaker club. We're working on a business plan for Sylvia. She's looking at starting an apiary in the community garden. Honey and beeswax are hot items right now."

"Won't have that if Clover and her daddy get their way." They wanted Wild West modern, which Danny imagined was like plopping Phoenix down into Angel Crossing.

"Is Clover there with you now?" he asked.

"Don't act like lions and puppies are lying down together. She's got ideas for the town. We wanted to hear them firsthand before the meeting. Plus, we heard about Melvin and his place. We wanted to ask her about that, too. You know Jones has explored there for his... Let's just say the place might be related to his research."

Danny couldn't puzzle out what his sister was not saying because of the angry roaring in his ears. How dare Clover come in here and act like she was the savior? He would go in there and set her and the Back Room Mafia straight.

"She's going to destroy the town," he said as he wrenched open a door. It would have made more of an impression if it hadn't led to the storage closet. "Damn it."

Lavonda said, "The next door on the right." He didn't turn. He didn't need to to know she was laughing at him. His neck burned with embarrassment. He yanked open the next door over and said, "Clover Van Camp is here to destroy Angel Crossing."

"Wow," said Marie, her round, wrinkled face grinning. "I didn't know she had so much power. We'll start calling her Clover-zilla. Wait. Wasn't there a monster movie called *Cloverfield*?"

"Not much of a movie," another woman said as she clacked away with two needles. "I like Clover-zilla. Now, that would be a movie. What do you think, Doris?"

Another woman with one flashing hooked needle nodded. "There are a couple of places I'd like to see blown up. Wait. Is that her superpower?"

"They'll get rid of the diner and charge you to have your meetings," he said, guessing that would be true under VCW. The plan was about making money, not a community. He looked around the table, making sure his gaze didn't land on Clover.

"The diner's nearly killed half the town at one time or another. Now they don't even have pie," Marie said. "The man making the desserts quit, or Chief Rudy suggested he move on. Something about counterfeit something or other."

"Danny," Clover said loudly enough that it cut through the "remember who used to live where" conversation around the table. "I'm just here to visit and answer questions."

"Do they know that your company plans to tear down most of the town, including Melvin's place, and put up condos?"

"We've talked about the housing. Not having to care for a yard sounds good to some residents," she said.

She just didn't get it. He knew what she and her father were planning. No matter what kind of lipstick you put on that porcupine, it would still stick it to you. "What about the cost? Did you tell them about that?"

"I'm answering questions. Not making a presentation. We'll do that at the meeting."

"Will it be everything you have mapped out? That you're going to make this an exclusive community, put a gate up?"

"It's going to be just what I talked about. If you think that's exclusive, then okay."

"That's enough, Danny," his sister said. "We all know you're mayor and you have your own plan. We've heard about it from you often enough."

"She's lying to you," he said, not willing to let this go. "She and her father are selling everyone a bill of goods."

"I am not lying," Clover said, standing. "I don't lie. Unlike you."

"Me?"

"Yes, you. You act like a stand-up cowboy. You act like what you're doing is best for Angel Crossing. It's not. It'll put money in your pocket so you can leave. Isn't that what you really want to do? Leave here and go back on the road. Isn't that what SAC is all about? Aren't you going to invite everyone to see you ride again so you can get sponsors?"

As he'd been working the bulls and training, he realized that having one gimpy arm wasn't as much of a handicap as he'd imagined. Recently, with VCW putting a wrench in his future, he figured he could still have a rehab business in Angel Crossing or Tucson, while he went back on the riding circuit. He'd hire a crew to do the work, checking on them between shows.

"Have you told Mama you want to ride again?" Lavonda asked, treating him like he was twelve.

"I don't need her permission or yours. In fact, I don't need anyone's permission to make decisions about my life."

"Right. Just walk away," Clover said, leaning forward. "What do you care? You'll get what you want. You'll smile and shake hands and walk away. You never cared anyway. This was all for fun. Or wait. Not for fun—it stroked your ego, and God knows you've got a big one of those."

"You didn't seem to mind 'stroking my ego.'"

A gasp went through the room and Clover stepped back like she'd been slapped.

"Danforth Clayton Leigh—" Lavonda said.

Before she could say she was disappointed in him, he went on. "I want to tell the truth. Isn't that what we're doing here? We had a good time but it's over. Just like that summer. I was some dumb cowboy that was available. I'm not so dumb anymore. I've learned a lot, including when to walk away."

Clover checked her suit one last time in the mirror over the bathroom sink in Dead Man's Cottage. She'd be out of here soon and back to New York with CFO as her title. If she said it often enough, it would be true. There wasn't an iota of the Texas beauty queen or the cowgirl who'd fallen for a bull rider with a bad arm. In the mirror was Clover Van Camp, an executive ready to break balls and build empires. Tonight at the town-council meeting of Angel Crossing, Arizona, her real career would begin. Her mother had called today, the first she'd heard from her since Clover had walked away from fashion and from the life her mother had dreamed would make Clover happy. She'd been so wrong.

Apparently, her mother had heard about the meeting. She'd also known about Rico Pueblo. She couldn't imagine her parents speaking about anything other than how horrible the other was. In any case, she'd told her mother she'd found her true calling, making the numbers and projects work for VCW.

"Cowgirls Don't Cry" rang out from her phone. Lavonda was calling. Clover hesitated, then picked up. The other woman had been friendly and sympathetic enough earlier.

"Are you ready?" she asked. "Jones is going to wear a kilt."

The non sequitur threw Clover for a moment. "Thanks for the heads-up. I've got my presentation memorized and I'm out the door right now."

"Pepper's mother is coming, too. Have you met Faye? She's a hoot and a half. She says Danny is a Taurus just like AJ. I'm not sure what that has to do with his plans, but that's Faye."

"Is the whole town coming out?"

"Nearly. Anita and Rita are even closing Jim's. Everyone, me included, wants to hear the whole plan again and see how council votes."

Clover got in the car, reminding herself that presenting to the council was no more intimidating than walking across a stage in a bathing suit. "I've got to go. I don't want to get pulled over for driving and talking."

Clover saw her father outside the town hall. He was on his phone and waved her away. She'd meet him inside. She knew what she had to do. He was here just to observe, despite what had happened at Melvin's. She went over the numbers in her head and quickly reviewed the bullet points. She'd blow the council and Danny out of the water with her grasp of the numbers. There would be no way for them to say no. She'd counter every possible argument. Having the time to stay in Angel Crossing had been a big help. She'd begun to understand the town and that had made the tweaks to her presentation even more compelling.

She was sorry that her success meant Danny would lose out, but that was the way of life. There were always winners and losers. She was going to be on the winning side this time. Plus, he was going back to the rodeo—that had become obvious. She didn't care what he did. He'd been a blip in her life, like he'd been that summer. Good to look back on as a fond memory and nothing more.

She walked into the packed room and saw two empty seats at the front. Those were for her and her father, she guessed. She kept her head up to match her confident strides. Tonight she'd be a winner in more ways than one. She'd finally get the job she should have had and she'd be moving on from Angel Crossing. After tonight, her life would really start. Everything that she'd been doing up until now had just been a prelude to her real work and life.

She pulled out the newly printed materials for the council and put one package at each of the places, including the mayor's. None of the members had been seated. That was unusual. And where was her father? They had exactly seven minutes until the start of the meeting.

"Oh, my," she heard a woman whisper, and she turned to look for Danny arriving. Instead, it was a tall man with auburn hair, wearing a kilt. On his right was Lavonda, looking tiny and happy. She waved at Clover as they took two of the few remaining seats. Pepper was there along with AJ and a woman who must be Pepper's mother.

Clover refused to check her watch again. She sat quietly, waiting. Waiting for the rest of her life to start.

Where was everyone?

As soon as she landed in New York, she'd look for a bigger apartment. With her salary as CFO, she could find a nice place, one that took dogs—which her current place didn't—because she thought she'd need a canine. It would be good for her health. There'd been studies—

Crack. "I call the meeting to order," Bobby Ames said, slamming down his gavel a second time.

When and how had the entire council, including Danny, come into the room without her noticing? Crap. She had to get her head back in the game. One more time through the bullet points as Bobby Ames explained the agenda for the meeting.

Where was her father? He should be here to see this. It was a project that would open new opportunities for VCW, usher in a new era. That was the speech she planned for the company's board when she got back to New York.

"We're ready for the vote," Bobby Ames said.

Before Clover could protest, Danny and a quarter of the audience shouted out.

Bobby pounded his gavel until there was quiet. "We had an executive session before the meeting to review new information. It seems Van Camp has expanded the scope of its work and will be assuring the town double its current property taxes as well as a substantial donation to the library and recreation funds. There is also talk of a fund for the garden."

Clover didn't allow herself to smile in triumph. So what if her father swooped in and took over the project. It sounded like he'd gotten the council to agree to what they were proposing and better for Angel Crossing. She was a little...hurt—that was probably the best word—that he hadn't included her on the negotiations. Did it really matter if they got the go-ahead?

"We can't be bought," Danny said, and two or three people, including his sister, agreed from the audience.

"We were elected to do what was best for the town. This is the best," said Irvin Miller.

"What about maintaining our independence? You know that money's got to have strings," Danny said. "Van Camp thinks we're just a bunch of dumb hicks."

"Mayor," Bobby said, "this is a good plan and your opinion might be a bit biased considering your property will no longer be eligible for residential development."

"Sounds like hooey to me," Anita said. "What about me? I've been paying taxes for years and what am I going to get out of the deal?"

"Yeah," said Rita. "Remember the mayor got us that money for the market and to save the theater? Will they keep that and all of the farm plots in town?"

More people from the audience spoke up now about what was working with the town. Clover needed to step in. Somehow the tide was beginning to shift despite Bobby's liberal use of the gavel.

"I'd like to address your concerns, if I may, Mr. President." She smiled brightly at Bobby Ames. "I've been in Angel Crossing for a few months now, speaking with residents, business owners and anyone who will listen.

What I've discovered is a town with a lot of heart and creativity. You've all worked hard to keep your town from dying. You've helped each other and lent a hand. Now it's time for you to benefit from all of that work. Van Camp Worldwide can be the partner to bring prosperity and jobs. To make sure your sons and daughters want to call Rico Pueblo home, too. I know the mayor has been one of your town's greatest advocates and his ideas had merit. But now you can see that VCW will make your town more than just a place to survive but one where you'll thrive." She saw heads nodding. She'd gotten the crowd back on her side.

"You think you know what's best for us, Clover Van Camp. You and your New York daddy? You're just a rodeo beauty queen who's lost her crown."

"Danny—" Lavonda started.

Clover didn't turn. Her gaze stayed on Danny. If he was prepared to fight dirty, so was she. "Those are big words from a bull rider who gave up because he was scared."

"I gave up bull riding because I became mayor."

"No, you didn't. You gave it up because you were afraid that a little damage to your arm was the end of your glory days and that you might actually have to work at winning those purses." The air was sucked out of the room and Danny's gaze went dark with an emotion she couldn't name. "I may not be a beauty queen anymore but I don't rely on people remembering that I once had a crown to make myself feel good. I don't come up with a plan to make a town feel grateful to me for just being there. And I certainly don't make anyone feel guilty for having a dream beyond the dust and dirt of a bull-riding arena. Angel Crossing doesn't need you as much as you need it, Danny. They'll be proving it by accepting VCW's offer."

Clover didn't move her gaze from Danny's and didn't acknowledge the glare she could feel from his sister. In the end, VCW's request was accepted and her father showed up just as she was having her picture taken for a business blog.

"Good job," he said. "I've got the demolition crews set up for next week, and the lawyers have the eviction notices all drawn up."

Chapter 13

Danny watched everyone file out of the meeting and saw that his sister and brother-in-law hadn't left. He wanted them to leave. He didn't want to speak with anyone. He didn't want to be a pathetic mess, punching a wall or wailing like a baby. Between losing his chance at changing Angel Crossing for the better and Clover's revealing his secret to the town and his family—the same thing, really—he wanted to crawl under a rock. He wished he was a hard-drinking, drown-his-sorrows-in-a-beer cowboy. He'd just never had many sorrows. He was making up for that now. He glared at Lavonda, telling her telepathically to get the hell out. She just gave him an indulgent smile—that was the trouble with being the youngest.

"Clover's plan will be good for *your* business," Danny said to his sister after strolling nonchalantly through the empty chamber.

"Possibly, although Jones isn't happy about what Melvin's doing." Lavonda's gaze didn't stray from Danny's face. "We'll talk about your bull riding later, with Mama and Jessie."

"There are artifacts on that property," Jones said, his Scottish accent not out of place with the kilt. "I told him that we could add his ranch to our tour and give him a percentage of our revenue."

"Can't you still do that?" Danny asked.

"Not once Van Camp starts its work. They have plans for that property to be a huge gated community. You know Melvin's property has some of the best views," Lavonda said.

"I was at Melvin's when Clover and Heyer, Clover's father, were there. I didn't know they wanted to put up gates, though." Danny was proud he hadn't stumbled over *her* name.

"We should talk with the state's historic commission about Melvin's. We should be able to get a stay on the sale," Jones said, his Scottish burr more obvious.

Danny had stopped listening because what had happened hit him in the face. He'd lost. His plan was done. He owned property that had worth only to VCW and all of his savings were tied up in it. He needed to move on. Angel Crossing had decided what they wanted and it wasn't him.

"Finally sunk in, huh?" Lavonda said, reaching out slowly to touch his arm. He jerked away.

"I've got a lot to do. I'll have to see what Van Camp will give me for my properties. If they don't pay well, I'll be stuck. It's time for me to come out of retirement anyway."

"What? Wait. You're really going to ride again?" Lavonda asked, her voice rising. Jones put a large hand on her shoulder. Danny's gut fell. That was the kind of gesture a couple made for each other without thinking. The kind of gesture that could turn a bad situation into something tolerable.

"There's not enough work here for me. I don't think Rico Pueblo will want me for mayor. Anyway, I'm a cowboy...a bull rider." Saying the words didn't feel as right as he'd hoped. "Gotta get home and let the dogs out." Danny made sure he sauntered from the building and strolled down the street. He was cool with what had happened. Sure. Initially it had been a slap in the face. Now that he thought on it, the whole situation was good. He'd never planned to settle in Angel Crossing. When he'd landed in the town, he was just waiting until his arm healed. So maybe it'd never heal entirely—that didn't mean he needed to stop riding. Like Pepper's mother, Faye, would say, this was the universe's way of telling him that he needed to change his path. He just wished the universe hadn't had to do its talking in front of the whole town.

The family who said they'd take on Hulk met him in the Angel Crossing all-purpose lot. They had two children, one of whom had a cochlear implant to help him hear, so they thought a dog with a similar challenge would be a good choice. His sister Jessie had recommended them. The son had been in one of her therapeutic riding camps at Hope's Ride. She'd vouched for him and his family. They'd met on a Friday afternoon as the vendors for Saturday's farmers' market started to mark out their stalls in the lot. Some would come in early tomorrow but many started their setup on Fridays.

Not everyone was an early riser like Pepper, who helped organize the market.

The family got back in their dusty SUV, just as Pepper pulled up to supervise the vendors and, of course, Clover came racing toward him.

"Is he gone?" she asked.

He hadn't seen her in the week since the council meeting. He'd been busy ramping up his training regime and discussing how to get back in the bull-riding game with AJ. He hadn't talked about Clover, even when AJ had asked him about her. He'd only just prevented himself from decking the man when he'd suggested that Danny should apologize to Clover (even if Danny hadn't done anything wrong), then beg her to take him back.

Clover stood with hands on hips in front of him, her soft mouth a hard line and her blue eyes flinty. "I asked you to let me know when you found a family for Hulk."

"You told me that VCW only wanted to help Angel Crossing."

"I know...in the long run...there's always pain with change, but it will be worth it."

"Worth it. Tearing down the town, destroying what everyone has been trying to save, chasing out all of the residents will be better?" Danny wasn't worried that his voice was carrying to the vendors or to Pepper. It was all true and they should know that Clover and her company were not their savior.

"We're making things better. There will be jobs."

"What kind of jobs? And where will people live?"

"Danny," Clover said in a reasonable tone that made his head explode.

"You think you know what's best for us? You think

because we live in a little town that's struggling, we should be happy for anything you're willing to offer us? We're not. We have a great town, an amazing community. That counts for a hell of a lot more than money."

"You talk a good game, but you're not staying and you didn't win the vote."

"I may not be staying, but I'm not leaving the town worse off than when I came. You and your father can't say the same thing."

"I'm not going to argue with you about this. We already did that at the meeting."

"Let's talk about the meeting." He stomped closer to her. He wanted to look her in the eye. "My hand and my arm were my business. Using them to win your case was low, even for a New York City diva. How would you like it if I aired the fact that your father has never thought you were competent enough to run any part of his business and that he came to Angel Crossing to clean up your 'mess.'" He made sure everyone heard the last sentence.

"Danny, I know you're upset but that gives you no right to treat me badly."

"You mean the way you let your daddy treat you. Please. You must like it or you would do something about it."

"I am doing something about it. I'm walking away."

"That's right," he yelled. "Run away. That's what you do best. When the going gets tough, then Clover gets going."

She turned and gave him a pitying look. What was that for? His phone pinged and he pulled it out. Hulk's new family had sent a picture of the puppy kissing the little boy. "Hell and damnation," he yelled, hurling his phone and hitting a car, dinging the door and shattering his phone.

"What bug crawled up your butt?" AJ asked as he strolled across the lot. "I see."

"What do you see?"

"An ass." AJ looked his friend up and down. "Feel better breaking your phone and putting a dent in Liddy's car? You'll owe her for that, by the way."

"I don't give a flying—"

"Don't say it, boy," Chief Rudy said. "I could hear you yelling over by Miss Faye's booth."

"Clover just left," AJ said.

"I see."

"If you *girls* think you know sh—" Danny said.

"No need for that," said the chief, who never swore. "I want you to go apologize to Liddy and promise to pay for the damage. Then you need to go speak with Miss Faye—you've upset her. Then you need to go after Clover and apologize for whatever you've done wrong."

"I have a daddy," Danny said, beyond annoyed with the two men. "I don't need you or AJ telling me what I should do. You don't see what *she's* done. *She* and Van Camp are going to ruin this town, and *she* lied about what they really have planned."

"Clover isn't the kind of woman to lie," AJ said. "She always seemed straightforward to me. I mean even back in the day. She wasn't snooty or anything. Didn't wear falsies—"

"Shut up," Danny said with a level of menace to let AJ know, friend or not, if he said another word, Danny would punch him.

"I'm not your daddy, right enough," the chief started, "but I am the law around here and there'll be no fighting, especially because you're too stubborn and bull-stupid to know you love that gal."

"Do not. It was just—" Danny stopped himself when he saw the chief's frown.

"Everyone knows it. She loves you back. And everyone knows that, too."

"Does everyone know," Danny said, "that she lied, that she's angling to be a bigwig at her daddy's business and that her idea of a perfect life is a Manhattan penthouse and a closet full of fancy purses?"

"Danny dear," Faye said, strolling up in a swirl of Stevie Nicks skirts and a cloud of patchouli. "It's always rocky when a Taurus—that's you—and a Leo get together. I told Rudy and Arthur John that before they came over. Did they explain?" she asked before going on without pause. "You need to help her with the next big decision in her life. You will be her protector by knocking all obstacles from her path and she'll calm your hot blood."

"Thank you?" Danny said, not sure what else he could answer, especially with the other two men staring at him.

"Oh, man," AJ finally said, "you are in big trouble if Faye thinks she needs to help."

"It's not me, Arthur John," she said to AJ. "It's the stars. I just interpret."

"Whatever any of you think, I am not in love with Clover."

"Yes, you are," Faye said, "and you loved Hulk. You're sad he went away today."

Danny's chest caved in with the picture in his mind of the puppy in his new home, quickly followed by the hurt on Clover's face as she left. He stared at Faye and she opened her arms. For a second, he wanted to lay his head on her shoulder and bawl like a baby. Except he was a big bad bull-riding cowboy. He didn't need to do either. "I've got work to do," he said lamely as he strode off with purpose. He certainly wasn't running. He'd made sure of that by slowing his steps to a stroll. He might not be a "drowning his sorrows in a beer" sort of cowboy, but he might change that because so far nothing else was working.

"Another beer, Anita," Danny said, drinking his lunch on Saturday since he wasn't hungry.

"Here you go."

He looked at the frosty mug of...root beer. "What the hell?"

"You've reached your limit, Mayor," Anita said with the sternness of a mother, one of which he already had and that was plenty.

"Two beers?"

"Yep. Heard what happened yesterday."

Great. Of course, the story had gotten around town. He never figured that the twins would turn down his business.

Anita went on. "And don't think Lem at the store will sell you liquor. I already called him."

"Tell Lavonda I don't need her to interfere."

"Didn't hear a peep from your sister."

Danny eyed Anita. Didn't look like she was lying. He put down his money and left Jim's. What was the point of being at the bar if he couldn't drink? He'd just go home and take care of his needs there. Damn.

His sisters and his baby niece stood on the sidewalk in front of him. How had they done that? Were the women in this town crazy? Something in the water? Maybe that was Clover's problem, too.

"We're taking you to lunch," Lavonda said, grabbing his arm.

"Your niece wants to have her lunch with Uncle Danny," Jessie added from his other side, her daughter settled comfortably on her hip.

He allowed them to drag him to the diner. Jessie made him sit with Gertie and help feed her.

"Here's your pie," Marlena said, setting down a slice that was covered in whipped cream, looking like a gallon had been dumped on it. "Heard about yesterday. Thought you might need extra."

"Don't get mad, Danny," Lavonda said. "Everyone feels bad about the meeting. Then you had to give up Hulk and then Clover dumped on you. I never expected that from her. She came to the Back Room."

Danny wasn't certain how being a part of the Devil's Food Diner's Back Room Mafia gave Clover Angel Crossing street cred. Was there such a thing?

"When you're done with that mountain of dessert—none of which you're going to feed to my daughter—we're going to the market," Jessie said firmly as she sipped her coffee, eyeing both him and Gertie. The little girl gave back a similarly stubborn stare.

He focused on the dessert but couldn't take a bite. He did not want to go back to the scene of the crime.

"Duncle," Gertie said. "Eat."

"I'm not hungry. Let's go play in the street."

"Danny," Jessie said. "Don't say things like that to her."

He shrugged, picked up his niece and left the diner. His sisters could pay since they seemed to have some plan for him that he wouldn't approve of. He knew the two of them and he'd seen the looks they'd shared.

He and Gertie gathered pretty rocks. Jessie deserved to carry them around in that suitcase she called a purse now. Nothing like the purses Clover coveted and used. Didn't matter anymore. He'd get back in the saddle in more ways than one soon enough. First he'd ride in the charity event. Then he'd be back in the ring. After that, he'd have no problem finding a new woman to squire around.

"Before we go to the market," Lavonda said, "I want to stop by your property."

"Real subtle, sis. What do you and Jessie have planned?" he asked. His niece was perched on his shoulders, wearing his hat, which she had to push at to keep it from covering her face.

"Nothing. I just have an idea for that space but need to see it before I make a decision," Lavonda insisted. Jessie wouldn't look him in the eye.

"You shouldn't fib. That's not right, is it, Gertie?"

His niece babbled nonsense in agreement.

He didn't say more but followed his sisters because now he was a little intrigued. He couldn't imagine what they had cooked up at his property. Had they kidnapped Clover and were holding her hostage there? No. Even his overprotective sisters wouldn't do that.

He saw a woman standing in front of the building. It wasn't Clover or anyone else he recognized.

"Surprise," Lavonda said. "This is Jolene. Nearly family. She's Olympia's sister, so by the transitive property she's related, right?" She looked at Jessie, Olympia's sister-in-law. "She's moving to Arizona—and she needs a place to open her business."

"Is that so?" Danny asked with sarcasm. He remembered Jolene from Olympia's wedding, which he'd officiated. She rescued animals or something like that. He couldn't imagine she was opening anything in Angel Crossing, which would soon be swanky Rico Pueblo. Way too soon for his sisters to be setting him up.

Jessie broke into the conversation. "It looks weird, we know, but really we hadn't planned this. Jolene called this morning to tell Lavonda she'd be in town and was looking at rentals. Blame the real-estate people. They suggested your property."

"Uh-huh," Danny said, believing only about half of what Jessie had just said. "Let's go say hello. She's not married, right?"

"No idea," Lavonda said quickly. "It's not a setup."

Danny kept his mouth shut as he put his niece on the ground and took back his hat. Today was as good a day as any to start his new life. Might be the beer and sugar talking, but it was a good idea. "Hello," he said, reaching out his hand. "I'm Danny and I understand you're looking to rent a place?"

"Jolene James," she said, shaking his hand with strength. "Maybe. Depends on what you want to charge me."

"Rent in Angel Crossing is reasonable. What kind of business are you considering?" He and Jolene toured the property as she explained she wanted to open a pet store that also offered homeopathic remedies and re-homing services for pets and ranch animals. It sounded overly ambitious to him, but more power to her if that was what she wanted.

"Thanks again for the tour," Jolene said. "It looks like it could work and the rent is very reasonable."

"I do want to let you know that a developer is coming to town and has plans."

"Heard about that. Rico Pueblo, right? It could work for me. Plus, it will be a while until that all gets done."

"News travels fast," Danny said.

"I heard there's a farmers' market here, too?"

"Yep," Lavonda said. "It'll be going on for another hour or so, if you want to stop by."

"I think I will. Can you give me directions?" Jolene asked.

"Why don't you come with us?" Jessie asked. Then Danny saw her nudge her daughter.

"Duncle, please." Or at least that was what Danny assumed the babble meant.

He stared at his sister. Really low using her little girl to force Danny into going with them. How could they be playing matchmaker? He didn't need their help. He was fine. What he and Clover had been doing was fun, but it wasn't more than skin deep. Any feelings he'd had were about his plans, not about him and Clover. He'd finally convinced himself of that after the beers, the pie and the tour of his building.

He walked down the street with his niece once again on his shoulders and wearing his hat. He heard the women speaking behind him about the possibilities of the property, how to best train horses and why jeans gaped at the waist.

"Duncle," Gertie said almost clearly.

"Yes, squirt?" She tried to lean down, almost falling to give him back his hat. He pushed her back in place and took the moist-around-the-brim hat. Then she started drumming her heels on his chest as she squealed long and loud.

"Gertie," Jessie said. "You stop that noise and kicking your uncle, or we won't go pick out a new lead rope for Molly. They have sparkly ones here."

"Darkles," Gertie said on a breath of love and joy. Danny knew that he'd lost her. He put her on the ground.

Lavonda said to Jessie, "What's that diva pony of yours up to? Is she teaching Gertie to ride, too? Or is she too busy starring on YouTube?" Lavonda turned to Jolene and said, "That pony is more famous than one of those viral video cats."

"Her last video did well," Jessie said of her childhood pony with diva tendencies.

"T'ome," Gertie said, tugging on her mother's hand. "Darkles."

"I better go help," Lavonda said as she hurried off.

"Not very subtle," Danny said to Jolene.

"My sister's about the same. Don't worry. I'm just here for the rental property and to buy salve that Lavonda told me about. She said she uses it on her donkey and it heals up anything."

He and Jolene strolled around the market. She was a good companion on a crappy day. See. He was an adult no matter what his sisters imagined. He was already making plans for the next stage of his life. It wouldn't include Jolene no matter what scheme his sisters had hatched. The woman had her own plan, which politely but firmly did not include a bull-riding cowboy.

"Thanks for telling me about the town. It sounds like the kind of place that might be open to what I want to do," Jolene said as the stands at the market started to close up.

"It's a good town. It'll be changing, though, so it's time for me to move on."

"I can understand. Good luck with SAC. I hope to be around for that. Sounds like a good time."

"It will be. We're just out to have fun. We even have an amateur event planned."

"Maybe I'll see you then," she said, waving as she walked away.

His sisters had said goodbye an hour ago, carrying a pink sequined lead rope for Molly along with a silver-and-pink halter. He was glad they'd already left because he needed to be on his own. He got stopped at least a half a dozen times as he tried to leave the market. He wouldn't miss this, would he? When he was out on the road and riding. It was a lot to feel responsible for an entire town. That had never been his intention. Plus, they didn't need him anymore. Right? They'd chosen Van Camp over him. He tried to convince himself he hadn't been hurt by that because it was all business.

He ignored the next three greetings. They didn't want his vision for a better Angel Crossing, fine. Good to remember that. He should be out of here not long after SAC.

"Hey, Mayor," Bobby Ames yelled out from his booth with stuffed and mounted animals in dioramas. "We need your signature on the agreement with VCW."

"No" shot out of his mouth before he could shut up.

"Don't be a sore loser."

"I'm not a loser. Angel Crossing is," Danny said close enough to Bobby to see the hairs in the stuffed animals. Danny wasn't sure where the words were coming from. "I resign as mayor because I can't agree to a project that will destroy the heart of this town."

"Don't you mean that will break your heart?" Bobby asked.

"Shut it or I'll...shove one of these damned football-playing squirrels where the sun don't shine."

His words echoed around the suddenly quiet market.

"That doesn't sound very mayoral," said Clover's daddy, who'd popped up like a gopher from a hole just behind him. He should be back in New York counting his money, not still hanging around the town he ruined. "But what can anyone expect from a bull rider whose brains have been rattled loose?"

The anger that Danny hadn't known he'd been holding back all day exploded. He turned to Heyer and grabbed him by the collar. "A bull rider who treats Clover with respect and love, unlike her own damned father."

Shit. He dropped his hands and stared at them. What had he just said? He couldn't mean it, could he? That he loved Clover.

Chapter 14

Clover looked around Dead Man's Cottage and sighed. She needed to pack. Her work here was done. She was going back to New York and her new office. How had the place gotten so full of her stuff when she was just renting? There had been trips to the farmers' market, where she'd picked up scarves and table runners from the weavers. Then she'd found out about a tag sale. *Thanks so much, Pepper.* That had added an old-fashioned sewing table, a kitschy lamp and a beautiful pot of Native American origin—although no one was exactly sure from which tribe or what decade. The closet in her bedroom, which had started out with a reasonable number of outfits, had exploded. Her mother had sent care packages of clothing.

Looking at it wouldn't get it packed or thrown away. She would have to jettison a lot of what she'd gathered here...including Danny and all of the memories they'd made. Wow. That was sappy. Maybe she needed to start a greeting-card company.

She was being too hard on herself. Every woman was allowed to revisit an old lover. Not that they'd been much to write home about when they'd been teens. Danny had certainly learned a lot since then, which didn't exactly make Clover feel any better about the situation.

Stop obsessing, she told herself. She was an MBA graduate of Wharton. She knew how to get things done. Yeah, hire someone. That made her laugh because that was one of her mama's sayings, much sassier and more understandable than Danny's mother's.

She might like to hire someone for the grunt work of packing, but she'd still have to decide what to keep and what to pitch. That was the real work. Maybe she should call Pepper and ask her to come over. Then she could give her the clothing and household items that others in Angel Crossing could use. The woman had an encyclopedic knowledge of everyone in town and what they might or might not be lacking. They could make it a girls' night. Did she have any wine and snacks to make it really fun?

Her phone rang. It was probably Pepper. No such luck. It was Mama.

"I understand that Van Camp owns Angel Crossing now," her mama said.

"Hello to you, too."

"This is a business call, darlin'. No time for hello."

"You don't care about Daddy's business, unless it means he can't make the next separation payment. I still don't know how you managed that."

"I care about you, and this plan… Well, I just don't think this is what you signed on for."

"I came up with the current plan," Clover said, frustrated that her mama was still trying to convince her to leave VCW.

"I don't think what your daddy is putting his money behind is your plan."

"Of course it's mine. Daddy sent me to Angel Crossing to fix Knox's mistake. Mama, just tell me what you're dying to say." Clover was so tired of the sniping her parents still indulged in after years of separation.

"You've spent too much time in New York. You know that I like to work up to saying things that aren't going to be heard well by others."

What the— "Mama," Clover said, hoping that her level of frustration was clear in those two syllables.

"If you insist, darlin'. Your father is building Rico Pueblo's gated section on a historic site that will be destroyed." Clover tried to interrupt. "He's working fast so the state doesn't find out. He's also lining up the same legislators and the lawyers to oust every one of the current residents. Then he'll build housing outside of town for a VCW workforce. A modern-day company town."

"I made sure the historic site was worked into the plan, and there's no way we can just kick people out of our houses." But she hadn't seen what her father had presented at that executive meeting, now that she thought about it. What had he shown them then? He'd been slick about telling her his paperwork was elsewhere. Damn.

"Darlin', I don't like to be the one to tell you this, but Knox called me."

"He's the reason I came out here." That and the promise of being CFO.

"Not exactly. He told your daddy no. That's when Heyer called you."

Her heart hurt. Why did she let herself think she was his first choice? Why? She wasn't a little girl anymore. "Daddy lied to me from the beginning, didn't he? I've got to stop him."

"I don't think even you can do that."

"We'll see," Clover said, tears in her eyes. She hung up before she started to cry. She wanted to be a CFO. Her response to a crisis was not tears. It was a new strategy.

Danny had been right, or something like right. Her reason for coming to Angel Crossing might have been all about business, but she didn't want to be in the business of running people out of their houses and destroying their community and its history.

Wait. Maybe her mother had misunderstood or was even using Clover as another means of getting back at her sort-of ex-husband. Clover would call Knox, or at least email him.

She'd been so sure she could do it herself and was getting what she wanted from her father, not just the title but also his respect. Now she couldn't understand why'd she ever wanted that from him.

Still, he was her daddy. First talk with Knox and find out if Mama had the right end of the bull.

"Mama said you'd call me," Knox said when he answered his phone.

"Why didn't you tell me?" Clover decided she should

be just as mad at Knox as at her father—if it was all true.

"I assumed you knew. You were the one telling Daddy how you'd fix anything I'd done to ruin the project."

"He told me it was a revitalization of the town. I created Rico Pueblo to provide VCW and the residents with a good deal. Everyone would have come out ahead."

"I find it hard to believe he didn't show you any of this. He was so proud. He was going to show Mama how her down-home folks really were willing to sell their history for the right price."

"Are you telling me this is still all about them and their marriage? This is getting beyond old, and now it could ruin the lives of a whole lot of people. We've got to stop them." Clover was ashamed for the first time in her life. Not that she'd never been embarrassed by her fast-talking, tailored-suit-wearing daddy. He'd never fit into Texas, where Clover had always felt most comfortable.

"This is your fight now. I already fought him and I'm done. I'm happy enough in Hong Kong, and I'll be back in New York in a year or so. I've got plans for my life, too, Clover."

She and her little brother had never been close—too much time spent apart with her in Texas and him in New York. She shouldn't have expected him to defy their father for a second time. After all, she was the big sister. Before she could tell him it was all right, he went on. "You can always run back to Mama and Cowgirl's Blues. I've got VCW and that's it. That's the way it's always been."

"I'm sorry. I don't want to make things harder for

you. I'll solve this myself. I'm not going to let Daddy change Angel Crossing. Rico Pueblo is dead."

"I wish you luck, and remember that the board still has to approve anything of this magnitude." Knox hung up. She guessed that was as much help as he was going to give. He was right. She could always crawl back to Mama and beg for a job. Where would Knox go? He'd worked only for VCW. He'd only ever had their father, who'd made sure his heir apparent had a Knickerbocker upbringing with private schools, nannies and a seat on the Van Camp board.

Hold on. Knox had a seat on the board. And Clover knew a number of the other longtime members. She couldn't imagine that they'd be thrilled with what her father had schemed to make happen.

She'd call Lavonda, who'd been in PR. Clover'd bet she could spin this so that Heyer would look bad enough the board would make him pull out of the deal. Since this was about Angel Crossing—Danny's town—Lavonda would help, right?

Visiting Lavonda had been a bust. She said that she wouldn't help Clover unless Danny said it was okay. She blamed Clover, more or less, for the mess the town was about to be in. She couldn't really blame the other woman for her attitude.

What next? Should Clover approach Danny? Did she want to? He'd called her names and treated her like dirt. Time, as they say, to put on her big-girl panties—which made her think *thong*, which made her think *hot nights*, which made her think seeing Danny again was a really, really bad idea.

She didn't usually walk away from a challenge and

this was more than a challenge. This was her saving the town that her father's plan—the one that she'd opened the door for—would destroy. Danny had been right. Wouldn't he love hearing those words from her? Yes, he would, but she didn't need to say them in front of the whole of Angel Crossing. She needed to find him alone. She knew how to do that. He might not be a creature of habit, but Maggie May was.

Clover waited quietly at the end of the lot behind the diner where Danny let the dog out in the evening. This was the last trip for the night. It had taken Clover that long to work up her courage, outline what she would say and gird her loins against the pull of Danny. She tried to smile at the last picture. It was up there with her big-girl thong.

Maggie May ran right up to her. Danny hung back, his face devoid of emotion. Fortunately, the dusk-to-dawn light and the full moon made the lot bright enough for Clover to read his face. She leaned down and rubbed the dog's head. "How did she take her last baby moving on?"

"Fine. She'll be ready to adopt as soon as I can find the time and money to have her spayed."

"Let me know how much and I can take care of that."

"Of course you can. I keep forgetting you just finished buying up the town."

"I just want to help."

"We don't need your kind of help." He turned away from her, leading Maggie May away with a signal from his hand. The dog looked over her shoulder, definitely letting Clover know that she didn't approve of Danny's rudeness.

"I have a plan." Clover started after him.

"Where have I heard that before?"

She didn't let his back or his cold tone stop her. "You were right." She held her breath but he didn't turn around and open his arms to her. But she hadn't expected him to. Not really. "Did you hear me?"

"I heard you."

"Aren't you going to say something else?"

"What is there to say?" He turned and Maggie May sat, her soft eyes looking at Clover with doggy pity as she leaned against Danny's leg. "You think admitting you were wrong makes it all better? This isn't about us or anything we did." His chest heaved once, twice, before he went on. "This isn't about winning or losing. This is about a town filled with good people who've been trying to survive. You and your father are going to finally break this place. The mine closing a decade ago didn't do what you and your millions in revitalization will do. How is this fixable? I didn't fight for Angel Crossing to prove I was right or even to make money. I did it because this place matters. These people matter."

"I know. That's why I—"

"I'm not going through this argument again. This is old ground. Come on, Maggie May." He started back to his apartment. The dog trotted at his booted heels, looking over her shoulder like she wanted Clover to follow.

"Danny," Clover said, not caring that her voice cracked with desperation. "I've got to make this right and I can. I care about Angel Crossing, too." She paused, trying to find the words that would change his mind. "I spoke with my brother, Knox, and we can fix this. He stepped away because of what Daddy wanted to do. He's with me... Danny, I know you don't believe me and I understand why, but believe this—I don't care if my father fires me. I'm going to make sure that Angel Crossing and its history is protected."

"Whatever," Danny said as he continued up the stairs.

"Why won't you listen to me? Don't you see? I'm doing this for you." *Wait. What?* Why had she just said that? Her chest tightened in surprise and fear.

"That's low even for you," Danny said, half turning to her. "Saying that you care about me, using what we—"

"That's not why I said that. I mean, I do care about you." She couldn't breathe because she didn't just care about him. She loved him. Her feet wouldn't move and her mouth wouldn't open.

"Yeah. That's what I thought you'd say. Go, Clover. Go back to New York. That's where you belong."

She watched him climb the last few steps. She wanted to shout to him to stop. She couldn't because she didn't understand what her heart had just relayed to her brain. She couldn't really be in love with Danny Leigh. That had been teenage beauty queen Clover Anastasia. Grown-up Ms. Van Camp, MBA, had much different tastes and plans.

Her feet finally moved. She found her car and drove back to Dead Man's Cottage. She'd told Danny she'd make things right and he still didn't believe her. How could he when she didn't believe what she'd just admitted to herself, that she loved him. She plopped down in the sagging armchair. She needed to examine all of this. Did she really love Danny? Was she imagining her feelings because she'd been deprived of his very fine body? No, that was stupid. Even as a shallow teen, she wouldn't have been able to convince herself that sex and love were the same thing. Making love with Danny had been, could be again... *Oh. My. God.* She'd loved him. Always. That was why they'd lost their virginity to each other more than a decade ago. They'd been in love.

Okay. Say she really did love Danny. What difference did it make? He hated her for good reason. She'd helped her father implement a plan that would ruin the town Danny loved.

Was she willing to give up on being CFO? Yes and yes. And not just because she loved a bull-riding cowboy. This decision was about her and what she wanted. What she needed. Her choice to fight VCW and save Angel Crossing was her choice because she had more than a shred of dignity and decency.

She pulled in a deep breath and let the tears stream down her face, the ones she'd been holding back since Danny had told her to go at the market. She ached deep inside and she couldn't hold it in anymore. She held her hand across her mouth so no one could hear her sobs, then gave a wet and hopeless laugh. Who would hear? Who would ever hear her? She was horrible at this relationship thing. She hadn't even known she'd loved Danny. Her first lover, her first real boyfriend, the man she'd measured every other boyfriend against. A sob deep from her soul slipped past her hand.

She wanted to run from the pain. She wanted to curl up in a ball and protect her soft underbelly. She wanted to call her mother and ask her to make it all better. The light of the single lamp blurred as tears couldn't fall fast enough from her eyes. Would this hurt ever stop? It had to because she wouldn't survive it.

Finally, her shirt collar a soggy mess from her tears and her eyes swollen to slits of misery, Clover pulled herself from the chair. After a night's sleep, she'd have a better idea how to go forward. Could she stay in the bed, though? Even though the room had been stripped of everything but the sheets, she and Danny had made love there. Dear Lord and his angels. She'd drive out of town and stay at a hotel. There wouldn't be any memories there. Then tomorrow, she'd hunt down her father and explain what she would do if he didn't amend the plan, pointing out that she'd make sure he didn't get any support from the VCW board. After that, Knox could step in and take care of things. Clover'd call Mama and beg her to give her a job at Cowgirl's Blues. She could let Lavonda know the gated community was gone and all the other parts of the plan that would have ruined the town, and *she* could tell Danny. That would be for the best.

She wiped tears from her eyes again and squinted to make sure that she didn't miss any of the twists on the road out of town. All for the best, she kept repeating, her heart skipping beat after beat as her rental moved farther and farther from Angel Crossing and Danny.

Chapter 15

Since the number of hours Danny had been able to sleep seemed to be in inverse proportion to the number of hours in the night, he'd had a lot of time to think and scheme. He might also have been dodging friends and family who wanted to know exactly what he'd said at the market and what he was going to do about Clover leaving. Nothing and nothing. Especially after going by Dead Man's Cottage and seeing she'd cleared out. Obviously Clover was smarter than him. Their...whatever it had been...had no future. Didn't really matter what he felt, right? It didn't matter that the floor had dropped out of his life, worse than when he'd thought he couldn't ride bulls anymore. That his injury had sidelined him in the crappiest of ways. No great wreck. No spectacular last ride.

The whole idea of going back on the circuit by

switching up his riding style wasn't what he wanted either. Right now, it didn't seem like he was getting much of anything he wanted, and that was because all he really wanted was Clover in his bed. In his life. His mama would tell him that if wishes were rubies then the whole world would look rosy. He gave a bark of a laugh, and Maggie May yipped. He still missed Hulk but an email with another photo from the puppy's new family convinced Danny he'd done the right thing. He also thought he might have a place for Maggie May: with his parents, which would be perfect because he'd get to see her. Instead, though, he should be focused on Angel Crossing. He was still the town's mayor. And he had a new tenant, Jolene James. She wanted to get her pet boutique up and running no matter what the town became. He had a lot to do to get the building ready.

It was time to snap out of his funk. He had other jobs to bid on and other life decisions to make. Was life in Angel Crossing or on the back of a bull, whether Clover was with him or not?

Regardless of what he wanted to do for the rest of his life, he'd promised Jolene that he'd get the first floor of the old building ready for her.

"Come on, Maggie May. Time to get some work done. Real work, not just thinking about what I want to do." The dog rushed to the apartment door, giving him a doggy smile of delight. Boy, he wished his life were that simple. Then he'd be a dog and he'd be neutered. Maybe not so fun.

"Hey, Danny," AJ said as he knocked on the door frame and came into the open space that would become Jolene's new store Pets! Pets! Pets!

"Working here." Danny didn't want to talk with his friend. He didn't want to explain what he'd said at the market and he certainly didn't want to talk about the town. The changes were going to ruin Pepper's ideas for improving the health of the residents with community gardens. Knowing his friend, he probably thought it was Danny's fault and he needed to fix it. AJ was all about making Pepper happy.

"I told those women you were busy and working hard. That argument went as far as a cat in the rain."

"The Back Room Mafia?"

"Who else? I was told to come and tell you to go after Clover."

"Ain't happening." Danny wasn't saying anything more on that subject. "Are you sure you don't want EllaJayne to compete at the rodeo?"

"No way." AJ walked over to Maggie May and gave her a pet. The dog licked his hand. "You found a way to save Pepper's plan last time, so what are you going to do this time? If we don't get Van Camp to move along, none of us will be here. I can't let that happen. Pepper and I are halfway done with our house. Faye has that whole alpaca and llama yarn thing going. We can't move along. We can't do that anywhere else."

"I tried. No one would listen to me."

"So you'll just take your lasso and go home? This is Angel Crossing. This is our home."

"Yours, maybe. I was just here because of Gene, and then I got tricked into being mayor. I think it's time for me to mosey down the road. I guess Van Camp showed me that."

"Really? You're going to let that New Yorker beat you?"

"It wasn't the New Yorker. I could have ignored anything he threw at me. It was the blasted whole town acting like I'd done something wrong."

"They got played. Can you blame them? What Clover—"

Danny couldn't stop his mouth from tightening.

AJ shook his head. "So? You weren't lying at the market when you used the L word. Damn, man, you're one sorry cowboy."

"I'm finally a smart cowboy," Danny argued. "I know when to wrap up my ropes and move to the next ranch."

AJ's expression turned serious as he stepped up to Danny. "If you care...if you love Clover, don't let pride or whatever else get in the way. I know how well that works. You were given a second chance with her. I'd say that was the universe telling you what you should do."

"You've been around Faye too long. Next thing you know, you'll be telling me that I've got a scorpion in my rising sun." Danny moved away from his friend, turning his back on what he was saying, the possibility he was holding out.

"It's Scorpio. And what I'm saying is that you loved Clover when you were sixteen. We all knew it. You had such a sappy expression. Then after you—"

"Enough," Danny snapped. "I know. I know. But I can't fix this with a little cowboy magic. This is the real world and Daddy Van Camp has a bottomless pocket. I'm done fighting the 'man.'"

"You're breaking your promise to Angel Crossing. You said that you'd make this a better place."

"It is a better place and will be even better when Van Camp is done."

"Sure, a bunch of gates and mansions and froufrou dogs. That's going to make this better. What about Anita and Rita? Jim's is all they have."

"It's not my problem."

"Maybe. But do you think you'll feel better ignoring it and not going after Clover?"

"You tell me to not abandon Angel Crossing. Then you tell me to go after Clover. Can't do both of them."

"You're the cowboy who rode Tito V, and you're the only bull rider I know who doesn't walk with a limp. You've got some kind of mojo. Use it now. Prove you're more than a pretty face."

"What if I don't want to fix this?"

"Then you're a liar on top of everything else."

"What do I get out of all of this but a lot more headaches? Just like when I agreed to be mayor…against my wishes."

"Why are you acting like such a little girl? You know you want to be the cowboy in the white hat saving Angel Crossing and getting the lady."

AJ might be just a little right, especially about the girl. He did want Clover. More than want her. She was that piece of his heart that he hadn't even known he'd been missing. He knew he couldn't make her stay, but he also couldn't let her walk away without understanding how he felt about her. Could he do the distance thing like his sister Jessie and her husband, Payson, had done? Hells yes, if it meant that Clover was his. Well, there was his answer. "All right," Danny said. "Help me finish up these shelves and the counter. Then I'll be off to save the day like the Lone Ranger and all before lunch."

"Hot damn," AJ said.

* * *

What the— Clover pulled over as the lights from the police cruiser were followed by blasts from the siren. She might have been speeding. She wasn't sure. She'd left Angel Crossing for the final time this morning, making sure Dead Man's Cottage was cleared of her stuff. She'd just... Well, she may have ruined her entire life. She sat waiting for the officer to tell her how much she owed so she could be on her way. She'd go to Tucson, get a flight to San Antonio and then ask her mother for a job, but not advice. She knew that Mama would probably agree with Knox. Clover wasn't up for another fight.

"Miss Clover," Chief Rudy said. "I need you to step out of the car."

She followed his order, not caring why he was here or what he thought she'd done.

"I need you to come with me," he said.

"Excuse me?" Why was the police chief out on the highway and why did she need to get in his car for a traffic violation?

"In the car. With me."

"Why?"

"I don't think you're in a position to ask that."

A pickup raced past, skidded to a halt and reversed, kicking up a sandstorm of dust. Clover and the chief coughed. But she thought she heard him say, "About time."

Out of the dust, his white hat (nearly white, anyway) tilted a little forward, strode Danny Leigh, looking like himself again with his straight even teeth, tanned skin and blond hair. Tall, powerful and slightly pissed off.

"Clover," he said, touching the brim of his hat. "I need to speak with you."

"I don't need to talk to you," she said. She didn't know that she had enough steel in her spine to have a conversation with him. She feared she'd break down and beg him to take her back. "Chief, just give me my ticket, and I'll be on my way out of here."

"I'm giving you a warning," the fatherly man said. "Don't be too proud to say you're sorry and don't be too scared to take the leap." He walked back to his patrol car. Clover snapped her mouth closed.

"What was that about?" Clover asked Danny—more accused than asked.

"I told the chief—" Danny stopped himself. "Hell's bells. I can't do this alongside the road."

"Do what? It doesn't matter. I'm going to Tucson. I need a flight to San Antonio."

"No."

"Danny, I wish you and Angel Crossing well," Clover said. Then she decided that really she wasn't a coward. "I'm a Van Camp. And I can tell you that VCW will not be turning Angel Crossing into Rico Pueblo."

The surprise on Danny's face was genuine, followed by something she couldn't name.

"My brother and I talked with the board and my father's project has been...defunded, is probably the easiest way to explain it. But what it means is that Angel Crossing will remain Angel Crossing. Knox and I are still working out some other details."

"Hell's to the double bells," Danny said, pulling his hat from his head. "That puts a big ol' pin in my plan."

"Not anymore. You can move forward with what you planned. I explained it to Knox and—"

"Not that plan. My other one."

"You mean the charity ride?" She was trying to fill in the blanks and could see from Danny's face that she wasn't doing a good job.

"Maybe I should have sent you a text. I'm messing this up." A car whizzed by, throwing gravel against them. "Come on. At least sit in my pickup. It's not safe standing here."

She hesitated for a moment, then remembered that she was fearless Clover. The teen beauty queen who'd gone after the best-looking boy on a bull. She went with him, working out how to tell him exactly what she thought of him—and of them together, no matter the consequences.

Thank God and his angels. She might have hesitated but now she was following him to his pickup. He had to tell her soon or he'd never get the words out. He also needed to find out more about what she'd said about her daddy and Rico Pueblo. The morning coffee sloshed uncomfortably in his gut. Maggie May gave a growling bark when Clover slid in.

"It's okay," he told the dog. "She'll be staying." Hell. Why had he said that? Because he had bull crap for brains.

"Sweetie," Clover said, holding out her hand to the dog, who'd poked her snout over the seat. "I'm here to... Well, I already told him about my daddy, and now I've got to say the rest of it."

"No." That had come out louder and a lot angrier than he'd wanted. "What I meant is that I've got something to tell you."

"I think it's ladies first," she said, swallowing hard.

Her throat moved and he wanted to kiss the ripples under the soft skin. He wanted to hold her hand and tell her that everything would be all right because... because—

"I love you," he blurted out. Silence filled the cab of the pickup. He saw her wide blue eyes, the blush, the clenched hands. Whatever she had to—

"I wanted to say it first," she finally said.

"What?"

"I love you. I wanted to say it first."

He laughed and Maggie May yipped along. "You love me?" He didn't wait for her to answer. He pulled her across the bench seat to him, locking his lips on hers. Clover. She was his. Her taste was like every good memory he'd ever had or ever would have.

Her hands pushed against him. He instantly lifted his head but didn't let her go. He was never doing that again.

"I had a speech. I want to give my speech," Clover said, although she remained so close her breath spread its warmth over his skin. His hands tightened on her shoulders. He wanted her mouth again. He wanted to drown in the taste of her. "I'll make it fast," she said, holding him off even as her eyes softened. "I realized I loved you because I didn't care about being CFO. I didn't care what Daddy thought of me. All I cared about was making this right for you because Angel Crossing is your place. Your heart."

"Not my heart," he said. Then he leaned in to nuzzle her ear and whisper, "You're my heart, my soul, my reason for getting out of bed every day."

She shivered as his lips found her neck. "Not sure I can live up to that."

"You already have." He pulled her to him again, kissing her hard but with a warmth that was for her alone. No other woman had ever made him hot and mushy at the same time. She was special.

"I love you," she said into his mouth.

He pulled her closer and finally into his lap. He wanted her against him, in the place that had felt like an empty gaping hole. Now with her here, it was completely and permanently filled.

Clover finally wiggled away from Danny, slowly, reluctantly, after the steering wheel had put a permanent crease in her back. He'd let her go grudgingly and with more kisses. She was as giddy as a girl with her first crush, which was just about right since Danny had been her first. She smiled.

"What?" he asked, adjusting his seat and smoothing his hair. It stood up in whorls and tufts where she'd run her hands through it.

"I was just remembering you were my first and now you'll be my last."

"Damned right," he said proudly. "You're a cougar."

"Two years' age difference doesn't make me a cougar."

"Hey, it's my fantasy. I get to say you're a cougar if I want to."

She would not blush but she couldn't stop the flush of heat that added to the near painful fullness between her thighs. She drew in a deep breath because he could take care of that later…and he would. Right now, they really did need to talk. There was so much that had happened and needed to happen.

"We can discuss your fantasies later." He gave her a

knowing smile and she shifted in the seat. Had the cab gotten even hotter?

"Not too much later."

She liked that he was anxious to be with her alone and horizontal. She made herself do return-on-investment calculations in her head to slow her heart and tamp down the heat. They needed to discuss what she and Danny could do to help Angel Crossing. Now that she knew he loved her—insert girlie squee—this part would be easier than she'd imagined. "I told you that my father's project is dead in the water. But VCW still owns or has an option on a number of properties. We don't want to just walk away."

"Good," Danny said fiercely, and Maggie May growled in agreement.

"That means making compromises on both sides." This really was a broad-strokes plan. She and Knox hadn't worked out the details... Maybe she should—

"Remember. I love you." Danny's smile lit up the entire cab. "Dear Lord, I do like saying that."

"I love hearing it, and you'd better love hearing me say it all of the time because you are not going to be able to out 'I love you' me."

She took his hand, marveling again at the callouses, its strength and the tenderness she knew he could show.

"Back to business. With a little work and an infusion of cash, I think we can create a strategy that will use some of what you'd been hoping to do along with some of what my original plan would have done. In other words, we could provide the housing and support to those residents who need it, while creating jobs and economic opportunity. It won't be Rico Pueblo, but we might use parts of that to ramp up the economic—"

He held her face and kissed her hard on the lips. "You make me hot when you talk all MBA." He kissed her deeply then softened his lips as he pulled away. She swayed toward him. His denim-blue eyes darkened to indigo. "How did you make me love you even more?"

"My special talent? If I'd known that when I went for Miss Texas, bet I would have won."

"You would have, but then I would have been arrested for punching every cowboy in the audience. Your sexy MBA talent is only for me."

"ROI," she whispered in his ear. "GDP." He chuckled as his mouth landed on hers and she worked on messing up his hair again.

Chapter 16

Clover tried to wipe the sappy grin off her face. Just not possible. She and Danny had played bull rider and the cowgirl go to the rodeo… Well, she had to giggle at the memory, or she'd end up all hot and bothered again.

"What?" Lavonda asked, sitting beside Clover in the metal stands of the small outdoor arena where Clover had watched Danny practice and now would watch him compete again. Lavonda had told her this was where she'd met her husband, who'd been competing at the Highland games here—a kilted cowboy with a passion for archaeology.

Clover was not telling Danny's sister about anything they'd been doing.

"Yuck," added Jessie, Danny's oldest sister, corralling her daughter between her long legs. "I know that kind of look because you get it, Lavonda. It has to do with—" she looked down at her little girl "—grown-up stuff."

Clover refused to blush because it clashed with her hair. "Look, it's the peewee riders," she said to distract the women.

SAC Bull-Riding Extravaganza, which was still raising money for the town's new revitalization projects, had everything from three-legged races to bull rides by the top professionals. Best of all, the stadium was full of spectators and every concession stand had a line, including the one run by Pepper's mother, Faye, where she and the ladies from the Back Room Mafia were telling fortunes and giving out horoscopes. They also had a "Take a Selfie with Ralph the Llama" booth, and the line was three deep. Apparently, Ralph had a big Instagram following.

Clover knew she should be nervous for Danny. He would be riding, just for fun—although she'd seen some betting going on between the men, when she'd gone down to wish him luck. He said he was in good shape, having worked on riding left-handed. Of course, she may have distracted him when he'd been working out. What could she say? A big blond cowboy doing push-ups was a thing of beauty. She'd needed to show him her true appreciation.

"Oh, crap," Pepper said from her seat next to Clover. Butch, her "herding" dog, had slipped into the arena, then proceeded to chase the children and the younger llamas who'd been recruited as "wild" bull substitutes. "Butch," Pepper yelled, standing and ready to run into the ring. Then a streak of red and white came hurtling into the fray. It was Maggie May. She'd attached herself to Butch, feeling the need to treat him like one of her pups, while he adored her with the burning love a teen boy had for his first crush. Maggie May nipped at Butch, who stopped what he was doing and lay on his back to show that he was defeated. Pepper laughed. "That silly dog. I'd better go help—"

"Never mind," said Lavonda. "The menfolk are taking care of it."

All four women laughed as Jones in his kilt, Danny in his white cowboy hat, AJ in ripped jeans and Payson in chinos began rounding up the llamas and the scared children. Danny turned and squinted into the stands. *He's looking for me*, Clover thought to herself as she waved. Her stomach dropped at the gorgeous sight of her cowboy. She lifted her matching white hat, with her signature dyed-pink snake-skin band to which a few rhinestones had been added to match one of the purses her mother had started to design with a little bit of input from Clover. She blew Danny a kiss and *wham*. One of the llamas rammed him bull-style then galloped over top of him.

Clover ran down the metal stairs, nearly decking a mom and her kid when they got in her path. She couldn't see the dirt of the arena because so many people had gathered around the railing to watch the kids and now Danny lying hurt on the ground as llamas and dogs raced around.

"Out of my way," Clover said, elbowing people as she'd learned to do at every New York City crosswalk. She got to the dirt and a security guard put out his hand. She growled just like Maggie May and the man shrank back. She sprinted to the circle of men, ignoring the two dogs now calmly rounding up the llamas.

She pushed at the kilted man and finally moved him

aside. Danny sat in the dirt, his cheek bruised and his hair matted with…green goop that smelled…worse than manure after a hot day in the sun. Yuck. "Are you okay? Do you have all of your teeth?"

"Teeth?" he asked blankly. "Nope. Didn't lose my cap. Just a little bruised," he said.

AJ added, "And you smell like crap. That's the first time any of the furballs has spit on a human. Feel privileged, Danny."

"Women somewhere probably pay good money to be slathered in llama spit."

"They do not," Clover said. "Let me help you up. Since your *friends* are being as helpful as a tiara on a pig, I'll take you to the showers. This is a college—they've got to have a locker room."

Danny stood on his own and Danny's brother-in-law, the surgeon who hadn't even been examining him—men!—handed him the dented and dirty white hat. She teared up looking at it. Wasn't that just like Danny? All white knight under the dirt and the dings.

He put his arm around her. "Maybe I need help getting into the showers?"

Did he just wiggle his eyebrows? She looked for help from the other men. They had scattered. "You stink," she said, pushing at him. Llama spit was nasty stuff.

"I'm sorry I scared you."

He did it again. Just when she thought he was nothing but a bullheaded cowboy, he'd say something sweet or smart or just so Danny.

"You did scare me. Why did you wave to me instead of watching for the animals? You're a cowboy. You should know better."

"I do know better. It was your rhinestones. They dazzled me."

"So, now it's my fault?"

"Sure is, ma'am. I'm just a cowboy in love and stupid with it." He kissed her before she could say no, and suddenly llama spit smelled a lot like sexy cowboy.

When they broke apart, both of them were breathless. Good. She didn't want to be the only one getting hot and bothered. Whew. He smelled horrible. Amazing what a kiss could make her forget. "Get in the showers now or you'll get kicked out of the competition."

"You, too."

"What?" She raised her hand to her face. Ee-ew. She had a blob of llama spit on her face. "Get it off."

"We will," he said calmly. "The locker rooms are right here. Too bad they're not coed." He gave her another eyebrow wiggle.

"You are one sick puppy." She hurried into the building. She had to get rid of this smelly mess so she could go check on Danny and make sure he wasn't hurt. She knew one thing about cowboys. They were never hurt until they passed out from loss of blood.

"I'm coming in," Clover yelled into the men's locker room five minutes later. No answer. That probably meant no one else was there—but it could also mean that Danny had passed out. She walked inside to stop her imagination from going any further. "Danny?" Then she heard the whistling. What was that? It couldn't be. "Barbie Girl"? Before she could shout his name, he belted out the chorus and now she laughed out loud. Her cowboy was a surprise every day, which made her love him even more. Darn him.

"Danny," she shouted as she stepped up to see him washing away in the large open shower area. He jerked around guiltily—as he should. "Practicing for karaoke night at Jim's?"

"You can't be in here."

"Really? I'm here."

"I mean this is the men's locker room."

"I know. But I'm here to check on you. To make sure you don't have a bone sticking out somewhere that you neglected to tell me about."

He gave her a grin that somehow married sexy man with immature teen. "Wow. You might be right." His eyes looked downward, which made her glance the same way. Darn him. They couldn't do anything about that particular problem right now. She was beginning to feel distinctly hot, too.

"Go back to 'Barbie.' I'm out of here."

"Sure you don't want to make sure nothing is broken?" How could he waggle his eyebrows with water running down his face?

"Later."

"But I'm not sure that I can sit a bull like this."

"You're not sitting a bull no matter what."

"I am."

"Are not."

She drew in a breath, refusing to get pulled into a juvenile argument. "Danny, you knocked your head when you fell. You had to. You've got a huge bruise on your face."

"It's a small bruise and I didn't hit my head, just got a tap on my cheek. I organized this whole thing… well, with Lavonda's help and maybe a few others, but

I can't not ride. People paid to see 'real' bull riders. I'm one of them."

"You *were* one of them."

"I'll always be a bull rider, just like you'll always be a beauty queen."

"Not the same thing. And I've not been one for a long time."

"To me you'll always be a beauty queen." He started out of the shower and she backed away.

"We'll talk about this when you're dressed. And saying silly things like I'm still a beauty queen will only convince me that you really did hit your head."

He moved faster than a wet, naked man should and pulled her into his arms, nuzzling into the crook of her neck so he could whisper in her ear, just a minor distraction from the big, wet, muscled male smashed all up against her. "I don't need a hit to the head to make me loopy. Seeing you in the stands with those tight white jeans and that hat is all it takes. What can I say? I'm a sucker for a Texas beauty queen." He kissed her neck and she held him and his lips there for a moment.

As she tugged on his hair so she could see his face, she said, "Flattery will not convince me you should jump on the back of a bull."

He moved his hips forward. "What about giving you a bull ride?"

"First, that's a bit of bragging, and, second, we're in a men's locker room. Now stop and listen to me." She stepped away from the temptation of him. Was she as juvenile and hormonal as he because she needed to put distance between them so she could talk to him like the rational, MBA-carrying woman that she was? "Everyone will understand why you can't ride. You've been hurt."

"I know you're trying to protect me."

"Darn right. Since you won't do it for yourself."

"Clover," he said softly. She turned to him again, unable to stop herself. He had a towel around his waist now and an earnest expression on his face. "I need to do this for me, too. You know, I never got a retirement ride."

How could she not have known that? She was supposed to love him. "Why didn't you tell me?"

"I'm telling you now because I just kind of figured it out. I'm good with not being a bull rider. I'm okay with that being my past, but I want to put a bow on it. I want to say goodbye."

"You want to leave on your own terms. I get that." She did. She understood needing to make your own way in the world. That was what she planned to do in Angel Crossing and with Danny. "Get dressed. You've got a bull to tame. Then later I'll ride the bull snake."

He laughed and hugged her. "That's not a thing, and it's about as sexy as granny panties."

"You've never seen *me* in granny panties, then." She kissed him long and hard, knowing once again that her future was here with Danny.

Danny settled himself onto the back of Thunder Jr. The bull was new to the ring, and SAC was the kind of ride that Dave the stockman insisted would provide a good show without testing the mettle of the riders too much. Danny thought that his mettle needed to be tested. This competition was his real retirement ride, win or lose, but he'd like to win. He owed it to himself, just like he'd told Clover. To say his final goodbye. He loved bull riding, but it wasn't number one in his life anymore. That was what it had to be for him to do it well. But now number one in his life was Clover, and Angel Crossing, his family, his friends.

"Yo, man, pay attention," AJ said as he thumped Danny on the back. "I thought you'd been practicing."

"I have been. I'm good." This really needed to be his final ride, if he couldn't even keep his head in the game while sitting on pounds of steely bull flesh ready to rid itself of the annoying cowboy on his back.

Dave said from his other side, "This little guy is new. Be nice. I've got big plans for him. Give them a good ride, but nothing fancy. Okay?"

Danny nodded, reached up and settled his slightly dinged-up hat on his head. Give the crowd a show. That was what he'd do. He'd enjoy the ride like he'd done as a teen, when not so much was at stake. Today was about giving the audience what it had come to see and raising money for Angel Crossing. Before he let his brain drift to places it didn't belong, he gave AJ the signal. The chute opened and Thunder Jr. didn't move. Hell's bells. Dave smacked the bull on his beefy haunch. He still didn't move. Frozen. Could a bull get performance anxiety?

"Give 'im a nudge, Danny," AJ counseled. Danny did and the audience yelled, expecting Thunder Jr. to explode out of the chute. But the large black-and-white bull took one dainty step after Danny urged him to move with a gentle nudge from the point of one boot in the bullish armpit. Thunder Jr. turned his head to give Danny a hurt look, like somehow he'd betrayed him.

He tried a tap of his heels, readjusting his grip. The bull stopped dead again, his large head turned so he could look at Danny with one brown eye. What did the animal want? This was a time for them both to shine. Next, the rodeo clowns came out. They looked at the animal warily but approached him, waving their arms. Thunder Jr. bellowed at them but didn't move.

"Okay, folks, it looks like Danny Leigh has already tamed this bull, so we'll be seeing him ride later."

The clowns carefully scooted to the rear of the bull and walked him with Danny on his back out of the arena. As they passed the fence, Danny lifted himself off the bull and waved to the crowd. He watched Thunder Jr. saunter away without a backward look.

What did Danny do now? Ride another bull? Was this the universe telling him that he'd pushed his luck as far as he should? Obviously, he'd been hanging around Faye too much if he thought that. Look at all of the good things he had. Did he really have to win this little bull-riding extravaganza to feel right with his retirement? Clover waved to him, the rhinestones on her headband and those decorating her shirt nearly blinding him in the Arizona sun. What did he need to ride a bull for? His life was going to be filled with more thrills and spills than he could imagine, hooked up to Clover. Time to give other cowboys a chance for glory. He was happy to be Mayor Danny of Angel Crossing and a cowboy for Clover Van Camp. What more could he want? *Babies*. Crap. Where had that thought come from? Thunder Jr. stopped, turned his front quarters and bellowed right at Danny. Dang. He must have hit his head when he and the llamas went two rounds.

"Hurry up," Lavonda said as she sprinted up to Danny after his "ride," then headed around the back to the arena.

Clover stood in front of him now, tugging on his hand. "Come on. We can't miss this. It's going to be the biggest thing in Angel Crossing since Anita got Jim's in her divorce."

He followed the women without argument. This day was supposed to be a good old-fashioned rodeo to raise a little bit of money and the hopes of Angel Crossing. They ended up just to the left of the chutes. AJ stood on top of the gate, decked out in his cowboy best. He must have changed. He'd mess up his clothes if he rode like that.

The announcer's voice boomed out. "We have a little change in the schedule, folks. Instead of AJ McCreary on Widowmaker, we will have a brief performance by AJ on banjo." There was a hushed silence. "Just kidding. That cowboy can't carry a tune in a bucket."

Danny saw AJ's horse Benny come into the arena. His friend jumped on the horse as he galloped past. "What the hell is going on?" he asked Clover, who shushed him.

He looked back to his friend, waiting for whatever was going to happen. His sister looked like she was about ready to explode. Then Jones came sidling up beside her and whispered something in her ear. Lavonda smiled and stared even more intently at AJ and Benny.

The audience stayed silent. Then the horse and rider made a perfect turn and magically AJ unfurled a banner. The rider and horse moved even faster around the ring as the banner whipped behind them. Finally, Danny saw it.

Pepper Bourne, Will You Marry Me? was written in large tie-dyed letters. Danny heard the crowd stirring, and then Pepper was flying down the stairs and into the dirt arena. Benny reared up, Trigger-style, before planting his feet well away from Pepper. AJ jumped off and went down on one knee. He held out the small box that stirred fear in every cowboy's heart. Pepper pushed it aside and landed on AJ, kissing his face and hugging him.

"Guess she said yes. Give them a hand, everyone," the announcer said. AJ and Pepper stood up, still kissing, until the announcer cleared his throat. AJ boosted Pepper onto Benny and led her and the horse out of the arena. He waved to the crowd and Pepper kept her eyes only on him.

Lavonda finally said, "Perfect. I knew he could do it."

"You planned this?" Danny turned to his sister.

"Helped. AJ had the idea. Those two are all about the public displays of affection."

"Don't think I'll do any such thing," Jones said to Lavonda.

"We're already married. You're safe for now. On our fiftieth anniversary, though, I'll be expecting something just as sappy." Lavonda took her Scotsman's hand and led him off.

Danny wasn't surprised that AJ and Pepper would make everything official. It was just that… Wow. He never would have imagined his honky-tonk buddy would go for something like that.

"It was very sweet. I wonder if anyone got a video. It could go viral, put Angel Crossing on the map."

He nodded absently. Why wasn't he thinking that AJ had gone loco? Not because he'd asked Pepper to marry him, but the way he'd asked. It just wasn't *cowboy*.

Clover stepped up and kissed him. He automatically

grabbed her around the waist, not caring who saw him kiss her.

"So how are you going to top that?" she whispered against his lips.

Chapter 17

Clover was supposed to be looking at the blueprints Danny had pinned to the wall—instead she was admiring his jean-clad, cowboy-muscled butt.

"You're going to make me blush," he said without turning around.

"Why would you be blushing?"

"Because you're ogling my butt."

"I am not." It wasn't like she was really all that embarrassed for admiring the view. She just didn't want Danny to think he was all of that and a case of Nutella. "There's no way—" Darn it. Clover hadn't noticed the dusty mirror that made up a section of the wall in the old warehouse building's office. "Guess the cowboy who worked here was vain, too."

Danny smiled and said, "Pay attention. This is the first work by Dan-Clover."

"We are not calling the business that. It sounds too much like 'Damn Clover.'"

Danny finally turned around. "If we don't come up with something, Lavonda will. She's already suggested Angelic Architects, which won't work since neither of us is an architect. Or Angel's Fancy, which sounds like a bordello to me."

Clover laughed because he was right and maybe—

"No. Don't even think about it. We are not naming our business that. Why can't it be Leigh Properties?"

"Because I'm not a Leigh. I like my last name just fine and don't see any reason to change it." She saw Danny's eyes go dark and his face tighten into unhappy lines.

"I wish you wouldn't say that."

"Forget about the name of the business or what I want my last name to stay. Let's talk plans." She walked over to the blueprint that laid out exactly what they wanted to do with the warehouse and the surrounding property. It would still be mixed use, but instead of business and residential, it was going to be old and young. Families and singles. She and Danny had plans for it all. They would make it affordable, a neighborhood within a neighborhood. Angel Crossing wasn't one of those places where people didn't know their neighbors, but over time it'd become segregated, mainly by who had how much money. This property would be a place to create a neighborhood that had it all. She was so proud—mainly of Danny. She'd primarily just made sure the numbers added up. He had the vision and creativity. Something she never would have imagined when she'd met the sixteen-year-old bull-riding champion and self-proclaimed (even though he'd been a virgin) ladies' man.

"These are going to look good and be functional, aren't they?"

"They are. I'm glad Knox finally convinced VCW to keep its investment in the business district and sell back the other properties at cost."

"Your daddy is still mad about it."

"Maybe." She shrugged. It hurt that her father had stopped talking to her after she and Knox had convinced the board to abandon his grand scheme. And scheme it had been. Even the board had been a little surprised by the direction her father had wanted to take the company.

Danny hugged her and kissed her temple. She let him, feeling happy and strong, not incompetent. Maybe that was what love was. "I love you," she said because you just couldn't say that often enough.

"That's good because I'm not going to be home tonight. Taking AJ out for his bachelor party. We've got a wild night all laid out. I want you to remember you said that you love me tomorrow morning."

"I've heard about the 'wild' night."

"Karaoke at Jim's can be very competitive, and Rita and Anita told AJ he can only come if he's in costume."

"They did not say that. You and Jones came up with that."

"Maybe. Back to Golden Acres."

"That's not the name of our development."

"Angelic Rest."

"Absolutely not. That sounds like a pet cemetery."

Suddenly Danny looked very serious. Scarily serious. He gently took her face between his hands, keeping his blue gaze locked on hers. "None of this would be happening without you. But that's not what has me puffed up like a rooster with a flock of happy hens." She knew her smile wobbled but his gaze didn't move. "You. Knowing you love me, that you believe in me and what I can do. I'm stunned, amazed every day that you're here. With me. Danny Leigh, big bad bull rider who never went to college and is content to live in a town small enough to make Mayberry look like a city."

"Stop," she said, putting her hands on his. "Who else would I be with? You're the man who knows me and doesn't flinch from the ugly parts—and there are some of those, and I'm not talking about how I'm knock-kneed. I mean that you don't flinch when I get petty and vain. *And* you make me not want to be any of those things. You make me want to be my best." Her smile got wobblier. "Where else would I want to be but in your arms as first lady of the town whose heart is big enough to accept a New York City cowgirl."

Danny's kiss was soft but not tentative. She could feel all of his love in that caress. She never wanted to be anywhere else but in his arms, no matter how clichéd that was.

This woman could turn him into a puddle of warm pudding with three words and the touch of her lips. He made sure all of his love, laughter and hope was in his gentle kiss. He wanted her to know she was cherished by him not because she slept with him or even because she made her special Texas brand of brownies. It was because of her. All of her curves and all the places she said were flaws. They were spice for him. They gave her shadows, making her highlights even brighter. Dear

Lord and his angels, he was sappy. He smiled against her lips. "Glad you can't read my mind."

She moved her mouth to whisper in his ear as her hips moved seductively forward. "Oh, yes, I can."

"Ha. I wasn't thinking about that."

"Somebody was."

"Always said Durango had a mind of his own." He buried his face into the curve of her neck where the special, never-found-in-a-bottle scent of Clover always was the strongest. He wrapped her tightly in his arms, whispering again and again. "I love you."

When he finally finished telling and showing her that he loved her, Danny carefully pulled away, his fast breathing matching hers. "Weren't we discussing Shady Cactus?"

"Lavonda said she'd come up with names for us, and," she added before he could break in, "we'll listen to her for our project because she's done this for very successful Fortune 500 companies."

"But we don't need to be on that list and look what she named her own company—Reese Tours. That's got no pizazz."

"Until everyone meets the little donkey she named the business after."

"I don't know what it is with my sisters and small equines. Jessie's pony Molly is famous around the world because of that video of her at the wedding."

"And for that one where she gives kisses to all of the children at Hope's Ride." Clover smiled at his cranky comments. His sisters still treated him like he was an annoying little brother.

"We'll listen to Lavonda but do what we want. Isn't

that what we've been doing since...well, since we met at that Texas rodeo?"

"I guess," Danny said. "We'll discuss the name later. We've got to make decisions about this rehab. The architect gets paid by the change, by the way, so let's keep it simple."

"You mean KISS."

"What?"

"Keep it simple, Sinbad."

"That's not how it goes," he said with a laugh.

"Could be."

"Are you saying the complex should be called Sinbad Acres."

"Now, *that* really doesn't make sense."

"You know what does make sense? You, me and Elvis. Come to Vegas with me and we'll get married now. Today."

"I'm not getting married by Elvis."

"Is that the only reason you're saying no to my proposal?" Clover's bluebonnet gaze went bright with tears and his chest caved in. "Forget I said anything."

"I want to say yes, but...not yet."

He pulled her into his arms because she was worth the wait. She was worth any trials she put him through. "I love you, with or without a ring, and until the cows and kittens come home."

She grabbed his face and pulled it to her, breathing out "I love you" as she devoured his mouth.

Of course, there was a pony with flowers and a lacy pillow walking down the aisle toward Pepper and AJ, with AJ's daughter, EllaJayne, leading Molly, the high-stepping Shetland pony. None of that mattered because

Clover really thought the star of the show was Danny standing at the end of the aisle with a folder of papers, the vows AJ and Pepper had written. The two hadn't wasted time after the SAC Bull-Riding Extravaganza, which had raised enough to fix up more vacant lots for gardens and start a little nest egg for beautification projects—the council was deciding between new trash cans and old-fashioned streetlights.

Clover was brought back to the wedding by the laughter rippling through the crowd, seated in folding chairs of all types in the recently dedicated Angel Crossing Parking and Multiuse District. Today was its first time as a wedding venue, but it made sense since this was where AJ and Pepper had first met, when his truck had broken down and his daughter had run away to be found by Pepper. Now whenever the two of them were together, their love was obvious to every single person there, including their daughter—Pepper had adopted the young girl with the inky curls and sparkling mahogany eyes.

"Molly—" Jessie's voice drifted over the crowd "—behave or no gummies." More laughter rippled through those seated.

EllaJayne said clearly, "Granny Faye told me we having sleepover so Mommy and Daddy can make a sissie for me."

Molly nodded her head in agreement. Clover couldn't read Danny's face exactly. He looked a little pained—maybe he shouldn't have worn his fancy boots, the ones he'd gotten for going eight seconds with some bull or another.

EllaJayne got Molly moving again and Rita and Anita, on cue, started the wedding-march music, which for this couple was "Baby Elephant Walk," chosen by EllaJayne. Then everyone turned as Pepper started down the aisle in a beautiful gown of blush pink with lace, sequins and pearls. The color made Pepper glow, or maybe that was love, Clover thought, smiling at her own fancy. Her gaze landed again on Danny, who wasn't looking at the bride but instead had his attention glued to her. *Oh, my.*

Danny had officiated at more weddings than he'd ever imagined he would when he agreed to be mayor, but this one had to top all of the others. All of Angel Crossing had turned out, plus a lot of friends from the rodeo and a contingent of family from all over the country. Even his daddy and mama had shown up. Their RV was parked at Lavonda's. AJ and Pepper had decided that their wedding would be something like a midsummer party. Faye had suggested the date because it was the longest day of the year, and it meant more party fun.

Danny thought that was about right. He took a sip from his longneck beer encased in a coozy that the couple had given out to everyone, which was embossed with the words *Love means never having to say you're sorry but always saying, "Yes, sweetheart."* :-)

He looked for Clover, who'd fit into Angel Crossing like a round peg in a pegboard, something his mama had said this morning. Clover had smiled and not pointed out to his mother that she might have that saying a little…or a lot…wrong. There Clover was with the bride, the pony, EllaJayne and the two dogs, as the photographer tried to snap a shot.

Jessie was there, too, looking hot, annoyed and ready to explode. Danny strolled over and met up with his brothers-in-law, Payson and Jones, and AJ. He knew that Spence—Payson's brother—and his wife, Olympia, and their children were around somewhere, along with Olympia's sister Jolene, who planned to open her shop in Danny's building next month. He already had another tenant lined up because of her. He might need to start an Angel Crossing family tree to keep everything straight.

"Need some help?" he asked Clover.

Jessie answered, "I don't need my baby brother fouling things up."

Payson walked over to his wife, took his daughter from her arms and kissed Jessie. Danny wanted to say "Yuck" like a twelve-year-old. That was his sister, man.

Pepper said, "We're just trying to get one picture that's a reenactment of the wedding procession. I want to make sure I have a good one."

"Molly says more gummies," EllaJayne wheedled.

"You've had enough of those," Pepper said firmly but with no anger. "Can you and she stand just like you did in the aisle?" EllaJayne tugged to get the pony beside her. Molly stamped her little hoof. The pony, who'd been Jessie's as a little girl, was a diva of epic proportions. Somehow they all gave in to her demands. He watched the little pony, and she stared right back at him. He might have been a bull rider but he knew that look.

"EllaJayne," he said as he walked over to Molly, "let me help." His sister Jessie relaxed a tad. She'd seen the look, too. He couldn't imagine that the pony would do anything to the little girl, but the adults and even the dogs might not have been so lucky. A braying started from somewhere over Danny's shoulder and a rumble of laughter and shouts followed. It couldn't be.

"Reese." He heard Jones's Scottish-accented voice above the crowd.

Crap. The miniature burro had more personality than Molly. Lavonda had insisted that he'd known he was missing something today.

The crowd parted and there was Reese, ears pricked forward before he opened his mouth and let out another hoarse bray. Molly tossed her head and whinnied back.

"Grab the beast," Jones said, still making his way through the crowd.

"I've got Molly," Clover said, taking the pony's rhinestone-studded halter from him, which looked a lot like her hatband. He grabbed Reese's black leather halter. Jones and his sister Lavonda stopped at the edge of the circle. And there was his mama and daddy along with Jolene, Lavonda... Hell's bells. It was everyone.

"Look, they kissing," EllaJayne said as the pony and the little burro touched noses. He'd barely noticed that the animal had reached out because after taking in the circle of friends and family, he'd had eyes only for Clover. Her blue gaze had locked on his. He couldn't hear anything beyond the beat of his own heart.

He wanted the words to come out of his mouth. He wanted to ask... Not that. Clover had made it clear she wasn't ready for that. "Ouch." He looked down and saw Molly's hoof on his shiny boot. She'd just stepped on him.

"Molly," Clover admonished, "that wasn't nice."

The pony lifted her foot and stamped it down again. He heard a number of female voices say the pony's name, and then Reese wrenched his head forward and bumped into Molly. She grinned at him before lashing out with her teeth, causing Reese to buck, kicking out his back legs, just missing Jones, who swore with proficiency.

"I told you, Molly..." His sister Jessie's voice lifted above the others as Danny saw her latch on to the pony's halter. "One wedding a year."

"Reese, my man," Jones said, pulling the burro toward him. "He doesn't need any help."

What was happening? "If a llama shows up, I'm out of here," Danny said.

"My beauties aren't close," Faye said.

"Uh-oh," Lavonda said. "He's got that look, and I don't mean Reese."

"Oh, man, you are so...twirly nailed," AJ amended, looking at his daughter playing with the two dogs who now stared at Danny with some expectation. Maggie May yipped and Butch whined.

"Everyone stop picking on Danny." Clover stepped up to him and took his hand. "Let's go try the Jell-O salad. I haven't had any of that since Mama's Nona Nancy made it."

"No. Wait," he gasped because he couldn't breathe; he couldn't move. This was worse than being thrown from a danged bull. "I... I want... Shi—"

"Don't say that. Little pitchers, big ears," Pepper yelled out.

This was not something he wanted to ask Clover with an audience.

"Danny?" Clover sounded worried.

"I'm fine," he answered with assurance. As sure as he'd been at sixteen and he'd known he had to ask out the eighteen-year-old beauty queen. "Clover Anastasia Van Camp, will you—"

"Don't you dare, Danforth Clayton Leigh," his mama said.

What sort of conspiracy was going on? He just wanted to get the question out. He just wanted to—

"Take this." His mother handed him her engagement ring, the one his daddy had given her and that had been his mother's mother's ring. "You can't ask a woman to marry you without a ring," his mother whispered into his ear with tears in her voice.

He took the ring and looked at Clover. Her eyes were wide, surprised, scared…and filled with love. Molly smacked him in the back with her bony head. He stumbled into Clover. She caught him and the two started to fall, but hands from the crowd around them kept them on their feet.

"I want to kneel," he said to no one and everyone.

"'Nother wedding," EllaJayne squealed.

"Shh," all of the women hissed at her.

He did kneel then, and the dogs came to his side, panting a little as everyone looked at Clover. Beautiful, funny, wonderful Clover. "Clover Anastasia Van Camp, will you—"

"Wait. I'm not—"

"Dear Lord, his angels and Corvairs. I just want to ask you to marry me." A stunned silence, a growl from Maggie May and another knock from Molly.

"Sure. But I'm not changing my name and I get to have as many rhinestones on my dress and hat as I want. And—" Danny grabbed her and the crowd erupted into Wild West shouts.

Clover couldn't catch her breath. What had she just said? Darn it. That wasn't how you answered a proposal. "I want a do-over."

Danny shook his head. "You heard her. She said 'Sure.'" He laughed, throwing back his head and ending it on a whoop of triumph.

She pulled his head down to her. "Wait."

"No more waiting." He kissed her and another cheer deafened her and shook her heart and soul.

"Danny," she whispered against his lips. "I love you."

"Good to know," he said. "I love you, too. But you will be Mrs. Danforth Leigh."

"As soon as you find a time machine and take us back to 1950."

"Is this our first fight?" Danny asked.

"Not a fight. A discussion."

"You go, son," his daddy said. "Start how you plan to go on."

"Gerald, that's horrible advice," his mama answered. Then everyone else got in on the discussion. Clover pulled Danny away and only Molly noticed them leaving. She gave a horsey smile and wink. Jessie had been right. There was something a little scary about the pony.

"Now, Danny, ask me properly and I'll answer you properly."

"There's no do-overs in proposals."

She didn't want her acceptance to be the word *sure*. "Then I'm proposing to you." She knelt and took his hand. "Danforth Clayton Leigh, will you be my husband, my lover and my best guy?"

"Sure," he said, pulling her to her feet and into his arms.

Dear Lord and his Corvairs, the man could kiss and, better, he could love her like no other.

When he finally gave her a little space for a breath, she said, "I expect this to last for more than eight seconds. I know how you bull riders can be."

"When you're riding the bull, time stands still, you know."

"I might know that but let's test it out again tonight while you show me again how much you love me."

"I'll do that. And I'll convince you that you want me to brand you with my name."

"I'll let you try, but it'll take you more than one night to change my mind."

"Is that a challenge?"

"Challenge or promise—I know that we'll both love it."

* * * * *

WE HOPE YOU ENJOYED THIS BOOK FROM

HARLEQUIN
SPECIAL EDITION

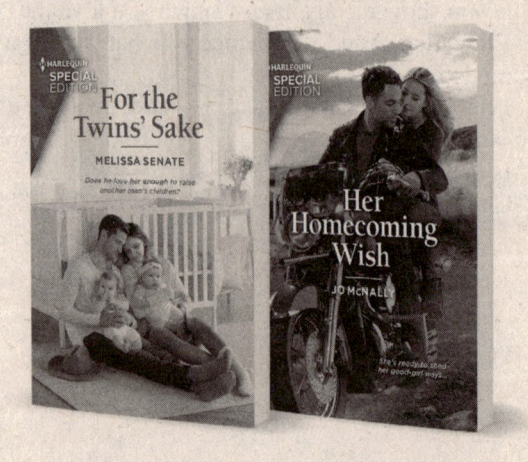

Believe in love. Overcome obstacles. Find happiness.

Relate to finding comfort and strength in the support of loved ones and enjoy the journey no matter what life throws your way.

6 NEW BOOKS AVAILABLE EVERY MONTH!

SPECIAL EXCERPT FROM

HARLEQUIN
SPECIAL EDITION

When Laurel Hudson is found—alive but with amnesia—no one is more relieved than Adam Fortune. He will do whatever it takes to reunite mother and son, even if it means a road trip in extremely close quarters. Will the long journey home remind Laurel how much they truly share?

Read on for a sneak preview of the final book in The Fortunes of Texas: Rambling Rose continuity, The Texan's Baby Bombshell *by Allison Leigh.*

He'd been falling for her from the very beginning. But that kiss had sealed the deal for him.

Now that glossy oak-barrel hair slid over her shoulder as Laurel's head turned and she looked his way.

His step faltered.

Her eyes were the same stunning shade of blue they'd always been. Her perfectly heart-shaped face was pale and delicate looking even without the pink scar on her forehead between her eyebrows.

Her eyebrows pulled together as their eyes met.

Remember me.

Remember us.

The words—unwanted and unexpected—pulsed through him, drowning out the splitting headache and the aching back and the impatience, the relief and the pain.

Then she blinked those incredible eyes of hers and he realized there was a flush on her cheeks and she was chewing at the corner of her lips. In contrast to her delicate features, her lips were just as full and pouty as they'd always been.

Kissing them had been an adventure in and of itself.

He pushed the pointless memory out of his head and then had to shove his hands in the pockets of his jeans because they were actually shaking.

"Hi." Puny first word to say to the woman who'd made a wreck out of him.

Still seated, she looked up at him. "Hi." She sounded breathless. "It's…it's Adam, right?"

The pain sitting in the pit of his stomach then had nothing to do with anything except her. He yanked his right hand from his pocket and held it out. "Adam Fortune."

She looked uncertain, then slowly settled her hand into his.

Unlike Dr. Granger's firm, brief clasp, Laurel's touch felt chilled and tentative. And it lingered. "I'm Lisa."

God help him. He was not strong enough for this.

Don't miss
The Texan's Baby Bombshell *by Allison Leigh, available June 2020 wherever Harlequin Special Edition books and ebooks are sold.*

Harlequin.com

Copyright © 2020 by Harlequin Books S.A.

IF YOU ENJOYED THIS BOOK WE THINK YOU WILL ALSO LOVE

LOVE INSPIRED SUSPENSE
INSPIRATIONAL ROMANCE

Courage. Danger. Faith.

Find strength and determination in stories of faith and love in the face of danger.

6 NEW BOOKS AVAILABLE EVERY MONTH!

SPECIAL EXCERPT FROM

LOVE INSPIRED SUSPENSE
INSPIRATIONAL ROMANCE

*They must work together to solve a cold case...
and to stay alive.*

Read on for a sneak preview of
Deadly Connection *by Lenora Worth,
the next book in the True Blue K-9 Unit: Brooklyn series,
available June 2020 from Love Inspired Suspense.*

Brooklyn K-9 Unit officer Belle Montera glanced back on the shortcut through Cadman Plaza Park, her K-9 partner, Justice, a sleek German shepherd, moving ahead of her as she held tightly to his leash. She had a weird sense she was being followed, but it had to be nothing.

Justice lifted his black nose and sniffed the humid air, then gave a soft woof. He might have seen a squirrel frolicking in the tall oaks, or he could have sensed Belle's agitation. Still on duty, she kept a keen eye on her surroundings.

"No time to go after innocent squirrels," she told Justice. "We're working, remember?"

Her faithful companion gave her a dark-eyed stare, his black K-9 unit protective vest cinched around his firm belly.

They were both on high alert.

"It's okay, boy," she said, giving Justice's shiny black-and-tan coat a soft rub. "Just my overactive imagination getting the best of me."

She had a meeting with a man who could have information regarding the McGregor murders. The DNA match from that case had indicated that US marshal Emmett Gage could be related to the killer.

The team had done a thorough background check on the marshal to eliminate him as a suspect, then Belle had been assigned to meet with him.

Justice lifted his head and sniffed again, his nose in the air. The big dog glanced back. Belle checked over her shoulder.

No one there.

She slowed and listened to hear if any footsteps hit the strip of pavement curving through the path toward the federal courthouse near the park.

Belle heard through the trees what sounded like a motorcycle revving, then nothing but the birds chirping. Minutes passed and then she heard a noise on the path, the crackle of a twig breaking, the slight shift of shoes hitting asphalt, a whiff of stale body odor wafting through the air. The hair on the back of her neck stood up and Belle knew then.

Someone is following me.

Don't miss
Deadly Connection *by Lenora Worth,*
available June 2020 wherever
Love Inspired Suspense books and ebooks are sold.

LoveInspired.com

Copyright © 2020 by Harlequin Books S.A.

HARLEQUIN

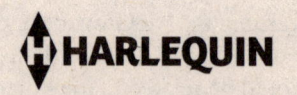

Heartfelt or suspenseful, inspiring or passionate, Harlequin has your happily-ever-after.

With new books published every month, you are sure to find the satisfying escape you know you deserve.

SIGN UP FOR THE HARLEQUIN NEWSLETTER

Be the first to hear about great new reads and exciting offers!

Harlequin.com/newsletters